An Anatomy

of Death

By
George Rees

Published by Accent Press Ltd – 2005
www.accentpress.co.uk

ISBN 0954709276

Printed and bound in the UK
by Clays, St Ives Plc

Cover Design by Rachel Loosmore
Accent Press Ltd.

One

I first met the famous – or infamous – Christopher Marlowe while looking after his horse outside the Curtain Playhouse in Shoreditch. A job better playmakers than I have done. I was feeling downcast. The actors were proving reluctant to buy my plays. I'd sold a few ballads to street singers. Failures according to them: 'Didn't hold them enough, Master Dekker,' they'd said as they negotiated a lower price for my next one. What that meant was the ballad had failed to lull the audience sufficiently for their mates to relieve the listeners of their purses. And when the poor devils were caught and hanged at Tyburn the ballad singer would be there hawking their last dying speech of repentance while a new mate worked the crowd. I know, having written a number of speeches for them. Still in my twenties, I've repented of being a murderer, cutpurse, housebreaker, coiner, highway robber – oh, and a Catholic priest. Bit awkward that last since he made his own speech which differed somewhat from mine. I'm a whole den of iniquity rolled into one.

But it is the theatre I long to write for. And not just because the rate is six pound a play. Although given my debts that is a powerful inducement. Even collaboration, the usual way to start, would be something. But getting actors to take my plays was like getting Puritans to take mass.

So I was feeling down. My girl, Elizabeth, was late with my bread and cheese and pot of ale. And when she did turn up I was going to have to ask her to pay for them.

Again. The heat was heavy, oppressive. Trying to cheer myself up with thoughts of my coming meal I heard a plop. Marlowe's horse had deposited his breakfast in a steaming heap on my shoes. Feeling down? I was lower than the Earl of Oxford's knees just after he'd farted in the Queen's presence.

A southerly breeze sprang up. That's a plus, you'd think. Especially as doctors say the south wind is healthy and dispels melancholy. Healthy? Not when it wafted the putrid mud of Moorditch up my nostrils. And into my eyes the smoke of London. Smoke from forges, foundries, smeltries – and bakeries. But no bread for me. My ears were assailed by the iron-wheeled carts rumbling along Bishopsgate Street carrying chickens, turkeys, geese, cheese, vegetables, past me and into the city.

London is my city. I grew up there and most of the time I love the bustling vulgar life of the place. Crowds of men and women jostling through the narrow streets; the babbling tongues of many nations; sailors, soldiers, merchants, chapmen, whores; apprentices in leather aprons, ladies in silk gowns, colliers heaving sacks of coal and gentlemen strolling in satin doublets. Yes, I love the city. Usually. But just now I could have preached a sermon on the place to a congregation of Puritans that would have got me elected as one of their elders. London is a suppurating sore on the body of England, brethren, I would say. Lance the luxury and drain off the pus of pride through the purity of the pious. My stomach growled. Where was my bread and cheese?

Just as I thought things could not get any worse I saw old man Cruickshank hobbling towards me. When he caught my glance he put his hand to his back and on his face his look of, 'I'm in pain but bearing it heroically'. With old Cruickshank there are two subjects you never raise. Illness and murder. Ask him how he is and he'll complain of more ailments than a true doctor's seen or a quack doctor could invent. The public executioner, fresh from disembowelling a batch of traitors, only brings his dinner back up when Cruickshank describes his haemorrhoids. Mention murder and for the thousandth time he'll tell you about the murder next door when he lived in Milk Street. Thence the palpitations he suffered – and we're back on his ailments.

'Hello, Master Cruickshank,' I said carefully. Nothing in that to get him going so he just nodded. Marlowe's horse deposited the remainder of his breakfast on the ground. Cruickshank looked envious. I think he was just going to start complaining about his constipation when an explosion from the playhouse almost cured him on the spot. They were acting The Battle of Alcazar and a cacophony of drums, trumpets and cannon announced that battle had commenced. Cruickshank, bad back forgotten, leapt in the air. He came down quivering with rage. Pointing at the archers practising in Finsbury Fields he said, 'When I was young that place was packed. We wanted to be ready to serve our country. Today's youngsters, they've got to be given guns 'cos they're too weak to draw a bow and too lazy to practise. All they wants to do is watch plays. When I was young plays had a moral. But now it's all fighting and killing and fornicating, teaching idle apprentices to beat their masters and bed their mistresses.'

I'm not interested in fighting and killing anyone but where is all this fornication? Elizabeth refuses to go to bed with me until we are married. Perhaps I should take her to more plays.

Cruickshank was glaring at me and complaining in his querulous whine, 'People are so used to gaping at the stage now, they can't hold an intelligent conversation with you any more.'

I sighed and was resigned to hearing a monologue on his health or his murder when a friend of his came along.

3

No maiden could have been more relieved to see a knight errant than I was to see him. Their friendship was explained by two facts. Cruickshank bought him ale and he was deaf.

'Quiet,' he said, as the Battle of Alcazar erupted from the playhouse with the din of all the devils in Hell being spewed out of Vesuvius. Taking his arm Cruickshank led his captive audience away saying, 'The only good modern play is Arden of Faversham though the murder in it is not a patch on my murder. Horrible she looked, Jack, horrible. It must have been witchcraft.'

Old Cruickshank was right about Arden. It is a good play. Popular too, even though it is about a fifty year old murder down in Kent. It set me thinking. Peele with his Alcazar, me with my (unacted, alas) Tragedy of Alexander the Great and other writers have, since its huge success, been trying to write plays as exotic as Marlowe's Tamburlaine. But Arden proves there is a market for plays about ordinary English people. Having been warned beforehand about Cruickshank as a bore I'd never really listened to his account of the Milk Street murder. Could there be a play in it? He had called it horrible and mentioned witchcraft. Having read Reginald Scott's book I am sceptical about witchcraft but most people still believe in it. If only I could keep Cruickshank off his health I might get something on the murder I could use.

Just as I was thinking of calling him back his health almost received a mortal blow. Finsbury Fields is used mainly by the lower classes but there was a young gentleman in a silk shirt learning to use the crossbow. Unable to wind it up he handed it to the man teaching him. Cruickshank snorted and turned to his friend. The words 'Youngsters today,' floated back from his diatribe. Meanwhile the young man was aiming the wound-up crossbow at the target and fiddling with the trigger. Nothing happened. He swung round with the bow to

4

consult the tutor who dived swearing to the ground. Jack knocked Cruickshank flat on his face and followed him down. The bolt whizzed over them to impale itself in a pig hanging outside a butcher's shop across the road. It did not seem the right time to ask old Cruickshank about his murder story. The tutor snatched the crossbow, reloaded it and sent the bolt smack into the centre of the target.

There's nothing like a bit of excitement to cheer you up but now it was back to waiting. This was a boring job. Marlowe's horse nuzzled my hand. I wished I had something for him to eat but I had nothing for myself. He was a fine looking animal but badly misused. As I looked at the flies buzzing around the blood on his flanks where Marlowe's spurs had raked the poor beast, I heard a footstep behind me. Turning I received a blast of tobacco smoke full in the face. Marlowe had left the play early.

Through watering eyes I peered at him, a young man about my age. His doublet was good quality, unlike mine. He gazed at the fiery redness in the bowl of his pipe then darted his hand at a fly. It buzzed in his fist. Holding it over the bowl he unclenched his hand then drew it away. The fly sizzled. The large brown eyes in the pale oval face gleamed as he murmured, 'A black soul burning in Hell.' Drawing on the pipe he blew out a cloud of smoke and remarked cheerfully, 'I like tobacco.'

I'm not sure I like you, I thought as I watched the smoke twisting about his head. This is how some wall paintings depict the Devil in Hell presiding over the torments of sinners. As well as tobacco many said there was also a smell of sulphur about Marlowe. Despite the warm day I shivered. As though having read my thoughts he said, 'I was meant for the church, think of that.'

I sniffed the air and replied, 'My nose detects rotting offal, stinking horse dung and the stench of a tallow chandler; but for certain there is no odour of sanctity.'

5

'An insolent horse holder,' he said with amused contempt as he threw me some coins. Contempt! And him the son of a shoemaker. Once men like him have been to university they think of themselves as gentry and want to forget where they came from. I did not go to university but I considered myself as good as Marlowe. Flinging the coins to the ground I looked him full in the face. But his eye had been caught by two horsemen approaching along the street while, over his shoulder, I saw Elizabeth pushing through a crowd of cursing porters and bawling hawkers. The smoke of London had not removed the country bloom from her cheeks; but serving in a tavern had sharpened her tongue. When I remarked on this at our first meeting she had replied, "The next man who says all roses have briars, I'll scratch." As if I, a poet, would be guilty of such a stale comparison.

As the two horsemen neared, a maid leaned from an overhanging window and shook a mop. Drawing his sword one of the horsemen sliced off the mop head catching it as it fell. Riding up he threw it at Marlowe's feet and laughed, 'The same fate to our enemies' heads, Kit. Come, we have some way to go.'

'Ingram Frizer,' said Marlowe coldly as he mounted his horse. 'Where to, Robert?' he asked the other man. Frizer cut in, chuckling: 'We've prepared a warm welcome for the poet of Tamburlaine and…' he leered – 'Edward the Second. And I hear you're writing another, Kit. About a man who sells his soul to the Devil? Faustus? Yes, a warm welcome at Master Walsingham's at Scadbury.'

Marlowe I've heard was a government intelligencer and spying is the Devil's business, for any side. I know that Robert Poley is a professional informer. As the poet says, "They cut men's throats with whispers."

'That's Marlowe the blasphemer,' said Elizabeth grimly as he rode away. 'He'll pay. The Devil always collects his debts.'

There's a Puritan minister in Elizabeth's family. And she is Puritan about sharing my bed. With the low-cut dresses women wear now it's hard for a man. In every sense. I think Elizabeth would like to turn me into a militant Protestant, writing fiery pamphlets against the Pope and all his works. I would not bet on the Pope in a face to face encounter with her. He wouldn't stand a chance against a woman who can subdue a bunch of roaring boys in a London inn with a single glance. But just as I'm beginning to wonder why I'm going to marry a woman who seems to be a cross between Queen Elizabeth and Joan of Acre, that severe Puritan countenance will light up with a smile. Like opening the bible and finding a picture of Venus in the Book of Job.

Handing over the bread and cheese and pot of ale, she picked up the coins and asked if they were mine. I shrugged and agreed they were.

'And what about your debts, Thomas? Are they paid?'

My mouth full of bread and cheese, I nodded. Well, why bother my lovely fair-haired beauty. She fixed her clear blue eyes on me and said, 'So I need not have troubled trying to shake off the two bailiffs who…'

Nearly choking on the bread and cheese I looked across the street. We saw each other simultaneously. Dropping the food and ale I ran.

'Henslowe wants you to collaborate on a play,' shouted Elizabeth as I belted down Bishopsgate Street hoping to lose my pursuers in the crowded streets of the city.

Two

Elizabeth's words put wings on my heels. Henslowe wanted me to write for his theatre. It was a start. But first I had to get away. Glancing back I saw they were gaining on me. Those two were stayers. The leader looked like a hog with his cropped hair and wart-encrusted nose.

Looking ahead I saw with dismay that a broken-wheeled cart was blocking the road. Swinging right into Finsbury Fields I ran behind the targets. No one bothered to stop shooting. Surely they wouldn't follow me here. They must have been desperate to earn the fee for catching me because looking back I saw them still grimly chasing. As we ran, heads down, arrows and bolts whistled past. Bailiffs are unpopular. The archers were gleefully taking the opportunity to wing one and claim they were shooting at the target. As I ran, panting, I had to agree with old Cruickshank on two things about modern youth. We lacked exercise and our aim with the bow was atrocious. Most of the arrows were coming my way.

I couldn't keep this pace up. I had to go to earth in London. They'd run me down in the open. The next entrance was Moorgate. Getting onto the road I groaned as I saw in front of me a great lumbering wagon heading for Moorgate. If it got there first I'd have a blocked gateway. Putting on a spurt I saw that it was going to be very close. If I could just squeeze through then my pursuers would be stuck. They'd have to wait until the wagon ground slowly through the gateway. Just as I reached the tail-end of the wagon the front was going under the archway. Trapped.

The bailiffs came running at me. As I was jumping onto the wagon Warthog grabbed my doublet ripping it from my back. But I was free, blundering through crates of squawking chickens, knocking them over, breaking them open. The driver turned, his mouth a gaping hole of black, broken teeth. Brushing past him I scrambled over the backs of the horses surrounded by flapping chickens and flying feathers. I jumped from the front horse and landed on a gallant bowing to a lady, knocking him flat. While disentangling myself I saw the driver furiously lashing the bailiffs with his whip as they blundered through the crates of chickens. Having got my breath back I made off down the street dodging in and out of the crowd.

I'd been given a slight start on them in the city but they still had me in sight. Swerving round a corner to my right I ran past shopkeepers shouting their call of, 'What do you lack?' then turned left into Ironmongers Lane. Taking a breather in a shop doorway I peered around the side and saw my pursuers arrive at the entrance to the lane. They stopped, looked down it, hesitated, then carried straight on. I'd shaken them off. Still looking to make sure they had gone I left the doorway and banged into a burly porter. He flung me aside and I crashed into a highly built pyramid of pots and pans bringing them clattering and clanging to the ground. Rushing out the shopkeeper swung a broomstick at my head, missed and hit the porter. He roared, dropped his pack, and began pelting the ironmonger with his own pots and pans. The two bailiffs came charging back round the corner and once again I was running.

Plunging into a maze of narrow, twisting alleys I ran with bursting lungs and aching legs. Sweat ran down into my eyes, sweat soaked my shirt. I ran seeing only the ground at my feet, hearing the thud of the carpenter's mallet give way to the ring of the blacksmith's hammer. And the smells. After the forge's hot metal I passed the acrid charcoal burner, the pungent tanyard then the heady brewery.

Outside the latter, two prentices had piled up a stack of empty barrels. They were resting on a piece of rope. In passing I bent and pulled out the rope bringing them tumbling down. Barrels bounced back from the opposite wall while others bounded along the alley at the pursuing bailiffs. Another respite gained.

I was completely lost when I suddenly emerged into St Laurence Lane. Turning left to get into the crowds of Cheapside I heard the tap, tap, tap of the cobbler's hammer and the cry, 'Yark and seam, yark and seam.' Crossing the road, I plunged into another alley.

That was my old master's voice, Daniel Clay, shoemaker. My father was Dutch and had been killed in the rising against Spain. When our village was burned by Spanish soldiers my mother had fled to relatives in London where I had been posthumously born. I had a grammar school education but could not afford to go to university. Although the money I had was not enough for a premium Master Clay had taken me on as an apprentice shoemaker. He and his wife had been another father and mother to me. I think my lean and hungry look brought out Mistress Clay's mothering instinct. 'Give him some more,' she'd tell the maid at meal times. Many a poor prentice goes short of food but not me. Yet I never took to shoemaking. Then I got in with a crowd of prentices who haunted the theatres and taverns and cobbling became more and more irksome. When I sold a pamphlet I thought I was a writer and decided to leave the trade. Master Clay begged me to stay but I was adamant and he would not use the force of law. He'd said that as a shoemaker I could earn a living anywhere in Europe. It

10

would grieve him and his wife to see me now being pursued by bailiffs. Master Clay was proud of "The gentle craft" and had wanted me to take a pride in it. I glanced back along the alley. Those two bailiffs also had professional pride. They were sticking to me like hounds to a fox.

Next I came out into Milk Street. As I ran down it I wondered which was the murder house. Old Cruickshank was sitting in the window of the Sun Tavern as I went haring past. He must have thought I'd taken his strictures on exercise to heart.

At last I was in Cheapside. But it was not as crowded as I would have wished. A fine coach with a familiar looking coat of arms on the door passed by. Through the window I saw a young woman with beautiful dark eyes. Fanning herself she looked at me labouring in a bath of sweat, an amused smile playing across her lovely face. If this had been a romance like Amadis de Gaul I would have been rescuing her from a band of outlaws instead of fleeing from a pair of bailiffs. But this was real life and the coach passed on.

I caught up with it at Cheap Cross. Cracking his whip the driver was forcing it through a crowd gathered around a preacher giving an impromptu sermon. There was no way through for me so I was forced to turn up Wood Street. The preacher was one of those who like to pluck their ideas from the passing scene: 'For what sin is that youth fleeing in this modern Babylon? Is he a haunter of the playhouse and the brothel? Learn from him brethren. For though he outrun the laws of man yet must he face…' 'Oh leave me alone' I thought. What had I done to deserve this? All I wanted to do was write plays.

Ahead of me loomed the Counter Prison. Standing at the door were two bailiffs waiting to enter with their prisoners. Seeing me being chased by their fellows, one of them moved across to intercept. I cut along a lane which eventually brought me back to Cheapside. Rounding a corner I saw the young woman from the coach standing before me. I tripped over a loose cobblestone and flung out my arms catching the front of her dress and ripping it down. It must have made a fine sight. Me on my knees gaping up at her bare breasts and panting like an ardent lover. Those lovely eyes blazed with anger. Then the absurdity of it must have struck her, for she burst out laughing.

'Bailiffs?' she asked quickly. I nodded. 'Into the coach.' I dived in and pulled the door shut. Just in time. As I crouched on the floor panting I heard my pursuers come pounding around the corner, shoes ringing on the cobbles.

'Look what the rogue's done to my dress,' shouted my rescuer, impersonating anger with a passion an actor would have been proud of.

'Which way?' was the terse response.

'Towards St Paul's.' They ran on and she came to the window of the coach: 'Stay there while I replace the dress you've ruined,' she said before walking away with her maid to find a clothes shop. Seeing the way her lovely white breasts had bulged over the dress she held against them I had no objection at all to staying. At the same time I felt apprehensive. I had recalled who the coat of arms on the door belonged to. Lord Hunsdon, her majesty's Lord Chamberlain, the man responsible for the performance of plays at court. The woman I was lusting for must be his mistress, Emelia Bassano. Heigh ho. If I did get my sinful way I wasn't sure who I'd be most afraid of finding out. Lord Hunsdon or Elizabeth.

But first things first. Stretching out on a seat, I had a much needed rest. Turning over, I saw a piece of paper flutter to the floor. When I picked it up I found a hand written poem. Having a professional interest, I read it. I was sure it was not by his lordship. He was a bluff

12

military man. Definitely not a soldier poet like Sidney or Raleigh. She had another admirer. It seemed an odd poem to write to your mistress. I read it aloud:

'*My mistress' eyes are nothing like the sun.*
Coral is far more red than her lips red.
If snow be white why then...'

'*her breasts are dun.*' completed Emelia getting into the coach and sitting opposite me. She had sent her maid on an errand. 'You read poetry, I see.'

'I write it too,' I replied with as careless an air as I could muster.

'Ah, a poet. That fits with being chased by bailiffs. Poetry and poverty go together like sweetmeats and toothache. The one causes the other. So what do you write? Epics, epigrams, sonnets, satires? Not satires I hope or I shall be afraid of you.'

Any woman who looked less likely to be afraid of a poet or any other man I have yet to see. 'I write plays,' I replied casually.

'Another playmaker. Should I have heard of you?'

'Not yet, madam. But I think one day you will hear the name Thomas Dekker.'

'So what do you think of my poet?'

'Saying your eyes are nothing like the sun is not doing justice to them.'

'Gaze into my eyes.'

'I could gaze into them all day,' I said looking deep into those lovely dark pools.'

'Oh I wouldn't like that, Tom – you don't mind if I call you Tom? – I should soon become bored.' She pointed to the window. 'Now gaze into the sun and tell me which is the brightest.' She patted the seat beside her and I leapt across with alacrity.

Breathing into my face she asked, 'Is my breath like perfume, Tom?'

'The very sweetest perfume,' I murmured, wondering whether it was time to take her in my arms. She drew back laughing: 'Oh, Tom. Try opening a perfumery and selling my bottled breath to fine ladies. You'd soon be bankrupt with a whole posse of bailiffs chasing you. You've seen roses, what do you think of the colour of my cheeks?'

'Well the red and white do suggest...'

Taking my hand she rubbed it gently against her face and said, 'You could say my smooth cheek is like the softness of the petals, but' – pulling my hand beneath her chin – 'where are the briars under them?'

'Your tongue?' I enquired dryly. She threw back her head and laughed: 'Good, Tom. I liked that.' She looked down at her bosom still showing a generous amount in the new gown: 'My breasts are not as white as snow, but then...' pressing my hand against them – 'they're warmer.'

I put my other arm around her shoulders and pulled her to me. She murmured in my ear, 'My poet also says he's never seen a goddess go and that I tread on the ground. Like a human being. And that's what I am, Tom, a woman. Not an old man's whore or a young man's goddess but a human being just like you. And like a man I challenge the right to follow my desires.' She kissed me full on the lips then called to the coachman to drive on and told me to pull down the blinds.

I'd heard of coaches being used for copulation, now I was experiencing it for myself. As I'd made a character in my (unacted, alas) comedy say, "Riding while riding."

'Slower,' gasped Emelia. She was talking to me of course but really should have been telling the driver. It was hard to slow down when he was bouncing the coach over the cobblestones. Then a series of potholes jolted me to a climax.

14

We dressed in silence. She pulled up the blinds and ordered the driver to stop. Opening the door she hissed, 'A woman's entitled to satisfaction as much as a man.' and gestured for me to leave. Watching the coach roll away, I thought of Phaeton who, trying to drive the chariot of the sun across the sky, had failed to control the mettlesome horses and been flung from the chariot down to earth. Then I cursed the Lord Mayor and the Council of London for the state of their roads.

Three

It was Sunday morning and I was sitting in the Cross Keys in Gracious Street. Elizabeth, skirt swinging, was bustling between the tables supervising the serving girls then springing up the stairs to check the guest rooms. As ever she was checking everything before leaving for church. She insisted on having most of Sunday off. The landlord, recognising her worth and anxious to keep her, had agreed.

I needed my beer. Today I was to meet the uncle and aunt Elizabeth was staying with in London. Then there was the vicar of St Olaves. He preached a long, long sermon. Some preachers can dramatise a sermon, make it as good as a play. You can smell the brimstone, hear the crackling hellfire and the shrieks of the sinners, feel their parched throats – I took a long swig of beer. Yes, some preachers can put heaven and hell in front of you. Well, at least hell. Not the Reverend Bracegirdle. He sounded like a schoolmaster interminably conjugating Latin verbs; or a long-winded lawyer pontificating on praemunires. Actually he does conjure up a kind of hell.

Elizabeth, guessing why I looked so glum, hissed as she passed, 'It's time you attended church or they'll think you're a catholic.'

True. And what was even more pertinent to my debt-ridden position was the threat of being fined for non-attendance. So it was St Olaves for me with Elizabeth and her uncle and aunt. I had another tankard of beer. They have a good full-bodied beer at the Cross Keys. And it felt

16

good to be able to slap down my own money for it. My first earnings from the theatre.

After my escape from the bailiffs (yes and being ejected from the coach) I was ejected from my lodgings. A lot of ejections last Friday, including my own pot hole propelled one. With little money for rent, I was forced to move into the tenements of Coldharbour in Thames Street. Your neighbours there do not include any aldermen in red robes from the city's Common Council. And you will not receive social visits from the Lord Mayor. (Private visits to Rosie upstairs, perhaps.) The previous addresses of my new neighbours included the Clink, the Fleet, the Marshallsea, Bridewell, Newgate and most of the other London prisons. And their visits are not social ones. So just enough money to keep me going. In beer, if not in board. Leastways not a board to which you could invite my lords Essex or Southampton. Always supposing you had their acquaintance.

Having fixed up my new lodgings I set off to see Henslowe at the Rose Playhouse in Southwark. First I called at the Sun in Milk Street. I wanted to hear old Cruickshank's story of the murder so that if there was a play in it I could outline it to Henslowe and his chief actor, Edward Alleyn.

Isn't it always the way? Now that I wanted to see Cruickshank he was nowhere to be found. On my way to the Bridge I tried another of his haunts, the Boar's Head in Eastcheap. Not there either.

Every time I cross London Bridge I feel proud to be a Londoner. I've heard foreigners describe it as one of the wonders of the world. And so it is with its high buildings on either side.

It makes an unpromising start. You pass from Fish Street Hill onto the Bridge with the waterwheel threshing on your right and the shouts of Billingsgate fishmongers on your left. There was a south wind that day so the pungent fish smells were gradually overpowered by the stench of smelting works, candle makers and tanneries blowing from Southwark. Then I was swept up in the bustle of the Bridge. A herd of lowing cattle followed by cackling geese with the barking of dogs and the yelling of drovers. Meeting them from the city end was a horse and cart, the driver cursing and cracking his whip striving to force a way through. There was hammering from workshops and behind stalls apprentices piping, 'What do you lack?' A fruiter beneath the sign of Adam and Eve crying, 'Best apples to tempt you.' A tobacconist crying, 'Finest Spanish,' under the sign of a Red Indian smoking a pipe. From above the shrieks of seagulls and, below, the roaring river gushing through the narrow arches with the shouts and screams of men and women as their boats shot beneath the Bridge. Occasional gaps in the buildings gave glimpses of the Thames glinting in the bright sun while from the landing stairs drifted faintly the cries of watermen calling, 'Eastward ho,' and 'Westward ho.' On I struggled through the tide of humanity past magnificent Nonesuch House, with its onion shaped cupolas at each corner surmounted by a gilded weather vane. Then I was outside the House with Many Windows, as it has been dubbed.

Passing through the Great Stone Gate into Southwark, I saw an obvious countryman in his russet-coloured hose and jerkin with a bundle on a stick over his shoulder. What we Londoners are used to he must have been seeing for the first time. He was gaping up at the heads of traitors stuck on poles above the arch of the gate.

'Looking for someone?' asked an idler outside the Bear Tavern to the guffaws of his companions. 'A relative? brother, father?'

Shooting them a surly glance the man passed onto the Bridge. The gate swallowed him like a mouth, another morsel for the city to digest. London needs its food and has a voracious stomach. Likely enough a greedy landlord, controlling the law, had enclosed his bit of land for more profitable sheep then spat him out like a plum-stone.

When I reached the Rose Playhouse they were rehearsing the play to be given that afternoon. I've got a good memory but actors, putting on a different play every day, need powerful memories to hold words like a magnet holds metal. They were going to perform Greene's Friar Bacon and Friar Bungay. Like Marlowe, Greene's another of the so-called university wits, looking down on the rest of us. Edward Alleyn interrupted his speech to tell me that the subject of the play I was to collaborate on was Sir Thomas More and that I would find Master Henslowe at the Mermaid Tavern. The other actors did not give me a glance. Writers are not much regarded except for Marlowe. To the chagrin of Greene.

So I retraced my steps, heading for Bread Street. Approaching London Bridge I looked up at the archway and thought, fifty odd years ago it had been decorated with More's head.

In the Mermaid, Henslowe was seated at a table with my two collaborators. There was Anthony Munday, often called a good plotter. Well, he would be, mixed up in the world of anti-catholic spying. The other was cheerful Henry Chettle, who'll write anything to turn a penny. How the university wits would have despised us. They despised Henslowe as a hog rooting money out of brothel and playhouse while destroying their poetry. But they were quick to lay out the money they got from him for their plays in his brothels. I'll say this for him. He paid promptly and was willing to give money to writers in advance. As with me now. And a bottle of wine for us.

Munday ran through the plot and I was assigned my part to write. Henslowe was particularly keen on the May Day riot by London apprentices against French

19

immigrants being included. Given the present day mutterings against Huguenot refugees, he was convinced it would soon be topical. Little did he know he would shortly have his fill of rioting.

Ideas raced through my mind as I walked home along Eastcheap. Then I saw old Cruickshank entering the Boar's Head. Hurrying in, I shocked him into silence buying him a pot of ale. We sat at a table and without preamble I told him I was writing for the theatre and might be interested in dramatising the Milk Street murder. While the faces of the other drinkers showed relief and incredulity at seeing someone actually seeking out Cruickshank's company, his face lit up. His murder story told from the stage.

'Mistress Wingfield,' he began solemnly, 'was murdered just over two years ago on the Eighth of February One Thousand Five Hundred and Ninety. And that was three years to the day after the execution of the Queen of Scots.'

'And time too for that Papist whore,' growled the landlord, who was violently anti-catholic. A murmur of assent travelled quickly round the room stopping at a young man dreamily puffing on a pipe. All eyes turned on him. Seeing their suspicion he said hastily, 'Yes, yes, like all good protestants I rejoiced to see her head taken off'.

Cruickshank put a hand to his neck muttering about a draught before going on with his story. 'Old Mother Wingfield was a witch,' he stated dogmatically. 'I know because she put a spell on me just before she was killed. She was looking out of her window at the back of Milk Street as I was coming from Wood Street along the lane by the prison. I'd often seen her there staring out with the window open so as the Devil could come and go as he pleased. But it was only that day she fixed her single, black, evil eye on me. And just as I reached my front door I fell down and broke my leg.' He looked around uncertainly. The pert young waiter placed the fresh pots of ale I'd ordered in front of us and said, 'You slipped on the ice, Master Cruickshank.'

'That ice had been there a week. Why didn't I slip before?'

Winking at the rest of the room, the waiter held up a pot of ale and said, 'You'd been drinking in here all day, Master Cruickshank, and we serve the strongest ale in London.'

'He's the reason a lot of people don't come in here,' said Cruickshank, jabbing a finger at the waiter's departing back. 'Could be the most popular tavern in Cheapside if he was got rid of.' I had to hear another diatribe against modern youth before we got back to the murder. 'She was found lying dead on the floor,' he said quietly and for the first time looked frightened. Perhaps the seriousness with which I was taking his account brought back the horror he had felt at the time. 'The door was bolted on the inside, Thomas,' he continued, his voice dropping to a whisper. 'We had a lodger, a felt maker's servant, a sober, religious young man. He was walking out with one of the old woman's maids. When she couldn't open the door she called him over and a couple of the watch who were passing. They broke the door down and found the old woman. Her eye had been gouged out and yet there was no weapon in the room. And the window was too high for anyone to have climbed in. Besides which they would have been seen. Thomas, what could it have been other than…?' His voice trailed away and he looked at me, an old man terrified by what he feared he had come into contact with. He made me shiver. I could see now why he had talked so compulsively about the murder. Despite his apparent anger at the jokes, they had calmed the surface of his mind; but deep down his terror had lurked like a sea-monster.

The landlord was a big man but he moved lightly and I had hardly been aware of his presence near our table. Now he leaned between us and said in a low voice, 'There were rumours about Mistress Wingfield knowing the secrets of men in high places. She moved to London from Kingston and she kept her door bolted, it is said, because she went in fear of her life. Courtiers plot against each other and have secrets they would kill to keep.'

If I got enough material from this affair for a play, would I get it past the censor? That would depend on whether or not he belonged to the faction whose guilty secret was being revealed. This was dangerous ground. Also intriguing, in both senses. Nothing moves a play along like intrigue.

The landlord's face hardened: 'And some courtiers plot against her majesty.' His voice became hoarse: 'Secret Catholics, Master Dekker.' He cast a bloodshot eye at the young man puffing on his pipe and whispered, 'They're everywhere. The defeat of the Armada was a sore blow to them so now they're trying to bring the Spanish in by treachery.'

'But many Catholics fought against the...'

'A blind, a blind. As a child I saw the protestant martyrs suffer at Smithfield under the Devil's whore Mary Tudor. The smell of their burning flesh is still in my nostrils.' Slipping a piece of paper into my hand he muttered, 'Burn it when you've read it,' and moved away to attend a customer. When I got outside I looked at the paper. It contained the address of the felt maker's servant and that of one of the watchmen. Was I going to go on with this business?, I wondered, while knowing that I would.

Four

'I hope you're more attentive in church, Thomas.' Elizabeth, dressed now in a sober black dress, was waving her hand in front of my face. I finished my beer and we left the Cross Keys.

Waiting outside were Elizabeth's uncle, Master Brayne, her aunt and their daughter, Chastity, who was about Elizabeth's age. Why do puritan families risk giving their offspring the names of virtues which so often seem to be contradicted by the children's nature? While her name was covered with frost, Chastity's eyes, raking me from under her demure bonnet, shot out fire. They say there are not many chaste maids in Cheapside. Chased, yes, caught, yes. Chaste, no. If Chastity was chaste it was not from choice. Perhaps she took after her father who had about him the look of a merry nature suppressed. Mistress Brayne, the undoubted suppressor, stood alongside him like a black bible next to a playbook. When Elizabeth introduced me the husband smiled, the daughter curtsied and Mistress Brayne said severely, 'I hope you remembered to bring your prayer book, young man.'

We set off for St Olaves along West Cheap. It being the Sabbath my attempts at light-hearted conversation were frozen out by the icicle at our centre. Respectful greetings from passers-by were met with a slight inclination of the head. When bawdy songs and banging tankards hit our ears from the doorway of an ale house, the temperature at our centre plummeted.

I wanted to make a good impression for Elizabeth's sake so, when we passed a crowd gathered around a ballad singer, I did not boast that he was singing one of mine. It was one I was proud of too. But its refrain was:

'With hey, trixy, terlery-whiskin,
The world it runs on wheels,
When the young man's in
Up goes the maiden's heels.'

Not exactly one of the psalms. It brought a glow to Chastity's cheek. And I fancied I saw Elizabeth and her uncle struggling to keep a smile from their faces. The only thing that would have brought a smile to Mistress Brayne's wintry features would have been the Archangel Gabriel asking her to ascend and reorganise heaven on puritan lines since Calvin and Knox were not up to the job.

I did not notice a ballad singer's mate working amongst the crowd. Perhaps they regarded my songs as a passport to Tyburn and refused to cut purses while they were being sung. That, "Doesn't hold them enough, Master Dekker," still rankled with me. At least Prigging Peter wasn't there to embarrass me with my present company. Peter was one of my neighbours in Coldharbour Tenements. Returning home I had met him coming out of my room.

'You're Tom, I hear,' he'd said holding out his hand. 'My name's Peter.'

'Prigging Peter,' cackled Rosie, who was taking a client up to her room. Prigging, I knew, was thieves' slang for stealing.

'It's by way of being a joke between me and Rosie,' he explained as I stared at my inkhorn protruding from his pocket. 'What happened, Tom, is, I heard a noise in your room and when I opened the door to see if anyone was stealing your stuff a rat shot past me and bolted down the passage. I goes in to make sure everything's alright and sees your inkhorn on the floor – which the rat must have knocked off the table – which must have been the noise I heard. Not wanting you to step on it when you comes home I puts it in my pocket while I checks round the room to see if the rat's knocked anything else off – over. He pressed the inkhorn into my hand and added, 'Don't thank me, Tom. What else are neighbours for?'

By now I had the feeling that he believed his own story. There is a lesson in that for we writers. But Peter is not a bad sort. We had a drink together later and I told him about the murder I was investigating for my play. My prestige rose when he knew I was a playmaker since he is a regular play goer. I thought ruefully that I would be providing the same kind of service for Peter and his kind with my plays as with my ballads. But he did let slip that he sometimes gets so engrossed by a play that the only purse he comes out with is his own. He promised to ask around about the Milk Street murder.

'Well done,' whispered Elizabeth, returning me to the present. 'For not chattering away,' she said in answer to my enquiring look. Mistress Brayne, who misses little, turned her eyes heavenward and said piously, 'We must hope his thoughts have been suitable for the Sabbath.'

I don't suppose she thought the street cries echoing along Cheapside were suitable. But for me, some of the London street cries are poetry. Perhaps not the hoarse voiced man pushing a barrow and bawling:

'My honest friend, will you buy a bowl,
A skimmer or a platter?
Come buy of me a rolling pin
Or spoon to beat your batter.'

But there is poetry in the lilting accent of a Welsh girl I sometimes hear in Holborn crying, 'My dill and cucumbers to pickle.' As there was in the sweet tones of a pretty young Irish woman behind us singing, 'Cherry ripe, cherry ripe, come buy my ripe cherries.' Her looks and voice brought a smile of pleasure to all faces with the one obvious exception.

Yes, if you know where to look for it, life is full of poetry. Then I saw Prigging Peter with his head stuck through the pillory. In addition to his usual broken teeth and broken nose he now had a puffed up right eye as black as Mistress Brayne's dress. I sidled behind her. I am not the kind to deliberately walk past someone I know but I did want to make a good impression for Elizabeth's sake.

Although Peter was his usual irrepressible self, a London crowd can be a fearsome thing and he needed to get them on his side. It must be terrifying to have your head exposed with your hands, wrists locked on either side, unable to defend it. More than one poor devil has been stoned to death by an angry crowd.

A young man overtook us, his satin and velvet clothes reeking of perfume, a scent bottle held to his nose against the street smells. His delicate face rose out of the frilly well-starched ruff around his neck.

'These wooden ruffs are the latest fashion, sir,' called Peter. 'Let me sell you one.' The crowd were silent and the man ignored him. 'Or you could use it in your privy. Just your size, sir.'

That brought a few guffaws. Unfortunately it also suggested an idea to a surly looking fellow who bent down and picked up a handful of horse dung. Peter raised a palm and said, 'If you're going to throw horse shit at me throw the bit that gentleman's just stepped in. It'll smell sweeter.'

The crowd laughed and the man, looking at his befouled shoe, shouted, 'This city is as dirty as the people who live in it.'

Rosie, who had just turned up, flounced over to him hands on hips and said, 'Pardon us for living, sir. Perhaps you'd like us to throw ourselves in the Thames.'

'It would wash some of the filth off you,' he sneered.

'You too,' shouted the surly man, splattering his satin doublet with the horse dung. When he began to draw his sword the crowd roared and a volley of dung and mud sent him flying down Cheapside. When the surly man looked at Peter and picked up another handful Rosie knocked it from his hand saying, 'Leave him alone, he's alright,' to a murmur of assent from the crowd.

'Mistress Brayne,' roared Peter, making her stiffen even more. Jerking his head at the crowd he said, 'Thanks to these good folk you'll soon have a new customer for your velvet and satin clothes.' He winked at the company: 'Finest mercers in Cheapside, I've had many a doublet and shirt from there.' Amid raucous laughter someone called, 'But when you going to pay for them, Peter?'

'When he's cut a few more purses,' chuckled Rosie. Peter shook his head as far as the pillory would allow and said with mock solemnity, 'Ah, Rosie, I'll wager you don't get any customers from Mistress Brayne's apprentices. She teaches them the virtues of chastity.'

'She hasn't got any virtues,' shouted a man, grinning at Chastity who giggled then put a hand over her mouth.

'Bloody amateurs,' said Rosie. 'They takes away our customers.'

When we got past a group of people blocking our way, Mistress Brayne put on a sudden spurt leaving me exposed.

'Tom,' yelled Peter. 'Come here.' When I went to him he said, 'I've been asking around about the Milk Street murder. That's how I got this black eye and was put in here. A poxy waterman said I must be an informer. Me,' he added indignantly. 'So naturally I thumped him. His mates joined in then my mates and I was the poor bastard who was grabbed by the Knight Marshall's men.' He sniffed my breath. 'You've been drinking, Tom. That's Cross Keys beer, the best. Now you've given me a thirst.'

27

I handed over some money and Rosie fetched him a pot of ale and held it to his lips. I was about to join my companions when I saw three horsemen approaching. It was Christopher Marlowe, Ingram Frizer and Robert Poley. A murmur that it was Poley the informer built up to an angry growl. Hearing it Poley swerved his horse aside putting the other two between himself and the crowd.

'He should be in here,' shouted Peter, 'for the innocent men his lies have hanged.'

Marlowe drew his sword and flourished it above his head. Frizer rode up to the crowd, took a handful of cherries from the girl's basket and squashed them into Peter's face. Rejoining his companions he laughed, 'Now he's like one of Raleigh's Red Indians.'

Marlowe, I think, was tiring of merely writing about powerful men like Tamburlaine and the Duke of Guise; he wanted a taste of real power. He was a baby in the hands of men like Frizer and Poley, though. Poley never smiled and Frizer's humour was like the devilish grin of a gargoyle. If someone had to be disposed of there would be no romantic flourish of a sword from Frizer, none of the glorious poetry of a Tamburlaine. It would be the prose of the assassin in Arden of Faversham, Black Will: "Give me the money and I'll stab him as he stands pissing against a wall but I'll kill him." To a master tradesman in murder like Frizer, Marlowe was an apprentice.

When I rejoined the others they were talking in scandalised tones of Marlowe the blasphemer and atheist. 'And,' they whispered, 'the sins of Sodom and Gomorrah.' No one paid any attention to Frizer, the most dangerous of the three. And so we made our way along West Cheap past Mercer's Hall and up to St Olave's.

It was good to get out of the hot sun beating down on the street and into the cool church. Not so good was changing the raucous poetry of the people for the dry tones of the Reverend Bracegirdle. When he stumbled

28

through the usual warning about wilful rebellion against the monarch appointed by God, I thought that the last one had been over twenty years ago, before I was born, the great catholic rising in the North. Moderate protestants were saying that now a rebellion was more likely from the puritans. With England still at war with Spain, that would be folly. During his achingly tedious sermon I reflected that if there were a rebellion it would be a good idea to send his reverence to preach to the rebels. That would dampen their ardour and extinguish the rising as quickly as a bucket of water poured on a penny candle. I prayed for his sermon to end, for the Lord to lead us out of the valley of tedium. At last it was over. I could tell everyone had been as wearied as me by our fervent singing of Psalm Four: "Hear me when I call, O God of my righteousness; thou hast enlarged me when I was in distress."

Now we were back in the bright sunshine walking out through Cripplegate to Islington. Mistress Brayne stared sternly ahead, probably meaning to have a word with the Reverend Bracegirdle about his sermons being too short. Chastity whispered in my left ear, 'Mother will be in a better mood when we reach Islington;' then Master Brayne in my right ear, 'My wife will be in a better mood when we reach Islington.' Next Elizabeth, 'Aunt Esther will be…'

'Yes, yes,' I said, 'at Islington. 'But what's at…' my heart sank. I groaned, 'It's not another sermon, is it?'

Elizabeth, in what I consider to be a most unchristian manner, let me stew for several minutes before whispering, 'Cakes and custard.'

Well of course I knew that Islington was famous for those. There were many other parties like us. It was a favourite Sunday walk after church. When I was an apprentice the Clays had often taken me out as a treat. Although we generally went to Hoxton which Master

Clay maintained had finer custard. 'It's their Derby ale he goes for, Tom,' Mistress Clay would say with a wink. And now as we walked from Golden Lane into Old Street and turned left I saw poor Master Brayne gazing wistfully at the men turning right for Hoxton. Nothing surprising in that. What puzzled me was the coupling of Mistress Brayne with cakes and custard. It was incongruous. Like coupling misers and free spending, lawyers and plain dealing, courtiers and humility, poets and plenty. But I suppose everyone is human; and the closer we were getting to Islington the more human she was looking.

Then the Sabbath quiet was shattered as across the fields from the theatre rolled beating drums, blaring trumpets, roaring cannon. You'd think they would have chosen a quieter play. They were not supposed to act on a Sunday but they sometimes said, to hell with it. And Hell is what it must have sounded like to Mistress Brayne who began gabbling like a turkey about temples of the Devil. She glared at her husband: 'How your brother, a respectable grocer, could have put money into building that den of iniquity – no one in my family would do such a thing. I had a cousin, twice removed, who was once heard whistling on a Sunday and none of us has spoken to him since.'

At last we reached Islington and entered one of the refreshment gardens. We sat at a table and gave our order to a pretty young girl who curtsied then brought our cakes and custards. The severe lines engraved in Mistress Brayne's face by the iniquities of this sinful world, by actors in playhouses and insulters in pillories, were filled in by the cakes and smoothed out by the custard. Replete she sat back in her chair, sighed with satisfaction and permitted herself a half smile, even though it was a Sunday. Elizabeth's Puritanism is tempered with good sense, good humour and a good heart; poor Master Brayne has to rely on cakes and custard.

Having digested our food we joined others strolling in the fields around the village. It was good to look back at the smoke of London while breathing the fresh country air. Citizens complain that they are condescended to by courtiers but they do their share of condescending. I heard a portly alderman, showing off his status in a red robe, say to his wife: 'It's good to get away from sophisticated city-dwellers for a while to be among the simple country-folk of Islington.'

'And may they always remain so,' said his wife.

'Amen to that.'

When Chastity took Elizabeth off to pick flowers and herbs, Mistress Brayne said firmly, 'The other way,' directing them away from a group of young men watching a wrestling match.

Lying on the grass, I listened drowsily to the twittering birds and buzzing bees. It took me back to summer days in school with the same sounds drifting in through the open window while the schoolmaster's voice droned the words of a Roman writer. I sat up abruptly. Why had the memory of a summer's day in school made me think of a winter's day in a locked room with old Mother Wingfield lying on her back, a black hole where her eye should have been? Because I'd been lying on my back? No. It was something to do with the Roman writer. A poet? A satirical one seemed likely. Horace, Persius, Martial, Juvenal? An historian? Livy, Tacitus? No. Suetonius had some lurid tales of the emperors. Although there had to be a question about the reliability of an historian one of whose books, lost unfortunately, was entitled Lives of the Great Whores. It could be Seneca's play, Oedipus. While translating the passage where he describes in horrific detail Oedipus gouging out his eyes, I had vomited in the classroom. Could the old woman have gouged out her own eye in a fit of madness? I must ask the watchman or the servant who had found her.

As we walked slowly home the warm summer lanes seemed as remote from that cold winter room as ancient Rome from modern London.

Five

The watch are a joke. On the stage constables are always portrayed as comic figures. So when I called to see Nicholas Winton, one of the watchmen who had found old Mother Wingfield's body, it was unwise of me to tell him that I wanted to write a play on the murder.

A pair of clear, intelligent eyes sized me up as he said, 'I was first into the room after we had broken the door down. However, I did not trip over the body and fall out of the window. But no doubt your chief comedian will put that right.'

'I'll be writing the play, Master Winton,' I replied firmly while knowing that Will Kempe would get his way over a mere writer.

Having closed his apothecary's shop for the day Winton motioned me to a chair. Taking out his pipe he lit it from the fire with a spill. Puffing out smoke he sighed contentedly and said, 'No doubt, as my wife says, a filthy habit but a major part of our livelihood and my pleasure. So you'll be writing the play, Master Dekker. But the actors will be paying you and he who pays the piper...'

After drawing on his pipe again he continued, 'Whether by accident or design you've come at just the right time of day, when I'm at my most mellow. With my pipe drawing well I enjoy holding forth to a willing listener.'

While he sucked on his pipe in silence, collecting his thoughts, I studied him, a thin-faced, sparsely-bearded, bony man, his eyes taking on a dreamy, contented look as the smoke curled about his head. I looked around the shop at a tortoise and a stuffed alligator hanging from the ceiling with skins of ill-shaped fishes; on his shelves empty boxes, green earthen pots, bladders, remnants of packthread; and cakes of pressed roses, their perfume mingling with musty seeds and the sweet or pungent smells of a variety of medicinal herbs. When my gaze returned to Winton's face his eyes beneath his beetle-brows were sharp, again appraising me.

'I had a couple of actors in here last week,' he said. 'One of them a writer, since his companion was urging him to write a tragedy about love. The writer's eyes made an inventory of me and my shop. Like yours.' He smiled: 'And mine when I'm called to the scene of a crime. It interests me. My wife complains it's what keeps us poor. True, no doubt, since, unlike my neighbours, I refuse to hive off my watch duties onto decrepit old men. And I suppose the actors are right enough since most of the constables and watchmen I work with have skulls as impenetrable as that tortoise shell. Besides, avoiding trouble and taking bribes are their sole interests. So what do you want to know about the murder of old Mother Wingfield?'

'You think it was murder, Master Winton?'

'What else?'

'Could she have gouged out her own eye in a fit of madness? There's an old play in which a man does just that.'

'This is real life, Master Dekker, not a play. People don't gouge out their own eyes. Besides, there was no blood under her fingernails.'

'People do stab themselves. Perhaps in her death throes she flung the knife through the window.'

'I checked the garden. There was a thin layer of snow on the ground. It had not been disturbed.'

'No footprints?'

34

'No footprints, no knife. Nothing.'

'And the door was bolted on the inside?'

He nodded.

'Could someone have got down the chimney?'

'No fireplace so no chimney. And before you ask, no priest hole. There were only two ways into that room, the door and the window. I wanted to solve that puzzle. Topcliffe hasn't racked his victims in the Tower harder than I've racked my brains for an answer. The snow had been there before the old woman went into the room so no one had come through the garden.'

'Could someone have climbed down a rope from the roof?'

He shook his head: 'The snow on the roof was undisturbed. And there were no windows close enough for the murderer to jump from.'

'They say witches can fly,' I said carefully.

'So I've heard, Master Dekker,' he replied, equally carefully.

'Do you believe in witchcraft, Master Winton?'

'I believe in Master Topcliffe's rack and if he asked me that question I should quote the bible, "Suffer not a witch to live." But I've never seen anyone fly. Not even,' he added dryly, 'a constable running away from a robber he's just bumped into.'

'Whoever killed her went to a lot of trouble. He must have had a strong motive.' Weighing my words carefully I added, 'I've heard rumours that she moved to London from Kingston where she had come into contact with powerful men, courtiers.'

He studied my face closely and remained silent.

'I'm no informer, Master Winton,' I said hotly, 'trying to trick you into incriminating yourself.'

He nodded: 'I think you're too honest to be a Robert Poley and I'm a good judge of character. When a woman asks me for a strong rat poison I have to be able to work out how many legs the rat she wants to kill has. Oh it's easy enough when the poor woman has bruises on her face. That's when I regret having to remind her that the penalty for a wife who kills her husband is burning at the stake.'

A new thought struck me: 'Could she have been poisoned earlier with something that would have later burned out her eye?'

He shook his head firmly: 'No, Master Dekker. There is no such poison. Besides which she had none of the symptoms of poisoning. As regards motive, I too have heard stories of great courtiers being involved. And religion.' He lowered his voice: 'Or even no religion, atheism. You got your information from old Cruickshank?' I nodded. He went on: 'A felt maker's servant, James Stour, was lodging with him. Stour was with us when we broke into the room. I've heard from various informants that he knew more about the affair than he let on. I had intended questioning him but I was warned to drop the enquiry. The warning, I was told, came from on high. Stour has moved away since.'

'To Southwark,' I said. 'I have his address. Where is the other watchman who was with you?'

'Moved away shortly after. Tribulation Cheadle's the name. A puritan name but not a puritan nature. I believe he's still in London.'

On my way to the apothecary's shop I'd passed the murder house and seen that it was now empty. When I expressed a wish to see the room, Winton offered to take me there. He was acting as an agent for the owner, who lived out of town. As we walked to the house he told me that when tenants heard about the murder they started hearing noises. Never the other way around. And they spoke in whispers to the neighbours about having felt a sense of evil on first entering the house: 'This would have

36

been just before they paid over the first year's rent in advance,' said Winton.

There were several people at their windows watching as we entered the house thinking, no doubt, another poor devil being gulled into renting a bewitched property. It was a three-storied building and as we climbed the stairs I thought I heard a noise. The room was on the top floor. Climbing the second flight again my ears seemed to detect a noise from above but again I kept silent. Through the gloom of the final flight came the patter of something moving above our heads.

'Rats,' said Winton. He pushed open the door of the room and we entered from the semi-dark of the corridor. A crimson light dazzled my eyes. On the floor alongside an overturned pot of vermilion paint the fragments of a broken mirror reflected the rays of a blood-red sun slanting through the window.

'The last tenants left in the middle of decorating,' explained Winton. He tapped the stout oak door and pointed to the two bolts. 'The old woman had those put on.'

'And they were both across?'

'Yes. And I've heard about bolts being slid across from outside with a piece of wire to give the impression the victim bolted the door. I examined the door carefully before we broke it down. It fitted tightly.'

We walked to the window and looked into the garden. The sun was setting behind the Counter Prison opposite, casting a long shadow across the grass and weeds. Winton pointed to the floor just behind us: 'That's where we found her, lying on her back. The chair she'd been sitting on was lying beside her.'

Looking at the spot I could imagine only too clearly that hole where her eye had been staring up at the ceiling.

'There's an attic above,' said Winton, following my gaze, 'but no trapdoors.'

I looked out of the window again and said, 'I believed in witchcraft as a child, of course, and I'm reluctant to return to my believe. But if Reginald Scott were here even his scepticism might be shaken.'

'Yes, I've also read his book.'

'Then how would he – how could he – account for what happened in this room?'

Glancing around the small room that the old woman must have thought was so effectively sealed off, Winton said, 'My sceptical attitude to magic derives not only from what I've read but also from what I've seen. As a young man I wandered around England and much of Europe searching for medicinal herbs. For a time I travelled with a troupe; acrobats, jugglers, conjurers. In return for my keep I helped set up their stage. Although I had seen them practising their tricks, in performance even I was almost induced to believe it was magic. Some of the country-folk called them wizards and drove us out of the village with stones.'

He swept his arm to indicate the room: 'Until I'm shown otherwise I shall continue to believe in a rational explanation.'

Before leaving I paced up and down the room. The floor was solid. No trapdoors. Walking from the house we discussed the affair. Winton said he was still interested in it and asked me to keep him informed. In return he promised to pass on any information he obtained and asked where I could be contacted. When I said Coldharbour Tenements he raised his eyebrows. The place is notorious. I explained my straitened circumstances and admitted its being a sanctuary had been useful.

'From bailiffs,' I added hastily. 'I'm no thief.'

'You could become the victim of a thief in Coldharbour, Master Dekker; and you're vulnerable to bailiffs outside it.'

'No. I've paid part of my debts and my creditors have suspended their action on my promise to settle when I'm paid for my share of the Thomas More play. So I must get on with it.'

I left Winton at his shop and carried on towards Cheapside. Having to look out for bailiffs had sharpened my perceptions and I thought I saw a movement in the shadows across the street. Had one of the creditors reneged on the deal? It was still light, with too many people about for there to be much danger from robbers. They come out after dark. Now the streets still belonged to kites and ravens swooping on the heaps of refuse thrown into the gutters. The visit to the murder house, I decided, was making me nervous.

On my way home I called at the Cross Keys to see Elizabeth. Working at an inn had been good for her. Coming from a puritan family in puritan Cambridgeshire she admitted she had once been as austere as a snow-covered tombstone. That was the gist of it, anyway. I came up with another good image (one I can use in a play) when I said that the inn had broken the stained glass windows over her eyes and let in the world's light. She replied with the old severity: that her people smashed stained glass windows and let God's light into the church. True. The smashing bit, I mean. I don't know about the other. If the puritans get their way then soon they'll all be smashed. Seems a pity to me since some of those windows are beautiful. But I keep quiet.

The Cross Keys was heaving with assorted humanity, talking, singing, laughing, banging and clinking their tankards. I found a seat and Elizabeth, telling one of the girls to take her place behind the bar, brought me a tankard of their best beer and sat beside me. When I leaned forward to kiss her she turned her face away saying primly, 'There's a time and place, Thomas.'

I'd told her to call me Tom and tried calling her Bess. She had nipped that in the bud like a late spring frost. How, I wondered, had she come to work at the Cross Keys? I expressed surprise that Mistress Brayne had consented to her working at an inn. The late frost thawed in one of her warm smiles as she said, 'Uncle is a friend of the landlord and he got me the position. At first Aunt Esther was strongly against it, complaining about the sin of drunkenness and being amongst the ungodly. I reminded her that our Lord had gone amongst publicans and sinners and had turned water into wine. Uncle said that since there was nothing else suitable I would have to remain at home instead of bringing in money. Aunt decided that perhaps, after all, I might spread the word amongst the benighted. So here I am, talking to you, Thomas,' she concluded with another smile.

'And practically running the place,' I said looking around. The singing and shouting near the door suddenly died down. Glancing over Elizabeth's shoulder I saw a man in the buff jerkin favoured by soldiers and their imitators standing in the doorway. His hesitancy went oddly with the arrogant tilt of his head. When he saw who was behind the bar he swaggered into the room, drew his sword, clapped it onto a table and said loudly, 'God send I have no need of you,' then glared around at the company. Elizabeth stood up and walked over to him. Looking him straight in the eye she said, 'I banned you, sir, and you remain banned.'

They locked eyes for half a minute then he picked up his sword and slouched out. As she walked back to our table a man stretched out his arms saying in an affected voice, 'Ah, Mistress Elizabeth, I would be a willing Adonis to your Venus.'

'No, Sir Ambrose,' she replied, 'I would be a willing Judith to your Holofernes.'

'Who are they?' he asked his companions.

40

'They're in the bible, you ignorant bastard,' answered one.

'Was she in love with him?' he asked hopefully.

'She cut his head off, man.'

Shortly after, I walked Elizabeth back to her uncle's house where Mistress Brayne had organised a prayer-meeting.

'Are you sure you've got a deal with your creditors, Thomas?' she asked, noticing my darting glances in the street.

'Habit,' I assured her. When we reached the house she asked me to come in but I declined saying, I had to get on with my portion of Sir Thomas More. Which was true enough. 'Better not mention that in there.'

'No indeed,' said Elizabeth. 'Aunt Esther groans over you enough as it is. I'm not going to tell her that you put your playmaking before her prayer-meeting.'

So I made my way home through the darkened streets. I'm a good protestant and I'm ready to shout, the devil take the Pope and God bless Queen Elizabeth, down with the King of Spain and up with Sir Francis Drake and so forth. Young as I'd been, I was at Tilbury in eighty-eight ready to fight for England. But attending one of Mistress Brayne's prayer-meetings was beyond the call of duty. Especially when I heard from the open window the soporific tones of the Reverend Bracegirdle praising the Lord through his nose.

Ahead of me loomed the high, black outline of Coldharbour Tenements and, beyond, the dark Thames. Then I heard the rumble of wheels and saw reflected lights dancing on the water. A fine coach surrounded by outriders carrying flaming torches passed across the head of the street. Some rich man on a – I was knocked to the ground while something thudded into the house alongside me. As I grappled with my attacker he gasped, 'It's me, Peter, Prigging Peter.'

I relaxed my grip on his throat and asked what the hell he thought he was doing.

'Only saving your life, Tom, that's all. I saw someone in the shadows across the street then the torch-light glinting on metal.'

I ran my hand over the wall where I'd heard the thud and felt something sticking in it. 'A crossbow bolt,' I said. 'He must have been following me waiting to get a clear shot.'

'And the torch-light gave him his chance. Let's get inside, Tom. I've got some information for you.'

In my room he told me what he had gleaned from London's underworld. A powerful courtier was getting disturbed at my enquiries and wanted my mouth stopped. I sighed: 'It looks as if it's time to find a safer subject for a play.'

'There could be a difficulty about that, Tom. Lord Powerful, whoever he is, may still get rid of you in case you've found out something dangerous to him.'

'What I like about you Peter is you're such a cheerful soul.'

'As a matter of fact I do have more cheerful news. Or at least rumours – after all we're not dealing with men whose word is their…'

'Yes, yes, the cheerful news, man. I need it.'

'Lord Powerful, surprise, surprise, has a rival at court who wants to see him damaged. He's ready to protect you. But of course, if you stop asking questions he'll have no motive to preserve you.'

'He may continue to look after me out of the goodness of his heart; but against that I have to weigh the fact that he's a courtier, a politician.' I sighed: 'It looks as if I'll have to go on with my enquiries.'

Six

'*No other noyse, nor peoples troublous cryes,*
*   As still are wont t'annoy the walled town,*
*   Might there be heard: but careless quiet lyes,*
*   Wrapt in eternall silence farre from enemyes.*'

I quoted wistfully as one of Rosie's clients rolled
crashing and cursing down the stairs.

'You accuse me of taking your fucking watch,' she
shouted, 'and I'll stick this knife in your gizzard.'

I looked out to make sure he hadn't broken his neck.

'I'll get the law,' he spluttered.

'And I'll tell your bishop what you wanted me to do.'

'He wouldn't believe a whore against a vicar.'

'I can describe the mole on your arse.'

Seeing me standing in the doorway, he jammed on his
hat, pulled it down over his eyes and made for the exit.

'Hello, Tom,' called Rosie, giving me a big smile and
waving the hand with the knife in it. For some reason
Rosie had taken a liking to me. I waved and went back
into my room. There's not much calm and quiet for
writing in Coldharbour Tenements. But I had stuck at my
part of Sir Thomas More for the last few days and now it
was finished. Heavy rain had helped by keeping me in my
room. But now the sun was shining and I decided I'd
earned a pot of the Cross Keys best. Also I wanted to
show what I had written to Elizabeth. She's a good judge
with a fine ear for dialogue.

After making myself presentable I left the room and
pulled the door shut. A pair of hands flung me against the

43

far wall and I was punched in the stomach. As I doubled up I felt a knife pressed against my throat. Then it was withdrawn and, gasping, I looked up and saw the bailiff, Warthog.

'The punch,' he said, 'was for making me chase half round London and still lose my fee. It's because of nimble-footed bastards like you I have to take on freelance work. The knife, would you believe it, was to make you trust me, as suggested by my employer, a clever bastard. If I'd been the man trying to kill you I could have slit your throat and been away. But I've been hired to protect you so don't go jumping me. Mind, I'd rather have the other man's job, but keeping you alive is what I'm being paid for. Also I've got a message from my paymaster. He thinks I didn't know him, hanging back in the shadows, but I recognised him. It was the sodomite playmaker, Marlowe. He's waiting to see the play you're planning to write and he'll be very disappointed if you don't finish it.'

I was beginning to get my breath back and I was angry. One side in a power struggle had tried to kill me now their opponents wanted to use me as a pawn. Warthog slid his knife back into the sheath, jerked his thumb at my room and said, 'So get the fuck on with it.'

All my anger and frustration boiled up and I flung myself at him. We struggled back and forth in the passage striving to throw each other. He pulled himself free gaining space to hit me hard in the face. Being bigger, heavier, he was like a bear broke loose from the stake rushing at one of the dogs baiting him. Another swinging punch smashed into my face knocking me against the wall. I bounced back cracking my skull on his nose. Roaring with pain he again rushed at me. While he was off balance I grasped his arms and swung my full weight sideways. He crashed to the floor with me on top ramming my knee into his stomach. Rosie ran down the stairs to look at my bruised face as a tenant came in, stepped over Warthog without a second glance and went up to his room. Fights were common in Coldharbour.

Warthog clambered to his feet, put a hand to his nose, stared at the blood and said to me, 'People in high places changes their minds. When the one who wants you protected changes his,' he tapped his knife, 'I'll be ready.'

As he left Rosie stroked my face and said, 'Come up to my room, Tom, and I'll tend those cuts.'

Her room was much like mine, sparsely furnished with table and chair but a bigger bed. She sat me down on the bed and dipping the hem of her skirt in a basin of water cleaned the blood from my face: 'Where did you learn to fight like that, Tom?'

'Oh, my uncle fought the Spaniards in the Low Countries and he taught me to use a sword and how to fight if you lost your sword. And I had plenty of practice at fighting in school where the other boys tried to bully me because I was Dutch.'

'Well you fought that man like a hero, Tom. And you beat him,' she added softly. It's very flattering to have a woman call you a hero while she's tending your wounds. Rosie was no great beauty but she was pretty enough with a fine pair of bubbies one of which had somehow popped out of her smock. I took it in my hand and gently squeezed. Rosie slipped out of her skirt and smock then pulled off my breeches. We rolled onto the bed. I sat astride her and with one hand on her breasts was struggling with the other to pull my shirt over my head when the door was banged and a woman shouted, 'Rosie, I just seen your slave lord through the window.'

'Sweet Jesus, I forgot about him,' said Rosie darting a hand beneath the pillow and pulling out a watch. 'It's his time.'

Slipping from under me she jumped to her feet and ran to a chest. Pulling up the lid she rummaged inside and threw a short Roman tunic on the bed. Then she took out what looked like an ancient Briton's dress and put it on.

'Come on, Tom,' she urged, 'you'll have to go.'

'Where are my breeches?' I asked looking around.

'Under the bed.'

'He's coming up the stairs, Rosie,' the woman called softly. I was hopping on one leg trying to get the other into my breeches while Rosie was putting on a breastplate. There was a tap on the door.

'You'll have to get out through the window,' she hissed.

'It's the top floor,' I yelped, falling over.

'There's a ledge. You can get into the next room,' she whispered, pushing me to the window.

'It is I,' called a man from behind the door, 'your Roman captive, Queen Boadicea.'

When I put the wrong foot in my breeches Rosie snatched them, pushed me through the window onto the ledge and handed them to me, whispering, 'Get dressed next door.' Running to the chest she pulled a whip out, cracked it, and cried sternly, 'Enter, slave.'

I've heard some of these aristocrats have strange tastes and it's true. Perhaps they get bored with being bowed and scraped to and want a change. As for Rosie, she'd make a fine player if women were allowed on the stage.

As I inched along the ledge, shirt flapping in the breeze, I looked down. A mistake. The ground looked a long way off. It was a long way off. I could imagine Mistress Brayne groaning about the ungodly if I ended up with a broken neck on the cobblestones below Rosie's window clad only in my shirt. The sudden crack of the whip nearly sent me leaping in the air. Pressing back against the wall I moved nearer to the other window. Another whip crack and I almost dropped my breeches. Don't look down, I told myself. Sweating profusely I rested and looked across the rooftops to the great bulk of

46

St Paul's dominating the skyline. To my left the silver Thames sparkled in the sun with gleaming white swans gliding between wherries and barges. Far away to my right were the green hills of Highgate and Hampstead. After a few more feet of shuffling I gained the window and climbed in with a gasp of relief.

Next door Rosie was barking orders. 'Yes, Queen Boadicea,' cried the abject aristocrat. Here a woman was lying on the bed drinking from a bottle of wine. Unsurprised by my unusual point of entry, she asked in a wheedling voice, 'Can I pleasure you, dearie? I can be Queen Elizabeth if you want. Lots of gentlemen like her.'

With the thick layer of paint on her face (now fissured by an earthquaking smile) she could have been Queen Elizabeth herself earning a bit of pin money. Pulling on my breeches I said, 'Some other time,' and hurried out. The Queen was magnificent at Tilbury with her, "I know I have the weak and feeble body of a woman but I have the heart and stomach of a king, and of a king of England too." I cheered as loudly as the best of them and was ready to die for her. But in battle, not bed.

I regained my room and stretched out on the bed exhausted. What an experience for a poet. I'll wager Edmund Spenser has never experienced anything like it. But then he's against

"Lustful lechery;
Who rough, and blacke, and filthy did appeare,
Unseemly man to please fair ladies eye:
Yet he of ladies oft was loved dear,
When fairer faces were bid standen bye:
O who does know the bent of women's fantasy?"

"Men's more likely," Rosie would say.

Before calling on Elizabeth I set off to see Nicholas Winton at his apothecary's shop. When we had talked he'd let drop a few remarks that seemed to show he knew something of court politics. I needed to find out who were the upper and lower millstones I was being ground between. Winton was behind the counter while his apprentice was boiling a pungent pot of herbs. We repaired to the nearest tavern after he had warned the boy not to sell any poison.

Once we had our pots of ale in front of us and Winton had got his pipe drawing I told him of my would-be assassin and unwilling protector. He thought for a moment then said, 'The murdered woman came to London from Kingston where I've heard she was involved with extreme puritans. They think the present government is soft on Catholics and the present church too popish. They're Calvinists who want to make her majesty subservient to their church. Some are trying to bring it about through arguments in pamphlets but others are ready to use violence.'

'The landlord of the Boar's Head suggested to me that Catholics were involved in her murder. Admittedly he's an anti-catholic fanatic.'

Winton shrugged: 'I'm no papist but my impression is that most Catholics have given up hope of restoring their religion and simply want to be left in peace to practise their faith. After all they caused no trouble in eighty-eight when the Armada threatened us. Indeed, I've heard that when the English victory was announced in Rome, the Englishmen there training to be priests burst out cheering.'

'The year before there was the Babbington plot.'

'Which led to the execution of Mary Queen of Scots, thus removing the main Catholic motive for killing Queen Elizabeth. Of course there is always the danger of some fanatic acting alone.'

'So you think it may lie in puritan politics?'

He nodded: 'I get courtiers coming into my shop so I hear gossip about rivalries at court. At the moment Sir Walter Raleigh and the Earl of Essex are vying to be accepted as leader of the puritans. Unofficially, of course.'

It made sense. They wanted a more solid power base than the Queen's favour. That could change quickly. Besides, I've heard it said that she did not consider either of them to be in the same class as old Lord Burghley or his son as administrators. 'Could it be,' I wondered aloud, 'that Mother Wingfield knew something about one of them that would disgust the puritans? After all, it doesn't take much to disgust them.'

'Having a powerful voice at court will outweigh much. And most people already know of Essex and Raleigh's reputation with women. Raleigh is known to speculate on things like the existence of the soul and rumours are circulating of a group that's formed around him called the School of Night. Marlowe is said to belong and you'll have heard of his blasphemies.' Winton coloured slightly, cleared his throat and added, 'He's got no reputation for womanising.'

'Quite the opposite,' I said, also a bit embarrassed. 'Anything against Essex, Master Winton?'

'Nothing about speculating on religion. The young Earl of Southampton has become a friend of the Earl of Essex. Which is somewhat surprising as he comes from a catholic family.' He coughed: 'I don't know what the world is coming to, Master Dekker, for there are similar rumours to those about Marlowe circulating on young Southampton. And I don't mean as a blasphemer.' He added hastily, 'But nothing like that concerning Raleigh or Essex. Women are their sole interest.' He got up and said heartily, 'Well, I must get back or the wife will come looking for me.'

Equally heartily I said, 'I'll just stay and get something to eat then I must go and see my girl, Elizabeth.'

It's a devilishly embarrassing subject for two men to discuss but I knew that my life might depend on finding

49

out the truth. We shook hands and I promised to keep him posted on future developments.

I still had money from the advance I'd been paid and now with the part written I would soon be getting more. So I decided to eat well. Calling over the serving-girl I ordered a plump chicken to be followed by plum pie and a bottle of wine. The girl who served me had long golden hair and a bosom as plump as the chicken. Leaning over the plate, carving knife poised, she asked, 'Which part would you like first, sir.'

'Breast,' I gulped. When I asked her to join me in a glass of wine she replied, 'Too busy, sir' and moved briskly, bubbies bobbing, to serve another man. The lust in his face must have mirrored mine. I sighed. Rosie had put business before pleasure. This girl had done the same. When I'd ordered the food I'd had an appetite for it. She had given me quite another appetite. But I like my food and was soon enjoying the chicken and the plum pie both of which were excellent. Having polished them off, I settled back with the wine which was a good one.

When I heard her behind me I could not resist turning my head. She was carving roast pig for a fat man with bulging cheeks. It was difficult to tell whether the gleam in his eyes was for the pig or the girl. A commotion at the door made me turn back.

'Just steadying you, Master Marlowe,' said the landlord.

'I don't need steadying, you bitch's spawn. Get me a bottle of sack.'

The landlord, glad to get off so lightly, hurried away. Marlowe drunk was trouble. It was well known that he had been in a number of street fights in which he'd been quick to draw his knife. He looked across the room and I saw the same lust in his eyes as I'd seen in those of the other men when gaping at the girl. The rumours about Marlowe were untrue then. In vino veritas. The wine was exhibiting his true nature. I grinned and turned to look at the girl. She'd gone. When I turned back to Marlowe, the lust was still in his eyes. He was looking at me.

'No,' I said, standing up and shaking my head. When he started towards me I turned and ran.

'Come back,' shouted Marlowe. I kept going. He roared with frustrated lust and a knife thudded into the wainscot near my head as I charged through a door into the kitchen. I ran past the startled cooks out into the yard and away down the street. Slowing to a walk, panting, I reflected on life's little ironies. One courtier wanted to kill me, his rival wanted to protect me, the man who'd been hired as my guard wanted to fight me while his paymaster wanted to – it didn't bear thinking about. And all I'd set out to do was write a play.

Seven

Elizabeth had introduced me to her relations and now I was taking her to see my mother who lived in Old Fish Street. An uncle had died and left her with enough to live on. She had re-married but I did not get on with my step-father.

On the way there we met my two maiden aunts, very respectable ladies, who had rooms in the same block. Approaching the costermonger they patronised ("Because he does not swear") they had a view of his broad backside straining against his breeches as he bent to pick up a crate of apples. While the two ladies averted their eyes I reflected that if I were to say that such a sight would have excited Marlowe, it would have confirmed all their prejudices about the theatre. Of course, I refrained. They would have had hysterics.

The crate slipped from the coster's hands and split open spilling out apples. He shouted, 'God dam...' saw my aunts and gulped '...aged.' With an oily smile he said, 'Codling damaged apples, ladies. I call them cod for short. Can I interest you in anything?'

'Ve vill let you know ven ve are in need, Master Smith,' said Aunt Bertha sailing by. Her sister, who had never learned English, contributed her usual, 'Ja.'

As we entered the apartment block I thought, how different from Coldharbour Tenements.

'And vare are you living now, nephew?' asked Aunt Bertha.

'In…' I began, then realised that Coldharbour was not the sort of address to give to my aunts or mother. 'Still in…' Elizabeth glared at me. She hates lies. 'Still in search of a permanent home.'

'But vare now are…'

'I've got him attending St Olave's Church,' said Elizabeth coming to my rescue. That "attending" was stretching things a bit for Elizabeth and I squeezed her hand in grateful acknowledgment.

'Goot, Ja,' chorused the aunts squeezing her other hand. Elizabeth's stock had risen with the two pious old dears.

My mother was equally pious but with a sharp intelligence that sliced through falsehood like a headsman's axe. But I felt no anxiety when I introduced the two because Elizabeth was also intelligent and genuine, qualities mother was quick to discern and respect. They also discovered a mutual belief in female education; one of the great debates of our age, of course.

Aunt Bertha voiced the doubts of many when she said, 'Eve gained knowledge through eating za apple and brought evil into za world. A voman's mind is not strong enough for knowing much.'

My mother, who had mastered English completely, said dryly, 'Deborah was wise enough to rule in Israel and Queen Elizabeth, despite evil men, still rules England.'

Next I came under mother's scrutiny. Where was I living? What was I doing? Apart from getting into debt. Once again Elizabeth helped out, telling mother about my play. Which I confirmed by pulling out the manuscript. Mother peered at it and exclaimed, 'Sir Thomas More. He was a papist who burned protestants.'

'He also stopped the London apprentices from attacking foreigners. And he gave his daughters a full education.'

53

But at the moment it was the extreme puritan sects I wanted to know about. One of them could be the source of my danger. These days I felt like the poor blind bear I saw in Paris Gardens chained to a stake beset by the pack of dogs. My mother was a Lutheran but she had carefully studied the other protestant sects saying that finding the surest way to heaven was more important than finding the shortest trade route to Cathay. So I asked her about them and was bombarded with Barrowists, Brownists, Anabaptists, Familists, Amsterdam Brethren, Consistarian Puritans and the Sabbatarian doctrine of the Disciplinarians. I smiled as I thought – that last sounds ideal for Rosie's lord and said aloud, 'Disciplinarians.'

'Yes, Thomas,' said mother severely; 'and some discipline is what you could do with in your life.' She shook her head and continued sorrowfully, 'That reminds me of poor Dr Udall. Two years he's been in prison for his book Demonstration of Discipline.'

'And only saved from the gallows,' said Elizabeth, 'by the intercession of Sir Walter Raleigh.'

Mother nodded: 'That man knows the right in religion.' Adding darkly, 'If not in other things.' She sighed: 'Poor Dr Udall, he's such a fine preacher.'

'Yes,' agreed Elizabeth eagerly. 'I heard him preach when we visited relations in Kingston.'

My ears twitched at the mention of Kingston. And Raleigh was involved.

'Was it just for writing this book?' I asked.

'Some say he was Martin Marprelate,' blurted out mother. Silence. Then the two aunts suddenly remembered they had important business and left hurriedly. I wasn't surprised. It was only two years since the Marprelate pamphlets had caused such an almighty row. They had attacked the bishops in some of the liveliest and funniest satire I have ever read. The government were furious. They had hired several writers

54

to reply but everyone agrees that Martin gored and threw them as if they had been dogs baiting a bull.

Finally the secret press for printing the pamphlets which had been moved from place to place was captured when the wagon carrying it overturned. It was destroyed but they still hadn't discovered the author's identity. People were worried about being associated with Martin Marprelate since the government were still anxious to find and, doubtless, do horrible things to him. Anyone suspected of knowing his identity might have horrible things done to them by Master Topcliffe in the Tower. The rack encourages people to adopt a sharing attitude to their information. If the poor devils have got it. Not for the first time I wished I was well out of this business. But I had to go on.

'So this Dr Udall preached a good sermon?' I enquired innocently.

Mother raised an eyebrow: 'Since when did you care about sermons, Thomas?'

Elizabeth smiled: 'I think he is looking for someone livelier than the Reverend Bracegirdle.'

Mother snorted: 'That man would send the seven wise virgins to sleep. All too often the fool of the family is sent into the church. It needs wise leaders to combat Satan and his legions of devils. Do we select the leaders of our armies from fools?'

'Many an old soldier would say we do,' I countered and was assailed from both flanks with 'Sidney,' 'Raleigh,' 'Drake,' 'Norris.' I beat a retreat.

Mother and Elizabeth kept up with the current situation. When I first met Elizabeth one of my companions had mentioned France and I, to impress her, had, perhaps condescendingly, tried to explain the military situation there. She had corrected my mistakes then given a brisk account of the Catholic League and Henry of Navarre's Protestants. It sounded to me as if she could have advised the Prince of Navarre on his enemies. Perhaps she could advise me.

So far I had told Elizabeth nothing, not wanting to involve her in my troubles. But if I were arrested she would be involved. It would be better to confide in her so that she would at least be forewarned. After we had left I told her. Everything. I didn't mean to but Elizabeth is a female Topcliffe who does not need torture to get the truth out of a man. When we get married I'll have to stay on the straight and narrow.

A lot of information can be gleaned at an inn and Elizabeth vowed to be vigilant. Meanwhile it was decided that today I should try and see Dr Udall in Newgate Prison. She thought I should be safe enough where there was an authority in control. I was not so sure but said nothing. For tomorrow it was agreed that she would accompany me when I delivered my manuscript to the Rose Playhouse in Southwark. Also when I went to see another man who had found Mistress Wingfield's body, James Stour.

'It's useless arguing, Thomas. I'm in this with you, so I'm coming.'

So while Elizabeth made her way back to the Cross Keys I headed for Newgate. On the way I caught a rare glimpse of Warthog shadowing me. I was still important enough to be safeguarded. I had to make sure I remained important. Also, dammit, I wanted to write that play.

Passing St Paul's, I met Sim Hicks, one of my drinking companions when we had been apprentices.

'I'm a tailor now,' he boasted. I'd heard he had only graduated to doing repairs and it must have shown in my face because he admitted sullenly, 'Alright, I'm just a botcher. But I'm better off than Cod bloody Randall. He's being botched in a sweating tub.'

I winced: 'Not syphilis?'

'No, only Monsieur Gonorrhoea. Lucky bastard.' He laughed harshly: 'He sweated over it being syphilis before ever he got in the sweating tub. It'll sweat some of that bloody belly off him. Boasting to me about marrying his master's daughter and being set up as a tailor with his own shop. Well now some whore has given him the pox. I wonder if he gave that to his wife.'

I never did like Sim Hicks. If there was a sweating tub for envy he ought to be in it. Cod Randall on the other hand was a good sort and I resolved to visit him. His wife, Sim told me gleefully, had refused to let him be treated at home so he was in the Spital in Shoreditch. But before my hospital visit there was my prison visit. I was beginning to feel like a clergyman. All I needed to complete the role was to accompany some poor devil to execution. And there were plenty of gallows-birds waiting to fly to Tyburn where I was going.

With a bribe, I passed through Newgate's grey portals and into hell. My ears were assailed by men groaning, women screeching, chains clanking, fetters scraping and jailors bawling. This pandemonium was enveloped in a miasma of stale sweat, sour beer, foul jakes and clouds of tobacco smoke through which the fiery bowls of the pipes burned like miniature hellfire. I felt like Dante in the Inferno. Although the jailor who was my guide was not exactly Virgil, that is what I silently named him. When I asked for Dr Udall, the preacher from Kingston, he cackled, 'He'll be able to preach to Southwark when his head's on London Bridge.'

We passed groups of prisoners holding mock trials to prepare them for the real ones. Others were being taught to pick pockets and cut purses. In thieves slang the jailor told me the pickpocket was called a foist and the cutpurse a nip. Since he did nothing to stop them practising I can well believe the stories about jailors letting thieves out at night in exchange for a share of their loot. Despite the high prison fees, some prisoners live very well.

Dr Udall looked as if he lived fairly well. That would be from the money of wealthy supporters. When I entered his cell he was, as you might expect, reading the bible. He continued reading until he had finished the passage, then looked up. I saw that he had the familiar prison pallor. After I had introduced myself he asked me to sit. How to introduce the subject of Mother Wingfield's murder and the attempt on my life? After all the man sitting opposite me faced being hanged, drawn and quartered. For attacking the bishops in a book. Some of them need attacking. Whores are called Winchester geese because so many of the buildings in Southwark which house brothels are rented from the Bishop of Winchester. Dr Udall might feel he had enough problems of his own without concerning himself with mine.

Also I had not thought out a line of questioning. Hearing of poor Cod Randall sitting in a sweating tub in the Spital had brought to mind my own encounters with Winchester geese. The thought had caused me to break out in a sweat without the need of a tub. No more such liaisons for me, I resolved. Tub-thumping preachers have got nothing on sweating tubs as persuaders from sin. Especially when you add the horrors of having to swallow mercury.

How was I to begin my interrogation? Interrogation! Who did I think I was? Topcliffe with his rack? Dear God, I was sitting there interrogating myself. I wished I had Nicholas Winton there. His experience of questioning while on watch duty was what was needed.

Udall snapped the bible shut, startling me from my reverie. He leaned forward, the paleness of his face making his eyes look bright. They were bright. Glowing. Were they burning with puritan fanaticism or prison fever? Or just plain madness?

Staring into my eyes he demanded, 'Do you have the inner light?'

That was it. The inner light. He was a spiritual lanthorn. I saw an opening.

'Yes, Dr Udall,' I said as fervently as I could. 'Ever since I heard you preach in Kingston. In fact you were recommended to me by a gentlewoman in Kingston, a Mistress Wingfield. Do you remember the lady?'

He stood abruptly. I did not like the look in his eyes so I stood too as he barked, 'Have you read my book?'

'Yes...' he might question me on it – 'no. I couldn't afford...'

'What's your name?'

'Thomas Dra...' I'd given my real one to the jailor who would have told him. 'Dekker,' I gulped.

'You're a spy,' he hissed advancing on me, eyes glaring. His voice rose: 'You've been sent to trap me.'

The door was open and the corridor was crowded with lounging prisoners. If they thought I was a spy I'd get badly beaten, perhaps killed. Standing my ground I said firmly, 'Dr Udall, I am not a spy. If I am attacked because of your suspicions it will be bad for your case. And you may have an innocent man's death on your conscience.'

I considered laying my case before him but he looked dangerously unstable. His imprisonment, the strain of being under sentence of death with his suspicion of me made a volatile mixture. I'd been trying to examine a barrel of gunpowder with a lighted candle. He followed as I backed to the doorway. In the corridor I forced myself to walk slowly through the throngs of prisoners. Unable to resist a glance back, I saw him standing in the corridor glaring after me.

Turning a corner, I looked back at him once more and walked into a card game scattering cards in all directions. Dodging and riding their blows I forced my way through checking the pocket where my money was. The players fell to fighting among themselves as to who had which cards.

Turning into another corridor I was halfway along it before realising it was the wrong direction. Retracing my steps I saw two men coming towards me. One held a bottle and was unsteady on his feet. As we passed he stumbled against me. Jumping forward the other put out his hands to prevent me falling. Being a Londoner I could recognise a foist. As his hand came away with my purse I caught the wrist and twisted hard. He screamed and dropped the purse. Bending to pick it up I missed the bottle his mate swung at my head. It shattered against the wall showering me with broken glass.

By now I was crouched, my knife out and held towards them. Others crept from their cells hungrily eyeing the purse. They were like a pack of wolves. Just as they were about to rush me my guide with another jailor ran up and scattered them with their truncheons. The pickpocket held up his broken wrist whining that I had attacked him for no reason.

Taking an arm each the jailors marched me away. Near the entrance they halted and pushed me against a wall. Virgil said to his mate, a heavy, sullen brute, 'I think we may have to hold Master Dekker while that gentleman's charge is investigated. But no matter, he's got the money to pay his fees until his trial.'

Of course I knew their game. I would most likely be acquitted but the trial might be put off for months. In the mean time I would have to pay the exorbitant rates for my bed and board. Unless I was prepared to be put with the poor unfortunates in the hole. The fee payable there would be chunks of my flesh to the rats. Besides taking my turn sitting in the cage hung outside the walls begging money from the passers-by to pay for our food. Cursing them for sharks I handed over my purse.

Virgil weighed it and said, 'Having given due consideration to the gentleman's charge I finds it groundless. So Master Dekker, having paid his prison fees, is hereby discharged.'

When I held out my hand to Sullen Brute for my knife the bastard growled, 'It's confiscated.' I would have been better letting the first pair of thieves rob me.

Eight

As Elizabeth and I crossed London Bridge into Southwark we saw a ladder against the archway. A man was placing the head of a Catholic priest who had been hanged, drawn and quartered, on a pole. Even we Londoners, however much we might pretend, are not completely hardened to such sights. Elizabeth, being from the country, recoiled.

She shuddered and gripped my arm: 'Oh Thomas, his suffering must have been terrible.'

'They're allowed to die on the gallows before being – before the rest of the sentence is carried out.'

This is true enough. Provided the condemned behaves well, doesn't curse the Queen, the crowd often will shout for the hangman to let him die before he's disembowelled. But not otherwise. When I was an apprentice Sim Hicks talked us into seeing a traitor executed. Just before being pushed off the ladder he called her majesty the whore of Babylon and the crowd roared for him to be cut down quickly. He died screaming and I vomited. The Pope did not help English Catholics when he declared it was their duty to kill Queen Elizabeth.

We called first at the house where James Stour, one of those who'd found Mother Wingfield's body, lodged. It was in a lane behind the White Hart Inn. When I asked the landlady for him she said, 'Does he owe you, as well?' When I replied that I had to see him on business she said, 'If you've got money for him then I want my rent.' Finally she told us, 'He'll be at the feltmakers in Clink Street, singing psalms with the brethren outside St

Saviour's, or, most likely, boozing in there,' and she jerked her thumb at the White Hart. As we left she shouted, 'Tell him I want my rent or he needn't come sneaking in here anymore.'

Her words brought back painful memories of my lodgings before Coldharbour when I had fallen behind with my rent. When the landlady banged on my door I'd keep very still. Sometimes I would hear her creeping up to the door where she would listen, her breath wheezing. On one such occasion I thought she had gone and continued with my writing. When my quill squeaked on the paper she shouted, 'I can hear you in there. Go and do some honest work instead of writing those heathen plays.'

She was a Puritan who drove her husband to drink. I'd meet him in the passage while I was sneaking out and he was sneaking in. We'd pass each other silently, fingers to our lips.

'Has that landlady brought back memories?' asked Elizabeth dryly.

'I was recalling that dragon in Shoreditch. She drove me into Coldharbour Tenements and her husband into the taverns.'

'She needed money from you to pay for her husband's drinking because he never worked. When landladies let rooms, Thomas, they expect to be paid for them. Just as writers expect to be paid for their plays.'

Socrates might have had an answer for that but I didn't.

The White Hart was the nearest so we called there first. James Stour was sitting in a corner holding a pot of beer, licking the froth from his lips. Nicholas Winton had given me a good description of his large, round head with sandy hair and cross-eyes set in a pale face. I ordered drinks for Elizabeth and myself and we joined him.

At first he looked suspicious but Elizabeth's presence must have reassured him. There are no female bailiffs.

Having made the introductions I ordered him a fresh pot of beer (with money from Elizabeth) and mentioned our mutual acquaintance, Winton. Stour shook his head, saying, 'I fear he is not one of the godly, Master Dekker,' drained his pot with one swallow, belched, then added, 'I only drink it for my health.'

Elizabeth said, 'Your health will not be improved, sir, if your landlady puts you onto the street.'

His face reddened, his nostrils flared and his squint worsened. He hissed, 'She's another of the ungodly. She persecutes me because I am one of the saints. My inner light shows up her darkness. I reported her for not attending church.'

He leaned towards us and said confidentially, 'It's my belief she's backsliding into Popery. They're everywhere. And not only among the lowly. There are secret Papists in high places.' – I thought of that poor priest's head only yards away up on London Bridge. Stour was still talking: 'They drink wine and call it Christ's blood but it is Protestants' blood they thirst for.' He took a draught of beer and continued, 'In eighty-eight they lit bonfires along the coast to guide Anti-Christ's Armada to England.'

'They were beacons warning people to be ready,' said an exasperated Elizabeth. He smiled at her as if she were a child and said, 'That's what they wanted you to believe. Those who work for the Devil are clever.'

I sighed at having to listen to another, "They'll murder us in our beds," bigot. It's they who are everywhere. While he took another swig of beer I said, 'Serving Satan is right. Witchcraft, Master Stour.'

He almost choked on the beer in his eagerness to agree while I felt Elizabeth stiffen against me. But I was learning that you have to tell lies in this game. Meanwhile I had started Stour off on another subject dear to his heart. It seems that witches too are everywhere. How do we survive? His enthusiasm was giving him a thirst and he drained his pot. I nudged Elizabeth and after a little hesitation she slipped me some more money. When he had taken a drink from the fresh pot I said, 'I have a good friend, a devout Calvinist, who thinks he was bewitched by old Mother Wingfield. Not Cruickshank,' I added hastily. 'Nicholas Winton told me all he knew about her then directed me to you as a man zealous to root out the evils of witchcraft.'

He nodded solemnly. Self-importance, bigotry and beer were going to work his tongue. 'I knew her when I lived in Kingston. There were many stories about that woman, Master Dekker. Some of the country people – simple folk,' he simpered at Elizabeth – 'went to her as a white witch to be cured of their ills. But that could have been a cover. Dr Udall was seen going into her house. Also a Welshman from the university – and a good Calvinist, I'm told – John Penry. I think they were trying to gather evidence against her so I resolved to keep a watch on her house.' He cast his eyes up at the ceiling then down into his three-quarters empty pot, saying, 'I'm full of zeal to do the Lord's work, Master Dekker.'

I had the pot refilled and he continued, 'One dark night I saw something being carried out on a shutter – the kind they use to carry dead bodies. The thing was covered with a blanket and the men loaded it onto a wagon which was then driven quietly away.'

Despite the drink, Stour's face as he talked had become paler and paler. He was telling the truth, I was sure. He went on, 'I saw a much greater man than Udall or Penry go into her house.'

'Who?' I asked eagerly. Too eagerly. Stour was now all suspicion. 'Why do you want to know about him? I thought your concern was with the old woman?'

I was saved from answering when a pert-faced youth wearing a leather apron came in and over to our table saying, 'Drinking, Jemmy Stour.'

'You don't talk to me like that,' grated Stour, turning on him a look of pure hatred. The youth replied, 'The master didn't excuse you from coming in early to go boozing. You told him you'd be singing psalms.'

'I only…'

'I only drink for my health,' mimicked the youth. 'Anyway, Jemmy lad, you should thank me for coming to warn you.' He pointed to the window: 'The master is standing just across the street.'

While Stour was peering through the window the youth picked up the pot and drank greedily. Turning back Stour said, 'I can't…' slamming down the pot his tormentor ran for the door shouting, 'You've got good taste in beer, Jemmy.'

Spitting with rage Stour pointed towards the Bridge and snarled, 'His head will end up on a pole and…' jabbing his finger at the floor – 'his soul down there.'

I muttered, 'He'll be happy enough in the White Hart's cellar.'

'He can't drink without his head,' giggled Elizabeth.

Stour drained the dregs of the pot then stood up to leave. As we followed suit I noticed a portrait of the Queen on the wall. It was the one painted full of eyes to signify her watchfulness. Turning to follow Stour I saw the informer, Poley. He had been seated quite close to us. How much had he heard? If a portraitist were to paint an emblematic picture of Robert Poley he would give him ears as big as clams, all the eyes of Argus, a bloodhound's nose and a dagger for his tongue.

Stour hurried on ahead. When we came up with him he was standing outside St Saviour's with his black-clothed brethren singing lustily. With his right eye turned towards the Clink and his left eye towards the Bridge he was doubtless seeing the progress of the beer-snatcher from prison to pole.

Me and Elizabeth walked on past the Clink to the Rose Playhouse. Away to our left the rose bushes for which the playhouse was named wafted their perfume to us while from the Bear Garden we heard barking dogs and roaring bears being prepared for that afternoon's baiting.

In the Rose the actors were preparing for their afternoon's performance. They were rehearsing the ever-popular The Spanish Tragedy. Although given the number of times they have played it they hardly need to rehearse. In fact they can put it on at a moment's notice, as one poor playmaker found. His new play was being acted. All his friends were present and he was pointing out the finest passages. After about twenty minutes the audience began getting restless. Soon they were hurling apple cores and nutshells at the players and calling for The Spanish Tragedy to be acted. Then we thrilled to Hieronimo going mad again and laughed at Pedringano's blackly comic death on the gallows. Little did I think I would one day see the latter in real life.

I handed my part of Sir Thomas More to Henslowe who glanced through it before showing it to my co-writers Munday and Chettle. We were standing in the yard in front of the stage. Elizabeth nudged me and pointed to the gallery. Gentry with time on their hands like to drop in on rehearsal, discuss the finer points of acting and amuse themselves with the latest stage gossip. Today there were a whole gaggle of them.

Lord Hunsdon was seated up there with Emelia Bassano. To his left I recognised the Earls of Essex and Southampton with a few followers and servants. They had just been joined by Ned Alleyn and another actor. To Hunsdon's right was Sir Walter Raleigh who, it was rumoured, had got one of the Queen's maids of honour with child. With him were Marlowe, Greene, Spenser and a few others I did not know. Also their servants. Beer and wine was being brought up to them and to the players who were taking a break from rehearsal.

Essex was complimenting Alleyn on his Hieronimo while the other actor, who had his back to us, talked with Southampton. Raleigh looked across at them and said loudly, 'I hear you have a rival, Kit, who is trying to out-Tamburlaine you by hanging the heavens with black, changing day to night and scourging the stars with the crystal tresses of comets. Rumour has it that a brace of lords are wooing him to be their poet. Now what is his name? Shakeshaft? Shakebag?'

Marlowe, leaning over the rail, half turned and suggested, 'Shagbag.'

Greene chuckled and said, 'I fancy it's Shakescene, Sir Walter.'

Henslowe looked up nervously, fearing trouble in his playhouse. Unlike brawling apprentices these were not people you could throw out. I told a blushing Elizabeth that the name was Shakespeare and he was a good writer and not a bad actor. He whispered something to Essex and Southampton who laughed.

'*A gentle knight was pricking on the plain,*' quoted Essex looking at Spenser. Southampton looked at Raleigh and said, 'Another knight was pricking in a bed.'

Elizabeth blushed scarlet and Henslowe resumed biting his nails. He had cause. In the gallery they had jumped to their feet hands on swords. Lord Hunsdon in the middle was trying to pacify them. Raleigh and Essex were glaring at each other, Emelia, with slightly parted lips, was gazing at Southampton who was looking at Marlowe while Shakespeare was staring at Emelia. The actors on the stage were now an audience wondering if the drama in the gallery was a play of love or hate. A comedy or a tragedy.

The front door of the playhouse opened and three men entered. The centre one was carrying what looked like a warrant.

'Cecil's agents,' muttered Henslowe. Going up to the gallery they bowed to Hunsdon and he was shown the warrant. He walked over to Raleigh and showed it to him. Raleigh drew his sword and gave it to one of the agents. Essex stepped forward and said, 'I'm sorry, sir. It was none of my doing.' Raleigh scowled as he was escorted away followed by his friends. Essex and Southampton came behind and left the playhouse. The talk was that the Queen had been told about Raleigh and Bess Throckmorton.

Meanwhile both sets of servants, having gathered the gentlemen's cloaks, descended from the gallery by different stairs and met at the bottom. One of Raleigh's servants said to Southampton's, 'You'll beg my pardon for your master's insult to Sir Walter.'

'I never beg pardon,' he replied, trying to look as proud as the earl in his servant's livery. His companion, saying, 'Sir Walter's done too much of this,' thrust his thumb into his mouth. Raleigh's servant swung one fist under his jaw the other down on top of his head. Biting his thumb he roared and all of them began fighting.

'Get them out of my theatre,' shrieked Henslowe dancing in his rage. With the actors I rushed forward. We pushed and pulled the seething mass bundling them through the door. Those servants had staged a burlesque of the faction fighting between courtiers. What worried me was that with Raleigh in prison was I going to lose my protection?

Henslowe told me that Munday and Chettle had agreed that my part of Sir Thomas More would do and paid me my share. Ned Alleyn showed greater enthusiasm generously saying it would act well. Proving they were not empty words he demonstrated his believe in my ability by giving me a further commission. Will Kempe wanted to expand his part in A Knack To Know A Knave and I was to do the job. Already I saw how a scene in my rejected comedy What Do You Lack? could be utilised. It was a cobbling job like taking leather from botched work to make a new shoe. I was confident I could make it a good fit for Kempe.

Walking back through Southwark with Elizabeth I noticed Warthog's relief guard, a tawny-bearded man, trailing us. How long before they abandoned me for lack of pay? Or went over to my enemies?

Nine

The money I received from Henslowe I gave to Elizabeth to look after. Coldharbour Tenements was not the place to hold onto money. You were expected to spend it treating your friends. If you didn't they would treat themselves to it. Even my good friend Prigging Peter begged me not to leave money in his way since withstanding temptation was bad for his health. As his friend, he said, he was sure I would not want him to injure his constitution. As it turned out the man it most needed safeguarding against was myself. The money Elizabeth insisted I keep to buy much-needed new clothes I spent in the taverns with my friends.

It all began when I was dutifully tramping around the clothes shops in the area comprising St Thomas the Apostle Street and College Hill. I hate shopping for clothes and would have much preferred to browse in the bookstalls around St Paul's. Elizabeth, knowing this, had intended accompanying me but the Cross Keys had been too busy for her to leave. If only I had gone to St Paul's, I kept telling myself that night.

Wandering into a clothes shop in College Street I met a sullen-faced Sim Hicks repairing a jerkin. 'At least it's honest work,' he said; adding with a sneer, 'How's the writing going?'

I was in no mood for Sim Hicks' envy-fuelled sneers. But if I left too abruptly he would tell people that now I was writing for the likes of Edward Alleyn I considered myself too good for a mere tailor. So I stayed and made conversation. As we talked another two of my old drinking companions came in to fetch Sim. We greeted each other with our old catch-phrase from The Spanish Tragedy, "Hieronimo is mad again." I was persuaded to join them by the one we called (with good reason) Wheedler. He even coaxed Sim's stern-faced mistress into letting him go early.

During our drinking years we had given each other nicknames (except Sim). I had tried to get them to call me Erasmus after the great writer from Rotterdam; but I had been dubbed with the obvious name.

'You're deep in thought, Dutch,' commented Wheedler.

'Thinking up his latest masterpiece,' said Sim.

Turning into St Thomas the Apostle Street, crowded as always with sailors from the fishing boats, we began the evening with one of the fish dinners for which the street is so famous. As I tried to explain to Elizabeth, it was the salted fish that was responsible for my thirst. When the dinner had been set in front of us Sim looked carefully round the table to see if anyone had a bigger portion than himself. Wheedler had. Sim protested but Wheedler and the waitress were too busy smiling at each other to take any notice. The joker of our group said, 'No use giving you Wheedler's fish because he'd wheedle it back. I think mine's bigger, have that,' and he switched plates. 'No it's not, it's Dutch's,' he switched again. 'No it...'

Sim, whose eyes were swivelling, shouted, 'Leave it, Tarlton.'

Heads turned with smiling faces at the name. 'Were you related?' asked a man. We explained it was a nickname. By now everyone was reminiscing about the late, much lamented, Dick Tarlton, the funniest man of the age. How the Queen, beset by Papist plotters and Puritan protesters, only had to see Tarlton's face peeping out from behind a curtain to burst out laughing.

I told my own story. In eighty-eight before leaving London for Tilbury I had gone to the Rose to see him but the playhouse was full. As I turned away disappointed I saw a worried looking man approaching. A roar of laughter from the theatre brought a look of astonishment to his face.

'Dick Tarlton's on stage,' I explained. Still looking baffled he said in a thick Dutch accent, 'I have just crossed from Flanders where I have seen the Duke of Parma's great army assembled on the coast. The Spanish Armada is sailing to escort him over and the English are laughing at some sort of clown.'

'He's not some sort of clown,' I said indignantly. 'He's Dick Tarlton.'

The man walked away shaking his head, muttering, 'They told me the English are lunatics and it is true. I have come into a madhouse.'

Having eaten our fish we set off on our drinking spree. I made it plain to the others that I could not spend the whole evening with them since I had promised to meet Elizabeth later. Wheedler solemnly assured me that no one would try and persuade me to stay longer. It would be charitable to believe he meant it at the time.

As we walked to the nearest tavern Sim asked, with a sly grin, if I had been to visit Cod Randall yet. The grin grew broader when I was forced to admit that I had not. Sim Hicks loves to have his low opinion of human beings confirmed. There and then I resolved to make time to visit Cod. A visit that was to have unfortunate consequences for another Spital inmate. And I still shudder at James Stour's fate. But that was in the future. Tonight was a feast of good fellowship with Sim as the vinegar.

In one tavern I met Peter who gave me some reassurance by telling me that I was, for the moment, still being protected. He had also heard of my meeting with Stour. Just as he was about to tell me something else a drunk blundered past purse jingling and reeled out of the door. Peter followed him.

At the Bull Inn an acquaintance who had visited Cod told us that the infection was almost gone but he was staying for a few weeks more to make sure.

'And to give him more time to persuade his wife to take him back,' said Sim.

Before hearing of Cod's recovery we had been arguing about whether to visit a bowling alley or a dicing house. Now the argument shifted as to where the best brothels were. The cheap, low leaping-houses of Turnbull Street in Clerkenwell, the bawdy-houses of Shoreditch, the vaulting-houses of St Katherine's. Tarlton pointed out that the last two were nearest.

We were served by a girl whose clear skin and strong Devonshire burr proclaimed her fresh to London from the country. In reply to Wheedler's praise of her service she said innocently, 'I hopes as how I gives satisfaction, sir.'

Sim leered at her and asked, 'Have you got any stewed prunes?'

'Do we have any stewed prunes, Moll?' she asked a trim young woman serving another table. Above the guffaws going round the room Moll, a Thameside tartar, called out, 'We don't have any but he can get stewed prunes in Shoreditch so hot he'll be glad to step into the Spital for a good sweat.'

Now everyone was laughing at Sim which he hates. Turning to the girl he said, 'You'll find out what a stewed prune is when you're lying on your back for a living,' sending her away in tears.

'You ripped that girl's innocence like you rip clothes,' I told him. 'Which is why you'll never be a true tailor or a true anything.'

'Listen to Master dewy-eyed Dekker.'

'You're a cynic, Sim, like Diogenes who was called a dog for snarling at human beings.'

Tarlton bounded round the table, dropped to his hands and knees and barked at Sim. Again he was laughed at. Holding onto his temper he stared at me and said with great deliberation, 'All women who work at inns are whores.'

Jumping up, I swung my fist at him, drawing blood from his lip. We were grabbed by the others who kept us apart. Wheedler, who until now had been urging me to stay, now advised me to go and see Elizabeth. 'Far better to sit with your girl than sit in the stocks all night for brawling.'

The German clock on the wall began striking. Ten o clock. The time I had promised to meet Elizabeth at the Cross Keys. I left. Hurrying along Gracious Street I thought, I won't be too late. By my standards hardly late at all. Elizabeth would be resigned rather than annoyed. Then I remembered I had not bought the new clothes. And most of the money was spent.

Just as I tripped over a pothole the watch came round a corner and stood in front of me. The Head Constable held up his lantern and peered at me.

'I'm in a hurry, masters,' I urged as I got up.

'He's in a hurry,' echoed the Constable nodding at his men. Circling round me he added, 'Dirty shoes, a threadbare doublet, but he's in a hurry.' Thrusting his face close to mine he said, 'Gentlemen, which to us is them that wears fine clothes, they can be in a hurry. They're privileged to beat the watch when we stops them. And if we complains, why, they'll have some lord to back them. That's to say, if they're not a lord themselves, which is not unknown. Being in a hurry is one of their God-given rights.'

Once again he circled me then spat out: 'But we don't allow as a broken-shoed, dirty-doubleted, shabby-shirted, lousy-haired rogue with a puke-coloured face has any right to be in a hurry. Not when we wants to examine him.' He gestured to his men to surround me then barked, 'Quick march.'

Of course they wanted a bribe to set me free. When I showed them the few coins I had left they laughed derisively and proceeded to escort me to the Counter Prison in the Poultry. On the way the Head Constable said, 'I have some watch business to attend to in Shoreditch, neighbours. I'll meet you at the Counter. Look you guard the prisoner sure.'

'Aye, Master Constable,' they chorused respectfully. Once he had gone their tone changed. 'Watch business,' said one scornfully. 'Whore's business, more like.'

Another cackled, 'He bears down hard on daughters of the game.'

'With all his weight.'

'The scourge of the Shoreditch sisterhood.'

'They've got to choose between the beadle's whip and the Constable's rod.'

'That great nose is not the only thing he pokes into their business.'

'Aye,' said one viciously, 'one day his poking will get him a pox that will rot his nose off.'

'The whores will have been a tribulation to him then. You,' he said turning to me, 'had better raise some money or Tribulation Cheadle will be a tribulation to you.'

'I'm a friend of a man he used to work with,' I said eagerly. 'The apothecary Nicholas Winton.'

They roared with laughter, slapping their knees. Finally one of them spluttered 'Cheadle hates his guts. Winton stood up for the doxies and I don't mean in his breeches.' The man spat: 'Believed in treating 'em fair. So he denied Cheadle many a fair, plump wench.'

The watchman who had told me the name said, 'Telling Cheadle you're a friend of Nicholas Winton would be like telling Philip of Spain you're a friend of Francis Drake.'

'Or telling Prigging Peter,' cut in another, 'that you're a friend of one of us.'

In view of what happened next I don't think that last was a very good analogy. We were passing the Exchange when three men emerged from an alley across the street. There was the ring of shoes landing on cobbles from a height and a forth emerged. In the fitful light of the watch lanterns they looked big, tough and armed. A linkboy was passing and his flaring torch momentarily lit up the heavily scarred face of one of the four. A young watchman said excitedly, 'He's wanted. It's –'

'No it's not,' said another, the rest murmuring their agreement.

'But they could have been robbing that house,' I said.

'You want to start a fight so as you can escape in the confusion,' I was told. I was hit in the ribs and a voice hissed, 'Our last orders was to take you to the Counter, so move.' Still keeping our eyes on the four we began slowly walking on while they moved in the opposite direction still keeping us under observation. When I was a child I remember seeing a big rat coming out of a house, a piece of cheese in its mouth. Approaching it was a cat. Eyes fixed on each other they slowly passed. London's watchmen have taken the preacher's warning to avoid bad company to heart.

As we approached the dismal Counter Prison in the Poultry I was slapped on the back and told, 'Cheer up, it's not as bad as the Wood Street Counter.'

The man who had hit me chuckled, 'But don't tell the jailor that or he'll think his standards are slipping and try to make it worse.'

The watch handed me over to the jailors who entered my name in the prison register or Black Book as it's better known. 'You're allowed your choice of quarters, friend,' I was informed. 'Master's Side, Knight's Ward or…'

'The Hole,' interrupted his companion. 'And judging by his clothes it'll be the Hole for this one.'

'Not so fast,' said the other. 'Master Dekker may be a wealthy man who chooses rather to keep his money for poor, honest jailors instead of wasting it on cheating tailors. Or he may be a footpad who has just robbed a wealthy man. Either way he will want the best, which is the Master's Side.'

I'd been in prison for debt so I was able to translate his eulogy into reality. On my way to the Master's Side at every doorway I'd have to pay the turnkey anything from a shilling to half-a-crown to have the door opened.

'And in the hall,' continued the jailor, having omitted to mention the en route expenses, 'you will see a tastefully decorated tapestry depicting the story of the Prodigal Son. Described by our guests in letters home, you'd be surprised how often it loosens the purse strings of a stern father. To our mutual benefit. And from the hall…' failing to mention a further garnish (bribe in plain English) – 'you would be conducted to a compact (narrow) uncluttered (bare) simply decorated (with cobwebs) room. You'd have your own bed (straw) with sheets (dirty). You can have a little gentlemanly gambling or drinking in convivial company or enjoy the privacy of your room (you'd have privacy whether you wanted it or not if you didn't pay the turnkey to let you out). And you'll eat well (and pay well). How does that sound?'

He beamed like an innkeeper, which in a way jailors are. Then frowning he added, 'Of course, there's the Knight's Ward which is cheaper but where you will be much less comfortable.'

'And there's the Hole,' said the other scowling, 'where you won't be comfortable at all.'

I sighed and said, 'The Twopenny Ward.'

Now they both looked ugly. The Innkeeper was hoping to get more than twopence out of me. As for Scowler I think he would have preferred to forgo the twopence for the pleasure of thrusting me into the Hole. Innkeeper said, 'If you have anyone with money, friend, I would strongly advise you to get in touch with them.' His face lightened when I asked for pen and paper. Of course I had to pay for them. I wrote to Elizabeth asking her to bring money and to get in touch with Nicholas Winton. It would not be sent until the morning. They would make sure of getting one night's payment out of me and more if it could be managed. The fee for sending it and the purchase of some stale bread and mouldy cheese took the last of my money.

Scowler escorted me to the Twopenny Ward which reeked of beer and vomit, tobacco and sweat. Some were crying out for more beer and tobacco with turnkeys bawling at them to get to their cells for the night while others groaned that they wanted to sleep. I was crammed into a small cell alongside five others with straw for a mattress and coal sacks for sheets.

'The Hole is even worse,' said one of my fellow lodgers.

'That,' I suggested, 'must be hell.'

'No, hell is the Wood Street Counter.'

That night I dreamed of a devil flying out of Wood Street Counter armed with a fiery spear and driving it into old Mother Wingfield's eye in Milk Street.

Ten

A week later I was walking across London Bridge heading for the Rose. One of many visits that week. Little did I realise the horror that was going to be this visit's climax.

The money Elizabeth had brought coupled with Nicholas Winton's persuasions had freed me from the Counter Prison. In the morning Tribulation Cheadle had turned up first with a magistrate. Judging by Cheadle's face his night's business in Shoreditch had not been very satisfactory. Puffing out his cheeks he began, 'In the course of my duties as Master Constable I apprehended...' then he was forced to adjourn the proceedings and hurry as fast as his short fat legs would carry him to the jakes. His groans brought smirks to the faces of his watchmen. By the time he returned Winton and Elizabeth had arrived and Winton took him aside.

When they re-joined us Cheadle said savagely, 'No charges.' Obviously Winton knew too much about him. The magistrate left, swearing at the incompetence of the watch, and I was free. Elizabeth had gone and Winton told me that he had been invited to accompany a merchant friend on a voyage to the Baltic where he was going to search for new medicinal herbs. He advised me to get out of London for a while. But with my playwriting career blossoming, I had to stay where the playhouses were.

When I caught up with Elizabeth she refused to look at or speak to me but silently handed back the money she had been looking after for me. I held the purse out pleading with her to take it back. A beggar squatting outside the Exchange held out his hand saying, 'Ask me, friend.'

I am a poet and from Cornhill round into Gracious Street and right along to the Cross Keys I used all my eloquence trying to persuade Elizabeth to take me back. Walking with rapid steps she stared straight ahead, her face set. I followed, disconsolate, into the Cross Keys and sat down. One of the girls brought me a tankard of beer and, sensing the strained atmosphere, whispered, 'Keep trying.'

Yes, I thought, don't give up. Elizabeth was bringing a tankard to her admirer, Sir Ambrose, at the next table and I said, 'In trying to find a route to your heart, Elizabeth, I'm like Martin Frobisher searching for the North West Passage; your every frown is an iceberg barring my way.'

She banged down the tankard making Sir Ambrose jump and hissed, 'Don't talk to me like that. I'm not a character in one of your plays.'

Of course, she was right. All the same it was a good simile for a future play.

Emerging from the Bridge into Southwark I glanced up at the heads on the archway. I was doing this a lot since getting involved with the Milk Street murder. Elizabeth would be sorry if my head ended up there. But not as sorry as me being dragged on a hurdle to Tyburn for the painful preliminaries of hanging, drawing and quartering. I shuddered at the thought that it could happen. Traitors were those who ended up on the losing side. There was a verse going around London said to have been written by the Queen's godson, Sir John Harrington.

Treason does never prosper, what's the reason?
For if it prosper none dare call it treason.

Passing the Marshalsea Prison did little to dispel my melancholy. Not that I had been in it. As yet. I had been inside the King's Bench Prison for debt, Newgate as a visitor and the Poultry Counter for no reason. It had cost me money to get out of all three. The grey-bricked building stood in front of a Thames that sparkled in the bright June sunshine, its surface cut by elegant gliding swans. The prison was like an ugly picture set in a beautiful frame.

Poor squint-eyed James Stour had been in there. Probably because of me. So his character was as unattractive as his face. He still didn't deserve to be hauled off to prison by the Knight Marshall's men. A brutal bunch. At least some of them were quickly repaid in kind.

My mind went back again to the day of my release from the Counter. I was still in the Cross Keys, staring into my tankard, memorising the North West Passage simile (not a good idea to write it down in Elizabeth's presence, I realised) when with a stomach-jolting start I remembered that A Knack To Know A Knave was being acted that afternoon. Kempe would want to run through my additional scene. Jumping up I made for the door.

'Don't do anything foolish, Tom,' said the girl who'd served me. 'She'll come round.' But I did not want to jump in the river, just get across it. Quickly.

I hared to my room, picked up the scene and ran to the riverside where I told a waterman to take me to the Rose. I sat getting my breath back as he pulled away from the landing stairs and said, 'You're an actor, I suppose. Late for rehearsal? You know, I don't think that Ned Alleyn is as good as he's cracked up to be. Give me Will Kempe. Laugh? I've pissed my breeches more times…'

'Double fare if you get me there double quick.' That stopped his mouth and got his arms going. We shot forward scattering the swans and cutting up another boat. Landing I paid him off with the other boatman's curses ringing in our ears.

When I arrived at the Rose Kempe cursed me and snatched the paper from my hand. Henslowe, who was looking gloomy, said, 'There'll be a riot. I know it. And they'll use my playhouse as a cover to assemble. Then the authorities will close us down.'

Alleyn, walking past, patted him on the shoulder and said, 'You worry too much, Master Henslowe.'

'It's alright for him,' fretted Henslowe. 'All he's got to do is act. I've got the playhouse to worry about. And when those damned prentices get one of their moral fits I've got the worry of my – other businesses.'

Brothels, he meant. 'But what's the trouble?' I asked.

'Those licensed ruffians, the Knight Marshall's men, had a warrant to arrest a man. They burst into the house where he was reported to be with daggers drawn, terrified the wife of the house who had a young child in her arms and dragged the man off to the Marshalsea.'

'What did he do?' I asked.

'No one knows because no charges have been laid against him. He was a feltmonger's servant so all those apprentices will be on the streets and they'll call the other prentices out.'

With a sinking feeling I asked what the servant looked like. Kempe, who was passing on his way to the stage, crossed his eyes.

I had dinner with the company at a nearby inn. The wit and laughter sparkled, flowing past a gloomy Henslowe like the Thames past the Tower. Then back to the Rose for A Knack To Know A Knave. Normally Henslowe would of course have been pleased to see a full house buying large quantities of his bottled ale. But it was plain that most of the audience were prentices their clothes bulging with what looked like clubs.

The play went well although the laughter became more and more strained as the tension in the audience and on stage grew. Then we came to my scene. The company had an Irish actor called Malone who was at his best in tragedy. He had perfected a dramatic pause of which he was very proud. At a moment of tension he would break off in the middle of a speech and hold the audience in suspense before continuing. I had seen how it could be used in my comic scene. After a long pause Kempe would burst up through the trapdoor while Malone shouted, "Mercy on us." Since he took himself very seriously he was not too keen. But Kempe liked it so he had to comply. I had parodied a popular play that would soon be on again.

You could tell that Malone had forgotten he was in a comedy which suited me fine. I wanted it played straight. The book holder was off ill and an apprentice actor, with good reason nicknamed Muffler, was prompting. In sonorous tones Malone said,

'*Lord, who would live turmoiled in the court,*
That may enjoy such quiet walks as...' a pause as Malone swept out his arm. From backstage a voice piped, '*Mercy on us.*' The look of serene content on Malone's face changed to a ferocious scowl. He strode off, we heard a thump, a yell, then he strode back on and said, 'Sure he prompted me in me grand pause.'

After the play Kempe's new jig was performed. It went down well. But with the state of the audience anything would have had them roaring. Despite (or because of the mishap) my scene was well liked and I was asked to write some comic relief for a tragedy. But Henslowe refused to give me an advance since he was convinced that the theatre would soon be closed down.

Outside the playhouse the apprentices were acting their own play. There were mock cries of army officers: 'Right about wheel.' 'Close ranks.' 'Present arms.' There was much drunken laughter and we heard a bottle smash against the theatre wall. A commanding voice shouted,

'Save those bottles for the Marshal's men. Enough playacting. To the Marshalsea.'

We went outside and watched them tramping away. Some ran up side streets shouting, 'Clubs, clubs,' the prentices cry to bring their fellows onto the streets. I've run along Cheapside myself shouting it. Most men are drawn to a fight so we followed.

The great seething, bawling mass gathered in front of the Marshalsea. There were shouts of, 'Let him go.' 'Release him.' Then began a steady chanting of 'James Stour, James Stour.' At a great roar we craned our necks and saw that the Marshal's men had emerged from the prison. They formed a line clubs and truncheons at the ready and, glinting in the sun, a few daggers. They were pelted with bottles, stones and gravel. A man near us prised loose a cobblestone, hurled it at them then asked, 'What's it about?'

There was a shout of, 'Advance,' and the Marshal's men charged the crowd truncheons swinging and knives slashing. Heads were cracked and faces gashed. A youth reeled away clasping his face, blood running between his fingers. When he removed his hands blood welled where his nose had been. Acrid smoke from burning bracken drifted across stinging our eyes and making the scene look like a pitched battle. Those at the front of the dense crowd with no room to swing their clubs tried to get away from the knives and truncheons but were pushed forward by the fury of those behind. Now the great weight of the crowd was beginning to tell. The line of Marshal's men forced back and back was starting to fracture. One of them went down and was dragged away screaming by the prentices. A red-haired fellow smashed a large stone down on his skull. Ravens and kites wheeled overhead as if they could smell the blood. Just as the line seemed about to break we heard the thunder of galloping horses and shouts of, 'The Mayor's men.'

85

We moved away from the crowd as the band of horsemen swept around the corner and charged full tilt into the prentices swords slashing. The Lord Mayor in his red robes of office directed them to the ringleaders. The Marshal's men, reformed, were attacking from the front. Now the great mass was being sliced into segments. Prentices were bound and pushed into the prison. These men did not bother about distinguishing between rioters and spectators so we left. The others back to the Rose and myself, by a circuitous route, to the Bridge.

Now a week later I was outside the Marshalsea again heading for the Rose. They were acting the third part of the ever-popular Harry the Sixth. Burbage would be coming into his own as Richard Crookback. I was hoping that James Stour had not played the part of Duke Humphrey who in part two had been murdered in prison. Rumours about Stour had been flying all over London. He was still in the Marshalsea being starved to death. His body had been seen floating under London Bridge. His ghost had been heard singing psalms outside St Saviour's.

I hurried on. At least I had the play to look forward to if nothing much else. Despite constant endeavour I had been unable to win back Elizabeth. The prospect of losing her had jolted me into realising how much she meant to me. Mistress Brayne and the Reverend Bracegirdle were doing their best to make the rift permanent. They had someone in mind for her. No doubt one of their psalm singing saints with short hair and a long face.

The playhouse trumpet rang out as I joined the crowd streaming towards the Rose. The watermen were doing a roaring trade ferrying people across the Thames. It was going to be another full house. Henslowe needed it with closure still a threat. There were two black clouds hanging over the London theatres. They could cause a storm of rioting that would sweep away the playhouses. The fate of James Stour and Midsummer. With or without a cause

Midsummer Eve is a traditional time of riot for apprentices. My head still carries the scar from a sergeant-at-arms truncheon.

I secured a place in the yard right in front of the stage. You can keep your bear-baiting, bull-baiting, cock-fighting, prize-fighting or sword-fighting. For me there is nothing like the excitement of waiting for the start of a play. Girls were moving among the audience selling apples, nuts and bottles of ale. The crack of nutshells, that could so put an actor out, was sounding across the theatre. Youths in the yard were casting their eyes around the galleries looking for the prettiest girls. Having settled on one they paid the extra to enter the gallery and hired a cushion to put behind her back and bought fruit for her to eat. Bona robas leaned over the rails breasts hanging out of gowns and beckoned to the men.

Ingram Frizer was up there too with that smile on his face that boded ill for someone. In the Mermaid one evening a writer, Peele, Kyd, Shakespeare, whoever, said something like, "Frizer smiles in such a sort as if he mocked himself that could be moved to smile at anything." Like Richard Crookback he's a murderous jester.

Now the buzz of conversation was drowned by beating drums and blaring trumpets and Alleyn as the Duke of York entered at the head of his followers all wearing white roses in their hats. But where was Burbage as Richard Crookback? During the opening lines I caught his voice backstage rising with anger: 'Find it or I'll take yours out there.'

'Someone's taken it, sir,' snivelled Muffler who was now in charge of the properties. He was going to get another clout around the ear. Then, 'I've found it, sir,' and Burbage hobbled on stage as Richard Crookback holding one arm behind him. The Yorkists, fresh from victory, were boasting of their exploits to the Duke. His eldest son,

Edward, who had slain the Duke of Buckingham, held up his sword crying

'*I Cleft his beaver with a downright blow.*
That this is true, father, behold his blood.'

Then Montague,

'*And, brother, here's the Earl of Wiltshire's blood,*
Whom I encountered as the battles joined.'

Now Richard stepped forward saying,

'*Speak thou for me and tell them what I did,*' throwing down the Duke of Somerset's head. It hit the stage with a heavier thud than usual and rolled towards the front. When it stopped I was looking straight into the wide open cross-eyes of James Stour.

Eleven

All the London playhouses were closed by order of the
Privy Council. The watch was increased for Midsummer
Eve and householders and tradesmen were instructed to
keep their servants and apprentices indoors. The ban on
the theatres was going to be a long one (if the Mayor and
the Common Council had their way it would be
permanent). So the companies at the Rose applied for a
licence to tour and began making preparations. The book
holder was too ill to travel and I accepted an offer from
Alleyn to take his place. Henslowe would stay in London
to look after his 'other businesses.' The inquest on James
Stour concluded that after being released from prison he
had been murdered by a person or persons unknown. The
rest of his body was never found.

Calling at the Cross Keys, I was told by the girl who
had urged me to keep trying that Elizabeth had gone
home.

'To Cambridge?' I yelped.

'No,' she said squeezing my hand, 'Cheapside.'

As I looked into her soulful eyes I had the feeling that
here was a haven to retreat to from the storm. But she
only made me realise how much I wanted Elizabeth back.
Having got over my self-pity and self-justifying I could
see now that Elizabeth had put up with a lot from me.
Instead of seeing my debts and unpunctuality as
fecklessness they had made me think of myself as a devil
of a fellow; one who flowed through life, like the Thames
through London, into the nooks of ale houses and the

inlets of gambling dens. One who lived for today and consigned tomorrow to the torments of Hell. Now I was worried. Had my night in prison been one tightening of the rack too many for Elizabeth's love?. Being put in the Counter was a kind of justice. If I had spent the money as I'd promised on decent clothes the watch might have passed me by.

Since I was in the Cross Keys I decided to have a beer. It was practically a necessity for visiting Mistress Brayne's house. The girl, whose name was Grace, brought the beer and said, 'If you wanted to find out whether Elizabeth still loves you or if,' she cast her eyes demurely down, 'or if – there was someone else who does, I know a very good astrologer you could ask.'

'No,' I said gently, not wanting to hurt her feelings. But it amazes me that people still go to astrologers. Their credibility had taken a bad knock four years earlier. Year in, year out, they had predicted disaster for England in 1588. So it was not only the Armada that was shattered that year. But the astrologers, like the Spaniards, were fighting back. I finished my beer and set off for Cheapside thinking, now I'm going to find out if my hopes have been wrecked or merely disabled.

The maid asked me to wait at the door of the Braynes' house. There was quite a lengthy consultation before I was admitted. They were all facing the door when I entered the room. There was a friendly, 'Hello, Tom,' from Master Brayne, a sniff for the reprobate from Mistress Brayne, an amorous glance from Chastity, a sigh for the sinner from the Reverend Bracegirdle, a sharp look from the young Puritan, John Mulcaster and a slight nod from Elizabeth.

Mistress Brayne engaged Bracegirdle in a conversation about the pride of players, jetting it in their fine clothes bought with the money they got by mouthing the lies of playmakers. Stung, I said, 'I'm happy your brother invested in a playhouse, Master Brayne. It's brought pleasure to many and a profit to him.'

His wife's savage look turned his grin to a frown. She said, 'Heathenish plays drawing people away from sermons,' to the vigorous nods of Bracegirdle who quoted, *'Will not one blast of the playhouse trumpet sooner call thither a thousand, than an hour's tolling of a bell bring to the church a hundred?'*

She groaned at the wickedness of the Londoners and went on, 'Violence on the stage spreading onto the streets from the theatre – yes Master Brayne, you might well blush for your brother – rioters inflamed by the players terrifying the godly of Southwark.'

'That was a comedy,' I argued, 'with no rioting in it.'

'But there are knavish tricks in your comedies,' she retorted, looking sharply at Chastity, 'teaching the young to deceive their parents and run away with rogues.'

'And there's immorality,' said Bracegirdle moistening his lips; 'filthiness, lust,' his face reddening at every word and his voice turning hoarse on, 'whoredom.'

'And now,' said Mulcaster, 'there is murder on the stage, as in Nero's Rome.'

'That did not happen on...' I began before being drowned by the exclamations of the others, who had not heard the news. Mulcaster told them of James Stour's first and last appearance on the stage ('On the stage,' groaned Mistress Brayne, 'and him one of the saints of Southwark.'); then the Cambridge-educated bastard quoted Greek at me. Naturally, we did Latin at grammar school but not much Greek. So I was floundering.

'I was quoting Plato,' explained Mulcaster. 'He would not admit poets or players in his Republic since he regarded them as disruptive and corrupting. Men acting evil may become evil.'

Well, I knew of Plato's arguments at second-hand. I replied with the usual defence of plays. They showed vice being punished and the evils of rebellion; they encouraged patriotism through depicting the brave deeds of English soldiers like Talbot and the Black Prince and great kings like Edward the Third and Henry the Fifth. I got quite carried away, and me of Dutch origin.

Mulcaster replied quietly that patriotism was best fostered by teaching the people about the evils of popery and exhorting them to be good Protestants. That, he concluded, could best be done by able, zealous preachers. I looked pointedly at the Reverend Bracegirdle who was smirking all over his fat face. Mulcaster grimaced and looked away which gave me a good opinion of his intelligence. But I did not like the admiring look Elizabeth was giving him so I went onto the attack, saying, 'You people criticise plays without having seen any.'

'I made a point of going to see them,' he replied.

'Purely from a sense of duty,' said Mistress Brayne.

'His money's as good as anyone's,' I said flippantly, then regretted it catching Elizabeth's scornful glance. Mulcaster continued, 'When they brought Jack Cade's rebellion onto the stage, up in the gallery I received the beer and garlic laden breath of the rabble in the yard cheering on the rebels, their counterparts in the play.'

Well I must admit I felt somewhat exhilarated at seeing the rebels capture Lord Say, a member of the government, and, when he tries to soothe them with, "These cheeks are pale for watching for your good," hearing Jack Cade's reply: "Give him a box o the ear, that'll make 'em red again." I argued that the rebels are shown defeated with their leader killed.

'But the playwright,' he said, emphasising Wright as in wheelwright or Cartwright to align him with Cade the plasterer and Dick the butcher, 'the playwright is at pains to let us know that Cade is killed by Iden only because he is weak from hunger.'

'But the poet does not hide the brutality of the rebels.'

'You dignify a playmaker with the name of poet?' he said disdainfully. 'I have some respect for true moral poets like Sidney and Spenser.'

Both with Puritan leanings, of course. I was about to mount a defence of Shakespeare's (and my own) profession when Master Brayne interrupted with, 'Come, we've had enough talk, time for some music.' He turned to Elizabeth: 'Will you play for us, my dear?' When she sat at the virginals he looked proudly at the instrument and said, 'It's the only one in the neighbourhood.'

'Vanity, Master Brayne,' warned his wife, 'vanity.'

Mulcaster got up and stood by Elizabeth, turning the music for her while she played. Earlier, in the Cross Keys, my jealousy had been in my head; I had been able to compose fancy metaphors for it. Now, seeing him looking down at her and she occasionally smiling up at him, I felt it in my gut. I was sick to my stomach. As the harmony filled the room all I felt was bitterness and anger. Knowing it was my fault made it worse. When Elizabeth finished Mistress Brayne said, 'Come Chastity, we'll hear you now. Music is better than talk of nasty plays with their murders and lusts.'

'There's murder and lust in the bible,' I said harshly. There was a shocked silence. I had gone too far. It's true enough but they were horrified at stage plays being compared to the holy scriptures. Mistress Brayne stood up: 'Get out of my house. Get out.'

Not daring to look at Elizabeth I left. I walked back along Cheapside utterly desolate. The cries of a girl selling flowers and herbs grated on my ears as much as the croaks of ravens from the rooftops; while the scent of her lavender was no more to me than the stink of the refuse carried along the gutters. Bounding dogs, bustling hawkers, jostling porters were completely at odds with my stagnant mind as I trailed down Gracious Street past the Cross Keys and into Thames Street.

Approaching Coldharbour Tenements I saw a posse of law officers running after two men one of whom looked like Prigging Peter. The two men ran into the Tenements hoping to lose themselves in the warren of passages. Meanwhile the posse was being pelted from the windows with pots, pans, brimming jordans and broken chairs. The Tenements are thought to be one of the sanctuaries but the leader shouted, 'Let's go in,' and with heads down they rushed through the entrance. I waited in the street listening to the uproar inside. After a while they came back out battered and bruised but dragging one of the fugitives. They would never have emerged alive if so many of the residents had not been out on business, conveying goods from shops and money from pockets. Conveyers they called themselves. As for the poor devil being hustled away, it looked as if his conveying days were over. He was likely to be conveyed himself, on a cart to Tyburn.

Peter was sitting on the stairs outside my room with Rosie and a few others. I joined them and asked, 'Any hope for your mate?'

Peter shook his head and pointed to his thumb. That meant that the man had been reprieved once and branded with a T for Tyburn.

'It was a last minute reprieve, too,' said Rosie. 'Me and Peter went to see him off.'

Peter nodded: 'Old Jack was game. Stood there with the rope round his neck, hangman alongside him, like he was at the alter waiting to be wed.'

'Some bloody bride,' said Rosie. 'Two reprieved out of how many? Eight?'

'Nine,' corrected Peter. 'Jack was the second to get his name read out.'

Rosie laughed: 'First one fainted and fell off the cart. If his mates hadn't run and got the noose off he'd have been stretched anyway.'

94

I think the authorities throw a few reprieves to the crowd to keep them happy. And last minute ones have more drama. A kind of theatre.

Rosie said, 'You'd better get out of London for a bit, Peter.' When he shrugged she held up his hand showing his thumb branded with a T. Peter grinned: 'I got off by pretending to read my neck verse. An old thief in Newgate taught me it just before my trial. Trouble was,' he added ruefully, 'I had to give him all my money so I had nothing to slip the jailor to use a cold iron on my thumb. I never did find out what it meant in English.'

'They nearly always give you the opening of the Fifty-First Psalm to read,' I explained: '*Have mercy upon me, O God, according to thy loving-kindness: according unto the multitude of thy tender mercies blot out my transgressions.*'

'Transgressions,' said Peter cheerfully. 'I've got plenty of them.'

'Why do they let you off for knowing Latin, Tom?' asked Rosie.

'It goes back to the time when the clergy could only be tried by the church. In those days it was mostly only the clergy who could read Latin and that's how they proved who they were. It's called Benefit of Clergy.'

'Well you can't use it twice, Peter, so you'd better get out of London,' warned Rosie. The woman who lived next door to her said, 'You'd do well to get away for a bit yourself, my dear. There's a whisper that someone's peached on you.'

'It's that bloody vicar with the mole on his arse,' said Rosie firing up. 'The one who tried to say I took his watch.'

'And you didn't get much for it, Rosie,' said Peter. She dissolved into giggles. 'Look,' he told her, 'I've got relations down at Faversham who I haven't troubled for years. They'd take me in for a while. Come down with me.'

I urged her to go. I had grown fond of Rosie and I did not want to see her whipped through the streets at the cart's tail. The local beadle, a cruel bastard, was said to lay it harder on a woman's back than a man's. I said, 'We'll be touring in Kent so I may see you down there.'

A Londoner, born in Bow, she was reluctant to leave but finally agreed. Peter told me that Wheedler had called and left a message to meet him at the Bull Inn.

When I arrived Wheedler was there with Tarlton and after a meal we set off for our long-promised visit to Cod Randall in the Spital. On the way we each bought sprigs of rosemary to stick in our coats from a girl in the street. It is said to give protection against infected air. Henry the Eighth accused Cardinal Wolsey of giving him syphilis by breathing on him. We all agreed it would be a sad thing to catch the pox without any of the pleasure.

When we entered the hospital the smell of sweat, urine and pus was heavy. Our sprigs of rosemary were as much use as a single drop of perfume in the sewer that is Fleet Ditch. Cod, in a gown, looked healthy enough. He got up from his chair and said cheerfully, 'You bastards might well be wearing rosemary for remembrance. It's taken you long enough to remember me.'

'You talk to us like that,' said Tarlton, 'and next time we'll bring Sim Hicks along.'

Cod took us to see the sweating tubs. It was a long room filled with high closed in tubs from which heads poked. Clouds of steam hung in the air giving it the appearance of Hell. And many of the heads looked as if they belonged to the damned. Bald heads glistened above noses half eaten away by syphilis. Some had the vacant eyes and hanging open mouths of insanity. Their howls and shrieks were increased by a devilishly grinning

96

dwarfish attendant with a steaming jug who reached up and poured hot water into the tubs.

Through the steam I discerned poking out of a tub the fat face and now very red cheeks of Tribulation Cheadle. When I walked over to him he gave me an evil scowl. I assured him that I had not come to gloat, just for information on the Milk Street murder. Naturally, he told me to go to hell. Resisting the temptation to reply that I was already there I said, 'Master Winton...' his scowl became ferocious – 'has come up with a new herbal remedy for the pox that several of my friends have used. They were cured quickly.' All lies. But Winton, like any apothecary, did have a medicine for the disease. And building up Cheadle's faith in it would make it more efficacious. Cheadle finally agreed to talk about the murder when I returned with the medicine.

'No tubs left,' said a voice behind me. I looked round then down. It was the attendant with his steaming jug. When he raised the jug Cheadle yelled, 'No!' But he got the lot. I left the Spital with his curses ringing in my ears.

This was too good an opportunity to miss. Another should come with the first stop of our tour, Kingston. I hurried along Bishopsgate Street past the grim Bedlam and back into the city. At the shop Winton's wife served me, her husband having gone on his voyage. I ordered the medicine, saying, 'It's for a friend.'

'It always is, dear,' she said with a smile. Back at the Spital I was met at the door of the sweating room by the attendant who grinned and said, 'We've got a place for you now, sir.'

I looked at the empty tub and asked, 'Where's Master Cheadle?'

He shook his head: 'Took a turn for the worse so we put him to bed. He doesn't want to see anyone.'

I looked around the room at the tubs, like bloated bodies, the small heads sticking out, sweat running down

97

the faces, then at Cheadle's empty tub with steam rising from the top. The dwarfish attendant, flanked by two pock-faced titans, stood blocking my way the jug, brimming with hot water, held before his chest.

Twelve

Rejoining my friends I asked Cod Randall to try and have a word with Cheadle. Now I sat in my room reviewing the situation.

Just before leaving for Faversham with Rosie, Peter had given me some information he had gleaned. I still had my protection. Raleigh's wealthy friend the Earl of Northumberland, popularly known as the Wizard Earl, had taken on the cost. He was known as the Wizard because it was rumoured he and Raleigh's circle, Marlowe, Hariot the mathematician and others, were engaged in alchemy and necromancy. Because of their supposed practise of black magic they were known as the School of Night. They protested that they were simply investigating the laws of nature.

While looking into the Milk Street murder, Nicholas Winton had heard stories that the School of Night had consulted Mother Wingfield for their experiments, then used magic to kill her because she tried to blackmail them. Being a sceptic, Winton discounted it. Or at least the killing by magic. If it was true why did they want me to continue my investigation? Unless they had manufactured evidence against Essex and wanted someone unconnected with their circle to uncover it. I hoped to find out more when I arrived at Kingston on our tour. That reminded me that I had to get across to the Rose. Henslowe wanted me to make a list of all his theatre's stage properties while I sorted out those to take with us. Also I had to consult with Will Shakespeare about a play he had been commissioned to write by the Earl of Essex. The ban on playing would not affect it since it was to be acted privately in the Earl's house.

Just as I was about to set off there was a knock at the door. Opening it I saw Warthog's big ugly face glowering at me.

'Marlowe wants to see you. Now.'

'Where?' I shot back, equally abrupt. Social niceties would be wasted on Warthog. As a bailiff his usual method of greeting people was to clap a hand on their shoulder and growl, 'You come with me.' From force of habit he almost replied to my question with 'The Counter' but changed in mid word to 'The Cross Keys.'

When I demurred, saying I did not want to go there for personal reasons, he half drew a club from under his doublet. On this occasion I decided not to argue. Warthog was too much on edge since he was taking a big risk coming into Coldharbour Tenements alone. If he had been recognised as a bailiff he would have received rough treatment. So he kept a hood on. Even though it was a hot June day this was not regarded as strange behaviour in Coldharbour. Many residents came and went hooded for fear of informers.

As we walked along Gracious Street, I tried to wheedle out of him why Marlowe wanted me. He responded with a coarse jest which had me hoping Marlowe was not drunk. Being desired by him and spurned by Elizabeth was the reverse of how I wanted things to be.

When we entered the Cross Keys Elizabeth was her usual animated bright-eyed self bustling about among the customers. Now that I seemed to have lost her I longed for her more than ever. Marlowe, who was sitting at a table writing, motioned me to a chair. He waved away the hovering Warthog, saying, 'Go, "walk abroad and kill sick people groaning under walls," or whatever takes your fancy.'

'*Go about and poison wells,*' I contributed, getting my own back for Warthog's jesting. Knowing he was being mocked but not understanding it changed Warthog's face from sullen to ferocious before he turned and left.

'So you've seen my Barabas, Tom.'

'Of course, Kit.' If he was going to patronise me by using my Christian name (shortened at that) I would do the same. 'It seemed to me that the governor of Malta and his fellow Christians were greater villains than the Jew. He had cause to be angry.'

'Yes,' agreed Marlowe. 'In truth, I'm fond of Barabas, my little Machievel. Christ may prevail in the next world but in this one our messiah must be Niccolo Machiavelli. And just as in my play there are greater villains than Barabas, so in England there are greater villains than my friends. And one of the greatest is my lord of Essex.'

'If it suits them your friends will crucify you between Robert Poley and Ingram Frizer.'

He smiled: 'I feel that Frizer and Poley would be the ones nailing my hands and feet to the cross. However, it's Essex the overreacher I want to speak of. He's hungry for power. I'm told' – with pride creeping into his voice – 'he has been many times to see my Tamburlaine. Essex certainly has the pride of a Tamburlaine and I'm sure lusts for his power.'

I was sceptical: 'He's not going to overthrow her majesty as if she were Queen of Persia or Empress of the Turks.'

Marlowe shook his head: 'It would not happen like that in England. Essex would gain control of the Queen, get rid of her other ministers, then govern in her name. I have some insight into the power-mad mind and I tell you, as I've told Raleigh, Essex is wild enough for it and even now may be plotting an uprising.' Marlowe's eyes shone as the words tumbled forth. It was plain to see that his all-conquering heroes came less from the chronicles and

101

more from his own "aspiring mind." How he must have wished he had been born higher than a shoemaker's son so that he could have been a leading player in the power game. Little wonder that Tamburlaine, a shepherd who had made himself ruler of half Asia, appealed to him.

'What do you know of this play Essex has commissioned to be acted in his house?' he asked looking directly at me.

'I'm to help in the staging of it but as yet I know very little,' I replied.

'What is its title?'

'Love's Labour's Lost,' I said, giving him the cover title. The true title had been given to me in confidence. It was The School of Night.

'So you'll be there for the performance,' mused Marlowe. 'As will I.'

When I looked surprised, he added with a smile, 'The Earl of Southampton has invited me.'

I was reminded of his smile in the tavern; though this time, thank God, his lust was directed at an image of Southampton in his imagination. Money was doubtless another factor. In a year or two the earl would be twenty-one and wealthy. Already poets were angling to catch him as patron. Another School of Night poet, George Chapman, was setting out his wares for the earl. I had to be content with Henslowe as patron, Prince of the Playhouse and Baron of the Brothel. And I was content. Having an aristocratic patron meant writing dedications greasy with flattery. With my plays if I pleased the people I pleased Henslowe.

Elizabeth was attending to guests and supervising staff with all her usual self-assurance. Treating the soulful Grace with a good-humoured sympathy.

'Could you lend me your attention, Master Dekker, if that is what you prefer to be called,' said an exasperated Marlowe. 'Now, a servant in the Essex house was offering to sell us a document that implicates his master in some kind of treason. There was an accident when Ingram Frizer was questioning the man so we failed to learn the exact whereabouts of the document. But we are reasonably sure that it is still in the house, probably hidden in the servants' quarters. You'll be there helping to put the play on which will give you a good opportunity to search for it.'

'What about you?' I said indignantly.

'I shall be there as a guest and have no doubt that my lord of Southampton will require my constant attendance. In any case, being a friend of Raleigh I will be closely watched.'

'So will I.'

'Your efforts have yielded so little that we think they no longer consider you a threat.'

'Well, that's not my impression. Another thing, are you sure Ingram Frizer is on your side?'

Marlowe's eyes gleamed: 'That's what is so fascinating about this business, you can be sure of no one. Don't you feel that excitement? No,' he concluded looking at my face.

'I get my excitement from seeing my plays performed. The other kind I'll leave to you.'

With a bleak smile he said, 'You can't get out now. As you observed, my friends are ruthless. To dismount in the middle of a cavalry charge is to be trampled beneath the horses' hooves.'

'Oh please, spare me the epic images.'

'Then here's an everyday one. You've been in a boat on the Thames going downstream and the waterman asks if you want to stay on and shoot the Bridge or alight and walk around. It's too late to get out when you're being whirled between the arches.' He stood up. 'I'll make you a present of the image, Tom, for one of your plays. You've got a promising career as a playmaker. Don't let it get cut short.' At the door he turned and said, 'I always stay in the boat and shoot the Bridge.'

So there I was, press-ganged. When I tilted my hat over my eyes and folded my arms I was not posing, being fashionably melancholy. Dammit I was melancholy. I had a lot to be melancholy about. Alright, I was also hoping Elizabeth would take pity on me. Squinting from beneath the brow of my hat I saw her glance in my direction. After attending to a guest she looked again and seemed about to move towards me when a pretty young woman came in and walked up to her. She looked familiar. Where had I seen her? Elizabeth pointed to me and the woman came over and said, 'My mistress wants to see you.'

'Emelia Bassano,' I said and she inclined her head; nothing so vulgar as a nod from a lady's maid. 'Now,' she added, presumably because I had not leapt to my feet immediately. Well it was Elizabeth I wanted not Emelia and I was not going to damn myself in her eyes by walking out of the Cross Keys with a pretty young woman. So I replied with a good vulgar headshake.

'It would distress my mistress to have to tell Lord Hunsdon how you forced your way into her coach,' she lisped. I groaned. A word from Hunsdon and Henslowe would drop me as a writer. Another word to the Knight Marshal's men and they would drop me in prison. In the philosophical debate on free-will and fate I know which side of the argument I'd be on, I thought as I stood up. For a moment I hoped that it might work for me by making Elizabeth jealous. Then I saw her laughing with that silken shirted, satin doubleted, essence haired, bejewelled popinjay, Sir Ambrose. Elizabeth would not care if I were going to see the Queen of Sheba with Salome on one arm and Bethsabe on the other.

The coach was waiting for us. As we got in the maid blushed and the coachman sniggered. Last time the bastard had driven over the potholes deliberately. And he did it again, sending the girl into a fit of giggles at every bump.

We were set down in a mews and entered a big house through the back door. I was taken up the stairs and into a room dominated by a big bed. Emelia, sitting in front of a looking-glass, said, 'Isn't my hair dreadful,' as she pulled a gold backed hairbrush through it. She turned and smiled: 'You're a man of the theatre, Tom, don't you recognise a cue for a compliment when you hear one? Or do you think, like my poet, "black wires grow on my head." ?'

'The last time I argued against your poet, madam, you told me to look into the sun.'

She laughed and dismissed the maid with a wave of her hand. Her beautiful dark eyes gazed up at me as if I were all that mattered in the world to her. Then she rose gracefully and put her arms around me. I guided her to the bed whispering in her ear, 'No potholes here, nothing to disturb us.' She blushed prettily as she sat on the edge of the bed, drawing me down beside her, and murmured, 'Love's labours won't be lost here, Tom.' Stroking my cheek with her soft hand she said, 'My spies tell me you're helping to stage a play with that title at the Earl of Essex's house. I'm sure your plays will soon be in demand there and at other great houses, like my lord of Southampton's. I suppose he'll be there for the play?'

I drew back: 'So that's why you brought me.'

'No,' she retorted, slapping my arm. Caressing it she said, 'We can't always follow our heart, Tom. I'm a woman without rich relations. You live on your wits writing plays. I have to live on my wits too but in my own way.' Her voice took on an edge of bitterness: 'I've written poems and I know I could write better plays than many of those I've seen. But would they put plays by a woman on the public stage? You know they wouldn't. Any more than they'd have women acting in them.'

'You'd be a fine actor, Mistress Bassano.'

105

She smiled: 'We'd need a new word. Actress, perhaps. No, I'd prefer actor.'

'Player would suit you best since you're playing at chess with me as one of your pawns.'

Putting her arm around me she said, 'Come, you have far less cause than me, or any woman in my position, to be bitter. But you shall decide whether or not to help me. It's you I love, Tom.'

'You threw me out of your coach,' I said reproachfully.

'And I've regretted it ever since,' she replied huskily. As we rolled onto the bed there was a ringing metallic sound that made me leap in the air. 'Don't worry,' she said, 'I've only knocked a bowl from the table.' While Emelia loosened her gown I shrugged off my doublet and began pulling down my breeches. Drawing me on top of her she murmured, 'We have all the time in the…' There was a rap on the door and the maid called, 'Lord Hunsdon has returned, Mistress.'

'Not again,' I groaned.

'Quick, Tom,' said Emelia. 'It's you I'm worried for if he finds us.'

'I'm not going on any more ledges.' Pushing me towards the door she kissed me and said, 'Down the back stairs. I'll see you at the play.'

As I trudged towards the river I thought, where's my good angel? To which my conscience whispered, 'Keeping me quiet by keeping you faithful to Elizabeth.' In trying to win Elizabeth I was beginning to feel that I was playing a game in which Fate was throwing a loaded dice. Conscience piped up again that it was not Fate but my fecklessness that had lost her. There are times when my head feels like a pulpit with a particularly strident Puritan preaching from it.

Hang the expense, I thought as I hailed a boat. Walking across the Bridge was too much effort for my present mood. Isn't it always the way that when you just want to be quiet, someone wants to talk. But then what waterman doesn't want to talk as he rows? Who he had in the boat the other day. What's wrong with the country.

He wrinkled his big, red nose and began: 'That Walter Raleigh, mate. Sir Walter. In the Tower? The Queen ought of took his head off. Bedding one of her maids of honour? Disrespectful to her majesty, God bless her. Many's the time I've had him in my boat, that Raleigh. Proud as Lucifer. Sitting where you are now looking straight over my head as if I weren't in the boat with him. And no thanks when I lands. Nor no extra money. Different to that Earl of Essex. He's always got a word for you. And a bit extra. Best man in her majesty's Council. He'll sort out these Catholics flooding in from France. Hugo-whatsits they calls themselves.'

'Huguenots,' I said. 'They're Protestants, man.'

'Protestants. Secret Catholics, mate. In league with that Philip of Spain. You can't trust any of these foreigners.'

Exasperated I said, 'I'm Dutch.'

'Are you? You speaks nearly as good English as me. I've got nothing against the Dutch. Well, nothing much. I'm no bigot but those French take liberties.'

'What about Italians?'

'Oh, they're worse. Sly. Knife you in the back or poison you.'

'The Portuguese?'

'Well they're Spanish, aren't they? Arrogant. Like Raleigh.' Nodding at another boat he said, 'I took him across earlier. Lord Chamberlain. He slipped me extra.'

It was Lord Hunsdon. The maid had not seen him. Emelia knocking over the bowl was a pre-arranged signal for her to interrupt us. Emelia was keeping me on the straight and narrow path of her cause with the promise of future heavenly bliss. She also had the threat of Hell with

107

Lord Hunsdon. Women have an old saying: "By keeping men off, you keep them on."

When we arrived at the landing stairs I gave the waterman his exact fare. So he had the mean Dutch to add to his list of no-good foreigners.

When I got to the Rose, Henslowe was grumbling about a play being written for private performance that was too short for the public playhouse. Shakespeare promised to stretch it out for him like one of Rackmaster Topcliffe's victims. Henslowe, with his theatre closed and increasing signs of plague deterring visits to his brothels, was looking for someone to grumble at. He started on me, wanting a list of all his stage properties. I also had to sort out what we needed for the plays we were taking on tour and consult with Shakespeare about what he needed for his play at Essex House. He wanted a tree for characters to hide behind. Then I set to on the full list:

1 bay tree, 1 cage, 1 hell mouth, 2 coffins. 1 tomb of Dido, 1 bedstead. 8 lances, 2 steeples, 1 chime of bells. (would bells ever ring for Elizabeth and me?) 1 golden sceptre, 1 Pope's mitre. 3 clubs, (a reminder of prentices' clubs would not improve Henslowe's temper.) 1 lion's skin, 1 bear's skin. Phaeton's chariot. (That reminded me of being ejected from Emelia's coach.) Cupid's bow, 1 little altar, Tamburlaine's bridel. 2 moss banks and 1 snake. 1 tree of golden apples. 1 frame for the beheading in Black Joan. (Poor James Stour) 1 black dog. 1 cauldron (Tribulation Cheadle had been in hot water in the Spital. What had become of him?)

I was interrupted by Shakespeare who wanted to go over his play with me. This was going to be my first play as book holder and I wanted to make a good impression. Snooping around Essex's house for Marlowe and carrying out whatever Emelia was going to foist on me, I could have done without .

Thirteen

The day of the play had arrived. We had rehearsed it on the stage of the Rose, our voices echoing back from the empty auditorium. Everyone knew their lines. Piling the costumes onto a hand-cart we pushed it down to the river then loaded them onto Essex's barge. Looking back I saw Shakespeare approaching. Behind him walked the accident-prone Muffler carrying the stage tree. Naturally, he slipped on some horse shit pitching into Shakespeare's back and knocking him to his knees. Now, the tree behind him, like a true poet his head seemed crowned with bay leaves. Rising, he laughed and said, 'They don't crown mere playmakers with the bays but one day I'll do something to deserve them.'

I thought, perhaps your sonnets to Emelia Bassano will earn them. Or earn something. Rumour had reinforced what I had observed; the way he had looked at her when she was at rehearsal on the day of Raleigh's arrest. Then the expression on his face when she had eyes only for the Earl of Southampton; as black as a lightening-struck tree.

With everything loaded and all aboard we pushed off from the landing. It felt good to be rowed along the Thames in a stately barge with the Essex pennant flying in the westerly breeze. Alleyn opened a bottle of sack and glasses were passed around. The boys, instead of conning their lines as ordered, were chasing each other around the boat. With the sun shining and the wine flowing no one felt in the mood to stop them. Instead Will Kempe began taking bets on how soon Muffler would fall into the water.

No one won since another boy fell in. Before they hauled him back on board one of them, mimicking a Puritan pastor, said, 'I christen thee Muffler Two.'

We rowed westward past the deserted Bear Garden, also closed down, its bears forced to tramp the roads and be baited in the country towns. Soon we would be following them with our loaded wagon traversing the dusty roads of Kent. But for now we lay back enjoying the sights and sounds of the river.

What shocks the chaste-eared visitor to London is the swearing of the Thames watermen. Essex House is in the Strand so we had to cross the river. The steersman swung round the tiller and we cut across a fleet of skullers, barges, cock-boats, pinnaces and yowls. Broadsides of Billingsgate language roared across the water. Blasphemies shrieked through the air like chain-shot. Oaths screeched at us like bullets. 'You lousy, scabby, beggarly, run-down, poxed-up pimps.'

'You pools of vomit spewed from a whore's mouth frightening the Queen's swans with your ugly faces.'

'You turd-begotten bastards born in a jakes and christened in a jordan.' This last had been shouted at us by the hard-faced oarsman of a boat we had almost swamped. His passenger, a young gallant, stood up water streaming from his silken clothes and screamed, 'You could have sunk us.'

Kempe ran to the side of the barge and pointed at the oarsman, shouting, 'Never, friend. Look at his gallows-face. As the proverb says, "He that is born to be hanged cannot be drowned." It's Tyburn not the Thames will claim him.'

From the surrounding boats came shouts of, 'It's Will Kempe.' Acknowledging their shouts Kempe danced around the barge somersaulting over the oars then leaping onto the bulwark and dancing along the edge his shadow capering on the water while passing between the cheering boatmen, their dripping oars glinting in the sun as they were raised in salute.

Landing at the stairs we unloaded our gear and carried it through the garden and into Essex House. We were met by the steward, a portly man who puffed out his chest to show off his gold chain of office. We named him Monsieur Malevolent for his affected airs and his first words to us: 'I don't like players but my lord has commanded me to receive you. Let me make it clear that I will have no drunkenness, no disturbance, no noise…' he howled as Muffler stumbled and dropped the bay tree on his foot.

We had a spacious hall in which to act the play. Entering it we found the maids busy sweeping away the old brown rushes covering the floor, together with bones and scraps of food from dinner which the dogs had not eaten. Women were bringing in armfuls of fresh green rushes from a cartload in the street to strew in their place. A maid flung sprays of meadowsweet and rosemary amongst them. The empty hearth had been filled with green boughs.

The oak beams supporting the high arched roof had been carved with intricate designs while images of birds and beasts were cut into the stone around the chimney piece. The walls were covered with woven Flemish tapestries and English painted cloths. On one wall, fitting in with our play, were depicted the Nine Worthies; Alexander the Great burning down Persepolis, the red flames seeming to leap from the cloth; Caesar crossing the Rubicon; King Arthur and Charlemagne laying about them. All ambitious, powerful men.

On other walls were biblical scenes. The Prodigal Son returning home in rags (my mother's prophecy for me). Daniel in the Lion's Den (how I felt in this house). Judith cutting off Holofernes' head (a strong woman was what I needed now).

The trestle tables and benches had been pushed back against the walls and we removed the great dining table at the end of the hall and began erecting a stage. The thudding of the carpenter's hammer was accompanied by "Fortune My Foe" and other strains as the musicians practised up in the gallery. Add to this all the actors testing the acoustics by simultaneously declaiming their lines at full pitch and it sounded as if we had brought to life the painted cloth depicting the Tower of Babel.

Shakespeare was on his favourite subject of trying to get the players to act more naturally, saying, 'Do not saw the air too much with your hand, sir,' and everyone else was occupied so I decided to slip away and investigate the house.

I climbed the broad oaken staircase looking furtively around for Monsieur Malevolent. Then I realised that this was the way to draw attention to myself. So I adopted a bold confident manner my hand gripping the banister in proprietary style. This hardly went well with my worsted doublet and homespun breeches, I thought, as I looked at the richly coloured pictures on the walls and the tinted windowpane, blood-red.

Not long after getting upstairs I was lost. It was the first time I had been in such a large rambling house. I wandered along corridors and into rooms which led into other rooms then back down the corridors. In some chambers from behind the closed bed curtains the sweet smell of perfume was accompanied by creaks and grunts and gasps. From somewhere I heard Ingram Frizer's sinister laugh. Rounding a corner I saw Shakespeare knocking at a door. I sidled into the shadows. No playmaker would be best pleased to see the book holder neglecting his play. When the door was opened the voice of Emelia Bassano's maid said, 'My mistress is not at home.'

'Oh don't be ridiculous, Joan,' said Shakespeare, pushing past her into the room.

'A gentleman would know what not in means,' came Emelia's cutting voice. It would certainly have cut poor old Will who was hoping to get a coat of arms.

'Emelia,' he responded in a conciliatory tone: 'You know how much I care for – no, love you.'

'You showed that by your last poem to me.'

'I was angry when I wrote it. Read my latest.' There was a ripping sound from the room. It was embarrassing listening to this but I was in a quandary. I did not want to go back and perhaps meet Frizer. Going forward would take me past the open door. So I stood irresolute. There was a rustle of paper then Emelia's voice: 'Here's what you think of my beauty:

"Yet in good faith some say that thee behold

Thy face hath not the power to make love groan."

'You know perfectly well,' said Will, 'that a fair not a dark complexion is the fashion for women's looks. You're selecting your quotes. I go on to say: "Thy black is fairest in my judgement's place."

'Yes, lulling me before attacking my character.' Again there was a rustle of paper then:

'*In nothing art thou black save in thy deeds,*

And thence this slander, as I think, proceeds.'

'Is it so untrue, Emelia?' he asked sadly at which she exploded: 'What do my morals have to do with you? I'm not your wife. She's being swived by all the country clowns of Warwickshire. What colour hair has your son got?'

'That's the judgement of a whore.'

'Go back to your little town and your shop-keeping father. You a gentleman? Everybody laughs at you.'

He came out red-faced and flung some coins at the feet of the maid, saying, 'We've done our course.'

The maid shouted, 'I'm no bawd. I'm a virtuous girl. I'm as good as you. Better, because you're just a player.' Turning she saw me and said, 'My mistress wants to speak with you.' Shakespeare turned and glared at me. I shrugged helplessly and went into the room. The maid stooped and swept up the coins then followed, closing the door. Emelia was fitting back the poem she had torn. Glancing over it she smiled and could not resist reading it out:

'*Thine eyes I love, and they, as pitying me,*
Knowing thy heart torment me with disdain,
Have put on black and loving mourners be,
Looking with pretty ruth upon my pain.
And truly not the morning sun of heaven
Better becomes the grey cheeks of the east
Nor that full star that ushers in the even
Doth half that glory to the sober west,
As those two mourning eyes become thy face.
O, let it then as well beseem thy heart
To mourn for me, since mourning doth thee grace,
And suit thy pity like in every part.
Then will I swear beauty herself is black,
And all they foul that thy complexion lack.'

'Perhaps I was too hard on him,' she sighed and caressed my cheek, adding, 'But a penniless woman has to be practical, otherwise…'

I could see how she had captivated Shakespeare. Even knowing what she was about I was almost falling. Almost. Now that Elizabeth seemed unattainable I was more desperate than ever to attain her. Not, admittedly, that I would have said no to a romp with Emelia. But it did not appear that she was going to give me another chance to say yes or no. She wanted me not as a bedfellow but as a broker.

'My lord of Southampton, I'm sure, is interested in me, Tom. He visits the playhouse a lot so you could act as

114

my…' 'Pimp,' I suggested – 'Agent,' she concluded firmly. 'You might even wrap it up tonight.'

'In your sheets,' I added sourly.

'Come, Tom. The Earl is rich, you're a poet. I could persuade him to be your patron.'

I was under no illusions about that. Marlowe and Shakespeare seemed to have the talent for the poetry that would appeal to a patron. I was a mere playmaker. No lord would give money to have a play dedicated to him. One imitating those of Greece and Rome and meant only to be read, perhaps; but not a play written for the popular stage. However, I decided to go along with this. Southampton being friendly with Essex I might pick up a clue to guide me through the labyrinth surrounding Mother Wingfield's death. At the same time I realised that using a woman as clever as Emelia would not be easy. I might end up like the spider described in traveller's tales. The male uses the female for his pleasure and is then gobbled up for her breakfast.

It seemed wise to return to the rehearsal and so, guided by Joan to the top of the stairs, I made my way back to the great hall. Frizer or no Frizer, after the play I would have to find the servants' quarters and search for that document.

Richard Burbage, who was playing the part of the young lover, Berowne, came over to me and said, 'Take me through this, Tom,' and handed me a paper. He added, 'At the last minute Will decide to give me some extra lines.' I followed the words as Burbage spoke them in the more naturalistic style Shakespeare liked:

'A whitely wanton with a velvet brow,
With two pitch-balls stuck in her face for eyes;
Ay and by heaven, one that will do the deed
Though Argus were her eunuch and her guard:
And I to sigh for her! to watch for her!
To pray for her! Go to; it is a plague

That Cupid will impose for my neglect
Of his almighty dreadful little might.
Well, I will love, write, sigh, pray, sue and groan:
Some must love my lady and some Joan.'

Burbage looked at Shakespeare and said, 'He seemed like a man possessed writing it and thrust the paper at me like a dagger.'

I looked forward with interest to Emelia's reaction when she heard the lines. Her temper was far fiercer than the glimpse I'd had in the coach. In fact with so many references to real people in the play I would be looking at the audience as much as the stage.

With all ready we had a quick meal then watched the audience filing in. There was a lot of manoeuvring as men tried to sit near ladies they were wooing for bed or lords they were flattering for patronage. Emelia had got next to Southampton who she wanted for both. But Marlowe was on his other side causing a diversion while Lord Hunsdon, her present keeper, sat next to Emelia, cramping her style.

The play rattled along well with Shakespeare, as usual, playing the king. The hits at Raleigh and others were much appreciated. Although a drunken soldier who had served with Essex in France felt the play needed livening up. At the line, "A lover's ear will hear the lowest sound," he belched resoundingly. We christened him Captain Belch. At the line, "One that will do the deed," it was not only Emelia's face that turned red.

After we had received our applause at the end Lord Essex came among us. He was at his most charming; shaking hands, patting shoulders, giving words of praise amidst good-natured banter. If he had lived in ancient democratic Athens he would have given Pericles a fight at election time. And even in a monarchy an ambitious man might think that being loved by the people could help him go far. As long as his popularity did not alarm the Queen. Well-liked though she was, a few grumbled at the favours she was thought to shower on her favourites. Some had compared her to Richard the Second who had really done so. It only needed some foolish friend to compare Essex to Bolingbroke, deposer of Richard, and her majesty would reflect that the Earl had Plantagenet blood. Then he would find that the Tudor Rose had a sharp thorn.

While the others were busy with wine and mutual praise I left my half finished glass on a window ledge and slipped away upstairs. Being a bit more familiar with the corridors I eventually found my way to the servants' quarters. I was about to enter when I stopped to consider. Had Marlowe sent me here to find papers or an assassin? My assassin. Glancing back along the darkening passage pierced only by a sliver of light from a half shuttered window, I was aware of the deathly silence. I was far away from the revelry up here in the attic of the great house.

Having come so far I had to go in. Slowly pushing open the door I peered round it into the long low room. The grotesque thought struck me that it looked like a coffin for a corpse that had been stretched on the rack. The room was lined with the usual straw pallets laid on the floor. No canopied beds and mattresses of down for servants.

Marlowe had told me that the dead servant had occupied a pallet on the right at the far end of the room. I walked between the pallets, crouching to avoid the low beams, and reached the end. Kneeling down I probed with my fingers the straw pallet while casting continual glances at the door. There was nothing in the straw. He might have had the papers in his box but that had been removed, by relatives no doubt. The doorknob rattled and I scrambled into the shadowy angle beneath the eaves.

Monsieur Malevolent entered. Full of self-importance he proceeded between the pallets on his tour of inspection. I was going to be discovered. But on reaching the first beam he stopped. Obviously it was beneath his dignity to go ducking and crouching. Instead he preened himself in front of a cracked mirror propped against the wall. Like an actor at rehearsal he tried different postures and expressions. Now fingering his chain and looking grave; then breaking into what he no doubt considered to be a lady-killing smile.

At last he left and I resumed my search. As an apprentice I had occupied just such a room and knew where to look. Running my hands along the floorboards beneath the pallet I felt one of them give slightly. Prising the board up I was about to thrust in my hand when I heard a noise. I hesitated. It might be a rat's nest. Without more ado I pushed my hand in and felt – paper. I pulled it out and thrust it into my doublet.

'I'll have that, Dekker.' My heart jumped. I looked up and saw Warthog standing just inside the door tapping his palm with the blade of a knife. Kicking the door shut he advanced on me ducking his head beneath the beams and grinning: 'No place to run now, friend.'

I was still kneeling with my hands on the boards as he ducked under the last beam. Jumping up with the pallet I rammed it in his face. Swearing through a cloud of musty straw he lunged with the knife as I darted past. While I dived under the beam the knife was driven into it. But his other hand grabbed my ankle. Wrenching the knife free he raised it above his head – then sneezed violently. I grabbed his hair and smashed his head down onto the beam. His grip loosened and I ran for the door. When I pulled it open Warthog yelled, 'Cutting Ball.'

Darting into the passage I saw Tawny Beard blocking the far end. The big knife in his hand and the name Cutting Ball sent me out through the window and onto the roof like a bat out of hell. When Cutting Ball thrust out his bull-like head I kicked the shutter against it. At least

I've given them both a headache, I thought, scrambling across the leads.

I regained entry through a window in the women's quarters and quickly made my way back downstairs. Picking up my glass of wine from the window ledge, I gratefully drained it. Elated at my escape I tried to cheer up a gloomy Shakespeare by describing the antics of Monsieur Malevolent in front of the mirror. He glared across the room at Emelia laughing gaily at a remark of Southampton and said harshly, 'Peers, poets and now perhaps a steward's gold chain for her spacious treasury.'

Fourteen

First chance I got I looked at the paper. Of course, it was in cipher. Who should I take it to? There was a brilliant mathematician in the Raleigh circle called Hariot. But could I trust him? Warthog was working for them and Marlowe could have got him into Essex House. But did Warthog have his knife out merely to threaten me? Or to dispatch me? Had Warthog changed sides? Whichever side he was on after what I'd done to his head sticking that knife into me would be a top priority. Not to mention the ominously named Cutting Ball. Probably the first part simply meant that he was a cutpurse while the second part (that sent shivers through my nether regions) was just his surname.

I was too vulnerable in Coldharbour Tenements and so I moved out. Cod put me up at his home. Since his nickname was short for Cod-piece he warned me not to use it in front of his wife. She was friendly enough once I had made it plain that I was not going to take her husband out drinking and whoring. In any case his sojourn in the Spital had put him off the latter. Nothing had been seen of Tribulation Cheadle since he had disappeared from the sweating tub. The prospect of my stay being short because of touring had no doubt also influenced Mistress Randall in accepting me. But it was taking time to get a licence to travel. Henslowe, I expect, was haggling over the amount of the bribes.

Edmund Tilney, Master of the Revels, had slashed our play of Sir Thomas More until it was like a Bedlam tailor's suit of clothes. Tilney's worry was the scene where apprentices rioted against foreign workers in London. Now, 75 years later, once more threats of riot hung in the air like thunder clouds. Ever since the St Bartholomew's Day Massacre, French Protestants (strangers, Londoners called them) had been fleeing to England from persecution and civil war. Naturally, I sympathised with the strangers. So it seemed did Shakespeare. (Though he has such a knack of entering the minds of a variety of characters that I'm never sure what he really thinks.) He had been brought in to write a speech for More eliciting sympathy for the strangers. When I showed it to my mother it brought back her flight from the Netherlands. She wept at the lines:

"Imagine that you see the wretched strangers,
Their babies at their backs, with their poor luggage
Plodding to the ports and coasts for transportation."

Henslowe wanted sympathy for himself. Being so topical the play would be almost certain to succeed. But despite having paid for it to be written he was still not allowed to stage it. Yet the government's apprehension was, I suppose, understandable. The situation was volatile. Courtiers like Raleigh and Essex were cannonading each other on a swelling sea of religious, national and social hatred. I quoted that line about Raleigh and Essex when drinking with my friends. Tarlton rephrased it as, 'A cockfight with the spectators joining in.'

We discussed the disappearance of Cheadle. Asking at the Spital we had been told that he had discharged himself. I was showing them the paper in cipher when Sim Hicks entered the tavern. When he came and joined us I quickly put it back in my pocket. I did not trust him.

Sim complained bitterly about strangers swarming into the country and taking the bread out of Englishmen's mouths. And getting the best jobs. 'I've got to work as a botcher because all the good tailoring jobs goes to the strangers.' When I argued that this was nonsense he said, 'You're Dutch so you would side with them.'

The others were quick to defend me; but they were also uneasy about foreign workers. It would not take much for London to erupt. And always there was the fear of Spain taking advantage with a surprise attack.

When I said, 'I'm going to water the roses,' Sim sprang up and accompanied me. As we walked into the yard he muttered, 'I've had a message from that constable you're looking for.'

'Tribulation Cheadle?' I asked eagerly. He nodded and went on: 'He's got some information for you and wants to arrange a meeting.'

'Did you see him?'

'No, he sent a man.'

'What did he look like?'

'I couldn't see. It was dark and he was muffled up'

'Where and when does he want to see me?'

'On Sunday, about noon. Do you know a piece of wooded land just beyond the Rose Playhouse?' I nodded. He looked nervously around then said, 'He'll be in there beside a large rose-bush. You're to go alone.'

It stank like the wall we were pissing against. When Sim made an excuse and left, I told the others. They agreed to accompany me at a distance. Cod was next to leave. As he stood up muttering, 'I'd better go,' Wheedler, out of sheer habit, tried to persuade him to stay.

'Let him go,' chuckled Tarlton, 'or he'll be in hot water again.'

'If you three go on brothelling,' he retorted, 'you'll be renting tubs in the Spital.'

Tarlton just grinned and said, 'At least we haven't got a wife to delude with a tale of a tub.'

'Get one boys and you'll be happier,' was Cod's parting shot. It struck home with me. I too left and set off to see Elizabeth at the Cross Keys.

It was still light when I stepped into Bishopsgate Street. The sun, beginning to set behind the Hampstead Hills, threw streaks of red across Finsbury Fields where a few archers were still shooting at the butts. I recognised the tutor who had dived to the ground when his pupil had accidentally loosed off a bolt. He seemed now to be engaged in a contest for money. His young opponent carefully levelled his crossbow and sent a bolt into the inner circle. He turned to his adversary with a look of triumph. The tutor, a big, black-bearded fellow, stepped up to the mark and, almost contemptuously, took the briefest of aims before sending his bolt smack into the centre. With a leer he held out his hand, palm up.

'Your shooting has improved remarkably, since we made our wager,' responded the young man. 'I think you have played me false, sir. You shot badly to draw me in. Well I'm no one's gull so you can whistle for your money.'

Blackbeard dropped his crossbow, caught the man's throat and whipped out a knife, snarling, 'Give me my money.'

The man reached into his pocket, gave Blackbeard some coins then hurried away. He wasn't a gull so much as a well-plucked chicken.

In Gracious Street I met Cheadle's watch. They were dragging a middle-aged woman out of a house. She had thickly painted cheeks and a mop of blonde hair with black roots showing through. 'Come on, you poxy whore,' growled a watchman.

'I'm not your wife,' she shrieked at him. Then adopting a haughty tone she said, 'I serve only gentlemen, so I'm a courtesan. Or, if you prefer, you may call me a bona roba.'

'Oh thank you my lady,' said another, bowing. 'Would your ladyship like to accompany us to Bridewell where I am sure your ladyship will find the accommodation and the company very much to your ladyship's taste.'

One of them spotted me and they came over. They suspected that I was involved in Cheadle's disappearance as revenge for his arrest of me. The man who had punched me said, 'We had a high regard for old Tribulation.'

'Yes,' I said. 'I heard you praise him as a fat, greedy, pox-ridden pig.'

He grabbed my doublet and hissed, 'If you've cut his throat we'll see you dance the Tyburn jig till your eyes pop.'

They watched me as I walked away. If Cheadle had been murdered the watch would be anxious to hang someone for it to discourage any more attacks on them. The question of whether that someone was guilty or innocent would not exercise their consciences too much.

When I entered the Cross Keys there was no sign of Elizabeth. Grace was bustling about among the guests with a tray of drinks. As I squeezed between the tables someone caught my arm. It was Richard Burbage. He was seated with Kempe and another actor. Not wanting to be in company when Elizabeth arrived I said that I would not join them.

'Indeed you won't, Tom,' said Kempe. 'We've got three wenches panting for us in a private room. We don't need any help from a playmaker for that performance.'

Burbage grinned: 'Tom would want to be a player himself.'

'The parts have been cast,' chuckled the other actor.

'Besides,' said Kempe, 'we've already got a poet player with Shakespeare.' Putting on a heavy Warwickshire accent he continued, '*Just speak what I've set down for you, Master Kempe; don't keep sticking in your own lines*. Well, Master Shakespeare's dear friend has stuck a line into Master Shakespeare's dear mistress, his dark-haired beauty. My lines are made of words but there the word is made flesh.'

'And since it belongs to an earl,' cut in the other man, 'I expect the lady thinks it's a pretty piece of flesh.'

Burbage smiled: 'Poor Will. One day we'll have that tragedy of love I've been urging him to write.'

They drank their wine, bought fresh bottles, then headed for the private room. Elizabeth did not approve of such goings on but the inn's owner had no objections to anything that brought in money; so Elizabeth, like the rest of us, had to compromise.

Finding myself a quiet niche I settled down with a tankard of beer and surveyed the scene. Alcohol-fuelled boasts were belched out all around me. Merchants overreached, money lenders tricked, taverns drunk dry, battles fought, duels won. But above all, women. Women the boaster had bedded, was bedding or was going to bed. If a tax could be levied on lies, all other taxes could be abolished. Her majesty would be the richest ruler in the world. My musing was broken into by Grace.

'Why so thoughtful, Tom?' she asked, pulling up a chair. 'Are you still thinking of Elizabeth? She has that young Puritan. I've heard he'll be minister of a rich parish 'cos he's got friends in high places.'

These words meant that I no longer needed to act melancholy. Now I felt it. Grace patted my hand and exuded sympathy. She said softly, 'There's others who like you, Tom.'

This surprised me. Grace was walking out with a man who owned a thriving draper's shop. Although I knew she liked me and was a rather romantic young woman, I was not vain enough to suppose that she would give up a wealthy draper for a penniless playmaker. That only happened on the stage. Yet she was gazing at me with her large soulful eyes. Was she ready for what some women do, a double marriage? An official one for prudence and an unofficial one for pleasure. Or was she really willing to throw over a rich draper for me? That was what my vanity was beginning to whisper. Leaving her hand lying on mine she murmured, 'Elizabeth won't come back to you, Tom.'

I was still undecided about how to proceed when Grace's draper came through the door. 'Ah, William,' said Grace smoothly. 'This is Mistress Elizabeth's young man,' the hand that had been covering mine now gesturing towards me. Rising she picked up my not quite empty tankard and putting her other arm around William's led him to the bar. My vanity collapsed like a pierced bagpipe. Unless she was ready for – but it didn't matter. I truly wanted Elizabeth back.

One of the other girls brought back my refilled tankard and I sipped it gloomily. Writing for a living is such an uncertain career that you can hardly blame a girl for preferring a fat draper for his fat profits. Elizabeth was different. She took life (this one and the one to come) more seriously than me. My comic plays ring truer than my tragic ones, I mused, staring into my tankard.

'You're looking unusually serious, Thomas,' said Elizabeth, sitting down. Taking off her bonnet she added, 'I think it's time we had a talk.'

Her sudden appearance drove out of my mind the fine, affecting speech I had composed for our meeting. Just as well. Elizabeth, as always, came straight to the point. Fixing her clear, grey eyes on me she said, 'I don't think there is any future for us as man and wife, Thomas.' Putting up her hand when I made to protest she continued, 'You seem content to drift along with no thought for tomorrow. You've hinted at marriage but without a firm proposal. And if you did ask me and I and my family consented how could you support a wife and, God willing, children?'

126

'I've been appointed book holder. Well, alright, temporary book holder. But my plays are being accepted and I'm getting money for collaborating.'

Still looking sceptical, Elizabeth said, 'Writing is a precarious living at the best of times as London's debtors prisons testify. And what of the worst of times, as now, when the playhouses are shut down? And according to John Mulcaster the government may order them demolished.'

'Yes, just what that damned hypocritical Puritan is working for.'

'He's no hypocrite,' retorted Elizabeth sharply. 'Although I have no objection to plays I can see that John is sincere and I respect his opinion.'

This talk was not going well. Desperate to say something positive I blurted out, 'I'm going on tour as a book holder so I'll have some money.'

She sighed: 'As a girl back home I crept in to see the players when they visited our little country town. The poor fellows looked half starved. I doubt they had much to send home to their families in London.'

'They were some threadbare, out at heel strollers. I'm going with the top London company who'll be resplendent in their rich costumes.' I added eagerly, 'The money will roll in from gawping, straw-chewing, hide-clad country clowns.'

'Thank you, Thomas,' responded Elizabeth dryly. After a brief silence she said casually (too casually) 'I was talking to Master Clay and his wife yesterday. Their shoemaker's shop is thriving.'

'How are they?' I asked in a neutral tone.

'Very well. They asked about you. Mistress Clay was concerned about you getting enough to eat.'

Mistress Clay was always concerned about me getting enough to eat. She had whispered to me when I had taken Elizabeth to meet her and Master Clay, 'She's a country girl like me, Tom, so I'm sure she'll feed you well when you're married.'

No doubt feeling she had prepared the ground well enough Elizabeth said, 'Master Clay is thinking of opening another shop. He'd be willing to put you in to run it. You know their only child died and they look on you almost as a son. It's a great opportunity, Thomas. And you'd be making them happy, too.'

'I was never very good at cobbling,' I countered.

'Master Clay said you were a fine shoemaker until your mind turned to the playhouses. They have a lot of affection for you and they worry about your future. With this you'd have security.'

'There's a future in theatre, Elizabeth. People need pleasure, recreation. I'm poised to be part of that future which I'm sure is going to be a great one.'

'It's the playhouse owners, Thomas, Henslowe, the Burbages, who'll make the money. Government and plague permitting.'

'*Man cannot live by bread alone,*' I quoted solemnly. 'As a good Christian, Elizabeth, you should realise that money is not everything.'

'Don't you quote the bible at me or tell me about being a good Christian. You go to sleep in church unless the preacher can turn his pulpit into a stage and his sermon into a play. I'm not mercenary but a woman with children to feed and clothe has to think about money. People can do without plays but they'll always need shoes.'

'My heart wouldn't be in it,' I protested. Unfortunately I was unable to resist adding, 'What shall it profit me to gain the whole world by mending soles if I lose my own soul.'

Two angry red spots burned in Elizabeth's cheeks as she stood up and said, 'When two people marry each has to make sacrifices. I think you're too selfish for marriage.' She stood up and left.

128

Am I selfish? Of course I am. For me writing comes before everything. When I should have been making shoes I was writing sonnets; and ballads instead of repairing boots. Scanning a line was more important than stitching a seam. I valued a lyric before a last, alliteration before an awl. I was taking refuge from disappointment in jokes, as usual. Our sins recoil on us like a soldier's musket. My selfishness would lose me Elizabeth. I thought of going after her to say I would take up the Clays' offer. Instead I made for my lodging.

When I got in I found Cod and his wife, Alice, at supper, a picture of domestic bliss. She was pouring ale into his tankard and they insisted that I join them. Sitting at the well-scrubbed table I looked round the room while Alice poured my ale. Pots and pans glinted in the candle light while the brass cauldrons hanging from hooks in the fireplace had been polished until they shone. How different from my room in Coldharbour Tenements.

With no appetite for food I soon made my way up to bed. There I dreamed that while standing at the alter with Elizabeth a hand was clapped on my shoulder and Tribulation Cheadle's voice boomed, 'I'm arresting you for selfishness. Take him away and lock him in the Spital.' There James Stour's head popped out of one sweating tub and John Mulcaster's, Cutting Ball's, Warthog's, Frizer's, Blackbeard's, out of others. Cheadle ran about knocking the heads with his truncheon until they all rose up and pitched him head first into a tub. Judge how prophetic this was.

Fifteen

When I called at the Rose next morning there was still no news about our licence to tour. Or anything from the censor about Sir Thomas More. We wanted to break it in when we toured the country towns before presenting it in London at our return. Henslowe was there grumbling about how much money he was paying out. Will Kempe, who had just finished arguing with him about money he claimed to be owed, said loudly, 'Why don't you write a play about a miser, Tom. You wouldn't have to look far for a model.'

Henslowe, wary about offending the crowd-pulling Kempe, took it out on me, saying querulously, 'Instead of standing idle, Dekker, you can call at the Revels Office and see if Tilney has made a decision on Sir Thomas More.'

So off I set. Coming from the Bridge into Thames Street I saw a small group of refugees, men, women and children, loaded down with luggage, asking at a butcher's stall for directions. Their broken English had a French accent, so, Huguenots. While they were talking the butcher kept working, his face growing redder and redder. When a Frenchman said, 'You tell me where we go, s'il vous plait,' the butcher swung his cleaver down hard sending the sliced off meat shooting into the mud. Waving his cleaver at the river he shouted, 'That's where you go, back where you come from.'

From a group of people who had drifted over, a man said, 'They're taking work off of Englishmen.' A woman

130

with a young girl complained, 'They takes the bread out of our children's mouths.' When a man shouted, 'They could be Catholic spies who'll murder us in our beds,' the woman clutched the child to her bosom. As I walked across to help them the Frenchman said, 'We are good Protestants. We wish only to live in peace.'

'Follow me,' I said. 'There's a Huguenot community in Spitalfields.'

Looking at a paper in his hand he nodded and ordered the others to follow. We were jostled as we left and the crowd followed us up Gracious Street shouting insults. They were working themselves up to attack us. We put the women and children in the centre as a youth darted from the mass swinging a club. Taking his blow on my arm I thumped him with the other sending him sprawling in the filth of the channel. We ducked and stumbled under a volley of apple cores, bones, dung and now a few stones. The red-faced butcher whirled a dead cat round his head by the tail and hurled it at us. At our centre women prayed, children screamed while their menfolk stood ready to defend them.

People were drawn by the clamour from shops and houses. A Constable waved his mace ineffectually at the roaring fist-shaking mass. A clergyman ran up and asked what the trouble was. When I explained he told us to stand our ground then strode back to the crowd. Spreading his arms he shouted, 'Are you men or beasts? Christians or heathens?'

'I'm as good a Christian as you,' bawled the butcher, 'but we're being overrun. Why should we keep taking in these strangers?' Above the roar of approval that greeted this the preacher shouted, '*For I was an hungered and ye gave me meat; I was thirsty and ye gave me drink: I was a stranger and ye took me in.*'

This was greeted with a sullen murmur as the crowd stood their ground. But from the shops people began coming over to us with meat, fruit, bottles of ale. A baker handed out some loaves saying, 'Not all Londoners are like those.'

Meanwhile, with the preacher staring them down, the crowd slowly dispersed. If only Elizabeth could see me now, I thought, as I led my flock towards the promised land of Spitalfields. Passing out of the city through Bishopsgate, ahead of us we heard the dreadful shrieks from Bedlam. It must have sounded ominous to the French after all they had been through. But as we turned right into Spitalfields the Bedlam cacophony was succeeded by a sweeter sound; sweetest of all to my companions who had told me that their trade was weaving. It was the rattle of the weaver's shuttle accompanied by voices singing in French. I recognised Psalm 4: '*Thou hast enlarged me when I was in distress.*' Many were in tears.

We were directed to the house of a man who helped Huguenot refugees to settle. His grave face became graver when I told him what had just happened. Shaking his head he said, 'We bring many new skills to England. France's loss is England's gain. And we'll be good Protestant subjects of Queen Elizabeth. So why do people hate us?' I assured him it was only some of the people.

On my way to the Revels Office I did a detour to tell my mother about the refugees. She also organised help for them. Under interrogation I was forced to admit that it seemed to be over between Elizabeth and me.

'Thomas, Thomas,' she scolded. 'How could you be such a fool? Well, I have heard of John Mulcaster as a man of principle.' Here she looked hard at me then continued, 'You have lost a good woman and she has gained a good man.' Thank you, mother, I thought, as I made for the Revels Office.

A clerk showed me into a room furnished with a few chairs and a desk. Behind the desk sat Edmund Tilney with a face as grave as the Huguenot leader and from much the same cause. When I explained the reason for my visit, he ordered the clerk to fetch the manuscript of Sir Thomas More. When the clerk returned Tilney showed me the parts he had censored. The play was disembowelled more thoroughly than a traitor at Tyburn. Of course his chief worry was still the riots against strangers. I pointed out the speech Shakespeare had given to More expressing sympathy for the strangers. He was not mollified: 'You would still be showing a riot on the stage directed against foreigners. And that,' he went on his voice rising, 'after the riot outside the Marshalsea, the rioters having met in your playhouse.'

'But that had a different cause. Besides, the city is fairly quiet now.' I salved my conscience with that, "fairly". But Tilney shook his head gloomily: 'There was trouble in Gracious Street over strangers today.'

I wish we received decisions on plays as quickly as the government receives intelligence of disturbances. Tilney, with growing impatience, said, 'In any case, the playhouses are closed, so there is no urgency.'

'But we want to take it on tour to try it out before – that is…'

'Before returning to London with it.'

'Well if you ban it in London, Master Tilney, there can surely be no harm in letting us act it in quiet country towns.'

'Precisely, sir. Quiet towns which the government wants to keep quiet. You're banned from playing to prevent spreading the plague and I won't have you spreading sedition.' A red-faced Tilney called to his clerk, 'Master Dekker is leaving. Show him out.'

Censors, I thought, as I was shown into the street. Tilney deserves far more than a bear to be tied to a stake and torn by dogs for the way he tears plays. Never mind my scenes, it would have done people a world of good to have heard that speech of Shakespeare's pleading for compassion for the refugees. Or do I have too much faith in words? Well just as the clergy need faith in God, so writers need faith in words. These thoughts carried me to Paul's Cross where a sermon was being preached. A sermon is always being preached at Paul's Cross. Judging by the sparseness of the crowd it was not one of the great preachers. Could it be the Reverend Bracegirdle? Looking over the heads in front of me I grinned. There in the pulpit, full of righteous indignation, was Rosie's client in Coldharbour Tenements, the one whose watch she had conveyed then sent him tumbling down the stairs. Rosie must still have rankled with him because the hypocrite was denouncing whoredom. He railed against scarlet women, Jesabels, Delilahs and the Great Whore of Babylon. Heads turned as a coach rumbled over the cobblestones and stopped. Out stepped Emelia Bassano. Jewels sparkled in her dark hair which set off the white breasts exposed by her low-cut dress. Emelia had a way of arching her black eyebrows that expressed scorn and a look in her dark eyes that said, you'll never enjoy my beauty because I despise you too much. It infuriated the preacher, whose name was Byrne. He must have recognised Lord Hunsdon's coat of arms on the coach and guessed who Emelia was because he pointed at her and shouted, 'The sewers of Italy pour their filth into England's silver stream.'

Emelia responded with spirit: 'I am proud of my Italian blood. Italians civilised Britain when your ancestors were savages in the forests of Germany.'

Working himself up to a fury with white flecks of spittle on his beard he screamed, 'Are you proud of your Jewish blood too?'

'Yes,' she cried fiercely. Controlling himself he swept his eyes around his audience and intoned solemnly, 'Then she is proud of being one with the slayers of our Lord.'

134

There were angry growls from the crowd of, 'Italian whore,' and 'Jewish harlot.'

Emelia stood her ground and said firmly, 'It pleased our Lord, without the assistance of man, to be begotten of a woman, born of a woman, nourished of a woman, obedient to a woman; and he healed women, pardoned women, comforted women; yes, even in his greatest agony and bloody sweat going to be crucified; after his resurrection appeared first to a woman, sent a woman to declare his glorious resurrection to the rest of his disciples.' Her voice hardened: 'Our Lord was slain by men. Are you, preacher, proud of being one with the slayers of Christ?'

The crowd had gaped, transfixed, at such an oration delivered by a woman. But now they began to growl menacingly. And from the gleam in his eyes and his finger pointed accusingly at Emelia I could see that Byrne was going to urge them on.

'Be careful, Reverend Byrne,' I called out. Every eye was on me as I added slowly, 'This lady has got friends in high places; she is not a denizen of Coldharbour Tenements.'

His Reverence's scornful expression at "friends in high places" changed to one of alarm at "Coldharbour Tenements." Looking closely he recognised me and said hurriedly, 'Brethren, we are enjoined to forgive, to hate the sin but love the sinner.'

Joining Emelia I said, 'In Coldharbour he loved the sin but hated the sinner,' as I hurried her to the coach. As we jolted and rattled over the cobblestones I told her about the Reverend's encounter with Rosie and she threw back her head and laughed. She wanted to return and ask him to show us the mole on his bum but I managed to dissuade her. No chance of us sinning in the coach today because her maid was there.

While Emelia talked of poetry, I was trying to find out if she'd heard from young Southampton what his friend Essex was up to. Using her subject as a bridge, I asked if Shakespeare was likely to obtain Southampton as a patron. But Emelia blocked it by wondering if he deserved such a patron; then questioned me on how poor besotted Will was taking her desertion. We struck a bargain. She would try and find out if Essex had any unpleasant plans for me; in return I would try and find out if Shakespeare meant to betray her to Lord Hunsdon in revenge for leaving him for Southampton. My head was starting to spin. Tom Nashe has told me that he once collaborated on a play with Marlowe and was trying to work out a plot while drunk and being chased around the room by his lust-crazed partner. I knew how he felt.

Emelia dropped me off at the Bridge and I walked across for the Rose. In Southwark High Street I met some of the actors who, after a meal at the George, were heading back to the playhouse. Shakespeare and Kempe were arguing about how big a role the clown should have in a tragedy.

'You of course,' said Shakespeare, 'would like him to be the king's constant companion.'

'Yes,' replied Kempe briskly; 'give the poor devil a few laughs before he meets his gory end.'

Shakespeare, walking nearest the wall and engrossed in the argument, did not see an astrologer in zodiac-decorated gown, head bent, hurrying towards him. Looking up they saw each other and stepped away from the wall then back to the wall then away from the wall.

'A dance,' shouted Kempe grabbing the astrologer's arm, whirling him round, grabbing Shakespeare's arm and whirling them both round until the astrologer, swearing, broke free and hurried on, calling down curses on Kempe who shouted after him, 'What's it feel like to be a whirligig?'

'If his predictions for you are accurate,' commented Shakespeare dryly, 'then the whirligig of time will bring in his revenges.'

Across the street we saw another collision looming. Two young gallants, both hugging the wall, approached each other. The closer they got the more they swaggered. Swords bounced on hips, heads tilted back in velvet ruffs; then hands went to hilts. Neither was going to step away from the wall and risk mud splashing on silken clothes from passing horses. Besides, it would have been like one ship striking sail to another, a loss of honour. They stopped, glared, then drew their rapiers, the blades flashing in the sun. A wagon lumbering past blocked our view. We heard a clash of steel and the wagoner roared, 'Go to it, my bully boys.'

The wagon passed and we saw the men fighting fiercely. Women with children scattered screaming. One of the fencers was much more skilful and he drove the other back steadily. But skipping forward for the coup de grace he tripped on a loose cobblestone and his opponent's lunging blade struck into his throat and out the other side. He sank to his knees, blood spurting from his mouth. To free his sword the other man put the sole of his boot against the face and pulled the blade out. His hand was shaking too much to sheathe his sword and he ran down the street slashing at those in his way. The dying man fell forward and rolled into the mud, his silken clothes stained red and brown.

On my way with Cod to meet Wheedler and Tarlton at the Boar's Head Tavern in Eastcheap, I kept my eyes peeled to see if we were being followed. Looking back along Fenchurch Street I thought I saw a familiar figure dodge into an alley. Despite sudden glances back as we walked down Gracious Street and Eastcheap I got no more sightings. Either I was mistaken or he was a skilful shadower.

The bells were calling the people to church as we entered the Boar's Head. Old Cruickshank, his tankard half-way to his lips, listened open-mouthed as Tarlton, between eating plums, told him (with many appeals for confirmation to a solemnly nodding Wheedler) of a sea-monster he had seen while on a voyage with Drake in the Pacific Ocean. 'We were chasing a great Spanish galleon, sir, that would have set every man of us up for life. The masts were made of chrysolite, the sails were cloth of gold; it had a ruby-encrusted bowsprit and the stern was another Golden Ass. Then up from the bowels of the deep rose a hugeous sea-serpent. Its massive jaws gaped wide and the galleon sailed between them, so,' and Tarlton popped a plum into Cruickshank's mouth.

We discussed our plans for the meeting with Tribulation Cheadle to the accompaniment of poor old Cruickshank spluttering on the plum, then on modern youth. The discussion was really a cover to give us time to sink plenty of ale.

In case someone had been following Cod and myself, we went out together, shook hands in the doorway and walked off in opposite directions. I turned left for the Bridge while Cod was to double back and join the others then all three were to follow me at a distance.

Whether it was the ale, the adventure or just the sunlight sparkling on the Thames I don't know but my spirits were high. Coming off the Bridge into Southwark I glanced up at the singing of a bird. It was perched on a traitor's head. On I walked past St Saviour's resounding to the 23rd Psalm, then past the Clink Prison. The prisons were full but the Rose, like the other playhouses, was empty. Getting a licence to tour was urgent and those holding out for a bigger bribe knew it.

Beyond the Rose the street ended in waste ground strewn with nutshells, apple cores and chicken bones. The black shape of a large rat scurried away from my feet in among the docks and thistles. Just ahead was the small wood. I knew where the rose-bush was that had been selected for my meeting with Cheadle. Striking up an acquaintance once with a young woman selling apples in the theatre, I had taken her there in the vain hope that the love scenes in the play coupled with the smell of the roses would induce her to yield. Of course I was indulging in these reminiscences to delay the moment of entering the wood. My high spirits had plummeted at the sight of those dark trees. Glancing back at the houses I saw no sign of my friends. But then I had told them to keep out of sight.

This was it. Swallowing hard I stepped amongst the trees, ears straining for the slightest sound. But the only sound was my feet rustling on the overgrown path. Then the sudden whirr of a bird's wings amongst the branches. That brought my knife into my hand. Reaching a fork in the path I stopped. Which way? A breeze wafted the scent of roses to me. But also the sweetly rotten smell of decay. Now I was straining with nose as well as ears. Damp wood? A dead animal? Following the mingled smells I came to a clearing. On the far side, beneath a tree, was the bush, its white roses bright in the sun. But one was red. As I stared another shook and turned red before my eyes. Blood was dripping from among the green leaves. Rustling in the undergrowth behind sent me running into the clearing. Head low I bounded across to the tree, leapt for the lowest branch and scrambled further up among the leaves.

A man was suspended by a rope round his feet tied to a branch. I cut through the rope and sent him head first into the rose-bush. Peering down through the leaves I stared into the sightless eyes of Tribulation Cheadle as he lay on his back with white rose petals falling on him and a red

139

gash across his throat. My foot slipped and I went plummeting down through the branches. As I grabbed at a branch there was a whirring noise and my hand was pinned to the tree. I heard someone crashing through the undergrowth towards me before I passed out.

Sixteen

When I came round I was lying on the ground with Cod, Wheedler and Tarlton bending over me. Stupefied, I looked at the hole in my left hand. Cod held up a crossbow. 'A bolt from this did it, Dutch. Pinned your hand to the tree.' He kicked the bloodstained bolt at his feet. 'We got there just in time to support you before your hand was ripped apart by your own weight.'

'It was a tall fellow with a big black beard,' added Wheedler. 'I saw him throw the bow down when he ran off. There was another man with him who I didn't get a clear look at.'

'There was a third,' said Tarlton. 'He was behind us and I heard him running through the bushes in the direction of the other two.'

Cod tore a piece of my shirt off and bound up my hand while I prayed it would not get infected. There was nothing we could do for poor Cheadle. We were gazing down at him when an old peddler came into the clearing on his way to Southwark. When he saw the body and my bloodstained hand he made off quickly the pack bouncing on his back. We shouted after him to tell the Constable but he did not look round.

I was sitting with my back against the tree having fainted again when the Constable arrived with the watch. His name was Miller and he was a short, tubby man perpetually fussing: 'What's this, what's this? Who is he?'

When I gave him Cheadle's name he told one of his men, 'Remember that.' Glancing from the slit throat to my bloodstained bandage he said, 'So you knew him?'

I nodded, adding, 'He was constable of the Bishopsgate Ward.'

'Constable! Bad business,' he said, his face growing grimmer. As his men lifted the body onto a litter Miller said, 'Show him respect, he was a constable.'

I did not like the way the rest of the watch surrounded us and took our knives. While being marched back into Southwark Cod whispered, 'It's only our word that anyone else was there.'

'No consulting,' shouted Constable Miller. 'I don't want you agreeing on a tale for the magistrate.'

Our fears were confirmed when we reached the Clink and were told we would be held there until the inquest. I was fast becoming a connoisseur of London's prisons. The Clink was one any self-respecting jailor would have been proud of. Perhaps it does not quite have the bouquet of Newgate or the pungency of the Poultry Counter. But it has its own special tang. When I put this into words to bring some cheer to our situation Tarlton said sourly, 'I'm the jester of this company, Dutch. Save your jests for your plays.'

'His next one may be the Tragedy of Tyburn,' said Cod glumly. That even had the usually optimistic Wheedler nervously putting a hand to his throat. We spent some of the little money we had left on beer. Prison beer or prison anything is ruinously expensive but we needed some solace. We'd even had to pay to remain together. Constable Miller had told the warder to keep us apart to prevent us agreeing on a tale. But our money was a more persuasive orator.

We paid out the last of our money sending messages to our families and a few hours later they arrived at the prison. Mothers, fathers, aunts and Cod's wife. Anger at us for getting into this scrape turned to anxiety at the possible outcome. While my aunts babbled away in Dutch my mother was planning the defence at my trial for murder. When Tarlton said to his mother, in reply to her wailing about him being hanged, 'Well you always wanted me to rise in the world, mother,' she had hysterics.

But the jokes were wearing thin with all of us. The authorities would want to hang someone for the murder of a constable and they would want to do it quickly. The inquest was to be held on Tuesday. A trial could be held two or three days after and two or three days after that ... There was a hollowness in the pit of my stomach as the thought hit me that next Sunday I, we, could be preparing for a Monday morning ride to Tyburn. They would transfer us to Newgate. I had watched the procession of death, men and women standing in the carts being carried through Holborn and along Oxford Street to that triple legged monster, Tyburn gallows.

When our visitors had left I sank into a slough of sad memories. Soon after I began my apprenticeship with Master Clay he suffered a loss. A heavy one because the Clays treated us all very much as family. One of the older apprentices, Roger, had been drinking with a friend. Seeing a miserly rack-renting landlord they decided to give him a fright. Covering their faces they robbed him and ran off leaving him wailing for his money. Five minutes later they had come back, faces uncovered, and returned his money saying they had got it back from the robbers. They had left him clutching his money bag like a long lost child, well satisfied with their sport. But Roger's companion had boasted about the prank in a tavern, been arrested and had saved himself by turning informer. Roger had been convicted and sentenced to death. The Clays had tried to save him, pleading that it had been youthful high spirits. But there had been a spate of street robberies and now that the authorities had someone, they were determined to make an example of him. He was nineteen.

We were taken to say farewell to him at Newgate on the last morning. I shall never forget seeing Roger, white-faced, trying not to cry, being put into the cart with the rest of the condemned. Mistress Clay and the maid-servants sobbed as they watched him being driven slowly westward between the crowds of people lining both sides of the street. Master Clay accompanied him to Tyburn. The hoped-for last minute reprieve did not come. A few days later a friend of Roger's, a carter who had just returned from a long trip, called at the shop. When he asked where Roger was he froze at the foreman's curt, 'Gone west.' For a long while after every time I was near the Thames and heard the waterman's cry of 'Westward ho,' I shuddered. Now soon people might be saying of me "Gone West."

None of us got much sleep that night. When I did doze off I was awakened by a drunk. He wanted to drink a toast to us for killing a constable and hanging him upside down like a pig.

Next day I was visited by my mother again; this time, to my surprise, she was accompanied by Elizabeth. Mother joined the others to let us talk. Any hope I had that Elizabeth was returning to me (assuming I had a future) was crushed when she said, 'John Mulcaster was willing to come and...'

'Gloat,' I interrupted angrily.

'No, Thomas. To see if he could help. You may not like his views but he is sincere. I did not bring him because I knew he would not be welcome.'

'Don't you find him dull, Elizabeth?'

She gave me a meaningful look and replied, 'I find him restful. No one, of course, could accuse you of being dull, in and out of debtor's prisons as you are. But with this you've excelled yourself.'

'I didn't kill him.'

'You don't have to tell me that, Thomas,' she said taking my hand. We were interrupted by the arrival of the Clays. She was a buxom, motherly woman who still, after forty years in the city, had a country air. Master Clay, a bred in the bone Londoner, as he always said, had a ruddy, cheerful countenance which only seemed to cloud over at other peoples troubles; his own he bore stoically. After the grief they had suffered over Roger's death God knew why they were laying themselves open to more with me. Typically Mistress Clay had brought a large basket of food, enough for all of us, while her husband had plenty of bottled ale. But what moved me was that they and Elizabeth still cared enough to visit me. I had to make an effort not to disgrace myself with tears. Seneca would have admired my stoicism.

Elizabeth seemed as surprised as me at the Clays' arrival so it was unlikely that she had arranged it to try and entice me into taking up the old offer of a shop. With all the excitement of late Elizabeth could easily have persuaded me to take up the quiet life of a shoemaker. But she seemed to have settled for John Mulcaster. Before leaving, our visitors promised to get Sim Hicks to testify about the message he had given me.

Now all we had to look forward to was tomorrow's inquest. If it went against us we would be on trial for our lives. Master Clay's bottled ale was our only comfort. That is until some of the actors from the Rose arrived. They cheered us up. Although one of Kempe's stories did not go down too well. He told us (suiting actions to words, as the players say) of the execution of a thief he'd witnessed. While being prayed over, the thief, to the amusement of the spectators, had stolen the chaplain's handkerchief. When Kempe mimicked the man's hanging

145

by clutching his throat and capering everyone felt it was in very poor taste. It was as well our senses were dulled by alcohol. The actors left soon after the last of the ale had been drunk. I had another restless night.

In the morning we were escorted in bright sunshine to the Rose Tavern where one of the rooms had been hired for the inquest. Henslowe and Ned Alleyn were standing outside beneath a window with a coloured pane depicting the Tudor Rose. Alleyn said, 'I've got the licence to tour, Tom.'

'With my money for lubrication,' grumbled Henslowe. 'I hope you're going to be available, Dekker. If a new book holder has to be found with all the delay and expense it will be my purse that will be called on again.'

'I'm sure Tom will clear himself,' said Alleyn heartily as the guards hustled me inside. Slowly my eyes took in the crowded room. The public were seated on benches, mother, the Clays and relations of the others among them. Lying on a table by the window was the body covered by a sheet. The sun had clouded over, leaving it looking sinister in the shade. Next to it, and facing the public, were the twelve jurymen occupying three benches. To their right, sitting in imposing isolation at a table, was the coroner, a thin man with a bristling white beard and sharp eyes. As I passed mother she caught my arm and whispered, 'Elizabeth will be here later.'

Constable Miller bustled forward and puffed, 'No consulting with the accused;' then sycophantically to the coroner, 'I don't want the accused in a tale, sir.'

'They are witnesses, Constable,' he replied sharply. 'For the moment. Bring them forward.'

The members of Cheadle's watch eyed us malevolently as we were escorted to the front. First the court proceeded to identification. Mistress Cheadle supported by three female friends, a handkerchief pressed to her eyes, was taken over to her husband's body. When the sheet was pulled down to reveal his face she groaned, 'Oh, my Tribulation,' and with one eye peeping from behind the handkerchief, looked round to make sure her friends were still there then fell back into their arms. As she was taken wailing back to her seat Cheadle's watch came forward one by one and gruffly identified him. Now it was our turn to identify him as the man we had found hanging from the tree with his throat cut. Complete silence descended on the room. As each of us looked down at his face and nodded I knew what everyone in the room was waiting for. It was the old superstition still believed in by a great many people. They were waiting for Cheadle's wound to start spouting fresh blood in the presence of his murderers. Of course, nothing happened. As we turned away a juryman muttered, 'Some say the murderer has to touch the body.'

'An old wives' tale,' said the coroner. But he was ignored as the cry was taken up by jurors and public of, 'Make them touch him.'

Cheadle's watch blocked our way hemming us in by the body. The coroner shrugged then waved his hand at us saying, 'Very well.'

The watch pushed Cod forward and he quickly touched Cheadle's arm.

'The wound,' growled a man. 'Touch the wound.' Necks were craned as one of the watch forced Cod's hand against the gaping wound in the throat. Wheedler and Tarlton followed quickly. Nothing. Now it was my turn. The air was thick with tension. There were murmurs of, 'He's the one Cheadle arrested.'

Shaking off the watchmen I stepped forward and put my hand on the wound. His skin was ice-cold. There was a loud gasp. I looked down in horror at a patch of red on the sheet. The shocked silence was broken by a voice from the doorway:

'That blood has been shed by the sun.'

We looked round. It was Nicholas Winton. He was pointing at the coloured window pane's entwined red and white Tudor Rose through which the sun was now shining. There was a cry of, 'It's still a sign from God of his guilt.'

Winton shook his head: 'God gave us the light of reason to search out evil. Let us use it.'

'And so we will,' said the coroner firmly. He ordered the door to be locked behind Winton to prevent further interruptions. And so we proceeded to the examination of witnesses. The peddler told how he had found us with the body. Then came Constable Miller and his watchmen. Next Cheadle's old watch told how they had arrested me on his orders. 'Disturbing the peace, he was,' growled the one who had punched me. The others foisted the bitter jokes they had made about their constable on to me. This was beginning to sound more like a trial than an inquest. And with the testimony piling up against me it would make my real trial (which now seemed a certainty) a mere formality. And my friends would be dragged down with me.

The warden of the Spital was called. He testified that we had been at the hospital about the time Cheadle had disappeared. The jurymen eyed us sternly. Most of them looked like strict Puritans in their sober black clothes. Psalm singing Southwark saints to a man, I had no doubt. Their train of thought was written on their long faces; it read, these young men were in the Spital therefore they had the pox; therefore they had consorted with whores. And fornication leads to murder as surely, in their view, as Papism leads to Hell. I could not say that Cod only had been in for treatment. Then it was our turn. I was cursing Sim Hicks for not coming when there was a knock on the door.

'It could be our witness,' we chorused. Reluctantly the coroner ordered the door to be unlocked. Elizabeth came in with a sullen-faced Sim.

'He claimed that he was too busy to attend so I reminded him that it was his duty,' she said. Elizabeth is good at reminding people of their duty as I have cause to know. Now I felt deeply grateful.

We gave an account of finding the body and my being shot through the hand. Our reason for being there I explained by referring to Sim's message. When he was called on to corroborate my testimony he put a hand to his forehead and said, 'I have certainly drank with Master Dekker and the others occasionally – in moderation,' he added, looking piously at the jury. 'But as for delivering such a message…'

'Perhaps I can give your memory a jog, Master Hicks,' interrupted Nicholas Winton standing up. When he introduced himself a juryman said to the coroner, 'I can vouch for Constable Winton since we are well acquainted.' Another juror said with emphasis, 'He has an honest face,' then looked hard at Sim and pointedly said nothing. I resolved in my next play to create a shrewd, sincere Puritan instead of the foolish, hypocritical ones we always portray.

Winton continued, 'Due to information I had been given I was following a certain John Williams, a notorious character. He met you at the Three Cranes near the Bridge, Master Hicks. I saw him give you money and was close enough to hear him mention Master Dekker and to refer to a meeting with Constable Cheadle. Williams is well known for giving archery lessons in Finsbury Fields as well as for less savoury activities. If necessary I can produce several witnesses to the meeting.'

Sim gulped, 'No, that won't be needed. I can remember now;' and words gushed from him like water out of the Pissing Conduit in Cheapside. Then Winton gave his account of how he had lost contact with Williams (who I think of as Blackbeard) and so had followed me and the others to the wood. He had not made contact with me in case I was being watched. His account corroborated ours, which was a huge relief. In addition he was able to testify to seeing Blackbeard throw down the crossbow before running off. Winton had followed him and another man. When they split up he kept after Blackbeard. But on reaching the Thames his quarry had jumped into a boat and pulled away leaving Winton helpless on the bank.

The jury of course found that Cheadle had been murdered and a search was ordered for Blackbeard and his accomplice. We were released though not without some murmurs and dark looks. None of us felt like remaining in the Rose so we repaired to another tavern for a much-needed drink. Winton told me that his ship had been driven back to England by gales. I gave him the coded paper I had obtained at Essex House. 'Stolen, I suppose, is the word a constable would use,' I said ruefully. He smiled: 'Let's settle for the word your friend Peter would employ, "conveyed."' He promised to let me know what it said as soon as he got it decoded.

When I asked Elizabeth if I could walk back to the Cross Keys with her, she shook her head and said she was meeting John Mulcaster. So I made my way to the Rose Playhouse where everyone was bustling about getting ready for the tour and announced that I could join them after all.

Seventeen

The next day I was up at dawn and saying goodbye to Cod and his wife. She, understandably, was relieved to see me go and in saying farewell was at her most friendly. Cod just groaned. I could measure the ache in his head by that in my own. We had celebrated our release the previous night with enough ale to float the Spanish Armada. Now its cannon seemed to roar in my ears as Cod's apprentices banged open the shutters. The light darted in like gun flashes. Slinging my pack over my shoulder, I left the shop and trudged down the street to the Thames.

'Eastward ho! 'shouted a waterman in my left ear. 'Westward ho! 'bawled another into my right ear. I stumbled into the latter's boat and mumbled, 'Rose Playhouse,' to his grinning face before my head slumped onto my chest. A stiff westerly breeze was making the water choppy. More and more I regretted not walking over the Bridge. To divert my mind from my stomach I silently recited:

"*Come live with me and be my love*
And we will all the pleasures prove
That hill or valley, dale or..."

Its smoothly flowing rhythm was beginning to have a soothing effect on my stomach when the waterman said in a Scottish burr, 'I'll wager I had more drams than you last night, laddie, but I'm just fine and I'm going to tell ye why. Thirty years I've been in this England of yours but I mind what my auld father had for his breakfast after a heavy night's quaffing. A big steaming heap of haggis, which for your information is sheep's heart, lungs and liver chopped up with suet, onions, oatmeal and boiled in a sheep's stomach'. I leaned over the side and emptied my stomach into the Thames.

Having prepared the day before, we were ready to depart soon after I arrived at the Rose. When we had secured the stage properties the wagons creaked forward through Southwark heading for the Bridge. Those like me, without a horse, walked, taking it in turns to ride on the wagons. When I was told to climb aboard I thought they were taking pity on my woebegone condition. Not so. Shakespeare had decided to remain in London and seek a patron by writing a long poem. The company wanted me to shorten his Henry VI plays to make them fit the smaller number of players we had on tour. So there I was on high, with each judder skewering my aching brain, trying to write while perched on a stage throne as shaky as King Henry's during the York – Lancaster wars.

The pungent smell of alcohol as we passed the Bear Tavern made my head reel. Then we rumbled through the Great Stone Gate and onto the Bridge, crowded already, early as it was. At the head of our little procession Edward Alleyn looked his usual stately self on a fine bay horse. A hatter's apprentice setting out his wares flourished a tall hat, struck a pose and cried, '*Is it not brave to be a king and ride in triumph through Persep* ...ow!' he yelled when his master walloped him across the ear.

It was nearly an hour before we rolled off the Bridge and into the tangy smells of Fish Street Hill. A fishwife held out her wares to us and sang, 'My mussels lily-white, herrings, sprats or plaice, or cockles for delight.'

We turned left into Cheapside as bleary-eyed London stretched and yawned. Past the appetising smell of a bakery, where they were well into baking fresh loaves for the day. Past Bread Street which no longer has any bakeries, but does have the Mermaid Tavern. Perched on my precarious throne I chewed my quill and stared at the white paper. Now I was swaying past the majestic bulk of St Paul's to my right with the booksellers opening up their stalls in the churchyard. Ahead on the left lay the great rambling Bel Savage Inn. John Holland said, 'I saw my first play there.'

'I acted in my first play there,' said the abnormally thin John Sinclair. 'Old James Burbage saw me and liked what he saw.'

'Wouldn't have seen you if you'd been standing sideways,' muttered Kempe who was not at his best this early. Not in any sense of the word. But neither was I. Poor as it was, Kempe had managed a joke. I still hadn't written a line even though it was only a matter of abridging another's work. There were no more thoughts in my alcohol-poisoned brain than there were fish in Fleet Ditch, London's most noisome sewer. Its stench was in our nostrils now. Any flower-sweet smells borne from the countryside on the wings of the western wind had been shot down by a volley of stinks from the Ditch. We crossed Fleet Bridge holding our noses.

There were calls for me to get down and let someone else ride if I was not going to do any writing. I hurriedly began scribbling. At Chelsea Village I was brought down when a wheel dropped into a pothole and the wagon lurched sideways breaking an axle.

'King Tom's deposed,' laughed Kempe clinging on in his privileged place beside the driver. The accident occurred outside a large house and a gentleman came out with several servants. Sending one off to the joiner, he invited us into his house. We were invited to stay the night and in return agreed to act a play in the great hall for him, Master Seldon, and his friends. It was a lucky accident since the inn we were booked to play at had been closed down by the magistrate as "a house of ill fame." Rubbing my bruised shoulder I said ruefully, 'Fortune's wheel has spun us up into soft beds but first it shot me down onto the hard ground.'

Slapping my injured shoulder Kempe chuckled, 'You're our saviour, Tom. Through your suffering you have taken our sins on your shoulder and gained us entry into heaven,' and he gestured to the great staircase. The mistress, who was giving directions about us to the steward, gasped and crossed herself. So did the steward. A Catholic household. She looked at Kempe as one lined up for a thunderbolt. He bowed to her saying, 'And here is one of the angels.'

Master Seldon bustled up all ginger whiskers and geniality playing the generous host with gusto, loudly telling his steward to, 'Take them to the buttery, give them all that my house affords;' adding in a low voice, 'Within reason.' Seeing that I'd overheard he grinned and shrugged. I liked him. Which of us wouldn't like to play the munificent lord while not wanting to be eaten out of house and home? For a band of actors can be to a house what the locusts were to Pharaoh's Egypt. The children of the house, a boy and two girls, came running to their father clamouring for a play about magic.

'You'll be in bed,' said the mother. Disappointed, they looked appealingly at their father who said to his wife, 'Come my dear, just this once.'

'*Just this once* is what you say every time you indulge them, sir. Have it your way.'

'Now sirs,' he said turning to us, 'have you a play about a magician who spirits away three mischievous children?'

Alleyn smiled and replied, 'We have a play about two magicians who will spirit your whole household away for two hours and return you safe and merry.'

So having eaten our fill of cold chicken and ham, plum pudding and clotted cream from the buttery washed down

154

with ale or beer, we began preparing the hall for our play: Friar Bacon and Friar Bungay.

It is not a favourite of mine but it held our audience. Especially Friar Bacon's magic mirror showing events hundreds of miles away. With so many characters and so few actors some had to juggle three parts. Kempe had two, the fool Miles and Friar Bungay. I was kept busy making sure they were ready for their cues and prompting them when they dried. What with the constant motion and the heat from the torches lighting the stage I was parched and sweating. When Kempe forgot a line and looked to me I opened my mouth and – croaked.

'Sweet Jesus, the prompter's dried,' bellowed Kempe, causing half the audience to cross themselves. He improvised brilliantly. I took a swig of ale and saw a servant run in and whisper something in Master Seldon's ear. His rubicund face paled and he jumped to his feet and hurried up the great staircase. Shortly after, there was a furious knocking at the door. The play stopped and the audience froze. Mistress Seldon held a servant back from answering the door and looked to the staircase.

'Open or we'll break the door down,' bawled a man. Seldon leaned over the banisters and nodded. His wife pushed the servant towards the door. As soon as he drew the bolts the door was forced open and a gang of men burst in. At their head were Robert Poley and Warthog. Between them stood a thin, anxious looking man. He looked at Seldon and said unhappily, 'I'm sorry Master Seldon, it's not of my choosing.'

'Do your duty, Master Magistrate,' ordered Poley while Warthog lead a bunch of men charging up the stairs. Others scattered through the ground floor rooms. The magistrate took out a paper and read, *'Acting on information that a Catholic priest has been seen in this house I hereby give order for a search of the said house.'*

'A search that began before I heard the warrant read,' pointed out Seldon bitterly.

'Leave off your legal niceties, sir,' interrupted Poley, 'and answer my questions. Do you have a priest in this house?'

'Do you hear any shouts of triumph from your creatures to announce that they have found one?'

'Yes, that's one of your Jesuit-taught tricks, to answer a question with a question. We know you're a Catholic.'

'There is no law against being a Catholic provided I am a loyal subject of her majesty. Which I am,' added Seldon firmly. Warthog came tramping down the stairs holding up a length of rope: 'The priest didn't need no priest-hole. We found this hanging from an open window. He must have escaped down it before we got the house surrounded.'

The son, who was about twelve, stepped forward and said, 'I'm sorry, father.'

Seldon shook his head and smiled at the magistrate: 'Adventurous youth cannot be confined. For his misdemeanours I told him he was not to go out of the door for a week. If he doesn't break his neck he'll grow up to be a brave subject of the Queen.'

'It's the priest you had here who'll break his neck,' said Poley. 'On the gallows.'

'Not so,' responded Warthog licking his lips. 'He'll be cut down first and disem…' he gaped and pointed to a figure with head covered in a cowl slinking to a doorway. Warthog plunged forward scattering audience and actors and flung himself at the man. They rolled on the floor and Warthog was pinned down with a knee in his stomach. The cowl was pulled back to reveal Kempe's grinning face. 'Greetings,' he said. 'I'm Friar Bungay. You must be the devil I conjured up.'

When they left Poley's silence, as always, felt more threatening than words. Warthog roared like an harquebus against players and – shooting a glance at me – those who scribbled for them. There was a general call for us to go on with the play. Everyone, including the non-Catholics in the audience, was in a good humour at the fooling of the priest hunters. No one had wanted to see the man dragged off to suffer the gruesome death for treason.

There was loud applause (demonstrating their loyalty?) for the compliment to Queen Elizabeth in Bacon's prophecy:

"From forth the royal garden of a king
Shall flourish out so rich and fair a bud,
Whose brightness shall deface proud Phoebus flower,
And overshadow Albion with her leaves."

Everyone cheered when the exuberant Kempe, booted and spurred as the foolish scholar, rode the Devil down to Hell. We laughed. But the devils who had just left the house were to prove that they were still very much with us in this world.

Next morning, after a generous breakfast, we were busy loading up our repaired wagon with the stage properties and costumes. The family were outside saying their farewells and urging us to call again while the children clambered onto the wagon and jostled each other to sit on the throne. Mistress Seldon shook her head at them but their father smiled indulgently. He patted his wife's arm: 'Perhaps Sir Thomas More's spirit still lingers in the house and has entered me. But although he indulged his children he worked them hard at their books as I do with ours. And they'll turn out just as well as his, you'll see.'

At the mention of More's name the pious Mistress Seldon had crossed herself. Many Catholics see More as a martyr to their faith. Doubtless another reason our play had difficulty with the censor. Everything was tied down and Alleyn's bay was being led out of the stable when a shouting, jeering crowd rounded a corner. Poley and

157

Warthog were again at their head. But this time a different man was between them. Pushed and jostled, he stumbled along in a priest's cassock his hands tied behind his back with a gold crucifix swinging from his neck. There were sobs from the women of the family. Seldon stepped towards him calling out, 'Father,' but was shoved away. As the priest was hustled on he called back, 'Be happy for me, my friends.'

And he looked happy. If he was acting then he was a better player than Alleyn and Burbage combined. He was utterly convinced that his inevitable execution would make him a martyr and carry him to heaven as surely as an east wind would blow a ship to the New World. Catholics believe they are saved. Anglicans believe they are saved. Calvinists believe both of them are damned. And from the Calvinists I've met, they're not too sure about each other.

So it was a sad farewell after all. We offered our awkward sympathy then resumed our journey. Passing the last house of the street we were in sight of the Thames, the morning sun sparkling on the water. At a landing stage the priest was being put into a boat for his journey to London. He was breathing in the fresh air of the river with that serene expression still on his face. For him Newgate Prison and Tyburn Gallows were merely staging posts to heaven. Poley's face had no more expression than a frozen pond. Warthog's sluggish smile was as putrid as Fleet Ditch. Both of them might have posed for devils in wall tapestries of the Harrowing of Hell.

As they got into the boat on either side of the priest, the oarsmen pushed away from the landing. Warthog turned and jeered at us from the statute against unlicensed actors: '*Rogues, vagabonds, strollers*. As for you, Dekker, I'm only sorry that I'll be cheated of my revenge. I'll tell my friend who pulls corpses out of the Thames to look out for you floating down from Kingston. Then I'll hang you up to dry on London Bridge.'

The watermen rowed the boat into mid-stream where the current helped it on its way to London. We trudged on to our next stop, Kingston.

Eighteen

The day that had begun with bright sunshine soon clouded over; great heavy, black clouds marching up from the south like an invading army. They seemed to come to a halt above our heads as though having found their target and were now taking aim. The air was clammy and our clothes stuck to our bodies as we hurried forward hoping to find shelter before the clouds opened. Lightning flashed, thunder rumbled; then it rained as though a giant bucket had been emptied on our heads. In minutes we were soaked.

We straggled into a small wood and huddled there. Not the safest of places with lightning forking across the sky. This was the unglamorous side of touring. In fact, to hear the players talk of small audiences, meagre payments, hostile councils, it was all unglamorous. Eventually the sun struggled out and we left the dripping leaves for a clearing. Here we managed to get a fire going to dry our clothes and cook a meal.

I had made some progress with the popular Henry VI plays which, it had been decided, would have to concentrate on the civil wars. What with the civil war raging in France it was topical. 'It will be a double play,' I told the company assembled around the fire. 'Part One I am calling The First Part of the Contention Betwixt the Two Famous Houses of York and Lancaster.'

'God help us,' exclaimed Kempe, standing up.

'And Part Two,' I continued firmly, 'will be called The True Tragedy of Richard Duke of York with the Death of Henry the Sixth.'

Kempe dashed the hat he was drying to the ground and shouted, 'Writers! He's got more words in those titles than a monkey's got fleas and nothing about me. It's my Jack Cade that pulled in the crowds.'

'Your Jack Cade,' I retorted. 'I think Will Shakespeare could have some claim to him.'

'He got him from a history book. I could have written the part.'

'Why didn't you?'

'We keep servants for drudgery.'

'You'd be lost without writers.'

'Writers. I shit 'em.'

'Then your arse must be even bigger than your mouth.'

Kempe's reply was lost in a general laugh and however good it may have been he was too experienced in comic timing to try repeating it. As Alleyn said, I had won that encounter. But he added, 'For God's sake, Tom, put Jack Cade into the title.' Soon I had half the company clamouring to have their parts included.

Plodding along a narrow track, the sun turning the Thames to gold and making us think of the beer we would be quaffing when we got to Kingston, a wheel skidded into a mud-filled ditch. We sprang into the ditch and braced ourselves against the side. But inexorably we were borne back as the wheels settled into the mud. All our pushing and pulling could not budge the wagon. In the end it took a farmer's oxen to drag it free.

It was a weary band that plodded into Kingston that evening. When a passer-by said to his companion, 'Strolling players,' we chorused back, 'Staggering players.' He carefully studied our bedraggled, mud-spattered clothes and said, 'Had some rain, have you? We could have done with it here.'

'We could have done with you having it here,' said Kempe. Tired, cold and hungry we finally found our inn, The Swan. The landlord looked us up and down then said, 'Had some rain, have you? Could have done with it here after our long dry spell.'

Actors are a resilient lot. Washed, combed and fed, sitting round a table enjoying the house's best wine, we were chattering like Barbary apes. Even Kempe, after a few cracks at pint pot poets, was in a cheerful mood. Then Ingram Frizer walked in. Of course the chatter went on because no one else had my suspicions of him. And if they'd had any they would have been drowned when he ordered drinks for the whole company. In addition he had thirty shillings if we would put on a play a friend of his particularly wanted to see. It was Marlowe's The Massacre at Paris which depicted in lurid detail the slaughter of Protestants by Catholics on St Bartholomew's Day twenty years earlier. Alleyn readily agreed. Kempe was not so keen since there was no major comic part. He grumbled, 'The people of Kingston will want to see my Jack Cade.'

Frizer took his arm saying, 'Play it the day after. I saw it at the Rose and I want to see it again. Above all I want to see again your capture of Lord Say.' He nudged the waiter who was clearing the table and said, 'Now lad, let's see how good you are at playing a lord,' then whispered in his ear. The waiter turned to Kempe, struck an exaggerated pose with one arm extended and declaimed, '*These cheeks are pale with watching for your good.*'

Kempe became Cade: '*Give him a box o' th' ear, that'll make 'em red again.*' Frizer thumped the waiter's ear sending him reeling. The lad shook his head then sprang forward in fury. Frizer was turned away from me so I could not see his face; but the waiter could and he stopped dead, his anger evaporating. He went back to clearing the table. Frizer ordered more drinks and

162

proposed a toast: 'Confusion to Catholics and a good old English box o' th' ear for the Spanish king.' He was patted on the back for his patriotic sentiments to the clinking of tankards. Kempe gleefully nudged him in the ribs and congratulated him on his jest with the waiter, a humour very much to Kempe's taste.

While everyone else was enjoying themselves, as book holder I thought it prudent to get out The Massacre at Paris and glance through it. One of Henslowe's other writers had shortened it for a previous tour. Frankly, he had massacred the poetry as ruthlessly as the Duke of Guise had massacred the Protestants. But all the killing was still in so the audience would be satisfied. And for once the Puritans would be less inclined to condemn violence on the stage.

Ensconced in a window-seat, I heard the creak of a cart entering the yard. After the driver had handed the horses over to the ostler he came in. He looked familiar. Standing in the doorway peering around the room through the cloud of tobacco smoke, his eyes came to rest on me. As he approached with a letter in his hand I recognised him. Nicholas Winton had pointed him out as a friend, adding, with his usual good humoured cynicism, "and more importantly, a friend who can be trusted."

I ordered him a pot of ale then read the letter. It was from Winton. He had broken the code in the paper I had taken from Essex House. There was no signature and no names. It detailed a plan to stir up anti-Catholic feeling in and around London; and to spread rumours of fresh plots to kill the Queen and bring in the Spanish army from the Low Countries. It was to be co-ordinated and built up to a climax in – then it broke off. Winton added that from information he had been gathering, Bolingbroke (our code name for the Earl of Essex) planned to build up a strong power base from the Puritan faction. Then organise an uprising to force the Queen to expel Essex's enemies from her council and make him her chief minister. He would, in effect, rule the country. It rang true. However much Queen Elizabeth was revered by the people many of the younger aristocrats like Essex resented being ruled by a woman. As one of her favourites there had been gibes about him being her minion. Winton thought that Essex's reckless nature would impel him into some rash act sooner or later.

More and more rumours were circulating that Protestants seeking refuge from war and persecution in France and the Netherlands were secret Catholics. This dovetailed people's hatred of foreigners and Catholics and took away feelings of guilt about wanting to turn away fellow Protestants. I've heard people say that true Protestants would stay home and fight. So the audience at tomorrow's play would easily reconcile sympathy for the St Bartholomew victims with their call to "Send the strangers back where they came from." People will believe what they want to believe.

When I looked up from the letter Ingram Frizer was staring across the room at me. The letter would have to be destroyed. I went into the kitchen and threw it in the fire. When I returned Kempe put his arm around my shoulder and said, 'I want us to be friends, Tom, and it's not the wine talking. Oh, you're right to give me that quizzical look and wonder what Will Kempe is up to,' he added chuckling while guiding me to a chair. Filling two glasses with wine he struck a solemn note: 'Ned Alleyn is a great tragic actor and he has Kit Marlowe to supply him with great tragic roles. I'm a comic actor, Tom, always will be. Many are speaking of you as a budding comic writer bidding fair to become an English Plautus.' He held up his hand: 'No modest disavowals, Tom. I would have seen it for myself but for...' striking the palm of his hand on his forehead – 'cursed envy. I envied you your gift with words. But I'm a performer, Tom, you're a writer. We're made for each other.'

All this was very pleasant to hear but I was still wary, waiting for Kempe to request a loan or ask me to sit up all night writing a major comic role into The Massacre at Paris. I was wrong. He pointed to a demure young woman and said, 'Her mistress saw us come into town and took a liking to one of us. Her description fits you, Tom. I must say I was tempted to send her away by saying you had found female company. But I realised I need you as a writer and this is my peace offering.'

I was flattered. What young writer wouldn't be at this praise from our best comic actor?. There was the obvious possibility that it was a trap. But I just could not see Kempe engaging in a plot to murder one of the company because of our spat. In that case most of us would have been victims, since he'd had fierce quarrels with almost everyone.

All of this I told myself as I accompanied the maid out of the inn and along Kingston's main street. But the real reason was that it was too long since I had lain with a woman. Kempe claimed to know the woman from a previous visit. His description of her charms and willingness to bestow them set my blood racing like the Thames under London Bridge. When a man's middle leg wants to go somewhere his two outer legs have to follow. That member was drawing me after it like a magnet. I was as wound up as a crossbow ready to shoot its bolt.

We had turned down a side street and ahead I could hear the lapping of the river. I suddenly remembered Warthog's gibe at Chelsea about his river-scavenging friend pulling my body out of the water. It was now twilight so I made sure we kept to the centre of the street while my eyes scanned the shadowy houses on either side. Putting a hand on the solid hilt of my dagger gave me some reassurance. Also I was feeling a little more secure from a direct attack. Questions were being asked in London about the murders of Stour and Cheadle and whether powerful men were responsible. My enemies must surely be getting a little apprehensive. And if Blackbeard were picked up he might have his tongue loosened. Unless he had been silenced.

As we came closer to the river I thought of the possibility of an accident being arranged. My prudence was getting the better of my lust and I was considering turning back when the girl pointed to a house and said, 'In here.'

As I hesitated I heard through the open window a lute being plucked accompanied by a sweet female voice singing, *'Bonny sweet Robin is all my joy.'* I wondered if she knew what Robin was slang for. I was going to give both of us joy with mine, I thought as I entered the house. The song of the siren luring men to their destruction was only a fable.

The woman seated on the couch plucking with slender white fingers on the lute, hair hanging loose about her shoulders, looked beautiful enough to entice an anchorite out of his cell. Either that or it was a case of any meal looks good to a hungry man. She patted the seat beside her and told the maid to bring us some wine. Propinquity and perfume drove all similes from my mind; her arms around me burnt up all words. I kissed her full red lips. Then the maid returned with the wine. My hand was shaking so much I almost spilled it.

'Careful,' she said, somewhat anxiously. Why? I took a sip. Smiling she put her hand to the glass and tipped more down my throat saying, 'Wine is a spur to love.'

Did I detect a strange taste? Poison? Or was I like the night time traveller who thinks every bush is a robber? The maid had left us so, keeping the woman occupied with a kiss, I tipped the rest of the wine over the back of the couch. Just in case. More kisses and murmured endearments. Then I began pulling her dress off. 'Slowly,' she whispered. 'It is better slowly. We have all night.'

She had a soft, smooth, languorous voice; a velvety voice that seemed to be stroking and soothing me into sleep. My lips moved down to hers but met only the cloth of the couch. Too tired to care I let my arm hang over the side while I drifted into sleep with the scent of her perfume in my nose.

I dreamed of making hot, passionate love to her. We were being consumed in a crackling, flaming furnace, lying on a bed of coals their smell acrid in my nostrils. Opening my eyes I thought I had fallen into Hell. The curtains were ablaze and I was choking on thick black smoke. I opened the door and staggered into the passage. It was on fire in front of the street door. No escape there. And the kitchen at the back was ablaze. The only way I could go was up the stairs. As I passed the room I'd just left the ceiling came crashing down and flames leapt into the upper part of the house. I ran up the stairs looking for a window to jump from. But they were all barred and shuttered. In the attic I stood on a chest and tore frantically at the thatched roof above my head. Making a hole, I pushed my head through out of the smoke-filled room and into the clear night air. But there was no time to waste. The front of the roof was burning. I wriggled through the hole. At the front of the house people were shouting for water. Here at the back was a narrow alley across from which was another house.

I jumped across and onto the roof, clutching desperately at the straw to stop myself sliding off. I scrambled up to the ridge. There was no time to linger. Sparks were being blown across and the thatch was already burning. The next house was further away but I had to jump. This time I only just made it. Even here I would not be safe for long. The fire had spread across the roof I had just jumped from and soon sparks would be blown across. But there were no other houses near enough for jumping. The Thames was below but not knowing its depth at this point I daren't risk diving in. So once again I tore at the thatch to make a hole.

I dropped into a room that was evidently used for storage. Lying invitingly on the floor was a palliasse. All the exertions I had been forced to make had banished the drug-induced drowsiness; but now it was returning. Just a few moments rest. But the rough straw of the palliasse felt like down and I was starting to doze off when I heard angry voices from downstairs. 'It's by order of the Mayor,' shouted someone. Then I heard the rumble of a barrel. Forcing myself up I went out onto the landing. The hall below was in darkness but I just made out a shadowy figure hurrying to the door. There was a shout of, 'Get clear,' then I saw a small flame spurting across the floor. Gunpowder. They were creating a fire-break. Running back into the room I opened the window and leapt onto the ledge. A tremendous explosion blew me from the house. Falling I prayed and took a deep breath before plunging into the river.

When I surfaced debris was raining down around me. The current whirled me past the burning houses and on before I gathered the strength to strike out for the bank. I hauled myself from the water, lay on the grass and slept.

When I awoke my clothes were steaming in the heat of the sun. I struggled to my feet and began trudging back to the inn. Passing the town's grammar school I heard the pupils chanting, 'Micher, micher, blackberry eater, miching by the riverside.' They were obviously greeting a boy who had played truant the day before. When we had miched as children we had begged bladders from the butchers and used them in the Thames as water-wings. I could have done with them last night, I thought, as well as the wings of Icarus. I had been burnt, blown up then ducked.

The town clock struck ten. I should have been with the company helping them rehearse. They would regard me as a micher. They did. But only after they had stopped falling about laughing at my lack of eyebrows and the burgeoning beard, of which I'd been so proud, burnt to a frazzle.

Nineteen

After my experiences I was not sorry to leave Kingston. Kempe, when I taxed him, had protested that Frizer had told him it was a joke. She was going to steal my breeches so that I would be forced to return in my shirt. Strangely prophetic, that. The fire was blamed on Papists. So one of Frizer's aims was achieved. My inquiries about the house James Stour had told me of yielded the information that there had been mysterious goings on there. Since I asked after the fire, most put it down to Catholic plotters. But one man claimed he had seen the well known Puritan John Penry going in.

Our plays had been well received. We had used the inn yard as our theatre and the weather had remained fine. However on our last day a carter with a wagon load of provisions had arrived a day early demanding to unload immediately. When he was refused the blood-thirsty threats of Richard Crookback before the audience were matched by the carter's hair-raising curses behind.

Now we were leaving Kingston and heading south. With the sun shining we were in high spirits. For the next few days we travelled at a leisurely pace, sometimes sleeping in the open since the weather was warm. From the hedges we picked blackberries for free; from orchards we had apples and plums for a speech by Alleyn or a jig by Kempe. We bathed in cool streams and with the constant sunshine were soon burnt as brown as the band of gypsies we met camped on a moor. They made us welcome and entertained us for a change with their dancing before we moved on. It was like an idyll, bringing to life the pastoral poetry I had found so dull in school.

In one village the less idyllic side of country life was seen. It was the centre of several villages and hamlets and Ned Alleyn had ridden on ahead to tell them of our coming. He returned with the news that we would be welcome and would have a sizeable audience. Our stage could be erected on the village green.

Arriving in the village we made our way to the green. A tavern had supplied us with six beer barrels and we laid boards across them watched by several villagers. One of the barrels was on uneven ground and when Kempe took a flying leap onto the stage it collapsed hurling him to the ground. In a good mood he joined in our laughter. The villagers did not. They muttered among themselves with dark looks.

We gave them The Comedy of Errors. The play began in bright sunshine which gradually clouded over. Later everyone claimed that it began to rain just as Alleyn spoke the lines:

'Dark-working sorcerers that change the mind,
Soul-killing witches that deform the body.'

Just as Alleyn was beginning to think of abandoning the play the rain stopped and the sun came back out. Soon after, the drumming of horses' hooves sounded. One of those late-comers who distract an audience just as you've captured them. As the rider swept around the bend his horse slipped on a muddy patch and he was thrown violently to the ground. The audience rushed over to him. He had been knocked unconscious. A villager told us that he was the son of a local landowner. As he was carried into the nearest house a rider was dispatched to bring his father. The crowd milling about outside the house were growing angry and the name Mother Naylor was being shouted. While the crowd were converging on a house opposite the green I asked a man who she was.

171

'A witch,' he growled and spat. 'The old bitch stopped my hens laying and gave my pigs swine-fever. I said she'd put a spell on me but no one would listen.'

'She put a curse on the play,' bawled a red-faced woman. 'She didn't want the noise so she stopped the play.'

She was getting plenty of noise now as people banged pots and pans together, hooted, jeered and hissed. Trying to make myself heard above the din I shouted, 'If we go on with the play that will prove she's got no power.'

'No power!' shrieked the woman. 'No power when she's half killed that young man?' By now we had reached the house and stones were clattering against the walls, door and shuttered windows. There were shouts of, 'Burn her out.'

The parson came hurrying up. Pushing his way through the crowd he stood in front of the house and addressed them: 'Like you good people I abhor the evil of witchcraft. But we must proceed according to law and that means a trial.' There were cries of, 'We don't need no trial, we know she's guilty.' 'She gave my children measles.' 'She made me miscarry.' 'She turned my milk sour.' 'Drag her out.' 'Hang her.' 'Give her the water test.'

This last was greeted with enthusiasm and the crowd were surging forward when we heard the clatter of hooves. Several horsemen galloped into the village. It was the sheriff, his officials and the father of the injured rider. The father was taken to see his son while the sheriff said to us, 'There's always trouble where you players are. I came here to move you on but it seems I wasn't quick enough.'

We protested our innocence but he was adamant: 'I won't have play-acting in my jurisdiction. Now get that stage down and move on.' Alleyn showed him the letter giving us permission to tour. He brushed it aside: 'If you

172

don't move on I'll arrest you for disturbing the peace. You can show your letter when you come up for trial.'

That could be weeks or even months away. Alleyn shrugged: 'We've lost our audience anyway, so we might as well leave.'

The sheriff went into the house and came out with the old woman. Trembling, she shrank back from the crowd's roar, the bleared eyes in her wrinkled face cast down. The sheriff shouted, 'She has been accused of witchcraft so who is prepared to bring a charge against her?'

'I will.' It was the father. The crowd parted to let him through. Shaking with grief and rage he sobbed, 'She has murdered my only son.' There were murmurs of sympathy and anger. The old woman whimpered. Ordering her hands to be bound, the sheriff turned to the father and said, 'You shall have justice, sir.'

As we dismantled the stage the woman was taken away in a cart. 'She'll hang for sure,' said Kempe. Adding savagely, 'And serve her right for stopping our play.'

'The sheriff stopped it,' pointed out Alleyn. I observed that although they both disliked the stage they would both appear on a stage called a scaffold when the sheriff officiated at her execution.

I reflected on people's belief in witchcraft as we left the village. If poor old Mother Naylor had all the power the villagers claimed, why was she living in poverty? And why did she allow herself to be arrested? Yet so many people believe in the power of witches. Including, I've heard, the Scottish king. He thinks they can go to sea in a sieve. I laughed at that after reading Reginald Scott's sceptical book. But the ugly scene I had just witnessed made me think of Mother Wingfield's mysterious death. Was there sorcery involved? How to account for it otherwise? The idyllic days after leaving Kingston had sent my mind back to Latin pastoral verse. Now as I trudged behind the wagon I was once more racking my brains to remember what, in my schooldays, I had read in a Latin author that would throw light on that strange death in a locked room.

We had good audiences at Rochester and Chatham, giving several plays at each. At Sittingbourne while Alleyn negotiated with a grasping council for the market hall I repaired to a quiet tavern. After a generous draught of their best beer I was ready to grapple with the play that I felt sure would make my name: The Tragical History of Priam, King of Troy. I laid the manuscript on the table with the inkhorn and pen beside it. Next I took out my penknife and sharpened the quill to a fine point. Then I dipped the pen in the ink, looked at the manuscript – and crossed out the last line.

When I had handed in my last script Hemmings had looked at it and said, pointedly, that there was scarcely a line blotted in Shakespeare's scripts. Condell had agreed. In fact they had waxed lyrical over it, like court ladies cooing over an apothecary's wrinkle-removing lotion. Should I have crossed that last line out? Wasn't it a good one?

"Hec: Your Hector, love, though armed, has arms for you."

Perhaps it was Priam in the title who should be crossed out and Hector substituted. What I'd written of the play was mostly about the latter. I was especially proud of the scene I was on between Hector and his wife, Andromanche. It was tender yet dignified. Just the kind of scene I could imagine between Elizabeth and myself if I were going to the war and she were still my sweetheart. Well she was; unfortunately I wasn't hers. I crossed out Priam and wrote Hector, Prince of Troy. I was desperate to write a successful tragedy because that is what brings a reputation. Look at Marlowe. Comedy, however, came more easily to me. Little did I know I was about to have a surfeit of real-life comedy.

174

A fine looking young woman accompanied by a much older man sat down at the next table. Her rich gown was cut very low showing ample white breasts. Sparkling rubies at her ears brought out the glossy blackness of her hair. A fair complexion might be the fashion but who cared with beauty like hers? Certainly not the men in the room who gazed at her with unconcealed longing. The man with her could not keep a smirk off his face at the sea of envy lapping around him.

'What will you drink, wife?' he asked, letting us know that he was the husband and therefore the bedfellow of this cynosure of lust-filled eyes. When the drawer brought their wine he carelessly tossed a gold piece onto the tray, said, 'Don't bother me with change,' and put an arm around his wife. She snuggled up against him but first her eyes from beneath her long dark lashes flickered around the room. They lingered on me. That's what every man is thinking about himself, I thought and returned to my play. After a few minutes I glanced up again. Had she just looked away from me? Loosening my collar I read over what I had just written.

"Oh Hector, husband, Trojan prince, you leave
Your Andromanche to bed her with the Greeks."

I sighed, drew a line through bed her and wrote battle. My manuscript was beginning to resemble the face of a veteran court lady who had run out of wrinkle-remover. Or a veteran court man who'd run out of it, come to that. The lovely lady opposite had no wrinkles. Her husband had plenty. But it would be difficult to say how many were the result of age and how many the result of his self-satisfied grin as he looked from the glittering rings on his fingers to the beautiful wife at his side.

Deciding that I could not work here, I bundled the paper, pen and inkhorn into my bag. I'd forgotten to put the cover on the inkhorn. Now the manuscript looked like the face of Aaron the Moor in Titus Andronicus.

As I walked back to our inn I reflected that it was just as well I'd had no chance of getting acquainted with the lady. Frizer, Blackbeard, Warthog, et al, were enough enemies to be going on with without adding one of Sittingbourne's wealthiest citizens. If the company were forced to leave town because I'd bedded his wife I would be as popular as a garlic-eater in a perfumery.

Back at the inn I got out Arden of Faversham to check we had all the props for it. Faversham was our next call so naturally we'd give them the play about the famous murder that had been committed there. Also I was looking forward to seeing Rosie and Peter. I hoped it would not entail a visit to the local prison.

Ned Alleyn returned bringing the news that he had agreed a price with the council for the market hall. The Mayor was too tight-fisted to pay for the usual Mayor's performance but a private citizen wanted to put on a play for his friends and was ready to fund it handsomely. Although, as Alleyn explained, it was more of a pageant than a play. The actors were to play famous men from history and each in turn was to try and seduce a beautiful young woman. Alexander was to offer all the lands he had conquered; Croesus fabulous wealth; Ovid was to woo her with his love poetry and Paris was to be ready to give up Helen and Anthony, Cleopatra, for her sake. The woman was to be played by the citizen's wife. At the end she would kneel in front of her husband, having rejected all the suitors, and say, "It is easy to be a Penelope when I have such a Ulysses as my lord and master."

My job was to write their speeches. For Alexander I could adapt a speech from my (alas unacted) tragedy on him. For Ovid I could translate from his Art of Love. Croesus? Lift something from Marlowe's wealthy Barabas. So I had just two speeches of seduction to write for Paris and Anthony. If the woman was who I suspected she was, that should not be too difficult.

It was a fine sunny day and I always think best when I'm walking so taking the bag with my writing gear I threw in Ovid's Art of Love and set out.

'Think of a role for me,' shouted Kempe. Sittingbourne's main street was not very long and soon instead of houses I was walking between hedges. The sun was warm on my back while my mind was hotter than a blacksmith's forge as I hammered out images of love. So absorbed was I that I only heard the carriage when it was almost upon me. I jumped into the hedge and cursed the driver. Reclining in the back of the carriage was the dark-haired beauty from the inn. Taken by surprise I croaked, 'Penelope.' She looked over the top of her fan at me while her maid giggled.

'Letting Bedlam madmen out to wander the country,' said the driver as they passed on round the bend. If I was mad it was through those burning eyes shooting their flames from behind her fan, enflaming my passions, firing my reason. I had the beginning of a speech there but what I needed was relief. Now.

Trying to calm myself I imagined that I was one of Penelope's suitors and had been able to bend Ulysses' bow. In my fevered mind it became Cupid's bow sending not an arrow into her heart but something else lower down. In short – then she was walking towards me, shimmering in the heat haze. I've gone mad, was my first thought. Smiling, she said in a pretty, lisping voice, 'I like to take a walk in the fine country air.' Leaning towards me in a conspiratorial manner she added, 'Also my maid and driver are in love so I'm leaving them alone together.' Laughing gaily she said, 'I'm playing Cupid.'

Here was my cue and I took it: 'You've played Cupid with me, madam, and my heart is still sore from your arrow.'

'Ah, poor man. Shall I rub it better?'

My 'Yes,' came out as a squeak. 'Yes,' I repeated in a deep voice. Now that she was circling her delicate white hand on my chest her plump breasts were right beneath my eyes. Wagging a finger at me she pouted, 'You're not the only one with a sore heart. I too have been wounded.'

'I'll rub it better,' I replied hoarsely and squeezed her left bubbie. When I pulled her to me she said, 'Not here, in that field.'

The gate was padlocked so we climbed over it. Pointing to an open gate at the far end she said, 'There's a little grove in there where we'll be safe. Keep close to the hedge so we won't be seen.' She had done this before. She said, 'He hits me so I don't see I'm doing wrong.'

In my view a husband who beats his wife deserves to be cuckolded. Usually it's her only means of revenge. Also it eased my, admittedly not very troublesome, conscience. It even gave me an idea for Kempe's role (a lover's brain races like a thoroughbred when he's about to perform as a stallion). Why a husband whose wife has been unfaithful is said to wear horns on his head I don't know; but many's the time I've seen a crowd outside the house of such a husband, banging pots and brandishing a set of antlers. And when he ventures out people make the sign of horns by putting their hands to their heads. Kempe could be Hercules and into his speech I would insert a joke about horns when he referred to his labour of capturing the Cretan Bull. Kempe was just the actor to suggest the innuendo without making it too obvious.

Penelope (as I thought of her now) stumbled and I caught her in my arms. We kissed fiercely. To hell with the grove. I popped her breasts out of her gown and she began pulling my breeches down. She fell to the ground and I fell on top of her, lips glued to a nipple, legs kicking off my breeches. Fondling her breasts with one hand with the other I hauled the gown up above her waist. She pulled me closer. Now I was kissing her lips hard and

178

moving my hand between her legs. She gurgled. Trying to push me away with one hand she pointed over my shoulder with the other. I looked round. Lumbering through the gate from the next field was the biggest bull I have ever seen, a huge black beast with long curving horns. Penelope wriggled from beneath me and, holding her gown above her knees, ran for the other gate. Keeping an eye on the bull I grabbed my breeches and tried to insert a wavering leg in them. The bull pawed the ground and lowered its head. I grabbed my shoes and, carrying my breeches, ran. Hooves pounded behind. Turning I flung my shoes at its head. They bounced off. It was gaining. When I caught up with Penelope she gasped, 'Don't leave me.'

I turned and held my breeches in front of me. The bull charged. At the last second I jumped aside. The breeches caught on the bull's horns and covered his eyes. He juddered to a halt and shook his head. I ran. Looking up I saw Penelope clamber over the gate while I tripped and fell flat on my face. Getting up I glanced back. The great beast was charging again my breeches streaming back from one of his horns. Reaching the gate I vaulted over as the bull crashed into it. Penelope was making off down the road as I lay gasping for breath and nursing a sore knee which I'd banged on the top bar.

A red-faced farmer came running up shouting, 'You poxy, whoring bastard exhausting that bull. It's going to stud tomorrow.'

'Going to stud,' I gasped, watching Penelope disappear round the bend. 'What about my breeches?' I demanded.

'Go in and get them,' he sneered. There was a rending sound. One leg of the breeches was hanging from the bull's horns while the other was on the ground being trampled by his hooves.

I limped back to Sittingbourne in my shirt, resolved to give up writing tragedies. Life just isn't like that. It's a bloody farce.

Twenty

We tramped out of Sittingbourne heading for Faversham. Everyone had enjoyed our stay except me. Takings had been high. What was termed my bull-baiting had quickly spread around town causing plenty of merriment. But they did not find out who the lady was. Now even the dullest in the company laboured to find a joke as we passed the Bull Inn. The sun shone, birds sang, bees buzzed and flowers perfumed the air. But I was homesick. I wanted the smoke of London, the songs of Gracious Street hawkers, the hum of Cheapside shoppers and the smells of Old Fish Street and Smithfield. Even the stink of Fleet Ditch – well, perhaps not that.

The morning after a heavy night's drinking I've often cursed the bells of London. But now I was longing for the bells of Shoreditch, Newgate, Ludgate, Southwark, Cheapside, as the bells of a village church floated across the fields. We were ascending a steep hill and it recalled for me the legend of Dick Whittington at Highgate hearing Bow Bells ringing, "Turn again Whittington, thrice Lord Mayor of London."

Breasting the hill we heard the blast of a hunting-horn accompanied by a baying pack of hounds. Well-tuned according to a countryman among us. He explained the pack would have five or six couples of bass mouths, about two couples of counter-tenors and a couple of roarers, the latter being heard mainly at opening or hitting of a scent. And the sound was pleasing to the ear. Though hardly to the poor hare we could see below us as he turned this way and that. Having been chased myself by everyone from bailiffs to bulls, with a few assassins in between, I had a fellow feeling for the poor little devil as he strove desperately to escape. Diving through a gap in the hedge, now running among a flock of sheep to make the hounds mistake their smell and now amongst rabbits scurrying into their burrows. When the hounds reached those spots they stopped and snuffled, noses to the earth. We could still see the hare on a rising standing on his hind legs listening. A loud baying gave warning that the hounds had his scent again. It was not difficult for me to imagine him feeling sick at heart as once again he began running. Now he was slower. The pack was gaining as he disappeared amongst a clump of bushes.

'They'll get him now,' said the countryman with satisfaction. The hunters felt the same, whooping and urging their horses on while those following on foot ran hard to be in at the kill. The other countryman in our company, Will Shakespeare, seems to sympathise with the one against the many, the hunted hare or the baited bear.

At the foot of the hill was a small village with a stream running through it. We stopped to water the horses and give them a rest. While the others lounged on the bank smoking pipes and playing cards, I strolled along the street. The houses were all one-storied, made of timber, their walls of dried mud with thatched roofs. Many were badly in need of repair, gaping holes in the roof and doors hanging off their hinges. At the end of the street was an ale house with a number of men seated on benches outside. I bought a pot of ale and joined them.

'We haven't got much money for players here,' said a grey-bearded old man, indicating the decaying houses. Even the red lion on the board above our heads looked mangy. A burly carter whose horse and cart stood nearby asked, 'Is Will Kempe with you?' I nodded. He grinned:

'I saw him at the Rose in Southwark playing Jack Cade. He made short work of lords.'

'Made them shorter by a head,' muttered a gap-toothed young man. 'A good Kentishman, Jack Cade. He reminded gentlemen that they got a joint in their necks like the rest of us.'

Grey-beard quavered:

When Adam delved and Eve span
Who was then the gentleman?'

'You tell 'em, gaffer,' responded Gap-tooth. Others nodded vigorously. One grumbled, 'They breaks our fences with hunting but don't repair them.'

'No, instead they fences off land that's been common time out of mind,' complained Gap-tooth to me. 'They can pay cheating lawyers to make it legal. There's many a poor man's got nowhere to graze his few geese and chickens.'

From the way Grey-beard was looking around I could see he was girding himself up for another recitation:

They hang the man and flog the woman
Who steal the goose from off the common;
But let the greater villain loose
That steals the common from the goose.'

'And we could put a name to the greater villain around here,' said Gap-tooth to nods of approval.

'Steady lads,' said the carter uneasily.

'Steady my arse. We're free-born Englishmen and we've got rights.'

'We've also got heads,' replied the carter looking nervously around. 'I travels to London regular where I sees what they sticks on London Bridge. It's where Jack Cade's head finished up.'

We turned round at the clip-clop of horses. Two riders approached along the street accompanied by a man on foot who was wearing the blue coat of a servant. A butcher nodded at them and said, 'Master Lovel is a gentleman by nature as well as name. If that boy of his grows up like his father he won't go far wrong.'

'I've got nothing against him or any man enjoying what's rightfully his,' said Gap-tooth firmly. 'I just want what's rightfully mine.'

When the riders came up they dismounted and handed the reins to the servant. The landlord came bustling out and Lovel ordered pots of ale for the three of them. Giving money to a man in patched clothes he said, 'I trampled some of your crops, Brown.'

The man touched his cap and mumbled out thanks. Gap-tooth said, 'It's no more than his right, Master Lovel. There'll be no compensation from – well, I'll just say a certain person since I know one gentleman don't like to hear abuse of another from what you're pleased to call your inferiors.'

Lovel banged his fist on the table making the tankards rattle. 'Brooke, by God. I'll name and abuse the rascal. The tricks he used to get an estate at Detling he's started using against me.'

'He's bought the estate on the far side of yours and now he wants yours to link it with his old estate,' suggested the butcher.

'That's what he wants,' said Lovel between clenched teeth; 'but he won't get it while there's breath in my body. Nearly three hundred years that land's been in my family. My father passed it on to me and I'll pass it on to this lad.'

'But he can't make you sell, Master Lovel,' said Grey-beard. 'So what can he do?'

'Do!' exploded a purple-faced Lovel. 'He'll do what he did at Detling. He's bought a cottage nearby and put in two rogues he calls tenants. They're no more tenants than the rats in my barns. I've already had fences torn down and crops trampled. This morning I found one of my cows with a broken leg. When I start bringing suits for trespass against those two rogues the suits will bring expenses which Brooke can spare but I can't. After he'd harried the owner at Detling like this for two or three years he pretended he had a title to the land. The long court action finally broke the man and he was forced to sell the estate to Brooke for half its value. But he won't do it to me. I'll accuse him to his face of putting those two rascals up to their tricks and if he denies it I'll call him a liar and strike him. He'll have to fight me after that.'

'A born gentleman like you can handle a sword better than an upstart like him, Master Lovel,' fawned the butcher. The prospect of a duel animated everyone.

'Well at least,' said Lovel, 'it will be in the hands of God instead of the mouths of lawyers.'

'And there too your honour will benefit because you haven't turned away your workers to rear sheep like that other,' said the butcher. 'He cheated me over sheep.'

Lovel nodded and said dryly, 'That's why he's got so much more money than I have. But I won't turn away men who worked for my father.'

Turning up his eyes the butcher said piously, 'The Lord will remember that in your hour of need, Master Lovel.'

'Can I help you fight Master Brooke, father?' asked the boy, who must have been all of ten years. Smiling Lovel said, 'No son, it must be one against one.'

'Then after you've killed him I'll help you fight the two rogues in the cottage.'

'Who are they, Master Lovel?' inquired the butcher. 'Where are they from?'

'Where are they from?' he snorted. 'Where do you think they're from, man? You go to Newcastle for coals and you go to London for rogues.'

All eyes turned to me. Lovel turned a deeper shade of puce and roared, 'Are you from London, sir? By God, he's brought you down to join them.' He stood up, towering over me: 'You've been spying on me.'

185

'I'm touring with a company of players,' I explained quickly.

'Accept my apologies, sir.' He held out his hand. 'And what's more, accept my hospitality. My father liked a play and so do I. I may not have much money but I can fill your bellies, give you beds for the night and send you off in the morning with a hearty breakfast. And by God you won't go away empty handed either. Jack,' he called to the servant. 'Run up to the house like a good fellow and tell your mistress to prepare plenty of food and beds. And Jack,' he shouted after him, 'don't forget to tell her that I'm sorry it's such short notice.'

His wife seemed to be the only one he had qualms about. No doubt he was a good sort, one of the traditional country landowners that London writers are always lamenting the demise of. But in the flesh I think they would find him a little overpowering. He had organised all this without asking any of the company whether they wanted to stay the night. Now he was ordering me another pot of ale without asking me if I wanted it or not. As it happened I did want it. But I might not have. I was pretty sure the company would welcome a break in the journey and beds for the night. But they might not. Yes, I'm still glad to be a city man. There is more independence. A man is free. Free to starve, it's true, but still free.

'Will Kempe is in the company,' said the carter wistfully. 'I saw him in...'

'Well break your journey, man, and see him again,' bellowed Lovel. 'And the rest of you. I want to see everyone at the Hall.'

Excited chatter about the play (and they knew there'd be plenty of ale) ceased abruptly as a body of horsemen clattered down the street. They were the rest of the huntsmen. At their head on a fine coal-black horse was a rider who looked the epitome of arrogance.

'His father was a damned botching tailor,' said Lovel, not bothering to keep his voice down. 'He made his money by cheating his customers. His son's inherited more than just his money.'

Brooke, an angry flush spreading across his face, reined up his horse. Lovel stood up and the hands of both men flew to their sword hilts. One of the huntsmen in the black coat of a parson said, 'Calm yourselves, gentlemen.'

Two horsemen moved forward on either side of Brooke. The nearest was Warthog. I might have guessed he would be one of the rogues from London. Craning my neck I saw that the other one was Blackbeard. Pointing, I shouted, 'That man is wanted for murder, there's a reward on his head.' Putting spurs to his horse Blackbeard galloped away.

'Hiring murderers, Brooke?' shouted Lovel jumping on his horse. 'Take my son's horse,' he called to me. Scrambling on, I was about to find out if it was true that you never forget how to ride a horse. As we galloped in pursuit Warthog shouted, 'I'm a law officer so I'll take him into custody.'

Then take a bribe to free him, I thought. Unless the reward was greater. The huntsmen had joined us, including a grim-faced Brooke. If Brooke got to him first Blackbeard might be killed "resisting arrest" to silence him. I wanted him alive. With his neck in danger of the noose he might be ready to talk about Mistress Wingfield's murder.

Although I had not ridden since I was a child staying at my uncle's estate I seemed to be doing quite well. It was probably due to a well-trained horse. Our chase was accompanied by whoops and yells from the hunters. They found hunting a man more exciting than a hare. And it must be admitted that after all the times I had been chased there was a pleasure in being one of the hunters. Also I had forgotten the sheer joy of racing along on a good horse.

Blackbeard rode with the recklessness of desperation. He splashed through streams and drove his horse at high hedges. After one such jump there were yells from the hunters when on landing he was almost thrown out of the saddle, just managing to cling to the horse's neck. Several riders prudently took the long way round. The chase went on for miles but we stuck to him. My shirt was soaked with sweat and the bones had been almost jolted out of my body; but I was determined to be there at the end.

Now he was forcing his tiring horse up a hill, digging his spurs in harder as the long slope steepened. He disappeared over the summit. Nearing it, we heard a roaring and shouting as if a pitched battle was being fought on the other side. Breasting the ridge we saw below us a seething mass of men, several hundred on each side, punching and kicking one another. Having taken part in one at my uncle's, I recognised it; a football match. The pitch would be the ground between the two villages, that on our right, close, that on the left about two miles off. Whoever forced the ball into the opposite village would win. Blackbeard had swerved to the left to ride round the back of the crowd but the huntsmen had anticipated such a move and were riding down hard to intercept him. Reining up his horse he turned it and rode to the right. But that also had been cut off. He jumped to the ground and forced himself in amongst the players. Lovel signalled to the riders on either side to continue around the backs of the crowd in case Blackbeard forced his way through. Then Lovel, Warthog and myself dismounted and plunged into the struggling mass.

We were buffeted, kicked and elbowed but just ahead of me I could see Blackbeard blocked by a huge snarling fellow who refused to let him pass. Blackbeard's head darted forward and when it came away the fellow was missing an ear. It was spat in his face and our quarry was past. We were still jammed in. Suddenly the ball appeared from the pack and was booted away to the side Blackbeard was making for. The surge after it carried us along. Men were more spread out now and we had room to run. Lovel, just ahead of me, was gaining on the fugitive when two players mistook him for an opponent. Catching Lovel between them one dashed him under the heart with an elbow while the other hit him under the ribs with his fist. Then the first kneed him in the groin and pitched him on his face. When they turned on Warthog he cracked their heads together leaving them staggering.

This gave me the chance to get ahead. We were clear of the players now and Blackbeard was running hard towards a wood. Just as we reached the first trees I was tripped and sent sprawling. A few minutes later I heard Warthog's triumphant cry, 'He's mine.' As I struggled to my feet, winded, Lovel and the horsemen arrived. Going further into the wood we found Warthog sitting on a struggling Blackbeard and binding his hands. Grinning broadly he said, 'I caught him so I'm claiming the reward.'

He would get it. The gentry would be too proud to claim it and what I wanted was information not blood-money. The gentry were looking down at the pair with utter disdain. Lovel nodded at them contemptuously and turned to Brooke saying, 'A fine pair of rogues for a gentleman to hire. The same dirty money that bought your coat of arms bought them.'

Brooke drew his sword and dagger with Lovel following suit. There was no parson to urge peace since he had been left far behind. One man made a half-hearted attempt to mediate but he was brushed aside. It was clear that this animosity had been building for some time and would be resolved only by bloodshed.

The clearing made a natural arena and the antagonists slowly circled each other. Both were the same stocky build but Lovel was lighter on his feet. This he showed at once by feinting a thrust with his rapier then darting in with his dagger and ripping up the sleeve of Brooke's doublet. The rich velvet hung flapping like the clothes on a scarecrow. The man who had tried to mediate stepped forward and said, 'If you gentlemen refuse to compromise then put yourselves in proper order.'

While the duellists eyed each other narrowly, friends removed their doublets. Once again they circled. Suddenly Brooke launched an attack, handling his rapier with skill, forcing Lovel to parry hurriedly and give ground. There were some murmurs of surprise from the onlookers. One man said dryly, 'He's had the best fencing lessons money can buy.'

But now Lovel's skill began to show. It was easy to see that he had been bred up on fencing from childhood. His rapier was like an extension of his arm. The end came suddenly. Lovel, side-stepping a savage upward swing of Brooke's dagger, caught his shirt in a bramble bush. Briars tore his shirt and skin as he ripped himself away just in time to avoid a rapier thrust. Falling to the ground Lovel rolled aside, again just avoiding Brooke's downward driving rapier, which thrust into the earth. Lovel leapt to his feet, dashing Brooke's dagger from his swinging left hand and hitting him on the jaw with the hilt of his sword, knocking him back into the brambles. Brooke frantically tore himself free lacerating his skin so that his face was a mask of blood. He was on his knees gasping while Lovel stood over him with upraised sword. There were shouts of, 'Spare him.'

'Ask for your life,' demanded Lovel. There were shouts of, 'Ask.' 'There's no disgrace, you've fought well.'

'I ask you to spare my life,' said Brooke sullenly.

190

'Swear to stop your damned practices against me.'

'That would be to admit my guilt,' hissed Brooke, 'and that I will never do.'

'Come Master Lovel,' said the mediator. 'He has asked for his life, you are honour bound to spare him.'

Lovel sheathed his sword, pulled Brooke's from the ground and broke it across his knee. We walked away, Brooke dabbing at his torn face, Warthog leading Blackbeard by a rope.

Twenty-One

Early next morning we said our farewells and resumed our journey. They loaded us with food for ourselves and messages from the Lovels and their servants for friends in Faversham. It was a bright day and everyone was in high spirits with plenty to talk about. Lovel, as a J P, had provided Warthog with an escort to make sure his prisoner arrived in London. Blackbeard had refused me any information, saying his friends in high places would not let him hang. Especially – here he looked meaningfully at me – as he had unfinished business to perform.

There was, as usual after staying at a big house, lots of boasting about who had slept with the maids. Most of it on a par with seafarers' tales of mermaids. But I did not doubt Kempe's boast was true. His fame, his self-assurance; and his ability to make women laugh, to jolly them into his bed. Although the girl he'd wanted had turned him down, I knew he had succeeded with his second choice of whom he boasted as we travelled: 'She won't forget her night with Will Kempe in a hurry. I seeded her, for sure. In nine months a little Kempe will come bouncing out of her belly like I do onto the stage.'

'Are you going to pay for its upbringing, Will?' asked Alleyn dryly.

'I've done my bit. It's up to her to provide a father from the footmen or kitchen staff.' Laughing maliciously he added, 'A Warwickshire man told me that's how our Will Shagspeare was caught in his country town. By a farmer's daughter eight years his senior. So our Will was marched to the altar with a pitchfork up his arse.'

Kempe did not like writers. He tried to rile me with remarks about playmakers who write double-Dutch that he has to translate into plain English. But he could not remove my self-satisfied smile. Although I said nothing he must have come to suspect the reason for my smugness because he began to grow surly. The pretty young maid who had rejected him had shared my bed.

So as we travelled past fields of waving corn and fruit-laden orchards towards Faversham, I was feeling in fine fettle. There is nothing like spending the night with a woman to make a man feel he can take on the world. Especially if she is the prettiest lass in the house. Yes, I was a fine fellow.

From behind we heard the drumming of hooves. They were closing on us fast. A cloud of dust enveloped the rider as he appeared around the bend galloping towards us. Reaching our column he reined in his horse. It was Christopher Marlowe. We gaped up at him expecting from his haste dreadful or at least urgent news. He threw back his head and laughed: 'You look like fish about to snap at the bait.' Dismounting he threw the reins to a young actor and said, 'Don't you know the sheer exhilaration of riding a mettlesome horse flat out just for the hell of it? There's the bright sun, the open road, the pleasure of being alive.'

Coming over to me he asked, 'Don't you feel the joy of life pulsing through your veins, Tom?' Putting an arm around my shoulder he added, 'Better than still, cold death, surely.'

I froze as I've noticed most men do when Marlowe puts an arm around them. But he is not someone you want to offend by throwing it off. He said sardonically, 'Don't worry, Tom, your virtue is safe. I'm going to visit my parents at Canterbury but first I shall meet a good friend

193

in Faversham. You will be breaking your journey there to perform a play and I...' he smiled – 'will also be performing there. Away from the prying eyes of neighbours and relations in Canterbury. You're doing too much prying, Tom. I heard about the questions you were asking in Kingston. And about your near fatal accident there. If you go on, so will the accidents. And sooner or later the theatre will lose a promising writer.' He stopped and looked me straight in the face saying, 'I'm advising you to forget about the Milk Street murder. If you want to write a play about murder, go back further in history or one day someone may be writing a play about your murder.'

I stared at him: 'Whose side are you on now?'

He laughed harshly: 'Shifting sands, Thomas. A hundred years ago it was said that men went to bed Lancaster and woke up York. Nowadays we go to bed Puritan and get up Papist.'

Observing him closely I said, 'That might depend on who we went to bed with. The Earl of Southampton is Papist, isn't he?'

Marlowe flushed and turned away, saying over his shoulder, 'But the Earl of Essex is not.' Mounting his horse he said, 'These are deep waters, my friend. I can swim in them but you'll drown. Give up politics or they'll be fishing your body out of the Thames.' Calling to Alleyn that he would tell the landlord of the Flower-de-Luce to prepare for our coming, Marlowe rode on.

This was the second warning I'd received about being pulled dead out of the Thames. And at Kingston I had almost drowned; and that just after being almost blown to pieces; and that just after being almost burned alive. Marlowe was right, all this was too much for me. My job was to create heroes for actors to play, not to be a hero myself. Especially a dead one. The time, I decided, had come to get out of politics and murder.

When we saw the smoke from Faversham's chimneys rising above the trees into the clear morning air, our spirits rose with it. 'Just in time for dinner,' was the general cry and we pushed on with fresh energy. With Faversham in sight we stopped and made our preparations. We had been so tired on reaching Kingston that we had straggled into town like a defeated army. No more such entries.

Our preparations complete, we marched into Faversham resplendent in our colourful stage clothes with flags flying, drums beating, trumpets blaring. Men, women and children ran from houses and shops to line either side of the street while others leaned from windows waving and shouting. Ned Alleyn at our head walked hat in hand bowing to either side while Kempe danced a jig around the wagons and between the actors. Passing a church we saw on the steps several black-clad saints rolling their eyes heavenwards and groaning at the vanity of strutting players and merrymaking people. Kempe jumped onto a wagon, donned a black steeple hat and reproved the onlookers as vain worldlings warning them not to repair to the Flower-de-Luce to watch the notorious murder play Arden of Faversham at two o clock on the morrow. Meanwhile Heminges and Condell were handing out playbills. A cheering crowd followed us to the inn, leaving the Puritans looking as miserable as a hangman and his assistants who have just lost their fee because the condemned have been reprieved.

'A triumphant entry,' said Alleyn as we supped the Flower-de-Luce's best beer while awaiting our dinner. One of the young actors came in from the kitchen, along with the smell of roast pork, licked his lips and said, 'One of the pigs has wept out an eye so it will soon be on our plates.'

And so it was. We tucked in with appetites sharpened by our walk in the fresh country air, keeping the waiters bustling back and forth. Replete we sat back and relaxed over a glass of wine. All the time gentlemen were coming in to talk with the players. Especially Alleyn and Kempe, whose fame had spread far beyond London. Footloose actors brought a sense of freedom to these settled communities; it was like peasants ploughing on the banks of the Thames pausing to watch a ship, all sails spread, cutting through the water towards the open sea.

Marlowe came in with a delicate-featured, fair-haired young man.

'His latest,' sniggered Kempe, looking the youth up and down. 'A fan would become him better than a sword.'

'Careful, Will,' warned Alleyn. 'You're too valuable to us to lose.'

'What! To that?'

'Remember another friend of Marlowe's a couple of years ago? The poet Tom Watson? When that innkeeper's son set on Marlowe in the street Watson stabbed him to death. This latest one may have some steel in that velvet scabbard.'

Marlowe, having bought wine for his friend, came to tell Alleyn about a strong part he had for him in his latest play. Poet and player withdrew into an alcove to discuss it.

Above the hum of conversation a vaguely familiar voice cried, 'God send I have no need of you,' as he clapped his sword on a table near me. I recognised him as the man Elizabeth had banned from the Cross Keys. He and his companion already had plenty of drink aboard as they bawled to the drawers to bring them wine:

'Best Toledo,' he said, tapping the sword lying on the table.

'So is mine,' responded his companion, half drawing it from the scabbard.

'This a Toledo? A Fleming, by God. You can buy them for a Guilder apiece. A poor army issue rapier.'

'But the man who sold it to me swore it was…'

'You should have consulted me, sir. I served under the Earl of Essex in France and when he wanted to buy a new sword he would say, "Send for Alexander Hay. Master Hay," he would say to me, "Master Hay, no man can use a rapier better than you and no man can select one better." I just bowed 'cos I wouldn't boast. A big Dutchman in our army was boasting about his swordsmanship. I walked over to him took his helmet off and spat in it. He did nothing. Knew my reputation.'

His companion pointed to Marlowe's friend: 'See that milksop. I kicked mud in his face once and he just walked away. I'll wager you could spit in his hat and he'd be too frightened to take offence.'

Hay got up, walked over to the youth, took off his hat, spat in it then handed it back. He returned to his seat with a broad grin on his slab-like face. His companion pointed at a man who had just come in and said, 'My mistake, that's the man I kicked mud at,' while the youth walked over to Marlowe and conferred with him. Marlowe came across and leaned on the table, his face inches from Hay's and said, 'I would have stuck my knife straight in you but my friend, Monsieur Tournay, is French and wishes to observe the niceties before sticking his dagger in your guts. Or his rapier. Or, as in his last duel, both. The most convenient place will be the field behind the inn, the most convenient time, now.'

Hay's face had turned white and he stuttered, 'W – Will your friend accept an apology, sir?'

Marlowe went back to his friend then returned to say, 'He will accept both an apology and a new hat. Come sir, I will accompany you to the hatter's'

They returned with a broad-brimmed hat sporting a large bunch of feathers. Marlowe had made him buy the most expensive hat in the shop. Hay took it to where

Monsieur Tournay was sitting and gave it to him while mumbling an apology.

'Take your hat off when apologising to a gentleman, sir,' snapped Marlowe snatching it from his head. Tournay examined the hat carefully, put it on then finally said, 'Qui.' Marlowe took his friend's hat and crammed it on Hay's head pulling it down over his ears. He pointed to the door and said, 'Now, sir, bundle yourself out of here double-quick.'

I was almost feeling sorry for poor Alexander Hay; but as he passed my table on his way out he said to his companion, 'By God, sir, but that fellow is fortunate. 'Twas only yesterday that I was bound over to keep the peace after beating a Surrey man who had insulted Kent.'

The story was soon all over Faversham and we had our play for the Mayor that evening. He had asked us to perform a short comedy at a banquet he was giving. We put on a translation of Plautus' Miles Gloriosus (The Boastful Soldier). As people looked at Monsieur Tournay with a new respect   fell to wondering if Marlowe had put on a short play with the same denouement as Miles Gloriosus. If he had it had saved his friend from the hazards of a duel. This led me on to wonder if I had been frightened off the Milk Street murder by a performance. But the deaths of Stour and Cheadle had been real.

Before getting down to rehearsing that evening's play I went out to see if I could find Peter and Rosie. Having heard where the company were staying they were coming along the street to see me. Peter was casting glances over his shoulder so I guessed he was in trouble. Sure enough five men emerged from a side street, caught sight of him and gave chase. Peter took to his heels and shot past me crying, 'See you later, Tom.'

Waddling a little way behind the men and urging them on was a stout man wielding the staff of a constable. Rosie bustled up to me and said, 'My gentleman will get him off, but follow them Tom to see they don't beat him amongst them.'

So I joined in another kind of manhunt. Chasing the watch chasing the thief. After doubling down streets and alleys and dodging round corners I saw, at the end of a long lane, the river glinting in the sun. On its bank a band of gypsy women were washing clothes while their children splashed in the water. In turning the corner Peter slipped and fell. Jumping to his feet he disappeared from sight. When I reached the corner I saw Peter helping a little girl out of the river. They stood on the bank water dripping from their clothes surrounded by the watch. The gypsy women gathered round and eventually the Constable joined us puffing and panting.

'I could have got clear away,' Peter was explaining, 'but I could not let this little child drown.'

The child was a girl of about ten with a snub nose and a determined expression on her freckled face. As if on cue she intoned, 'He saved my life, he did.'

'I wants that told to the Justice,' asserted Peter.

'That's what they calls mitigating,' said a watchman, nodding wisely.

'Ho, I got a lawyer 'mongst my men, have I?' asked the Constable. 'Well I don't believe a word of it.'

'He saved my life,' repeated the girl after a nudge from Peter. The Constable pointed to her clenched right hand and demanded, 'What you got there?'

'Nothing,' she said defiantly. He forced her fingers apart and took out a penny. 'He gave you that to say he saved your life, didn't he?'

Several men and women from the town had gathered now and a woman shouted, 'Not as big a bribe as you gets, you old rascal,' to loud cackles. Ignoring them the Constable said solemnly, 'If you tells me lies, girl, you'll go to Hell.'

199

'It's mine,' said the girl stubbornly, 'and I wants it back.'

'You damned rogue,' shouted a man; 'taking pennies from a child.'

There were cries of, 'Give the little girl her money or we'll throw you in the river.' Handing back the penny he said, 'Anyway, he won't be mitigated just for saving a gypsy's brat. Take him, men.' As Peter limped forward the Constable said scornfully 'Could have got clear away, could you?'

While Peter was being taken to the lock-up Rosie managed to whisper to him that he need not worry, her gentleman friend would take care of him tomorrow. I got back to the inn with time to spare for rehearsal and that evening the play went well. Kempe as the swaggering, boastful soldier excelled himself. We got our fee from the Mayor and a handsome collection from the guests.

I was up early next morning to get out the properties for the afternoon's play. We did not bother with a rehearsal. Arden was and is a popular play always in demand so the actors could have played it in their sleep. And the Mayor had been so generous with his wine that many of them almost did. So, soon after breakfast, I set off for the Toll Booth where the court was held.

When I entered, the room was crowded with townsfolk, among them some gypsy women with the little girl. A few minutes later the Justice of the Peace, a thin, sharp-eyed man, wearing a red velvet doublet and fur trimmed cloak, entered the room. He was followed by the Mayor, two aldermen and the Constable. They paced in a dignified manner to the end of the room where a table and five carved wooden chairs were placed upon a raised platform.

The first offender to appear was a householder who had failed to clear away a heap of dung outside his house. He was fined sixpence. Then Peter was brought in still

200

limping. The Constable told the Justice that he had stolen a piece of beef from a butcher's stall.

'The butcher threw it away 'cos it was rotten,' protested Peter; 'and I picked it up for my dog.'

'I did not,' declared the butcher standing up.

'Him throw meat away,' cackled a woman. 'The maggots carried it off more likely.'

'Silence,' shouted the Justice, banging down his gavel. 'What do you do for a living?' he asked Peter.

'I can't work because of my bad leg, your worship.'

'He got that running from us,' said the Constable indignantly. Unperturbed Peter added, 'And I've got a sore neck.'

'Got,' replied the Justice grimly, 'in the pillory, no doubt. Well I am going to give you a sore back to go with it. You will be whipped at the cart's tail from here to the end of the High Street and back.'

I looked around for Rosie and saw her leaving the court with a richly-clad man of middling years. Meanwhile Peter was putting forward a plea of mitigation for saving the gypsy child's life.

'Irrelevant,' barked the Justice to the delight of the Constable who crowed, 'You can't deceive his worship no more than you could me. He bribed the child to lie, your worship.'

'I will not tolerate bribery,' said the Justice sternly. 'In any quarter,' he added staring hard at the Constable who flushed scarlet. Peter was taken outside where the cart was waiting, the Beadle standing beside it holding his whip. Rosie was with him although her gentleman friend had left. The Beadle removed Peter's shirt then tied his wrists to the back of the cart. Rosie came over to me and from her breath she'd had more wine for breakfast than food. After hiccupping she giggled then whispered in my ear, 'I just hope Peter's not tickled to death,' and pointed to the

Beadle's left hand which was clenched. 'Your actors could learn something from this, Tom.'

The driver shook the reins and the horse ambled forward with the cart creaking over the cobbles. Peter plodded behind followed by the Beadle who made a great show of cracking his whip in the air. Bringing up the rear was the Constable, chest puffed out, flourishing his staff of office.

'Begin the punishment, Beadle,' he ordered. The whip whistled through the air but seemed to slow just before falling on Peter's back. I could see no mark on the skin as the Beadle drew the lash through his left hand before raising and swinging it down once more onto the back. Again it seemed to fall lightly but this time the skin was marked with a thin red line. Stallkeepers and customers stopped to watch our progress through the market as the Beadle methodically drew the whip through his hand then lightly lashed the back. Several onlookers were smiling and I had just guessed what was happening when Rosie whispered in my ear, 'Red ochre. My gentleman has paid him well.'

We were in the High Street now proceeding at a stately pace. Peter it seems was popular in his home town. Perhaps because London had been the scene of his activities for so long. At any rate there were more smiling than angry faces as they became alive to the imposture. One man chuckled, 'They should both be on the stage.'

Finally the Constable, who seemed to be somewhat slow-witted, began to sense that something was wrong and ordered the Beadle to lay it on harder. The light whipping continued. Incensed at being disobeyed he struck the Beadle's back with his staff. A woman sweeping dirt in front of a shop waved her broom at him and shouted, 'You great hulking bully.'

Ignoring her he hit the Beadle again and again as the man stubbornly refused to whip harder. Rosie grabbed the broom, ran up behind the Constable and hit him on the back. He swung round with his staff but she skipped away to the cheers of the crowd. Turning again he belaboured the Beadle's back and shoulders while Rosie darted back and forth hitting him with the broom. And so they proceeded up then back down the High Street; and the one who suffered least was Peter the thief.

I walked back to the Flower-de-Luce to prepare for the play that afternoon, thinking of the line, "This stage-play world." That little gypsy girl had been paid a fee to act and she had played her part well. Then she had stood up to the Constable. In contrast I had allowed myself to be intimidated by Marlowe into giving up my enquiry. I had been closer to the braggart Hay than the gallant gypsy girl. I resolved to go on with the investigation into Mother Wingfield's murder when I returned to London. That was to be sooner than I expected and I was to witness more treachery through play-acting.

Twenty-Two

More than once I have heard stories of people in the audience watching a play about murder being moved to confess to a murder. I have never seen it and those telling me have always heard it from someone else. It did not happen during the performance of Arden. As the audience gathered in front of the stage we had erected in the yard of the Flower-de-Luce some of us looked down on them from a gallery, picking out likely murderers. Kempe said, 'If a woman did shout out that she had murdered her husband years ago we could forget about playbills for Canterbury. Her confession would give us a sell-out.'

Quick as lightening I said, 'She'd sell-out herself and sell-out us.'

'I do the jokes in this company,' growled Kempe.

'Careful, Tom,' laughed Alleyn, 'or we'll have another murder play; Dekker of Faversham.'

'And they wouldn't hang me,' said Kempe. 'I've made her majesty laugh, so she'd give me a reprieve.'

And so she might, I thought; players are more highly valued than playmakers, the gaudy, gabbling parrot more than the wise old owl. The relationship between writers and actors is like the marriage in The Taming of the Shrew with Kempe as an especially exasperating shrew. Little did I realise that I was soon to be involved in a real-life drama similar to Kempe's vainglorious fantasy.

The play went well before a large audience. With reason. Even fifty years on, the murder was well remembered in the area. Some older people told us that as

204

children they had seen the executions that followed. And to give the play its due, it has convincing characterisation with the two villains, Black Will and Shakebag, reminding me of Blackbeard and Warthog.

After loud and prolonged applause with repeated calls for Kempe and Alleyn to take fresh bows we all trooped into the inn. The landlord had prepared a good supper for us and we tucked into it with gusto. Applause is better than fresh air for giving actors an appetite. And the bond between player and playmaker is renewed by applause like a marriage after a night of twanging bedsprings.

At the end of the week we were packing up to begin our journey next day to Canterbury when a self-important looking man presented me with an official document. It was a sub-poena to appear as a witness in the trial of Blackbeard for the murder of Tribulation Cheadle. Someone had moved fast. Perhaps because they wanted him out of the way. It meant the end of my tour. It was awkward for the company too, since someone now had to take on my work in addition to their own. The court official said we would set out in the morning for Rochester when the tide would be right to take a ship to London. This gave me a chance to call on Peter and Rosie for a farewell drink. In the alehouse Peter was greeted with cries of, 'How's the back?.'

'I expect your back's sorer, Rosie,' sneered a man.

'There's a pile of horse shit in here, landlord,' she shouted. He tossed her a broom from behind the counter. Catching it she swung it at the man's head. He took it on the arm then ran through the door to the jeers of the room.

'If you were fighting for the Dutch, Rosie,' I said, 'you'd sweep the Spaniards out of the Low Countries single-handed.'

'I may have to go and serve the soldiers out there,' she said gloomily as we sat at a table. 'My gentleman's just told me he has to give me up because his wife has found

205

out. That means that poxy constable will be able to have me whipped through the town. I think I'll take my chances back in London.'

When I told them that I had to end my tour and return to London for the trial Peter grinned and said, 'I think I'd better end my tour of Kent. I've performed in markets and taverns in Canterbury, Maidstone, Sittingbourne, Ashford. Wherever there's an audience listening to a ballad or...' he winked – 'watching a play. Faversham was my base so I laid off it 'til yesterday.'

'But a piece of beef, Peter,' I said.

'Rosie said she fancied it for dinner.'

'But I didn't mean for you to steal it, you bloody fool,' she snapped.

'Anyway,' said Peter, 'if they catch me again it's not my back will suffer but my neck. They'll truss me up for sure. So I'll come back to London with you two. If I'm going to swing I'd rather swing there so as not to disgrace my family.'

'You mean being whipped through your home town is not a disgrace to them, Peter,' said Rosie dryly. Taking her face between his hands he chuckled, 'But I wasn't, properly speaking, whipped, thanks to my little gentleman-charmer. But you've lost your gentleman which means we've both lost our protector. So it's back to London.'

A carter bound for Rochester was staying at the Flower-de-Luce so we agreed a price to ride on his cart and early next morning off we set. The court official had a hired horse so he rode alongside. Despite the hardships of touring it was a wrench parting from the company. I promised, after the trial was over, that if I could get the money I would re-join them at Ashford or Maidstone. It always came back to money. Henslowe might lend it to me. But he had nothing coming from his playhouse. And with the plague increasing in London he had less

206

customers for his other businesses. I was determined to make another attempt to win back Elizabeth. And I wanted to see Nicholas Winton to find out if he had any fresh information on Mother Wingfield's death. Seeing Arden of Faversham performed again had fired me up to go on with my play. It could be called A London Tragedy (although Henslowe would demand something sensational like A Horrid Murder in Milk Street). Whatever it was called it would, after all, gain me more of a reputation than comedy; and the confidence to write even better plays. I was right in the middle of a private audience with her majesty who was congratulating me on raising playmaking to a higher level when Rosie asked, 'What are you day-dreaming about, Tom?'

'Oh, nothing,' I replied. 'Unlike Peter, who's having a real dream and a pleasant one at that.'

We were trundling along Watling Street now but the shaking of the cart failed to dislodge the broad smile from Peter's face as he lay against a woolpack. The driver turned his head and looked, a big grin splitting his face. This carter had endeared himself to us all the previous evening. We were drinking heavily and Kempe had said loudly, 'We're imbibing copiously to celebrate Tom's leaving,' slurring his words but managing to pronounce "celebrate" clearly. Just then the carter had entered and said in awed tones, "The Earl of Brayfield was at the play and wants to reward Will Kempe for his performance. He said when Kempe was on he was all ears." Looking past the half open door he proclaimed, "And here is my Lord." Pushing everyone away Kempe had stationed himself directly opposite the door. As it was pushed open he bowed low then looked up to see an ass standing in the doorway staring at him. How we laughed. Kempe spent the rest of the evening explaining to anyone who would listen that while the jokes he played on others were funny, this one played on him was not.

Peter was still sleeping, the smile on his face even broader. Meanwhile the carter had looped his horsewhip into a noose which he gently placed around Peter's neck. That removed Peter's smile and set his eyes, nose and lips twitching. Then the carter carefully took off the whip. Peter opened his eyes and started up. When we asked what he had been dreaming about he said, 'I was in bed with a beautiful lady. She said I was the best lover she'd ever had. When we'd finished she told me to take everything in the house I wanted. I loaded pictures, curtains, tapestries, chests of gold and jewels onto a cart and drove away. Then the cart was the hangman's cart jolting through Holborn. Then I was at Tyburn with the noose around my neck. That's when I woke up, thank God.'

The court official riding alongside said to me, 'Give your testimony without fear or favour and you'll help put a noose around a villain's neck.'

It was not something I looked forward to doing but I was sure Blackbeard deserved hanging far more than Peter. We reached Rochester without incident. Although passing through Sittingbourne Peter suddenly felt tired again and lay in the bottom of the wagon covered with a cloak.

When our ship, a small coastal trader, had taken on its cargo, just in time to catch the tide, we set sail. The tide took us smoothly down the Medway but emerging from the shelter of the Isle of Sheppey we caught a stiff east wind. It was a great relief to our stomachs to round the headland and get into the Thames.

Passing Tilbury revived memories of eighty-eight. It seemed longer ago than four years. We wanted the Spaniards to land, we told ourselves, so that we could drive them back into the sea. When the news came that fireships had scattered the Armada and strong winds driven it north we cheered lustily. Mixed in with the patriotic cheers were, I think, a few of relief. Spanish soldiers are reputed to be the best in Europe. I had since toyed with the idea of going to the Netherlands as a volunteer to fight the Spanish in order to experience war. It would be interesting to find out how I stood up under fire. Later I did find out, without having volunteered.

We disembarked at Billingsgate, the old familiar roar of water under London Bridge in our ears and the smell of the fishmarket in our nostrils. It was back to Coldharbour Tenements for a room. As we parted the court official muttered, 'A den of thieves.'

From Coldharbour I walked to the Cross Keys and looked through the window for Elizabeth. She did not appear to be there. I did not go in and ask for her since I did not want her told in advance. It would give her a chance to fortify her position. I wanted to make a surprise attack. Tilbury must have sparked this military imagery like a match firing a musket.

The trial had been postponed for a couple of days so I called to see my mother, then on to find out if Henslowe had anything for me. He had two offers. Holding horses outside one of his brothels or doing painting and repairs to the Rose. The latter paid less because there were no tips but that is the one I took. It would be sinking very low holding a four-legged stallion outside while a two-legged stallion performed inside.

'Don't make too much noise hammering,' warned Henslowe, 'or I'll have the joiners after me.'

I made some money by writing a ballad on Blackbeard's trial, anticipating the outcome to get in ahead of other writers. There would be others on his execution. We were like vultures hovering over a dying animal. However, if Blackbeard was an animal then it was one any vulture would have broken its beak on; a dragon or another minotaur. At his trial accusations rebounded from his hide of arrogance and scales of contempt. He pleaded not guilty with an air of unconcern about whether he was believed or not. And that was his demeanour throughout his trial. He glared at witnesses (particularly me) as if he could kill with looks like another basilisk. But for the most part he showed a deep contempt for the proceedings. He was as sure of his reprieve as the court was of his guilt. For it needed no Theseus to grope his way through a labyrinth to find out this minotaur.

The jury were out only a little while before returning with a verdict of guilty. The inevitable sentence of being hanged by the neck until dead was passed with the judge stipulating that it be carried out where Cheadle's body had been found. He even suggested that it would be appropriate to hang Blackbeard on the same tree on which the Constable's body had been hung. But the joiners protested that it would do one of them out of a job and set a precedent. So a temporary gallows was erected alongside the tree.

I tried to borrow money from Henslowe to bribe my way into the Clink to question Blackbeard. To no avail. So on the day of the execution I stationed myself outside the prison. A large crowd had gathered by the time Blackbeard was led out. On his head was the usual nightcap giving that ferocious face a slightly comical look. His irons would have been struck off inside and now just his hands were tied in front of him.

'So as he can raise his hands in prayer at the gallows,' a bystander solemnly informed us. A Barbary ape was more likely to raise its hands in prayer than Blackbeard. From between the bars of a prison window a woman screeched, 'You didn't pay me for last night, you poxy bastard.'

'If I'm poxed,' bawled Blackbeard, 'you gave it to me, you leperous whore.'

'I've put a curse on the man carrying your reprieve to stop him delivering it. You'll drop off the gallows straight into Hell.'

'I'll still be here to watch you hang, you scabby witch.'

Unedifying words in front of a Puritan clergyman, I thought as I adjusted the steeple hat and smoothed down the black gown I had borrowed from the playhouse wardrobe. Thus attired I persuaded the guards to let me walk beside Blackbeard to wrestle with his soul. He growled, 'I said I didn't want a...' then recognised me. His scowl changed to a grin as he said, 'I'm glad you're here, Dekker. You've come to watch me hang. Instead you'll see me get off. Then you'd better start worrying 'cos I'm going to kill you. And I'm going to do it slowly. It won't just be business, it'll be pleasure as well.'

As we walked between the crowds lining the street I tried to convince him that he had been abandoned by his high placed friends. If he gave me enough information, I would be able to see that he was avenged.

'I could tell you what you want to know,' he said; 'and if I'd been abandoned I might. But I haven't. They know my value from what I've done for them. They've got no one else who could replace me.'

The man was positively swelling with pride. Could I play on that? We were passing the Rose Playhouse and for some reason the play that sprang to mind was The Spanish Tragedy. Dismissing it I returned to my task saying in an insinuating manner, 'Whoever planned and carried out the killing of Mother Wingfield had genius. Unless it was, as many believe, the Devil.'

He snorted: 'I didn't believe that witch back at the Clink so don't you believe that the Devil was in Milk Street. You nor all London can puzzle that out. No, nor never will unless you're told.'

211

'It's a pity the man behind such an ingenious stratagem will never receive the credit; that it is going to die now, with you.'

'I've told you I'm not going to die,' he hissed. 'You're going to die, Dekker. Slowly.'

His confidence was beginning to infect me. Was he really going to get his reprieve? Certainly the men behind him would be able to obtain one. We had reached the wood now and I had to drop behind on the narrow path. The wood was buzzing with people. We reached the clearing and Blackbeard stopped. At the far end was the murder tree. Next to it stood the gallows. Derrick, the hangman, sat on the crossbeam smoking a pipe, one foot resting on the top of the ladder, the other dangling in the air. On the ground stood his assistant with a clergyman. Blackbeard's eyes were raking the crowd ringing the clearing. They came to rest on Ingram Frizer who patted his doublet. Blackbeard nodded. Stepping forward the clergyman said, '*Perfect love casteth out fear.*'

'I'm not afraid,' shouted Blackbeard, grinning at Frizer who grinned back. Something in Frizer's grin and remembering that he liked plays made me think again of The Spanish Tragedy. Of course. There was an assassin in the play called Pedringano hanged while expecting a reprieve. It might be a way to pierce Blackbeard's armour-plated arrogance. Catching hold of his arm I asked, 'Have you seen The Spanish Tragedy?'

'Plays,' he said contemptuously. 'I wouldn't watch a play to save my life.'

With the usual Puritan sense of proportion about the theatre, the clergyman trumpeted, 'Scorn for acting is gracious in the eyes of the Almighty.'

'All I hate more than whining players,' said Blackbeard staring at him, 'is fucking preachers.'

The hangman's assistant took Blackbeard's arm but he shook himself free, strode to the ladder and began

212

climbing it. At the top he turned towards us and the hangman slipped the noose around his neck, pulling it tight. Then Derrick grasped the nightcap to pull it down over the face but Blackbeard shook his head free. There were shouts of, 'He wants to speak,' 'Let him speak.'

'Confess for the sake of your soul,' cried the preacher. Blackbeard looked at Frizer who half pulled a document from his pocket.

'The damned villain's going to get a last-minute reprieve,' shouted a man. An angry murmur ran through the crowd. Blackbeard smiled and leaned his head back against the ladder. Derrick pulled the nightcap down over his face, patted him on the shoulder and looked at Frizer. The crowd fell silent. Frizer rammed the document back into his pocket and the hangman pushed Blackbeard off the ladder. Blackbeard's roar ended in a gurgle. He really should have gone to see The Spanish Tragedy.

Twenty-Three

Every week there was a rise in deaths from the plague. Crowds now were seen only in a church or at a hanging. The streets were quieter. Rumours abounded. It was whispered that fanatical Jesuits were getting themselves infected in order to spread it amongst Protestants. Then there were war rumours. A great Spanish fleet was ready to sail. The English Jesuit Father Parsons was with it together with a large supply of thumbscrews. There were grumbles about our Dutch allies. People said we had gone to war to defend the Netherlands who were now trading freely with the Spanish while we were barred. So Holland and Zeeland had grown rich while England was impoverished.

'It's always the way,' said a man in the Bear Tavern. 'We let foreigners fool us.' Another tapped the table and said solemnly, 'My brother's wife's uncle was told by the landlord of the Cranes in the Vintry that he had a Dutch merchant in there as fat as a tub of lard taking bets on how long they could go on cozening the English. I tell you friends, we'll all end up on the parish.'

It was certainly where I was going to end up if I did not get some work. The money I got for the ballad on Blackbeard's execution would not go far. And there were no more repairs to do at the Rose. My clothes were now so ragged that I was ashamed to call on Elizabeth. But I still had enough pride to refuse work as a horse-holder for a pimp outside one of Henslowe's brothels. He was part owner of a tavern and said he could get me work there as a waiter. At reckoning figures I'm as slow as a lawyer who's paid by the hour, so I said I'd think about it. Given the state I was in I could understand Henslowe's look of incredulity. Work, any work, was a necessity. After the way the Clays had stood by me when Cheadle's inquest was hanging over my head I knew I should visit them. But I was afraid the shoemaking job would still be on offer and that in my parlous state I would take it. I could not let them down by leaving a second time. No, I had chosen my career; writing for the theatre supplemented with ballads and pamphlets.

Nicholas Winton had no ambitions to turn me into an apothecary so I called at his shop. He was enjoying a pipe of tobacco and waved me to a chair. While he finished his pipe I glanced around the shop. The tortoise and the stuffed alligator still hung there. Nor did the number of ill-shaped fishes appear to have diminished. Was Winton as reluctant to part with his wares as some sellers of used books I have known? He chuckled: 'Look carefully Master Dekker and you will observe that there has been a run on bladders and packthread. As for tobacco, my wife tells me that our best customer is my poor self. I'm afraid my smoke drives her out of the shop as the plague does the rich out of London.'

After commiserating with me over the closure of the playhouses he got down to business: 'The Earl of Essex is as unstable as he is ambitious. He is frustrated at not being able to turn the favour of the Queen into solid political gain. Raleigh, through his own folly, is no longer an obstacle. But Lord Burghley and his son don't have an ounce of folly in them. Essex is brilliant; quick and therefore in danger of tripping. Burghley is a plodder, steady and reliable. Essex is the hare and Burghley the tortoise.'

215

I nodded in agreement and said, 'With Ingram Frizer as the very much unstuffed alligator waiting to gobble up – who?'

'You and me, Master Dekker, if we're not careful. As for the two runners; the race, you'll remember, was won by the tortoise. Essex should be careful his ambition or his hot-headed followers don't put him in the power of men like Frizer. The document you found makes it clear he has been encouraging extreme Puritans.'

'And Mother Wingfield, Stour and Cheadle were murdered because they knew something,' I concluded. I left Winton and set off to see Henslowe feeling melancholy. It was no fashionable pose. My enquiries and therefore my play were getting nowhere. In any case with the plague worsening there was not going to be any market for plays for some time. Now, with my money almost gone, I would have to serve in Henslowe's tavern.

It was to the Sun Tavern in Milk Street that I made my way having bought second-hand clothes with a small advance from Henslowe. The tavern was almost opposite the house where Mother Wingfield had met her strange end. There could be a chance that someone had seen something.

Old Cruickshank was sitting in his favourite window seat sipping his ale when I went in. I said, 'Soaking up the sun, sir?'

He nodded suspiciously, not sure if the joke was aimed at him or not. The landlord, Lancelot Gort, was a small man who tried to increase his height with built up shoes. He was bowing and bobbing across the room like a dinghy amongst a fleet of galleons. Reaching me, he read Henslowe's note, frowned, then said, 'Very well, I'll take you on as a favour to Master Henslowe. But I warn you, I run a tight ship. My aim is to attract the man of fashion. Here his word is law.'

'*This gallant will command the Sun,*' I quoted; explaining, 'From one of Master Henslowe's poets.'

'I don't care what you provide playhouse patrons with, Dekker. You are here to provide my patrons with pots of ale and fish suppers. Do I make myself clear?'

'As clear as, well, the sun.'

'A gentleman has spewed up in the Apollo Room. You will get a bucket and mop and clean it up.' And that was my introduction to the serving side of tavern life.

The days went by in a flurry of foaming tankards and appetizing fish suppers. I kept my hand in for the re-opening of the playhouses by writing ballads and pamphlets. Old Cruickshank came to the Sun much less now. The murders of Stour and Cheadle had shook him and he did not want to be seen talking to me. None of my friends or theatrical acquaintances came in, for which I was grateful. I did not want them to see me being ordered about by the diminutive Gort. It was hard to refrain from hitting someone who went from cringing to a customer to lording it over the staff. If he had been better born, better looking, better built, he would have made a good toadying courtier.

My luck in not meeting any acquaintances while working at the Sun did not hold. Fortune, looking down to see who she could discompose, spotted me, gave her wheel a flick and in walked Marlowe, Greene and Nashe, three of the so-called university wits. I am not eaten up with envy for those who have had a university education. Learning is something I honour. But it is possible to read books without having attended Oxford or Cambridge. In an argument at the Mermaid once Marlowe quoted Ovid and Greene nodded approvingly. But when I reinforced my point with an equally apt line from Juvenal, Greene sneered about my being a "Perkin Warbeck pretender to learning."

217

Now when I brought in their order of Rhenish wine and pickled herrings Greene held up his brimming glass to the light and said, 'Your wine has more sparkle than your verse, Dekker, and a better measure.'

I shot back, 'I hope you don't choke on a fish bone like audiences choke on your plays.'

'Henslowe's made money on my plays.'

'Not nearly as much as he's made on Shakespeare's.' That stuck in his gullet, turning his face as red as his long pointed beard. His friend, gag-toothed Nashe, (most feared satirist of the day) was glaring at me and when I heard the gnash of his teeth I got out quick.

Next time I went in the wine and food was being attacked with gusto. Greene especially was tucking into the pickled herrings. They were abusing the players, calling them squeaking puppets, parasites sucking the life-blood of poets.

'At least our friend here is not a player,' said Marlowe clapping me on the back. Was it, I wondered, a coincidence that he was here? Was he keeping an eye on me? Since he now had the Frenchman as a friend it was not, I hoped, for personal reasons. They left full of wine and (especially Greene) pickled herrings.

Now that I had presentable clothes I called at the Cross Keys and enquired about Elizabeth. Grace said she had fallen ill and was with her aunt and uncle. When I went to the Brayne's shop their apprentice told me to wait while he fetched Mistress Brayne from upstairs.

When she came into the shop her stern face blocked my way more effectively than her body. She said, 'Master Mulcaster is giving my niece spiritual comfort. You are not wanted in this house,' and she stood at the foot of the stairs until I left.

Disconsolate, I wandered away down the street. But I could not leave without learning whether or not Elizabeth was seriously ill. I walked back and stood irresolute

218

outside the shop. The door opened and the apprentice hurried out. Blocking his path I demanded to know how Elizabeth was.

'She has smallpox and the doctor fears for her life. I'm going to the apothecary,' and he pushed past me. While he ran down the street, I re-entered the shop and mounted the stairs. Chastity, her eyes red-rimmed, stood at the top and pointed to Elizabeth's room. Mistress Brayne was just inside the doorway but I pushed past her. Elizabeth was lying in bed, eyes closed, sweat heavy on her forehead. Seated beside the bed was John Mulcaster holding her hand, a prayer book in his other hand. When I walked to the chair on the far side Mulcaster said to Mistress Brayne, who had caught my arm, 'Please, let him stay.'

The hours passed as we watched Elizabeth shivering and sweating in the grip of the fever. For a time we were relieved by Master and Mistress Brayne. It was a day and night of watching and praying with snatches of sleep.

Next day I returned to the Sun and told Gort why I had been absent and that I would need more time off. He was, predictably, unsympathetic, telling me that I had all the time in the world since I was not wanted back at the tavern. Ever. So I returned to my vigil beside Elizabeth. Mistress Brayne raised no more objections and I was provided with food although I ate little of it. There was a dull, dead ache in my stomach as the hours dragged past with the fever getting worse. Never had I longed for anything more than her recovery. When I looked across the bed at John Mulcaster's haggard face it must have mirrored my own. He cared for her as deeply as I did. His request to let me stay had been generous. If Elizabeth recovered it seemed likely that I would lose her to Mulcaster.

The doctor came and went, looking graver each time. To me he also looked more and more helpless. I called the others together and said I wanted to try someone else. It was strange but since meeting Nicholas Winton I had heard his name again and again. Not only as a conscientious and skilful Head Constable, but also for his medical abilities. Perhaps I had heard the name before but it had not registered. I had hinted at it earlier but got no response. Now I urged trying Winton.

'It is in the hands of God,' said Mistress Brayne. 'We must pray harder.'

'Yes,' agreed Mulcaster, 'but we are also enjoined to strive ourselves. I think we should try the apothecary.'

She had great respect for Mulcaster and with her husband joining us she agreed. The doctor had to be handled tactfully. We assured him that as a mere apothecary Winton would be under his direction. Having obtained his reluctant assent, I hurried over to the shop and appraised Winton of the situation. While he mixed his ingredients I lay down exhausted in body and mind. Soon he was shaking me awake. As we hurried through the streets Winton counselled me to moderate my hopes. He'd had successes but failures too.

Winton worked with the doctor, deferred to him while persuading him that he had bled Elizabeth enough. No doubt doctors are right in claiming that draining blood from the patient drains away the impurities that feed the disease. But surely the loss of blood must weaken them? At any rate everything humanly possible had been done for Elizabeth. Now, as Mulcaster said, it was in the hands of God.

I was awakened from a doze by Winton. Elizabeth was breathing easier. Mistress Brayne, with surprising tenderness, leaned over and wiped the sweat from her brow. Elizabeth's eyes opened and she gazed at each of us in turn. Taking my hand she whispered, 'Tom.'

Unable to speak I simply squeezed her hand. Her other hand flew to her face. Winton said gently, 'It's alright, my dear, they've come out on your arm,' and he rolled back the sleeve of her nightgown. She smiled at the red pitted scars then said ruefully, 'Vanity.'

Master Brayne patted her arm and murmured, 'Don't fret yourself, niece. We're all sinners.'

'Yes, indeed,' said Mistress Brayne looking hard at me. Mulcaster said quietly, 'Let us give thanks for our sister's deliverance,' and we knelt around the bed in prayer.

Before the amens had died away the doctor was asserting his authority, telling us to let Elizabeth rest. Chastity, who has a delicate skin, said defiantly, 'Well I don't think it's vanity for Elizabeth to be glad her face was saved.'

'You've got vanity enough for the whole household, Miss Minx,' replied her mother sharply. The doctor remarked complacently, 'My treatment not only saves the life but ensures that the face is unscarred. You might spread that among your friends, Miss Chastity.'

'She'll do no such thing,' said Mistress Brayne. 'Beauty is nothing but a snare.'

Elizabeth held out her hand to Mulcaster saying, 'Thank you for everything, John.' He took it briefly, bowed, then left the room. I said, 'You called me Tom, does that mean I am occasionally permitted to call you Bess?'

She kissed me and replied, 'That means yes. Occasionally.'

Then I was ushered out with the rest by the doctor. I had no job, no money and Winton now informed me that Warthog was watching the house. But I was back with Elizabeth.

Twenty-Four

Over the next few days I tramped the streets looking for work. The sale of a few ballads supplied my present needs. Henslowe had nothing for me. London had nothing for me. In Fleet Street I saw a tiny incident that seemed symbolic; although in view of what transpired later an astrologer might have described it as an omen. An old and mangy dog tottered along the street near collapse. Several kites and ravens who had picked the bones outside a butcher's shop clean watched its progress. They followed. Birds on the rooftops followed, flitting from house to house. The dog staggered then fell in convulsions. The fit subsided then it stretched out and lay still. The ravens and kites advanced on it croaking while others swooped down from the rooftops. A girl in the blue livery of a servant watched the birds pecking at the dog and began crying. Passers-by laughed while others looked on incredulous at someone crying over the death of a dog. The girl's mistress angrily shouted at her to come away. We're all pecking at the body of London, trying to survive. Or perhaps we are the food for a living, growing beast.

I was getting so desperate I tentatively approached Peter but he shook his head saying, 'You'd bring us both to Tyburn quicker than a dead lawyer's soul goes to Hell.'

He was right, of course. Not that I'd been serious about stealing. Elizabeth had forgiven me a lot but she would hardly marry a thief. But it was Peter who gave me the chance of temporary work. Not, though, before I'd had a grim encounter that put me off theft even more.

222

Bartholomew Fair would be opening soon and Peter knew a puppet master who was looking for an assistant: 'He's good, Tom.'

'Grabs the full attention of the audience does he, Peter?' I said with heavy sarcasm. But he only grinned. When Peter introduced me to the puppeteer, Master Blague, a white-bearded, venerable-looking old man, I was able to assure him that I had got my love of theatre from playing with puppets my uncle had bought me. He said, 'Do as I say and don't try any fucking fancy stuff.'

I had enough money from ballads to tide me over until the Fair opened so I set off for Smithfield to find a room near the site. As I approached Newgate Prison I saw a batch of prisoners being brought out for their last journey to Tyburn. One of them was Greene's protector, Cutting Ball, who had cut one purse too many. In our last encounter he had tried to cut my throat but I felt a bit sorry for him. Hanging men and women for stealing may deter some but other cutpurses and pickpockets would be plying their trade while the crowd gawped at their fellow thieves being strung up. A shapely young woman with tears channelling her painted face clutched at Cutting Ball's hand as he was pushed up onto the cart.

'His whore?' asked a hard-faced woman. A man replied, 'No, his sister. She's the poet Greene's whore.'

As the cart rumbled away Ball's sister turned and came over to me. Dabbing her eyes with the sleeve of her dress she said, 'I've seen you at the playhouse. I wish you'd come to Robert – that is, Master Greene. He's very sick and all his friends have deserted him.'

When praying for Elizabeth's recovery I had promised God that if he spared her I would show more Christian compassion. Here was my first test. Mistress Ball did not have much faith in my Christian compassion because before I could say yes she added a sweetener: 'Robert –

Master Greene – says he has a secret many would like to know.'

Off we set for Greene's lodgings. His room was almost as bare as mine in Coldharbour Tenements. Greene looked ill but was writing furiously when we entered. Throwing down his pen he motioned me to sit on the bed and said to his mistress, 'Bring us some wine.'

Hands on hips she replied, 'Give me some money then.'

When Greene turned to me I handed over enough for a cheap bottle. He gave it to her and she flounced out and slammed the door.

'Her brother…' he began. I nodded and said I'd seen him. Greene sighed: 'Poor Ball was a thief but he had formed an attachment to me.' He added fiercely, 'He stood by me better than many who called themselves friends. I don't allude to you, Master Dekker. You have just shown you have Christian feelings.'

I thought, I have more of those than I have money. He was looking very ill and went on in a melancholy tone, 'That girl will leave me soon and who shall blame her? It's a judgment on me for having abandoned my dear wife.' Shivering, he wrapped his gown tighter around his body. He continued bitterly, 'That atheist Marlowe laughs at my illness being a sign of God's wrath and says it was the pickled herrings.' His voice sank to a whisper: 'It may be poison, Master Dekker, from people who would feel safer if I were dead.'

Now I shivered. And I might have more cause for shivering after he had imparted his secret to me. Naturally, I thought it might concern the rumours that the Earl of Essex was plotting an uprising to sweep away his enemies on the Queen's council. Of course, spies and informers have an interest in spreading such rumours; it gives them more work. But Nicholas Winton, a shrewd judge of character, believed that Essex, being reckless and unstable, would sooner or later take such a course.

Greene tapped the paper he had been writing on: 'The man, the tiger, I have exposed here would like to see me dead.' His eyes were bright with fever as with an effort he controlled his shaking and continued, 'At least he would if he knew I had his secret. The only reason he does not want me dead now is that I owe him money. A paltry sum. The damned usurer flung it in my face when in my need I asked him for another loan.' He sank into a bitter, brooding silence. Suddenly he burst out: 'I would scorn to take money from him now if I were dying in the street. But I want you to tell him that if he prosecutes me I will reveal his secret.'

'Who, Master Greene?'

'Why, that "Tiger's heart wrapped in a player's hide." Shake-scene. He's bedding Lord Hunsdon's whore, Emelia Bassano.'

Mistress Ball returned with a half empty bottle of wine. We said nothing as she poured each of us a glass. Raising her glass she said defiantly, 'To my brother.'

We drank. He had tried to kill me but doubtless he would have said, 'No malice, just business.' We finished the wine and I left after promising to deliver Greene's warning to Shakespeare.

After finding a room convenient for Smithfield and my new career as a puppeteer, I set out with my message. Shakespeare was staying at the Earl of Southampton's house in Holborn so I did not have far to walk. I walked slowly, regretting my promise to Greene. He might have protested that he would take no money but his straits were so desperate he must have been hoping for some. I did not believe his claim that Shakespeare would have him arrested for debt. So it looked uncomfortably like blackmail, with me as Greene's agent. On the other hand I felt that Shakespeare should be warned. His career could be damaged since Lord Hunsdon decided what plays were shown at court.

Reaching the house I presented myself at the gatehouse. The porter looked at my mud-spattered, unfashionable clothes and said, 'I think you visited a draper's shop called Tyburn Tree, friend. I recognise that wine-stained, flea-ridden, tobacco-stinking doublet as belonging to a man who was hanged this very day.'

As he bowed low while ushering a satin-clad exquisite ahead of me I said, 'Rest assured, porter, I won't buy your servant's livery when you come to the Tree because I don't have the matching servility.'

Grumbling he went and fetched the steward who fingered his chain of office and looked at me disdainfully. When I said I wanted to see Master Shakespeare he replied, 'I'll see if the...' he coughed – 'gentleman will receive you.'

Those who feel most looked down on must have someone they can look down on. He returned accompanied by Will Shakespeare who took me into a side room and ordered wine. The steward stood still long enough to impress on us that he considered it beneath his dignity to take orders from a couple of playmakers before saying, 'I'll send a lower servant with it.'

Shakespeare gestured at his departing back: 'No one believes in degree more than your servant. I'm sorry I have to see you in this out of the way place, Tom.'

I indicated the state of my clothes (the mud and smoke of London soon begrimes them) and assured him that I had not expected to be introduced to the family. He said, 'No one is completely at ease with a poet in the household because no one is sure of his exact place.'

'I've just come from a poet who had a cutpurse in his household.'

'Robert Greene,' he muttered. I explained the situation. When I mentioned Greene's charge of usury he flushed with anger: 'Far from charging a high rate of interest I charged him none at all. Instead of paying me back he asked me for another loan. I refused, pointing out that I had a wife and three children in Stratford to support. I think that what angered him as much as the refusal was being reminded that he was not supporting his wife.'

I had never seen him so angry. Usually his feelings were concealed by an enigmatic smile. Now he was Will Shake-fist. And he had not finished: 'It's not only Greene who's lost money from the closing of the playhouses. So have I, so have you. I am dependent on the kindness of my Lord Southampton for food and shelter.' Darting a searching look at me, he asked, 'How likely is it that Greene will – inform on me to Lord Hunsdon?'

'He's ill, poor and bitter. Any of those might impel him to betray your secret.'

He paced up and down the room then turned to me: 'Even if I were willing to be intimidated, I have no money for him. A poet, like a performing bear, is given food and shelter but no money. At least not until I complete my poem which will not be for some time. I'm fairly safe from Lord Hunsdon while I enjoy the protection of my Lords Essex and Southampton. It's Emelia I'm concerned about;' adding bitterly, 'Though God knows why I should be after the way she has treated me.'

As soon as he put an arm around my shoulder I knew that a favour was about to be requested. And so, after he had explained that he was too well known at her apartment, I left promising to call and warn her. Will can "Play the orator as well Nestor."

When I called to see Emelia, I was told she was out. So on to my mother's place. She had promised me a gold ring of my father's to give to the girl I was going to marry. When I asked for it she hugged me not needing to be told who it was for. Now she told me that when praying for Elizabeth's recovery she had also prayed for us to be re-united.

As I walked up Bread Street and into Cheapside, the ring nestling inside my doublet secure from pickpockets, even the croaking ravens were music in my ears. To a peddler who thrust his tray at me shouting, 'What do you lack?' I called back, 'Nothing.'

Although I found there was something when amidst the smells of strong beer, freshly baked bread and roast pork my nose picked up the scent of flowers. I bought a bunch and took them into the Brayne's shop. The prentice grinned while Master Brayne slapped me on the back and jerked his thumb at the stairs. Mistress Brayne sniffed and it wasn't at the flowers. Mounting the stairs two at a time I burst open the door of Elizabeth's room and found her briskly sweeping the floor. Taking the broom I said, 'Your arms will be better employed holding me,' and kissed her. She still looked a little pale: 'You should be in bed, Bess.'

'Not with you in the room, Master Dekker. That will be when I can call myself Mistress Dekker.'

Taking the ring out I explained its significance and offered to put it on her finger. She looked at me with those beautiful eyes, serious now, then walked over to a chest of drawers and opened one. Returning with a ring she said, 'If we exchange these, Thomas, then it will be a solemn pledge to marry on my part.'

'On my part too, Elizabeth.' Taking her hand I placed my ring on her finger and she placed hers on mine. Everything, the scent of the flowers, being alone together, touching her, was having its effect. I said, 'We could marry today with troth-plight.'

'No,' she replied firmly.

'We could take our vows in church later,' I urged.

'No, Thomas. I believe marriage should be solemnised in church. Not a handfast contract. Church.'

228

I sighed and said, 'I'll see about the reading of the banns.'

'Don't be in such a rush. I must write and tell my parents. They have always trusted my judgment so I'm sure they'll agree. But I want their blessing on our marriage. And Tom, I would like to be married in my home town. It would also be a chance for you to meet my mother and father.'

I was ready to agree to all this although plenty of couples have begun with a hand-hold marriage. But there was still the ticklish question of how I was to earn a living. Master Clay, I was sure, would take me on as a shoemaker; Master Henslowe, because of the Privy Council's ban, could not give me employment as a playmaker. But the latter was all I wanted to do. Now it was Elizabeth's turn to sigh: 'My parents will, of course, want to know what you do for a living. When I tell them you're a writer they'll think I mean a scrivener.'

'Well you could go on letting them think that, Elizabeth.' I answered her look of exasperation by protesting that she would not be telling a lie.

'Thomas, I will not equivocate with my parents in such a Jesuitical manner.'

I grinned: 'Puritan jargon sounds delightful when it comes out of such a pretty mouth.' I was relieved that no pressure was, apparently, going to be put on me to give up writing. There was a knock at the door and Mistress Brayne stalked in: 'You should be in bed, Elizabeth.'

'That's what I've been urging on her,' I said. Elizabeth stuffed a handkerchief in her mouth as Mistress Brayne whisked across the room to straighten a chair as if it had been a backsliding Calvinist and banged to the open drawer as if she were shutting up a Popish priest. Turning back to us she said sternly, 'You should not be in here unchaperoned.'

We held up our hands to show the rings and Elizabeth said, 'We are betrothed, Aunt Esther.'

'I hope you realise that it legally binds you to marry.' We held hands and nodded. She added sharply, 'And I will not have any handfast marriages in this house. Do you hear?'

'Both Elizabeth and I are determined to be married in church, Mistress Brayne,' I replied, acting sincerity as well as Alleyn. Elizabeth suddenly looked as stern as her aunt. Well, almost. As she led the way down the stairs Mistress Brayne said over her shoulder, 'I trust now young man you will leave your ungodly profession and find yourself respectable work. I don't want any playhouse connections in this family.'

Under Elizabeth's quizzical eyes I held up our ringed hands so that my mumbled reply was lost amidst the congratulations of the rest of the family. Master Brayne insisted on sending the apprentice out for a bottle of wine to toast us.

When I left the shop Warthog shouted from across the street, 'Celebrate while you can, Dekker,' before disappearing into the crowd.

Twenty-Five

Next day I called again at Emelia Bassano's apartment. Warning her was now a task I somewhat regretted taking on. After all I might be suspected of couching her. Of course, I had. At least I'd coached her, if there is such a word. There probably is since coaches are now commonly called mobile brothels. Couched or coached, Lord Hunsdon would not care. He would be concerned not with the semantics but the sex. He would be more inclined, I felt, to see it as a former shoemaker's apprentice and prospective puppet master's assistant making free with his mistress. I had enough enemies without making one of Her Majesty's Lord Chamberlain. But I had promised to warn her so, after cautiously circling the building a few times, I went in and climbed the stairs to Emelia's room.

Her maid, Joan, answered the door. After she had consulted her mistress I was shown in. Emelia had obviously just got out of bed. Seated on a couch her hair hung loose over her shoulders while her satin gown was open almost to the waist. I took my betrothal to Elizabeth seriously. At least, I wanted to take it seriously. I was glad Joan was there. Emelia was eating figs and waving her hand at the bowl drawled, 'Figs are said to be an aphrodisiac. Help yourself, Tom.'

With her breasts almost falling out of her gown an aphrodisiac was the last thing I needed. I was doubly glad Joan was there.

'Joan,' said Emelia; 'would you go and see if my dresses have been cleaned. Then why don't you visit your sister.'

Joan curtseyed her thanks then hurried out. Emelia poured two glasses of wine and patted the couch, saying in a husky voice, 'Come and sit beside me, Tom.'

I sat down trying to keep a space between us without appearing discourteous by sitting too far away. I took the glass of wine she handed me but waved away the figs. She held the figs to my mouth her breasts pressing against my arm, her long, black, perfumed hair brushing my face and purred, 'Take what I'm offering you, Tom.'

Sliding away I held up the finger with the ring and gulped, 'I'm betrothed. I came here to warn...' jumping up she grabbed the fig bowl and shouted, 'When I offer, you take,' and threw it at my head followed by her glass. I was running for the door as the bottle hurtled past my ear and shattered on the wall splashing me with wine. When the table followed I was out of the room and heading for the stairs. From the bottom I heard Hunsdon bellow, 'What's going on up there?' then his heavy footsteps on the stairs. There was an open window on the landing and I was quickly out of it and perching precariously on the ledge. Once again I had a fine view across London. But it's true what they say: you can have too much of a good thing. I could hear Emelia sobbing, 'You don't come near me for days then I send my maid out on an errand hours ago and she does not return,' followed by Hunsdon's soothing words then the door being closed. With a sob of relief I got back onto the landing and raced down the stairs and away.

On returning to my room near Smithfield I found Greene's mistress waiting for me. When she handed me a letter from Greene I pointed out that the wax was broken. She replied, 'He was shaking too much to seal it proper,' and stared at me defiantly. The letter was brief. Greene said he was ashamed of threatening to inform on Emelia and Shakespeare and his threat was to be disregarded. He wanted to be at peace with the world when he died. I gave the girl a few coins and promised to visit Greene at the first opportunity.

Bartholomew Fair was in full swing: a roaring, jostling, tumbling torrent eddying around the booths and flowing between the stalls that stood like rocks in this river of humanity. Above their heads chattering monkeys dangled from poles while rope dancers skipped and somersaulted. At the mouth of an alley a company of dancing dogs performed while nearby Morocco, the famous counting horse, was tapping out numbers with his hoof. A man roared when a corn-cutter stepped on his toes while yelling, 'Any corns to cut.'

A peddler shouted, 'What do you lack? Mousetraps, mousetraps, a tormentor for your fleas,' before being swallowed up in the crowd. A mountebank held up a bottle of his medicine, The Universal Panacea. Acrobats cartwheeled around a dancing bear. A row flared between a hobby-horse seller and a gingerbread woman when he bawled, 'Your stall's blocking the view of mine,' to which she screeched, 'I've paid for my ground as well as you.'

'Move it, old woman, or I'll tell what's in your gingerbread.'

'What's in it? Nothing but what's wholesome.'

'Yes, stale bread, rotten eggs, musty ginger and dead honey.'

'I'll have you up afore his worship.' Turning to the passers-by she cried, 'Buy any gingerbread, gilt gingerbread.'

'You tell him, girl,' bellowed Ursula the pig-woman, swigging bottled ale at the entrance of her tent, the sweat running down her red face, the delicious smell of roast pork wafting from the tent. Making my way to the large

233

booth I'd helped erect I passed dicers groaning and exulting; the giant man and miniature woman; whores leading men into alleys; and other puppet shows proclaiming The Siege of Troy, Jonah and the Whale, The Destruction of Jerusalem. Drums beat, fiddles scraped, rattles rattled.

Our main attraction was a topical play about a London murder in which the wife had poisoned her husband. Just two months earlier the wife and her lover had been executed here in Smithfield; he being hanged before her eyes while she was burned at the stake. As in Arden of Faversham.

Master Blague swore as he hurried to get his puppets ready, his violent language belying his venerable looks. With everything in place I stood at the entrance taking the pennies. It was hot work; now jumping in amongst the jostling crowd to pull back a man trying to evade payment, now picking up a child who had been knocked down and trampled; and all the time checking I'd been given a penny and not a button. With the house full, I went and assisted behind the scenes. We worked hard. The next week was a riot of knock-about comedies and bloody tragedies; The St Bartholomew's Day Massacre, Keep the Wenches Waking, The Destruction of Sodom and Gomorrah and many more.

During a performance of The Constable and the Calvinist's Wife a black-clad man in the audience began shouting that he was being slandered and that puppets were Popish idols, an affront to the saints of Smithfield. Blague made the puppet Calvinist squeak, 'I agree with you, sir.' When the puppet constable belaboured him with his truncheon the wife squeaked, 'Have you another truncheon for me, sir?'

The man, infuriated by the audience's laughter and joined by some fellow saints, tried to rush the stage. The ensuing fight rocked the booth and was only stopped when some real constables rushed in and dragged away the offenders. Later I saw the man who had started it sitting in the stocks while his fellow Puritans stood around him singing psalms, all glorying in the martyrdom being conferred by the showers of stale fruit and rotten eggs.

When the Head Constable warned us that if we did not keep better order we would be closed down, Blague put on his most venerable look accompanied by reassuring words in honeyed tones. But most effective of all would have been the hard silver coins he slipped into the Constable's hand.

Next day as I stood at the entrance taking money, Peter turned up. Seeing the anxiety on my face he said, 'Don't worry, I won't be working here. I've got my own patch. Besides, I wouldn't poach on this man's territory, he's a tartar. Take my word, Tom, if he's caught in your booth don't be a witness against him. As well as a cutpurse he's a cut-throat with powerful friends in the thieves' fraternity.'

So far we had been lucky with no big losses amongst our audiences. That changed. We had a spate of cut purses and picked pockets. But still no big losses. Then just before the start of a performance, as I was pushing through the audience with the takings, a man fell against me knocking the box to the ground. The rattling pennies, my cry of, 'Thief,' set the audience shouting and surging. When the hubbub had died down a richly-clad man shouted, 'I've been robbed,' and he held up the thongs on his belt from which his purse had been cut. He roared, 'I've lost twenty pound.'

After a constable had been called someone pointed at me and said, 'I think he was in league with the thief. He dropped the box to cause a diversion.'

When I looked round for the man who had fallen against me he had gone. Blague came from behind and said to the constable, 'I'd begun to have my doubts about him. I was about to give him his marching orders.'

He was making me a scapegoat. And standing there red-faced and confused beside the venerable looking Blague with his white hair and beard I must have appeared deeply guilty. At any rate the constable arrested me and I was hauled off to Newgate. Passing through that dreadful gate felt like the journey from life to death. An abrupt passage from sunlight to gloom. From the fair where yells of laughter and cries of delight drowned discordant quarrels; to the prison where the only relief from cursing brawls was the silence of despair. Once again I faced the possibility of death. So much depended on who you got as judge. And what I was charged with. Conspiracy, I presumed. I was no lawyer and so was not sure whether benefit of clergy could be claimed.

I hated bothering Nicholas Winton again but he had told me to get in touch if I was in trouble. So I sent a message with a trusted girl who was being let out to earn her prison fees. I had prudently paid mine so when the other prisoners demanded I buy drinks as a newcomer I had only a few pence. They took them and cursed me for not having any more.

A few hours later Winton arrived with, to my surprise, John Mulcaster. The latter, after Cambridge, had studied law at the Inns of Court. I was annoyed when Winton said he had found Mulcaster through Elizabeth since I did not want her to know that I was in jail yet again. But I ended up being grateful for Mulcaster's knowledge of law. Or at least his ability to spout legal jargon. Really there was no evidence against me but when I had threatened an action for wrongful arrest and imprisonment they had laughed in my face. It was a different matter when they were told the same thing in legal language by a former law student. It was clinched when the constables returned with the actual thief. The man had his purse back and I walked free.

236

Trying to get my prison fees back from the jailors though was like trying to get a bucket of water out of a frost-bound Thames. But I was free.

I had made plenty of sarcastic remarks about Puritans and lawyers but John Mulcaster was a man of integrity. It was easy to see what had attracted Elizabeth to him. Less easy to see what had brought her back to me. The only reason I can think of is that man or woman does not live by logic.

When I reached my lodging I was confronted by the landlord demanding his rent. He was not interested in my explanation about Newgate, simply repeating, 'I want my rent;' adding, 'You won't stay here rent-free. I'll put you in prison until you do produce it.'

I groaned. He was on the point of sending his son to fetch the bailiffs when a deus ex machina turned up in the unlikely shape of Henslowe. He paid my rent and even advanced me a little for myself. Here was someone else I had showered with gibes. I was in the middle of praising his disinterested generosity when he said casually, 'There is a small thing you can do for me.'

I was wary. What did he have in store for me? He continued, 'Greene has died. I want you to search among his papers for any plays.' My thoughts about ravens and kites preying on carrion must have shown on my face because he justified himself with, 'I advanced him money for a play which I never had.'

That was feckless, improvident Greene. Who was I calling feckless and improvident? Henslowe was still rambling on: 'The playhouses must re-open soon and his plays did quite well. Not as well as Marlowe's and Shakespeare's, of course.'

Poor Greene. Less than the blasphemer and the player. If Greene's soul were hovering above us now it would say, 'Take me to Hell so it is from here.'

237

'Still at the same lodgings?' I asked. Looking uncomfortable, Henslowe replied, 'No. He couldn't pay the rent and was forced to leave. I've written the new address down.' He fished in his pocket and produced a scrap of paper. Henslowe's handwriting and spelling are notoriously bad and eccentric but here he had excelled himself. I read: "grene nuy adris. Dygeate wyrffe." If we all wrote like Henslowe, scriveners would be as rich as goldsmiths. Shaking my head I confessed myself defeated.

'Dowgate Wharf, man. It's plain enough.' So off I set, wishing I had been able to visit Greene before he had died.

The house belonged to a poor shoemaker called Isam and was a ramshackle building that looked ready to fall into the Thames over which it hung. Mistress Isam answered the door and took me up the stairs saying, 'The poor gentleman fell down in the street and my husband took him in.'

I had to duck going into the room and the first thing I saw was Henry Chettle on his knees in front of an open chest rummaging through it. He raised his hand to me and grinned then went on examining the papers. Mistress Isam whispered, 'Said he was a friend of Master Greene. None of the friends he sent messages to came to him.' I followed her gaze to the low bed on which Greene's body lay, his hands folded on his chest. On his head was a wreath of bay leaves. She adjusted it and murmured, 'At the end he kept saying he was a poet an' when he died he'd go to the Lizion Fields an' they'd crown his head with bay leaves. My husband said it's proper for poets so I made a wreath of them for him.'

'I heard at the end he was crying for Malmsey wine,' said Chettle. She bridled: 'What if he was? Wine is given us for a comfort which he got precious little of from his friends. He thought of his poor wife near the end and wrote a letter to her.'

There was a sound of footsteps running up the stairs and Robert Poley burst into the room. He went straight to the chest saying, 'I see you're here scavenging already, Chettle.'

I did not have the heart for it and after giving Mistress Isam the few coins I could afford and promising to be back for the funeral, I left. In the street I glanced I up at Greene's window. Poley was looking down at me like a hawk at its prey.

Twenty-Six

I felt as a scout must feel as he reconnoitres hostile
territory, every sense alert for an ambush. Was I just being
kept under observation or were they waiting for the right
moment to strike? Winton had gone on a herb gathering
trip to the West Country. Peter and Rosie were keeping
their ears open in London's underworld for information.
Elizabeth was back at the Cross Keys to the joy of her
regulars. Especially Sir Ambrose who, hearing some
fanciful story of Sir Walter Raleigh and Queen Elizabeth,
had welcomed her back by laying down his velvet cloak at
the entrance for her to walk over.

Henslowe was in no mood to welcome me back with a
cloak for a doormat. He complained that while Chettle
had got something rumoured to be juicy which he was
rushing into print, I had returned empty-handed. The
plague was getting worse so there was little prospect of
the playhouses re-opening. Ballads and pamphlets were
bringing in just enough to live on provided I did not eat
and drink too much. But that income fluctuated wildly.
There was too much competition from unemployed
scholars. At least those whose pens were not constipated
with pedantry.

One evening in the Cross Keys I was eking out my
tankard of ale with sips that an abstentious flea would
have regarded as small while just such a pedant harangued
the company about the book he was writing on English
pronunciation: 'God has blessed us with a beautiful

language; after Greek, Latin and Hebrew, of course; a long way after. Where was I?'

'Just leaving,' suggested a man hopefully.

'A beautiful language,' he went on sternly. 'To mispronounce it is wrong, wrong – I mean w-rong, w-rong, w-rong.'

'You have powerful ale, Mistress Elizabeth,' called out another man. Ignoring him the scholar continued, 'Chaucer always said k-nife.'

'I expect he got his ale here too,' said the mocker. Sir Ambrose, with a coy glance at Elizabeth, said, 'If I tie a love-knot in my handkerchief for a certain lady how would I say it?'

'Love-k-not,' replied the scholar.

'Not for me, Sir Ambrose,' said Elizabeth.

'You should say k-not, Mistress Elizabeth,' said Sir Ambrose archly.

'No,' groaned the scholar. 'Only words with a k. You, for instance, are a k-night.'

'I'm k-not, I'm a baronet.'

'And you, sir,' said the mocker, 'are a k-nave to call a baronet a k-night.'

The scholar folded his arms and fell silent with the look of the refined man patiently enduring martyrdom by the vulgar.

I walked Elizabeth home through the moonlit streets. But it was difficult to strike a romantic note when my eyes were continually darting to the shadows. Elizabeth had insisted on walking to the Thames first and while she rhapsodised about the beauty of the moonlight glinting on the water I was worried about it glinting on the blade of a knife. As we walked back up Gracious Street I jumped when a signboard creaked above our heads. We talked of our future. She had written to her parents telling them about our betrothal and asking for their blessing. But it might be weeks before a reply reached her via some

241

plodding carter. Not that there was any urgency given my financial position. Of course there was no problem about getting my mother's blessing. She told me roundly that I was getting the best of the bargain since Elizabeth was just what I needed.

When we reached the Brayne's house I did not go in, saying that the less Mistress Brayne saw of me the better for her temper. 'Now isn't that a Christian act?' I murmured as I kissed her.

'It would be, Master Dekker, if you weren't thinking of yourself as much as her.'

'But I'm doing unto her what I would be done to.'

She slapped my arm. 'Thomas! It's that kind of talk that inflames her temper. And with reason. You know what happened the last time you misapplied the words of the bible. Blasphemy Aunt Esther called it. She imputes it to your consorting with the actors.'

'If I were to use my experience of consorting with the actors, I could win golden opinions from the godly by acting the pious man. But reformation is my watchword,' I added hastily.

'Make sure it is.'

'It will be. So let's put aside controversy for kissing.' And we suited the action to the word.

Walking back to Coldharbour Tenements I heard a step behind me and whirled round. It was Peter: 'She's a fine looking girl, Tom. Not that I was spying on you. The fact is Rosie worries about you and has asked me to keep an eye on you. I've also heard rumours about you, the Lord Chamberlain's mistress and the seat of a coach. What's the secret? Have you got a love potion from your apothecary friend?'

'Nicholas Winton is like yourself, Peter, somewhat of a cynic. He maintains that the most effective love potion for a woman can be bought from the goldsmith or the jeweller. But I'm grateful to Rosie for worrying.'

242

'Well she may have cause. Those who want you dead may be growing more determined than those who want to keep you alive. And some of the reasons could be personal. Even a vicious bastard like Blackbeard had friends. I've heard that the bailiff you call Warthog had to use the blood money he got for Blackbeard to buy off those friends. You've got no money.'

"For lack of money I could not speed." London Lickpenny was written over 200 years ago and today it is truer than ever. Everything is up for sale in London, including revenge. Murderers will be setting up a guild soon and crying not "What do you lack?" but "Who would you like to lack?" I had the feeling that I would be safer in the American wilderness than on the streets of this city. I would have rejoined the tour but lack of money and reluctance to leave Elizabeth kept me in London.

A week or so later I was in the Cross Keys at Elizabeth's insistence for a mid-afternoon meal when Alexander Hay came cautiously in. He had bought a new hat since I had seen him at Faversham. One with a very tall feather that bowed and bobbed as he walked. When he saw Elizabeth he bowed himself, sweeping off his hat and saying, 'Madam, pray accept the humble apology of a rough soldier unskilled in the art of the courtier.'

He had learned his lines well and Elizabeth nodded briskly and bade him sit down. He was soon moving pepper pots, mustard pots and wine glasses around the table to demonstrate to the company how he would have defeated the Duke of Parma in the last campaign if he had been general instead of a captain. Sir Ambrose was much impressed with him, especially his colourful oaths ("By Pharaoh's foot") asking, 'Could you teach me to swear like a soldier, captain?'

'To swear like a soldier, sir, you must be a soldier. You must see a line of Spanish pikemen advancing and you alone with only your trusty...' he had his sword half out of the scabbard when Elizabeth caught his eye and he hastily pushed it back in.

Elizabeth was discussing with me my future prospects while cutting off a slice of beef for my meal when a man rushed in and said breathlessly, 'There's constables pressing men for soldiers for the French war.'

Panic. Men ran for the back door blocking the way. Elizabeth hissed, 'Quickly,' as I dived beneath a table. All round the room men were doing the same. Poking up from behind the back of a settle I could see Alexander Hay's feather. There was a pounding of boots as the constables burst in; shouts of, 'Grab them,' yells as truncheons thudded on bone. Meanwhile Elizabeth sauntered over to the settle and with a discreet swing of the carving knife sliced off the feather. The constables left dragging out those they had collared and we could all breathe again.

Alexander Hay stood up with the feather in his hand and said, 'Any other time I would have been glad to go but tomorrow I have to travel down to Faversham to fight a duel. When a man's personal honour is at stake ...' his sad shake of the head was meant to convey his deep regret at being forced to miss a chance to fight the Spaniards. Given the inadequate rations, the disease-ridden camps and soldiers cheated of their pay by corrupt officers it is little wonder everyone tries to evade military service. It was a different matter in eighty-eight when England was directly threatened by the Armada. But no one wanted to fight in France's civil war.

Next day I was browsing at the bookstalls in Paul's Churchyard, particularly among the Roman writers. There was still a vague memory niggling at the back of my mind of something I'd read in one of them that would help to explain Mother Wingfield's murder. At another stall I saw Shakespeare reading a pamphlet and looking extremely annoyed. When I went over he thrust it into my hand and said, 'Read that.' The bookseller took the pamphlet from me and said, 'If either of you gentlemen care to buy it you can read it at your leisure.'

Neither of us was prepared to lay out sixpence from our limited funds so Shakespeare told me what was in it: 'Chettle claims that Greene wrote it although I have my suspicions. It's a personal attack on me. I'm practically accused of causing Greene's death, of being a plagiarist, of being proud, of thinking I am, in his words, "The only Shake-scene in a country." He calls me an upstart crow, an ape, a Johannes Factotum and to cap it all misquotes one of my own lines to say I've got a "Tiger's heart wrapped in a player's hide." These fly-blown lies will attract all the envious kites and ravens of literary London.'

He was right, of course. And not only writers. I'm sure the same aristocrats who backed him would read the pamphlet with as much pleasure as they'd watch a cockfight. They must feel some resentment about so much talent being lavished on a tradesman's son. It undermines, just a little, their claim to be all that is best in the country. But, after all, they'd see Shakespeare as theirs so in the end they would back him. They'd want him to be literary cock of the walk. But it seemed to me that the insights exhibited in his plays showed that he was clever enough to use them for his own purposes. Unless his mind was clouded by love. He groaned, 'And now I hear that Emelia is with child and old Hunsdon is going to marry her off to a court musician.'

We parted in Paternoster Row, he turning left for the lords and ladies at the Earl of Southampton's house in Holborn while I turned right to join the thieves and whores of Coldharbour Tenements.

When I got back to the tenements Rosie invited me into her room where she and Peter had just opened a bottle of wine. She winked and said, 'A part payment.'

I had not seen them for several days and now she urged Peter to tell me his story. He said: 'I was scouting along Cheapside and I went into the Mitre where I struck lucky. My coney was a big man with a red sash round his waist. He was sitting at a table belching over a pot of beer. The room was packed so I was able to sidle up and cut his purse without him feeling a thing. As soon as I was out of the door I pocketed the money and threw away the purse.'

'You're taking a big chance doing it without a mate to slip it to, Peter,' warned Rosie. He shrugged and continued: 'My first job of the day and I'd got a handsome haul, a rich booty. I was strolling along thinking I might take the rest of the day off when I felt a hand on my shoulder. Jesus, I thought, they've got me. It was a constable and he said, 'You're going to be a soldier, lad.' So there I was with the other poor devils being marched along Cheapside.'

'Couldn't you make a run for it?' I asked.

'Bit difficult that, mate. They'd cut the tags holding our breeches up so we had to use our hands. Well I tells one of the constables escorting us that much as I wants to serve my Queen and country, I have urgent business to attend to down on my estate in Kent. So could we come to some arrangement? He pats my pockets, hears the coins clink, pulls me out of the line and takes me into – the Mitre. The fat fellow with the red sash was still seated behind the table belching over his beer.

"Got a gentleman to see you, captain," says the constable then whispers in his ear.

"Show me what you've got," orders the captain. "All of it."

'You bastard, I'm thinking as I plonks the lot on the table with the constable patting my pockets to make sure I have. As the captain starts counting it he chuckles, "I'll take my oath you've not come by this honestly." Then it occurs to me that he's going to think, that's strange, it's exactly the same amount as I've got in my purse, which he'll then reach for. So I says, "Look captain, you've got

246

my discharge money, I've got urgent business, so could you sign me as unfit and let me go?'

'He took a docket from a pile at his side, wrote on it and handed it to me. Then he returned to his counting, a big smile on his fat face. Just as I was turning into the street I heard him roar, "My purse is gone."

'Holding up my breeches I ran along Cheapside, cut down Friday Street, up Ram Alley and into Mother Moorcock's whorehouse. She hid me and even got one of the girls to sew the tags back on my breeches.'

After a few glasses I walked up to the Cross Keys. It was quiet so Elizabeth was able to leave it for a couple of hours. We walked down to the Thames meaning to take a boat to Westminister. But for the moment all the boats were occupied. So we strolled on hand in hand waiting for a vacant one to turn up. A barge had just finished loading barrels onto a cart and the carter had secured them swiftly and deftly with a rope. Now he was lashing the straining horse into the narrow Trig Lane.

Coming out of the next alley along I saw Warthog with three other men, hard-faced bastards. Warthog pointed at us then scurried away. A wherry had just drawn into the stair vacated by the barge and I pulled Elizabeth towards it. But a silk and satin young man jumped into it and the waterman pulled away. We ran into Trig Lane the three men close behind. Drawing my knife I cut the rope holding the barrels on the cart and they cascaded off bouncing and rolling at our pursuers. Squeezing past the cart Elizabeth held up her dress and we ran.

Hoping to throw them off, we dodged down a side alley, turned a corner and came to a high wall. Hurrying back we found ourselves facing the three men, each holding a knife.

'What about the woman?' asked one.

'You want to leave a witness to put a rope round our necks?' said a scarred-faced villain as all three advanced towards us.

Twenty-Seven

'Let her go,' I shouted; but I might as well have been talking to three tigers as they advanced inexorably. While Elizabeth quietly prayed I had my knife out; although I would have been hard pressed with just one of them. They held their knives as naturally as if they were extensions of their arms, swinging them from side to side as they crept forward. The only sounds were the watermen's cries from the river and the muted rumble and hum from the city. The scarred-faced one stopped and signalled to his companions to halt. They say a rogue's ear can detect the slightest sound and this one was listening intently. Then he darted back to the alley's entrance, shouted, 'The law,' and ran. His companions followed suit. A posse of men with truncheons passed the entrance in pursuit. When two of them stopped and turned towards us I said, 'Am I glad to see you fellows.'

'Hear that, Jack?' said one. 'At last we've met someone who wants to be a soldier,' and they grabbed my arms. As they hustled me away Elizabeth shouted, 'I'll raise the money to release you, Tom.'

'You'll have to be quick, sweetheart,' chuckled Jack; 'his ship leaves on today's tide.'

When we caught up with the other constables the slashed faces of two of them and the death of a third testified that they had caught up with our attackers; but they had failed to hold them. I was put in a wherry and rowed down to Wapping. After we had been buffeted and bounced shooting the Bridge the Welsh waterman

249

cackled, 'Wait 'til you hit the channel, boy, that'll test your belly.'

On the Surrey bank of the river a line of trees were shedding their leaves in the light breeze while I felt like shedding tears. I was worried sick about Elizabeth. She had been left alone. What if those ruffians doubled back? My promises to pay the constables later if they released me moved them only to laughter.

When I was put aboard the Goodwill at Wapping they said to an official with a list, 'This one fufils our quota.' Then I was pushed down into the hold and the hatch closed. In the dim light of a small lantern I saw a scene of crowded misery. Some men sat in silent despair, heads buried in their hands. Others swore, groaned, quarrelled, wept. A few were stoically playing dice or cards. A number were lying dead drunk. Filling the hold, the stale smell of sweat and vomit was almost eclipsed by the fouler stench of bilge-water. Above our heads casks and crates thudded onto the deck as the sailors completed the loading of the stores. Soon we heard the order shouted to cast off and then we felt the movement as the ship glided down the Thames towards the open sea.

The hatch was lifted and we looked up, blinking at the light. A heavy man with short hair and a pock-marked face began descending the ladder. Half way down he stopped and looked us over, his small fierce eyes raking every corner of the hold. He said, 'You're going to fight for old England, lads; so fucking cheer up. My name's Krake. Sergeant Krake. One day, if you live, you'll frighten your children with my name. You'll say, "Do what you're told or Sergeant Krake will get you." I'm going to cause you grief. I'm going to make you weep. I'm going to terrify you. You'll charge into the mouth of the cannon and throw yourselves onto the Spanish pikes just to get away from me.'

250

Climbing up and out of the hold he poked his head back in and said, 'Wind's getting up. It's going to be rough when we hit the open sea. But I promise you I'll make you sicker than any sea will.' He slammed down the hatch.

We knew when we were in the Channel. While the ship rolled one way my stomach lurched the other. I thought if Krake is really going to be rougher than this then we're in for a bad time. But soon my thoughts went the same way as my food and my mind was as empty as my stomach. Now I joined in the chorus of groaning and retching. Please God, I prayed, please God stop the ship rolling. Just for a few minutes. The hatch was lifted and I saw two faces grinning down at us. To my mind we were in Hell being mocked by devils. Hours later (or was it days?) the groaning subsided and we lay in a silent misery that was just about endurable. Then again the hatch was opened and a cheery voice called, 'Anyone for boiled bacon?' That set off a fresh round of retching and groaning while the sailor's devilish laughter echoed around the hold.

But gradually our stomachs got more or less used to the motion, enabling us to take a little food. This cheered us. I felt more hopeful about Elizabeth's safety reasoning that after their tussle with the constables the three rogues would have made off rapidly. Dice and card games started up again.

Several of us were watching a game of hazard, including a tubby haberdasher's apprentice, Timothy Firth. With only a gentle swell he had indulged his taste for boiled bacon. There were a few gold pieces in the pot so the tension was high. The player had chosen eight as his main number. He threw the two dice and got a four and three. Seven was now the player's chance number, the one he needed to win. If he now threw eight the pot was the banker's. Calling on Dame Fortune not to play the

251

whore he rattled the dice in his hands. A sudden gust of wind hit the ship, making it roll. Timothy spewed up just as the player threw the dice. One dice showed three but the other stuck on edge in the vomit, showing four to the player and five to the banker. There was a violent argument with each one claiming that more of his number was showing than his opponent's. Sides were taken. Other men, trying to be impartial, went down on hands and knees carefully studying the dice. Neither party would agree to throw again. The banker grabbed the pot and the player leapt at him, slipped in the vomit and brought down the banker. When the coins spilled from the pot there was a wild scramble for them with kicking and punching, shouting and swearing. I had a punch in the mouth that made my teeth feel as loose as those hung on a string outside a barber-surgeon's shop to advertise his tooth drawing skill. From the hatchway Sergeant Krake roared, 'Order.' The fight got worse men, hitting each other with pots and bottles. Through the hatchway came the flash and roar of a musket. The fighting stopped abruptly. Everyone gaped up. Three muskets were poked through the opening, each sailor holding a lighted match, ready to fire. Krake shouted, 'The next shots fired will be into you.'

He descended the ladder and walked around the hold men jumping out of his way. Those who were not quick enough were kicked aside. Having demonstrated his ascendancy he climbed back up the ladder. Turning at the top he said, 'I'll be ratsbane to you Newgate vermin.'

They allowed us on deck to exercise now. One man, seeing the coast of England receding, tried to jump overboard, shouting, 'I'll swim home;' fortunately for him he was overpowered and put in irons. Rumours abounded about our destination. I said France but many disagreed, wagering on their choice. One man bet on the Low Countries; that was soon ruled out by our continuing southward course. Those who knew we had troops in France plumped for Brittany or Normandy. Wilder guesses got better odds; Lisbon, Cadiz, even inland Madrid. Some said we were going to fight the Algerian corsairs or the American Indians.

'You're not fit to fight anyone nor won't be 'til I've trained you,' said Sergeant Krake. But he refused to tell us where we were bound for. We continued down the Channel before a gentle breeze until it shifted and strengthened, blowing us westward along the south coast of England. Sails were shortened as we ran before what was now a gale. There was terror in the pitch-black hold where we were battened down. Waves pounded the side of the ship hurling us against each other to a medley of cursing and praying. Suddenly the hatch was thrown open and a sailor shouted, 'Up, up or you'll be drowned like rats.' Men were scrambling up the ladder before he had finished speaking. A violent lurch threw them off and onto the heads of those below. I leapt at the ladder and shimmied up and out onto the deck. When I stood a gust of wind almost blew me back down the hatchway.

'Down with the topmast,' bawled the boatswain. 'Lower, lower,' while the master's whistle shrilled through howling wind and roaring water. Driving rain stung my face as I clung to a bulwark.

'The Lizard,' shouted a seaman beside me as he pulled on a rope. 'We'll never clear it.' Through the thickening rain I made out the dark bulk of land, with waves crashing thunderously onto the rocks. They seemed horribly close.

'Look out,' shouted the seaman as the topmast tottered, then crashed onto the deck. It hung half over the side making the ship list badly. A sailor with an axe hacked at the rigging until the mast slid into the sea.

'What's the use,' snarled the seaman beside me. He snatched the axe from the man's hand and ran towards the storehouse at the rear shouting, 'We're lost, mates.'

253

Others followed him. When the captain stepped in front of them he was knocked to the deck. The boatswain shouted, 'It's all over if they get to the drink.'

Krake grabbed my arm and ordered, 'Follow me.' As we ran back we heard the splintering of wood. Bottles of wine were being handed out when we arrived. Krake snatched a bottle from a man and smashed it over his head. While I was struggling with the axe-wielder Krake wrested the axe from his hand and brained him. When he turned, blood-bespattered, on the others they fled back on deck.

We just cleared the Lizard but it was close. 'Close?' said one sailor. 'I spit on it as we passed.' The man Krake had killed was thrown overboard without ceremony.

'No burial service for mutineers,' said the captain grimly. As his body disappeared beneath the waves, I'm sure the thought in every mind was, there but for the grace of God go I. We were tired, wet and cold but exhilarated at being alive.

The gale blew us far into the Atlantic before it subsided. While the sailors worked at repairs we idled. Krake vowed to make up for it once he got us ashore. From the sailors we learned that our destination was Brittany. We were going to join the English soldiers already there fighting for the Protestant King Henry. The Catholics had the Spanish on their side. The best troops in Europe. Until we got to know each other better no one would admit that they were afraid. We all boasted and talked loud to conceal our fear, as a drum is beaten outside a barber-surgeon's tent in Bartholomew Fair to cover the screams of those having teeth pulled out. Krake smoked his pipe and listened, a sardonic expression on his face.

After the tempest we now lay becalmed. We were bored. Gambling was officially banned but in practice it was winked at. When Timothy Firth, chewing on a piece

254

of boiled bacon, wandered over to watch a card game there was a roar. He was hustled away protesting that he would not be sick in a dead calm. The sailors took a delight in making our flesh creep, telling us tales of ships becalmed so long they had run out of food and water. One ghoul said, 'When your tongue is so swollen with thirst it's poking out of your mouth, your own piss will taste as sweet as wine. And you'll be looking for someone to kill so as you can eat his flesh.'

Krake jabbed his pipe at an alarmed Timothy and said, 'He'll be the most nourishing with all that boiled bacon he's gorged on.' Having witnessed Krake's axe work I had no doubt as to who would act as butcher. At last a breeze sprang up and Timothy breathed easily again.

'Sail to the south,' shouted the look-out from the crow's nest. We all crowded to the side while the captain altered course. After several hours sailing we had got close enough for the sharper-eyed sailors to see that it was a Spanish ship. There was a buzz of speculation about prize-money. She might be carrying gold.

Krake and the captain were arguing on the poop with several glances at us. Finally the captain gave the order to hand out weapons to us as well as the crew. Clearly there was a fear that, still angry at being pressed as soldiers, we might take the opportunity to seize the ship and return to England. There was now little reason to fear. Every eye was bright with gold fever. Swords, partizans, axes, pikes were handed to us. Firearms went to trained members of the crew.

We were gaining on the Spaniard but night was drawing on, when we would almost certainly lose our prize. The gunner was ordered to shoot down her topsail. He fired the cannon in the bow. The ball fell short, bouncing on the water and just missing the ship's waterline. He was roundly cursed. If the Spaniard was sunk it would take our prize money down with it.

'It's poor quality powder,' he grumbled. Poor powder or poor gunnery, he kept missing. The gap was closing but the sun was going down. A bonus was offered to any musketeer who could bring down the helmsman. With the sea choppy aiming was difficult. Several holes appeared in the sails above the man's head. Now we ourselves were under fire from the cannon at the stern and muskets from the bulwarks. A cheer rang out as the helmsman staggered and fell. Another quickly took his place. The cannons and muskets flashed red in the twilight. Another helmsman went down while someone on our ship screamed. Then as one of their musketeers was about to fire he was hit and fell back. His lighted match must have ignited some powder because there was an explosion. Sparks flew up and a sail caught fire. It was now quite dark but we had the blaze as our guide. We closed in. Some of their crew were fighting the fire while others opposed our boarding party. Krake, sword in hand, led the charge amidships while the captain shouted, 'Some of you help the Dons with the fire or we lose the prize.'

It was an odd situation with some of us fighting the Spaniards and others working alongside them. We quickly prevailed against the men who began throwing down their weapons; but the fire was putting up a harder fight. Then another explosion scattered blazing timbers that started fresh fires. I sniffed the air and was thinking, who the hell is smoking a pipe at a time like this when the order, 'Abandon ship,' was shouted. We scrambled back aboard the Goodwill and pushed off. Then we watched the Spanish ship burn, the lurid red flames dancing on the water.

'Richest cargo of tobacco I ever have,' said the Spanish captain sadly. 'It would have bring me much gold in Cadiz.'

'And me in London,' responded our captain glumly. Krake sniffed the tobacco rich air and said, 'Dearest smoke I've ever had.'

It was a gloomy bunch the Goodwill bore eastwards to Brittany. All except Houndsditch Harry Potts, that is. He was a perky little cockney with an eye for the main chance, combining the cheekiness of the sparrow with the rapaciousness of the raven. As soon as he was brought aboard he was telling the crew, who were mostly West Country men, that nowhere could beat London. To his fellow Londoners he boasted that the parish he was born in topped all others. 'Which one?' we asked. A little defiantly he replied, 'Houndsditch.' We fell about laughing and gave him the nickname. Now as we sat down to breakfast he grinned and said, 'I did alright out of the Dons last night.'

'Yes, yes, Houndsditch, of course you did,' we responded sarcastically. 'You always do.' Pulling a purse from his pocket he flourished it, clinking, and said, 'I took it from a dead Don.' He opened it displaying gold coins. Grinning he held a couple up: 'They'll buy me plenty of booze and whores in Brittany.'

We regarded him sourly and began tapping our iron-hard ship-biscuits on the table to get the weevils out. His grin broadened as he held up his biscuit: 'I slipped the steward something to supply me from the captain's store. Fresher ones with no weevils.'

'No weevils,' bellowed an Irishman. 'No weevils. Well have my fooking weevils,' and threw his biscuit at Houndsditch's head. Others shouted, 'And mine,' and followed suit. Everyone joined in and Houndsditch fled under a hail of biscuits.

At last we entered the harbour of Brest. We lined the sides, grateful for the sight of land.

'I wish it was England instead of France, though,' sighed Timothy. Thinking of Elizabeth, I felt the same and said, 'I was the last bastard to make up the quota.'

'Yes, Dekker,' said Krake who had strolled over pipe in hand. 'We had our full complement until a cunning rogue gave us the slip. The jest was he paid for his release with money he'd stolen from Captain Sarsfield earlier. I pity the men the captain conducted out here. When I last saw him in the Mitre he was in a foul mood. If he could have got his hands on that villain...' and Krake walked away chuckling over what Sarsfield would have done to him while I thought, I'm here in place of Prigging bloody Peter.

Twenty-Eight

We unloaded the arms from the ship into carts on the quay. Krake said, 'You'll carry weapons when you're more like soldiers than scarecrows.' Then he lined us up with corporals on either side and off we set through the town. Krake bawled, 'You're supposed to march, Potts, not mince like the Houndsditch whore your mother.'

When the rest of us laughed he roared, 'What have you bastards got to laugh at? Stand up straight. You're drooping like poxed up pricks in the Spital.'

And so we marched, or in Krake's view, shuffled, through the town. Just before we reached the camp on the outskirts we passed two men hanging from a tree. Pinned to their chests were papers saying, "Deserter."

When we straggled into the camp men came out of tents and makeshift huts to stare or jeer. Krake lined us up for an inspection by Captain Sarsfield. After looking us up and down he said, 'I pity you, Sergeant Krake, having to walk through Brest with these bits and bobs. But you have my permission to knock them into shape.'

'Thank you, sir,' said Krake with relish.

'Work the rascals hard, sergeant.'

'I will, sir. When I'm finished with them they'll be shadows of their former selves.'

'Yes, we need plenty of shadows for the muster book,' said Sarsfield with a nasty laugh. I knew what the corrupt bastards were joking about. Shadows, or deadheads, were soldiers killed or missing that rogue captains would keep on the books to pocket their pay. At least it meant that if

259

Elizabeth could raise the money Sarsfield would be willing to let me go. In addition to that, he would go on claiming for my pay. I had volunteered in eighty-eight but I was damned if I was going to give my life to make money for the likes of Sarsfield.

We had been sworn in and received our first pay on the ship. The blankets they issued to us were full of holes. 'Rats,' grinned an old soldier. Coats, they told us, had not yet arrived. The soldier spat and said, 'The money for 'em's arrived, though. You'll find it in Sarsfield's pocket.' And there everyone knew it would stay.

In the mess tent I was carrying my beer, bread and cheese away when a soldier seated at a table with his back to me half turned his head. He had a black patch over his left eye. I was wondering how he had lost it when he turned his head full round. The right socket oozed blood and pus. I dropped my beer to a roar of laughter. He pulled the patch from his left eye which was good and grinned: 'It always gets 'em.'

I was billeted with Houndsditch Harry and Fat Tim as the latter was now called. Our billet was on the ground under the stars. Not that we could see any stars that night because it rained.

Next day Krake began our drilling. At Tilbury I had joined too late to receive training. That was about to be remedied. Most of us clamoured for muskets but men who had arrived earlier had received these. They gave us pikes. At least we did not have to expend any of our meagre pay on powder and shot. From the expression of disgust on Krake's face it was obvious that our deportment did not meet with his full approval. Not a good time to ask him questions about our lack of equipment. Which is exactly what the not very bright Fat Timothy Firth did. He'd been talked into it by that sharp witted, smooth-tongued grinning joker, Houndsditch, who was nudging me in the ribs as Tim raised his hand and asked, 'Why haven't we got no armour, sergeant?'

Krake walked slowly over to him and said softly, 'You don't need no armour, lad. Not with all that flesh. That's thick enough to stop a bullet'. Circling him Krake added, his voice rising to a crescendo, 'The only thing thicker than your body is your fucking head.' Pushing his face to within an inch of Tim's he screamed, 'Straighten your back. Pull your stomach in. I can't see your feet Firth. Get your guts in.' Tim's face had turned purple by the time Krake moved away.

Taking a pike from a corporal Krake said, 'Don't let me hear anyone call this a spear. It's a pike.' Planting the butt firmly on the ground he tilted his head back to look up its 18 feet length to the sharp steel point. Then he looked at us and barked, 'You'd like pintles as long as this to impress your sweethearts. Especially Potts there. We got Potts out of a brothel in Houndsditch. I dragged him off a whore by his heels.' I couldn't help smiling as he went on, 'She didn't even know he was out of her, went on grinding away.' Now he turned to me: 'I'm glad I made you laugh, Dekker, because now you're going to give me a laugh when you use your pike, aren't you?'

'Yes, sergeant.'

He pointed to a hedge about fifty yards away: 'That's a line of Spanish infantry and you, God help us, are the English army. Advance.'

Lowering my pike I began advancing on the hedge with Krake walking alongside exercising his tongue: 'Move man, you're not out for a Sunday stroll, you're under fire. Keep your pike up. Not too fast or you'll get there like a spent prick. Not too high, keep it level. Now into the hedge with it. Use it, man. Harder, it's not for tickling your girl's nonny-no, it's for sticking in a Spaniard's guts.'

We grew to hate that hedge far more than we ever hated the Spaniards. Krake kept us at it for hour after hour, day after day. We learned to advance and retreat in formation; to debouch from column into line; to form a square; to combine with musketeers, halberdiers and billmen. And we practised push of pike against each other while trying not to trip over the swords we had to wear. We had to learn drum and fife signals, hand signals and word of mouth commands: 'Faces to your right hand;' 'Double your ranks;' 'As you were.'

Among ourselves we grumbled about being sent into battle without armour. Then it arrived. It was battered and partly rusted but still armour. We put it on, struggling with the unfamiliar straps and buckles. There was a corselet to protect the torso, pouldrons for the shoulders, vambraces for the arms, tasses (overlapping plate armour) and gauntlets. For helmet there was the burgonet or morion. We now found that extra safety meant extra weight. Cold as it was, we sweated. 'How's it going to be in hot weather?' we asked. In fact much of it was thrown away. But for training it all had to be worn. At least the extra weight we had to carry made us all the fitter.

We were melding, becoming a unified company; and the greatest unifying force was not loyalty to the crown, nor fervour for the Protestant religion, nor patriotic feeling for England. It was hatred; not hatred for Catholics, Spaniards or even that damned hedge; it was hatred for Krake. As the days grew into weeks and the weeks into months he worked us and worked us. Of Captain Sarsfield we saw little. He spent his ill gotten gains in the taverns and brothels of Brest. The old soldiers agreed that Krake was a bastard; but they said that he was the best trainer of recruits in the army and that we would be grateful to him when we had to fight. Perhaps, some said. Others of us would have preferred to learn while fighting. I must admit it is the fittest I have ever been; but also the most bored.

The only ray of light was a letter from Elizabeth that finally got through to me. She was trying to raise the money to buy me out. Although now that I was here I thought it would be interesting to see what it felt like under fire. I was to find out with a vengeance. In an effort to cheer my spirits, Elizabeth gave me some of the latest theatrical news. Ned Alleyn had married Henslowe's step-daughter. And a piece of scandal. Emelia Bassano, being with child, had been married off by Lord Hunsdon to a court musician called Lanier. Emelia would not, I felt sure, be pleased. And poor love-sick Shakespeare would be feeling sorry for himself now that he had a husband to contend with. Come to that, I was feeling sorry for myself with all these weddings taking place and me separated from Elizabeth.

And I could not find solace in getting drunk because our pay, as usual, was in arrears. Parliament wanted us to defend the country but they begrudged spending money on it. As well expect a water-mill to turn without water as fight a war without money. And when our pay did arrive I could hardly spend money on my pleasures when Elizabeth was making such an effort. I may not have such a strict conscience as a Calvin or a Knox but I have got one, even if, like London watchmen, it slopes off when most needed.

I was hearing more and more talk about the Earl of Essex as the man for England. Many of the soldiers had served under him the previous year when he had commanded in Brittany. The one-eyed soldier (a giant of a man, inevitably nicknamed Cyclops) seemed to be his greatest advocate. In every company he argued that Essex was the man England needed. Essex knew what had to be done and therefore should be supported whatever he did. When the time came Essex would know how to deal with the faint-hearts in the Queen's Council. And – here his voice would sink to a whisper – the worse than faint-hearted, those in the pay of Spain. This was dangerous talk and at first his listeners were few. But with sickness increasing through not having enough to eat and inadequate shelter from the cold, discontent was growing. Now our pay was late again.

Contrast this with the delicious smells emanating from the well-appointed tents of captains like Sarsfield; add to it the number of pretty young women seen leaving his tent; multiply these by the number of days he spent living in a house in Brest and the answer you'll get is mutiny.

The high command, seeing the discontent coming to the boil, must have decided that action was the best way to counter it. Orders were given that we were to be ready to move out on the morrow. Early next morning we assembled in ranks carrying our weapons. But when Krake gave the order to form into columns, we stood stock still. Sarsfield raged at us to no avail. The Colonel came forward and with icy contempt called us mutineers and traitors. Still no one moved. While the officers conferred, I noticed Cyclops nudging the man standing next to him and indicating that he go forward. The man had been amongst the loudest in complaint. Now, with others also urging him on, he moved, reluctantly, to the front. Here he was confronted by the Colonel flanked by Krake and Sarsfield. With many a nervous backward glance at the men he awkwardly articulated our grievances. The officers listened, not bothering to conceal their contempt. This set off a sullen muttering among the men. From the vicinity of Cyclops someone shouted, 'We were better off under Essex.'

'You've got just as fine a leader in Sir John Norris,' shouted the Colonel. 'And by God he'll show you how he deals with mutineers. I have orders to join him for a siege. I am ordering you to form into columns.'

There were shouts of, 'We'll confer,' as we broke up into groups. The old soldier I had spoken to on my first day in camp came over. He was a Dutchman called Antoon Haaker. Tapping the remnants of his tobacco pouch into his pipe he said, 'I hope there is a good store of this in town when we capture it.'

'You think the men will march on it then?' I asked.

'Oh, they will march. And the fellow that speak, who they push to front, he will also be in front when we attack town.' Looking in the bowl of his pipe, he sighed over how short his smoke was going to be, lit it and said, 'Spanish tobacco is the only good thing about them. And even that they rob from the poor Indians. Some soldiers miss the wine, some the women; me, I miss the tobacco.'

The Colonel threatened to send to Norris for troops but still we refused to move. There was a messenger standing by booted and spurred but the Colonel hesitated. I could see his dilemma. Sending to the General for help was a confession that he could not manage his men. The situation was volatile with the officers growing angrier and some of the men saying they would shoot the messenger if he tried to ride out. Then along the road from the town we heard the pounding of horses' hooves. As he rode into the camp the rider waved his hat and shouted, 'An English ship has just entered the harbour.'

There was a loud cheer although no one knew if there was anything on board. The messenger was dispatched to the town. Meanwhile in the camp card and dice games started up on drumheads as men gambled with the money they were confident was on the ship. The officers looked nervous, knowing there would be serious trouble if it was not.

With the short days the sun was declining before we again heard the drumming of hooves followed by the entry of two riders. There was no cause to shoot the messenger with the news he brought. He was cheered.

The wagons with the pay and other stores were being escorted to the camp now. Some men put their ears to the ground and claimed they could hear the wagon wheels rumbling. Others laughed and capered. Now the mood was festive. I joined in until I saw who had returned with the messenger. Ingram Frizer. I'd heard of his trips to the continent from Nicholas Winton, so it might not be my presence that brought him here. He could be here to further the Essex conspiracy. Keeping myself concealed among the troops, I resolved to follow his movements in the camp. The document he showed to the Colonel must have been satisfactory because it was handed back to him with a nod of approval and he was offered a glass of wine.

Twilight was upon us when the wagons rolled into the camp. While the men were being lined up to receive their pay I noticed Frizer slip away from the officers. I followed him to one of the camp-fires where another man half hidden in the billowing smoke was standing. As they began conferring I crept closer, sheltered by a tent. They spoke in low tones and only snatches of their conversation reached me. But from Frizer's talk of, 'He must be persuaded he is the man England needs and his friends are working on that,' I guessed who they were discussing. When Frizer urged, 'Those who support him will be well rewarded,' the fire suddenly flared up to reveal Cyclops, his one eye gleaming as he said eagerly, 'I can swing the soldiers behind Essex.'

'Quiet, man,' said Frizer fiercely. 'Come, we'd better get back before we're missed.' As they moved in my direction I turned quickly and tripped over a rope. Jumping up, I ran into the bushes hotly pursued. Looking back I saw the gleam of a knife in the firelight. 'Who goes there?' shouted a sentry. 'Halt or I shoot.' Since the pair of them were silhouetted against the fire they stopped and Cyclops called out the password. Crawling on my belly I got clear and joined the queue for my pay.

Early next morning we were again ready to march off. But this time ready in every sense. Last night's festive mood was still there. Even those clutching their foreheads joked about their helmets holding their splitting heads together. There were some grumbles about not being allowed into Brest to find women. A stock of tobacco had been brought so Antoon Haaker was puffing contentedly on his pipe. After the months of training everyone looked forward to putting it into action. The veterans smiled but we were confident. And there was the chance of plunder. Houndsditch said to Fat Tim, 'Like a few others you'll need loot to pay the interest on what I lent you.' Punching his stomach he added, 'My money kept that fat body stocked up.'

'You're getting very unpopular, Houndsditch,' said Tim rubbing his stomach.

'So long as I gets my money I don't care a cardinal's fart.'

Haaker shook his head and said gravely, 'I have known some men not liked who died facing the enemy with their wounds all behind.'

Just then I saw Frizer standing next to Cyclops. Both were staring at me. Then Krake shouted, 'Shoulder your pikes. March.' And the long column began snaking out of the camp.

Twenty-Nine

Spirits were high. Men joked, laughed and sang as they marched. Although I joined in all the time, I felt that Cyclops's baleful eye was boring into the back of my head. Frizer had left us. At least I hoped he had. You could never tell with him.

The spirits of we new recruits began falling somewhat as the countryside showed more of the devastation of war. The vine that had cheered our hearts last evening had died unpruned and ploughshares in the fields had rusted while nearby cottages lay in ruins, roofless, with fire-blackened walls. This, I thought, could have been England if the Spaniards had landed in eighty-eight. Still could be if Essex's wild ambition started a civil war like the one we and Spain were intervening in now.

A few coins were tossed to emaciated beggars, while other people fled into the woods at our approach. At a village that had escaped complete destruction the villagers sold us a few things, but with a sullen air. No doubt to the French the English are still the enemy. And now, Huguenots apart, we were heretics fighting for an heretical king. The faces of the peasants were as bleak as the war-scarred winter landscape.

After a few days hard marching we came up with the rest of the army, encamped outside a small town. Although a day late we had, as Houndsditch said, brought our welcome with us in the wagon containing the pay. To my, admittedly inexperienced, eye the town looked strongly fortified with its ditches and walls and a marsh to the north. Haaker agreed.

The position allotted to us was opposite the west wall. It looked like we had only a watching brief with the action elsewhere. Trenches were being dug on the south side and passages smashed through old houses right up to the counterscarp. Then we heard that a long trench was being dug on the east side with a platform of earth in the middle for the cannon. There were grumbles that others would get into the town first and grab all the plunder. Blowing out a cloud of smoke Haaker jabbed his pipe at it and said, 'In England you say the screen of smoke, ja?'

'Smoke-screen, Dutchy,' replied Houndsditch. 'Talk proper English, for Gawd's sake. Anyway, what's that got to do with us getting our fair share of the loot?'

Houndsditch got his answer that evening at dusk when a company of sappers arrived and began digging a mine. The extra picks and shovels they had brought were handed to us and we began digging gun emplacements. Since for several years I had used only a pen, my hands were soon a mass of blisters. But at least it looked like we would have first chance of plunder. Also a chance of getting killed as we fought our way in. But no one thought of that.

As we ate our supper around the campfire the talk soon turned to what we would spend our anticipated wealth on. Naturally, most plumped for women. Although after our long marches and hard digging I doubt that many of us would have had the strength to do anything just then. Houndsditch would have been one of the exceptions. He had let one of his debtors off the interest in return for doing his share of the digging. The other exception would have been a scout who had lain all day in a forward position keeping the town under observation, making notes of its strengths and as a guard against surprise attack. He and Houndsditch lovingly discussed the

269

London bawdy-houses from Shoreditch to Turnbull Street, Picket-hatch to Southwark.

'Yes,' said Houndsditch dreamily; 'once we're in the town it's the ladies I'll spend my loot on.'

'You won't need to spend any money,' said the scout licking his lips. 'You can just take them. And that's how I likes it.'

'Christ, man,' croaked a red-faced Houndsditch; 'I wish we hadn't started this talk. I'm as randy as the town bull and not a heifer in sight.'

'Me too,' growled the other. 'There's a few wenches in that town will get it hot and hard when I gets in there.'

Like most of the others I was too tired to contemplate anything but the deep sleep into which I quickly fell. Next day everyone was hard at work again. Except of course for Houndsditch and the scout, with the latter lying in his forward position. As I was digging, a sudden shouting and pointing at the town made me turn my head. From a postern gate had emerged a party of women, heads modestly lowered, apparently out to enjoy a walk in the sun. No one, of course, would fire on women. Female-starved, we gaped. The scout did more. Jumping to his feet he ran towards them.

'I'm going to get some too,' said Houndsditch. Some of us held him back saying he would be shot for deserting his post. Struggling free he said, 'There's no officers about.'

'Let him go,' urged one of his debtors. By now the scout had reached the women. Throwing back their hoods to reveal beards they grabbed him and hustled him in through the gate. Not long after his head appeared impaled on a church steeple. Houndsditch turned white.

That night there was a raid from the town on the decoy trenches. Their mistake was brought home to them next day when cannon were dragged into our section to bombard the western wall. Now we could rest while the

270

gunners scurried to and fro carrying powder and shot. They poured in the powder, rammed down wadding and ball and the cannoneer applied match to touch hole. We cheered as the cannon roared, belching fire and smoke, sending a ball crashing against the wall. Our position was out of musket range so we lay on the grass feeling completely safe. Like an audience watching a tragedy being enacted on the stage. Without warning a cannon ball whistled over our heads, sending us diving into the trench. The defenders had placed a cannon on a church steeple. Some of our gunners were told to bombard it. Shortly after, they hit the steeple bringing down cannon, cannoneers and the scout's head.

Gradually the relentless pounding of the same small area of wall had its effect. The masonry cracked, crumbled and fell. The parapet was battered down and a small breach made. But it was continually repaired by the defenders who maintained the rampart by flinging in feather beds, horse dung, bags of earth. More guns were brought to bear. Now the breach was looking assailable. When General Sir John Norris asked for a volunteer to examine it, Sergeant Krake stepped forward. The musketeers advanced to give him covering fire and the cannoneers played their shot along the parapet.

Krake had courage. Although under fire he took time to inspect the breach thoroughly. The lives of a lot of men could depend on his report. We learned later that the assessment he gave the General was negative; the approach to the breach was steep and sliding. Krake was to prove right. Our French allies urged an assault but Norris was not in favour, especially as the mine had not yet been pushed far enough. Still they clamoured for an attack saying that if the English were afraid then the French would launch it. That settled it. Norris had no option but to undertake it.

'The honour of you Englanders is at stake,' said Haaker gravely. Fat Tim solemnly nodded his agreement and Houndsditch said, 'Yes. Plus we'll get first chance at looting the place.'

I saw Cyclops cleaning his musket and felt more afraid of him behind me than the enemy in front. But it turned out that our company was not to be in the first attack. We formed the reserve. I, and I suspect others, felt relief. From the moment preparations for the assault began, that breach in the wall seemed to grow narrower and steeper. And behind it would be a formidable array of weapons. It would be like rushing into a dragon's mouth. The attackers would be pierced with swords and pikes while muskets and cannon spat fire.

After a final cannonade and volleys of musketry the pikemen advanced with drums beating and flags flying. Many fell from musket balls. After struggling up the slope they fought a fierce bout of push at pike for half an hour. But eventually the accuracy of Krake's report had to be recognised and the bugle sounded the retreat. Our spokesman back at the camp had, as Haaker predicted, been put in the front rank. He did not return.

Another disaster quickly followed. Perhaps because of so many men trampling over it there had been an earth fall in the mine. Many of the sappers had been buried alive. The others were exhausted. On top of working long and hard to finish the mine they had been digging frantically to rescue their buried comrades. Mostly in vain. Those of us who had been held in reserve were now drafted in to help finish the work. It was hot, hard and confined; and at the earth-face, dark. Frightening. We eased the tension by making jokes about having to enlarge the tunnel to accommodate Fat Tim. Surprisingly the one who took to it best was Houndsditch. He had gone down the opening like a ferret after a rabbit. Perhaps all that lurking in London's lowest dens had acclimatised him.

272

One of the sappers had been put with us to supervise setting the pit props. While I was taking a break from the earth-face he told me he was a Durham coal-miner and had volunteered for the army to have a break from the mines. Letting slip the nature of his job, he had been drafted into the sappers. Breaking off abruptly, he ordered the digging to stop. Lying down he put his ear to the earth.

'They're digging a countermine,' he said.

In the heat of that tunnel I felt a sudden chill. To die under the ground seemed worse than dying in the open air. It had been bad enough before but now we had to live with the fear that at any moment the ground beneath our feet might be blown up bringing the earth above down on our heads. I had to fight against the terror of that dank smelling earth filling my mouth and nostrils. Being from Holland my mother had instilled in me the belief that we should tolerate those of other nationalities and religions. Now, under my breath, I cursed, with the vilest words I could think of, Frenchmen, Spaniards and Catholics. It helped.

The attack when it came was not, as I expected, from below but from alongside. Just before the miner covered the lantern I saw the gleam of a pick head as it poked through the wall of the tunnel. In the darkness the smell of damp earth seemed stronger. Without being aware of it I had picked up an axe used for trimming the pit props. In the stillness my ears strained for the sound of the pick enlarging the hole. Stripped to the waist, I felt a trickle of earth falling onto my back. Was the digging going to bring down the roof on us? Trapped in stifling blackness I fought down rising panic. If the trickling earth had not stopped I might have broke and run. From the wall I heard a fall of earth and a man's grunt. The lantern flashed out and in its glare appeared the startled face of the digger. The miner drove a dagger into his throat. When a man behind him levelled a pistol I swung my axe. I felt it jar on bone. He screamed and the pistol flamed and roared. Someone on our side was screaming and earth was falling rapidly from the roof.

'Get out,' shouted the miner. Tim was groaning, 'My leg, my leg.' Men from the earth-face pushed past. I grabbed one of Tim's arms while the miner grabbed the other and we dragged him bumping and sobbing along the tunnel and into the open.

Tim was carried to the surgeon's tent and laid on a table. The surgeon cut away his stocking to reveal his leg shattered below the knee with the bone sticking out. He said briskly, 'It'll have to come off.' We stopped Tim's protests with a bottle of acqua vitae to his lips. Then he was transferred to a strong, steady bench and laid near an end. One assistant bestrode the bench behind him and held both his arms. Another man bestrode the leg to be cut off and held it with a good firm grip above where the cut was to be made. A third held the leg below the knee. When the surgeon picked up his knife I made to leave but Tim begged me to stay. With a quick, steady hand the surgeon cut away the flesh around the wound. Ignoring Tim's screams, he picked up his saw and with a light hand speedily sawed off the leg. Mercifully, Tim fainted. Haaker, who was standing beside me, said approvingly, 'A surgeon must have a good eye, a strong arm and a stout heart.'

Everything was ready, if negotiations failed, to assault the breach. Fresh troops had gone in, secured the tunnel and blocked up the enemy one. Then we had pushed on with the mine. There had been greater urgency because news had come through that an army of crack Spanish troops from the Netherlands had traversed Normandy and was marching through Brittany to relieve the town. This was good news for Haaker because it took the pressure off his countrymen; but bad news for us since we would be heavily outnumbered. However, since the town was completely sealed off, they would not know of the approaching army so Norris might be able to browbeat them into surrendering.

They were invited to inspect the mine and saw it packed with barrels of gunpowder all ready to be blown. Then, in the middle of the negotiations, a lone rider burst through our lines and under a hail of musket fire got into the town. When the Governor of the town asked for time to consider the proposals Norris knew that the talking was over. He had to withdraw or make an immediate attack. A council of war had been called and we awaited its decision. Ever since being pulled out of the mine and told to rest we had known what our position would be in the event of an attack; leading it.

Our cannon had knocked down more of the wall, widening the breach; the mine should widen it further and, we hoped, flatten the slope. The risk was we might be caught fighting in the town with the Spanish army attacking our rear. But so much effort had been put into the siege and we seemed so close to taking the town that for Norris the temptation to gamble on the assault succeeding quickly must have been great. Also he knew that it would be bad for morale to withdraw without making another attempt. The Governor was also gambling. Having turned down an offer of terms after his walls had been breached meant that the town could, by the rules of war, be sacked and the garrison put to the sword.

While we waited dice rattled onto the drumheads as men whose lives might be part of a gamble themselves gambled pay, future pay and even future plunder. Tim was recovering and waiting to be fitted with a wooden leg. Gangrene carried off most wounded men so Tim was lucky. He kept asking people if they thought it would be difficult to make a living with only one leg. We tried to reassure him except for Houndsditch who joked, 'You'll save a fortune in shoes and stockings.'

275

Captain Sarsfield returned from the council of war with his orders. Immediate attack. We quickly lined up; then, with shouldered pikes, began advancing – drums beating, fifes screaming. Cannonballs tore through our ranks while from the walls we came under heavy musket fire. Our musketeers in front of us fired back; Cyclops among them. I hoped he would get shot because soon I would be in advance of him. The breach was unmanned. They would be holding its defenders back ready to rush forward once the mine had been blown. We passed the musketeers and Krake shouted, 'Halt. Lower your pikes.' The points came down forming a steel hedgehog. Musketeers on the walls moved further from the breach while we waited, heads lowered. Then the ground ahead of us erupted with a tremendous roar and I felt a tremor beneath my feet while earth and stones rattled down on our helmets. For a moment we stood stock still with shock then Captain Sarsfield waved his sword and Krake bawled, 'Charge.'

We charged into the swirling smoke and dust screaming like devils. They met us with roaring cannon, their flames stabbing through the murk. A body was flung against me and my face was wet with blood. Bursting from the dust-cloud we ran into a line of pikemen. We thrust and jabbed at each other until pressure from behind forced us right up against them. Now it was push and shove as with our pikes upright we battered at each other with the butt ends. It was a hard, bruising fight with musketeers on the walls firing into us. The defenders were desperate knowing what their fate would be if they lost. But slowly, by weight of numbers, we were pushing them back. The end was close when we broke through their line and began herding them into small groups.

Winded by a blow to the stomach, I paused to regain my breath. I looked around at the smoke-blackened faces of my comrades exultant with the prospect of plunder. No mercy was shown to the defeated. Men lying on the ground pleading for their lives were run through with swords and pikes or had their brains battered out with musket butts. Cyclops was reloading his musket his one eye darting this way and that.

A corporal grabbed my arm and pointed at a line of enemy pikemen across the entrance to a street. Gathering others we charged, driving them back. The street was lined with rich-looking shops; drapers, mercers and a jeweller's. Some of our men deserted the line to break into them. When the corporal intervened he was knocked to the ground. Suddenly from the walls we heard shouting and cheering and cries of, 'The Spaniards.' The line of defenders took up the cry and attacked us with renewed vigour. Our men coming out of the shops laden with robes and jewellery were cut down. Now we were being driven back, while all through the town rang their rallying cry, 'The Spaniards, the Spaniards.'

'We're trapped,' shouted the man next to me. I looked round. The entrance to the street was blocked by another line of enemy pikemen. Then, like a death knell, we heard our bugles sounding the retreat.

Thirty

Several men threw down their weapons and begged for mercy. But after the slaughter our troops had committed it was obvious that none of us was going to get out of that street alive. It showed in the grim faces of the soldiers advancing on either side of us with levelled pikes. Throwing down my pike I jumped through the broken window of a tavern. An English soldier, snoring heavily, was lying on the floor dead drunk. That would soon be literally true, I thought, running for the back door. Coming out into a yard I could hear men pounding through the tavern behind me. Whether friends or foes, I did not stop to look but leaped at a wall, clawing my way to the top. Across the roofs of a row of houses was the town wall. It was crowded with musketeers firing at our men trapped in the town.

From the tavern the corporal burst into the yard, blood streaming down his face. He jumped for the top of the wall and I caught his wrist to help him up. But from the tavern doorway a soldier fired a pistol hitting the corporal in the back. He fell to the ground, groaned, then lay still. A musket ball whistled past my ear. The soldiers on the ramparts were firing at me. Bent double, I ran along the wall then dropped down into a garden. I hurriedly cast off my cumbersome armour and scrambled through a hedge.

Now I knew how the fox felt as those trapped inside the walls were hunted through the town. And we had no earths to bolt to. I did find one later and the memory of it can still make my stomach heave. But for now I was in a lane, listening to the sounds of battle inside and outside the town. How to get outside and rejoin my comrades? At the end of the lane was the town wall. Lying at the foot of it was the body of a soldier, a musket beside him. The rampart was deserted. Picking up the musket as a cover I ran up the steps and looked over the parapet.

Our army was in retreat. A rearguard was covering it against attack by the garrison who had issued out through the breach and the main gate. From the east a cloud of dust signalled the advancing Spanish infantry. Some squadrons of their cavalry were just beginning to engage the English cavalry. There was no hope of me rejoining my company. Haaker, Fat Tim and Houndsditch, even Krake and the corrupt Sarsfield, seemed like brothers now. How I longed to be with them.

From the foot of the steps came a shout in French. Looking round I saw a group of soldiers. Although my French was quite good it was difficult to penetrate the thick Breton accent. But picking out 'Anglais', coupled with the waving of his sword towards the breach, made it clear that he wanted me to join the attack on the besiegers. Pointing over the wall I laid the musket on the parapet and pretended to take careful aim. My ears strained to pick out from the din of battle their tread on the steps. If they came up to investigate me I would be betrayed by my lack of a Breton accent. Aiming the musket at random I applied the match to the touch-hole. The roar and hard recoil against my shoulder surprised me. I peered through the smoke, shouted, 'Oui,' and turned with a triumphant face as though I had hit my man. But I was playing to an empty theatre; my audience had moved on.

Haaker had taught me the rudiments of musketry so I reloaded then moved in the opposite direction to the soldiers. That end of the town, I reasoned, would be deserted and I would have a chance of going over the wall. A detour should eventually bring me back to the

English army. First I came down from the wall. It was too conspicuous up there.

I also found that working my way eastwards through back lanes and alleys made me conspicuous. Being alone I stood out like a scarecrow at a wedding. People looked out of windows and stared at me. An old man shouted something. From around a corner I heard someone begging for mercy in English. His offer of being ransomed was followed by a scream. Either they did not understand English or had no interest in money. I jumped over a wall into a garden with a pungent smell. Just in time; for I heard boots tramping past. Then in the distance I heard the quavering voice of the old man followed by the tramping boots returning. Since I had not passed them they would have an idea of where I'd gone. The stench in the garden was coming from a pigsty. Without hesitation I dived into it. The pigs looked at me, decided I wasn't a trough-looter and stuck their snouts back in the swill. The snuffling pigs were music in my ears compared to the thud of boots landing in the garden. And give me honking porkers anytime before ferocious Bretons bellowing, 'Merde Anglais.'

The soldiers' voices and boots passed on to be succeeded by female voices. It was obvious who they were talking about. Their use of 'Anglais' was coupled with 'Gorge.' They were afraid I was going to break into their houses and cut their throats. I did not want to get in anywhere; all I wanted was to get out. Out of the pigsty, out of the town, out of the country. But still the women went on talking. At least I was getting to hear the Breton accent. It could prove useful since I have a good ear for dialect. But the stench of the pigsty was becoming overpowering. Those women seemed to talk for hours. It was hours because when I finally heard their doors being shut and bolted it was growing dark. Thankfully I took my leave of my unfragrant hosts who gave me a farewell

280

honk. In a Breton accent, I expect. The musket was clogged with pig shit so I left it.

Celebrations for the town's deliverance were well underway. Wine was flowing and people were dancing in the streets by the light of torches. There were also more sinister sights. Bodies were being dragged towards the town centre, kicked and spat at by the dancers. I stumbled over a drunk lying senseless, a half-empty bottle of wine beside him. Wine was what I needed. Picking it up I took a good long drink

Another English body was being dragged past. A grossly fat man in a butcher's apron kicked it savagely. Looking at me he pointed, inviting me to do the same. To refuse could be dangerous but I was damned if I was going to kick a fallen comrade. Not if I could help it, anyway. Time for some more acting. Waving the wine bottle I took a running kick at the body, missed and fell flat on my back. The onlookers roared with laughter. Eat your heart out, Kempe, I thought as I lay on the ground. The butcher, who was truly well stewed, staggered over with outstretched hand to help me up. Bending over me he caught the full blast of the pigsty and spewed his guts into the gutter. Getting up I ambled on through the crowds disguised as a drunkard and armoured in a stink. I had no need to risk a Breton accent. Real topers who approached me as another maltworm soon forgot about convivial conversation as they struggled to retain the contents of their stomachs.

Although I had no appetite then, I would need to have food when I left the town. Having only English money was the problem. Until it occurred to me that I could act as if I had taken it from an English soldier. In the fighting I had received a cut face and a swollen eye so I must have looked as terrible as I smelt. Holding up some coins at a pie stall I slurred, 'Anglais.' The pieman looked dubious but other customers were holding their noses and turning away so he took the money. When I dithered over a beef pie and a venison pie he thrust both into my hands and shooed me away.

The crowds were thinning now as I moved in the direction of the wall. Soon the streets were deserted and I had no need to act drunk. But the wine was acting on my empty stomach and I was feeling drunk. I could not eat anything until I had washed off at least some of the pigsty. Now I was getting drowsy. But knowing that I must escape from the town while it was dark kept me going. The only light was from the stars. Ahead of me loomed the dark bulk of the wall. But which part? I searched the sky for the Pole Star but had to stop when my head began spinning.

Groping my way along the wall I came to a stairway. I climbed it on hands and knees, keeping an eye out for sentries. But with the English army in full retreat they would be relaxed about keeping a look-out. On the rampart it struck me that I had no rope to climb down. That blow on the head must have been harder than I realized because I'd not given it a thought. The wall was surely too high to risk dropping. There would likely be a ditch making the drop steeper. I might break a leg. But I was desperate. I had to get out of the town before morning. Either it was the lack of food or the wine or more likely both but as I leaned over the wall trying to make out how far off the ground was, my head swam and I toppled forward.

A soft landing told me that I had fallen from the north wall into the marsh. Thank God, I thought, until trying to get up I only sank deeper. Panic sent me struggling forward. Reaching firmer ground I dragged my legs from the morass. Then began a nightmare, hours long, of hauling myself from island to island of firm ground through what seemed miles of the clinging, sucking, slimy quagmire. At last I came out of the slough onto ground

282

that remained firm. Crawling amongst some bushes I fell into an exhausted sleep.

When I awoke the sun was up. My clothes were steaming and I stunk. The stink of the pigsty was overlaid by the far worse stench of the swamp. I smelt like a night-soil man who has been for a swim in Fleet Ditch. As for sight I must have looked like one of the Bedlam beggars who roam around England. Even the thought of Fleet Ditch and Bedlam made me homesick for London. Elizabeth would be told I was missing, probably dead. And now the sun clouded over, leaving me shivering with cold. The food in my pocket had been spoilt by the marsh so I was also hungry. The Reverend Bracegirdle would have said, "These things are sent to try our souls," and I would have kicked him into the marsh and when, slime-encrusted as me, he had crawled out, would have asked him if he still felt the same. This thought cheered me slightly as I walked away from the town swinging my arms to keep warm.

In the distance I saw a group of travellers walking beside laden mules. My first thought was to take cover; but it was an open plain. There was a wood some way off but running there would make them suspicious. Search parties I did not want. In my opinion I had given a good performance the previous night of a drunken Breton; so why not now play a Bedlam beggar or whatever was the French equivalent? Twisting my mouth awry, I adopted a shuffling, lopsided gait. As we neared I saw that having the wind behind me was proving a help. The travellers were wrinkling their noses and moving to the other side of the road. When I put my hand up to my mouth and made chewing motions they placed a generous amount of bread and cheese with a bottle of ale on the ground before hurrying on.

Food and drink feed the spirit as much as the body. After I had eaten I thought less about returning to England

and more about rejoining the army. What Haaker had said was true. If the war was not fought in France it would be fought in England. Shortly after I found a stream and cold as it was plunged in. At last I cleaned the filth off my body, even if I could not get it all out of my clothes. After rubbing myself dry I set off westward at a brisk pace my skin glowing.

Increasing numbers of coaches, carts and horsemen on the road indicated I was approaching a town. A few, a very few, coins were thrown to me which I picked up eagerly. Using my English money would be risky now. Large numbers of people were thronging into the town, most of them thin with sad, pinched faces, the debris of a country broken by war. But their faces also had a fevered excitement which I thought I recognised. The crowd carried me into the market-square and I saw the grim reason for the excitement. In the centre was a stake surrounded by faggots. Because I was a Protestant surrounded by Catholics I naturally thought they were burning a Huguenot. But they were going to burn a witch. Stories were swapped of curses, healthy cattle and poultry suddenly dying, inexplicable accidents occurring. She had given information to the heretic English soldiers; hadn't people seen her flying through the air to the English camp? Anyone casting doubt would have been in grave danger of being charged as an accomplice. These people needed a scapegoat. I had no stomach for this and pushed out of the crowd. As I was leaving the town the breeze carried to my nostrils the sickly sweet smell of burning flesh.

Through sleet, hail, wind and rain I trudged westwards begging my food and sleeping in barns or under hedges. One freezing night I slept in a cave. Next morning a row of icicles hung down at the entrance like lion's teeth. Alternately shivering and sweating I wandered, lost, through a forest unable to tell if its noises were animal,

284

human or delusions of my fevered brain. Covering myself with a blanket I had found some days earlier drying on a hedge, I fell into a troubled sleep. In my nightmare figures leapt at me from the undergrowth as I ran through the forest: Cyclops with one eye in the middle of his forehead spouting blood; Ingram Frizer brandishing the head of James Stour. Running between the trees I collided with the body of Tribulation Cheadle hanging upside down and recoiled into Blackbeard hanging by the neck, his tongue sticking out of his mouth. Fleeing from these into a clearing I came on a witch burning at the stake the flesh running off her face to reveal a grinning demon beneath.

I awoke with my head clear to find three armed men staring down at me.

Thirty-One

Unless I kept my nerve my nightmare would soon be reality. Adopting the lopsided expression of the idiot, I mumbled some French words.

'We know you are English,' said the tall man in the centre. My stomach was knotted with fear. I had heard in taverns and from pulpits the tortures Catholics inflicted on Protestants. And as a child I'd had nightmares from the horrors related in Foxe's Book of Martyrs.

'Do not fear,' said the tall man. 'We are Huguenots and we believe you are a soldier trying to rejoin the English army at Brest.'

'How did you know I was English?' I asked, a split-second before it occurred to me that it might be a trick.

'You were talking in your sleep,' he replied simply. Taking me into a clearing where there were several men, women and children he said, 'We too are trying to reach Brest, with our families, to take ship for England.'

I was invited to join them for a meal and while they ate they told me of their life in France. The tall man's name was Jean Bodin and he was the only one who spoke English. He said, 'We are from a small town and for many years we lived in peace with our Catholic neighbours. For the most part they were good people and were horrified by the massacre of St Bartholomew's Day. But as the fighting dragged on their fanatics, well, yes, ours also, began making trouble. But the good people on both sides were able to control them. Save for one who hated we Calvinists. Ragueneau.'

At the name the heads of the others jerked round with several looking frightened. Bodin continued, 'Many think Ragueneau is the devil.' I must have looked sceptical because he added, 'I too used to argue against this, saying he was merely a bad man. From a child he played cruel tricks and jokes on our community. He told a mother her child had fallen in the river and drowned and acted it so well she was screaming. My people said it was his devil's nature showing through. But I said no, it is just that he is a bad human being. This I said until a few weeks ago, until just before we are forced to leave our home town. Then Ragueneau brought an assassin to our town and when he had done his work Ragueneau made him disappear. Sent him back to Hell, my people say.

'One of our leaders was allowed on the town's Common Council to represent our community. Of course, some Catholics, with Ragueneau urging them on, were angered. As the council walked in procession through the town a man dressed in black stabbed the Calvinist member to the heart and ran off. When we got over the shock we ran in pursuit. Ragueneau and his friends blocked our way holding us up for a few minutes but we got past them. We came to a long lane and on the corner this good lady...' he pointed to one of the women and explained in French what he was telling me. She nodded vigorously.

Turning back to me he continued, 'She told us that a man clad in black with his clothes bloodstained had run down the lane. We followed. The lane led out of the town onto a large open moor. There was no sign of the murderer – only a procession of about a dozen Carmelite Friars.'

At the name there were angry words from the others. Bodin said, 'They say the friars were devils from Hell and the smoke swirling around them was a sign from God to warn us.'

287

'What smoke?' I asked.

'There was a fire by a garden wall burning fallen leaves. But of the murderer there was no sign. The only men – if they were so – were the Carmelite Friars in their white overmantles.'

I said, 'He took his clothes off and threw them on the fire and the friars had a white mantle ready for him.'

Bodin shook his head: 'There would have been no time for the clothes to burn; also, when we raked the fire there was no trace of cloth.'

'He put the mantle over his clothes,' I suggested.

'Although the Mayor was a Catholic he wanted to find the murderer. He was a just man. And most of us did not want religious strife in our town. So the friars were searched thoroughly. None of them had clothes beneath their mantles. The moor is flat and bare so if he had run across it he would have still been in sight. The garden walls along the lane were too high for him to have climbed over. And it was the Protestant quarter so no one would have taken him in. We searched the gardens and found nothing. The friars claimed they had seen no one.

'After that, tension in the town built up. Ragueneau was imprisoned but had to be released for lack of evidence. He joined the Catholic League and when rumours reached the town that he was returning with an armed force, some of us decided to leave. We heard later that those of our friends who stayed behind were massacred by Ragueneau's men. Since then he has been seeking us.'

It was time to move on. I looked around at the careworn faces of the men, women and children plodding towards Brest and thought that a short while ago they had been leading happy, prosperous lives. Now they were carrying everything they owned. Many of the women had babies on their backs.

With scouts ahead of us we moved slowly through the forest, swords and daggers drawn. Every rustle of an animal in the bushes, every flutter of a bird in the treetops stretched our nerves. But at least the trees and bushes concealed us. The time to fear would be when we had to emerge into the open. And so it proved.

A scout returned from the edge of the forest to report horsemen. They were too far off for him to make out whether they were English, French or Spanish. We halted. Then another scout arrived to say that all was clear. We moved on to the edge, then halted again. Ahead was open country. Some wanted to wait until dark before leaving the forest. Others were for pushing on arguing that almost all the food was gone and many of the children were sick. And with the weather getting much colder, some might die. Everyone turned to Bodin. He said that the scouts believed we were either in the territory controlled by the English army or very close to it. If we waited for night we might lose our way and wander into enemy territory. So, full of trepidation, we moved into the open.

Before we had got far, horsemen appeared on the horizon. While we stood irresolute Bodin sent the scouts to investigate them. Through the clear frosty air shots rang out and the riders charged towards us. While some of us were forming a circle around the women and children others wanted to flee back to the forest. Women and children screamed as Bodin roared at them to stay or they would be rode down. In the event of being captured some hoped the enemy were French while others said the Spanish would be better than their own countrymen. As the horsemen approached in two long lines swords glittering in the bright sunshine we saw that they heavily outnumbered us. The leader held up his hand and they halted. He shouted at us to lay down our arms. They were French. No one answered. A bugle rang out and he pointed to our right. Another line of riders was galloping

289

towards our small band. They could sweep right around us. The position was hopeless. When Bodin tried to ask for terms he was told to surrender immediately or take the consequences. Bodin looked at the faces of the men and women around him, just one or two despairing but most, now that the first panic was over, resigned to their fate. Telling them that it was the will of God, Bodin laid down his sword and the rest of us followed suit. All I had left of the weapons the government had provided me with was my dagger. I had been anticipating the rough edge of Krake's tongue when I rejoined the army. That was now the least of my worries.

The horsemen rode up and took possession of the arms. As the second band of horsemen approached the Huguenots had need of all the stoicism they could muster. The name whispered among them sounded in their mouths like the wings of the angel of death; Ragueneau.

Dismounting he strode up to us. He was solidly built with a thin smile across his clean-shaven white face, like wintry sunlight on a tombstone. Tension rose as he slowly looked us over. He snapped an order and our hands were bound. Another order and some of his men remounted and rode to the edge of the forest. We watched in silence as they threw ropes with nooses over the branches. Ragueneau said, 'You have a last chance to convert to the true religion before you die.'

'We have the true religion,' said Bodin. 'It is for you to convert.'

Ragueneau's face turned whiter still. He drew his dagger, grasped Bodin's hair, said, 'You have hearkened to the blasphemies of Calvin for too long, my friend,' and sliced off his ears. Bodin responded with a fervent plea to God to show this disciple of Baal the true light. Ragueneau slit his nose to the bone grunting, 'That's for your damned nasal whining.' To his men he shouted, 'Hang them up.'

Telling them I was an English soldier was useless. Prisoners were not being taken in this war. They marched us towards the trees. Bodin, who had fainted with pain, had to be supported. But he still managed to join in the communal prayer. I knew I should be praying but all I could think of was the bitterness of death; and so close to the English lines. Elizabeth would have urged me to make my peace with God but all I could think of was her. Determined not to give my captors the satisfaction of seeing me break down I stiffened my resolve with the commonplace, death is a debt that must be paid. Perhaps I would go as quickly as Blackbeard. But then he'd had Derrick, a professional hangman, while I had a bunch of bloody amateurs. Anyway, they would probably consider Derrick a milksop for finishing his victims off so quickly. With them a bit of suffering would not be out of order.

Gallows humour runs dry as you near the gallows. I was finding it more and more difficult to put one foot in front of the other and was pushed several times by my captors. The deep faith of the Huguenots was making it easier for them to accept death. Then the psalm they were singing was interrupted by a bugle. My heart flew up like a lark.

The Catholic Leaguers hastily remounted and rode to meet the English cavalry charging across the plain, banners streaming. Now it was the turn of our captors to be outnumbered. While they clashed with the main body of the English, another squadron wheeled around to outflank them. With our hands tied we could only stand and look on at the fight that would decide our fate. Swords clashed and rang on helmet and breastplate, horses neighed, men cursed and cheered as the Catholic troops were gradually forced back. When the English launched an attack on their other flank the Catholic line began to break up. Men were turning their horses to flee. Surrounded on three sides their only way was through the forest. At a rustling behind me I turned and saw English pikemen with Krake at their head advancing from between the trees. The trap had snapped shut.

There was a fierce fight in which few prisoners were taken. Ragueneau was one of them, having been clubbed from his horse with the butt end of a pistol. I saw Houndsditch rummage through the saddlebag and pull out a bottle of wine, brandishing it triumphantly.

The officer commanding the cavalry had been killed so Krake took command. After ordering the prisoners bound and us freed he said, 'We'll take two back for questioning. One for Captain Sarsfield and one for me. Keep them separate. Hang the rest.'

One of the women shouted at Ragueneau, 'Now you'll hang, like Haman, on a gallows you designed for others.'

When he swore at her Krake said, 'Save your breath, you'll need it when the rope's around your neck.'

'Protestant pig,' said Ragueneau in English and made a squealing noise. Krake forced his mouth open with one hand and with the other drew a knife and cut out his tongue. He threw it at me and said, 'I know I'm a bastard, Dekker, but I'm a Protestant bastard.'

Ragueneau was hanged with the blood spurting from his mouth. Houndsditch took a swig of his wine then handed the bottle to me saying, 'Cheer up, Tom. Don't you know?, it's Christmas Day.'

Thirty-Two

On the way back to the camp I got all the news. Antoon Haaker had been wounded at the siege but was recovering. Fat Tim was hobbling around on crutches. Captain Sarsfield was in a cheerful mood because, it was believed, (rightly in my view) that he was keeping the names of men who had been killed on the books and pocketing their pay. He was going to be disappointed when I came back from the dead. When I made this last remark to Houndsditch he said, 'Well I'm glad you realised we all thought you were dead, Tom, because it makes it easier to explain about your parcel.'

'My parcel?'

'Yes. We thought you'd want us to have the food. We drank a toast to your memory.'

'A toast?'

'Yes. There was a bottle of wine in there as well. And I knew you'd want your old friend Houndsditch Harry Potts to have the stockings.'

'Stockings as well.'

'Yes. I know you won't want them now after they've been on my foul-smelling feet. Very warm they are, too.'

'Can you tell me who the parcel was from?'

'Certainly. It was in the letter.'

'Which, of course, you opened.'

'Of course. There might have been important news in it. As it is I can tell you that the parcel was from your dearest Elizabeth and your loving mother. I almost shed a

293

tear. It was with great regret that we wrote to tell them of your sad demise.'

'You did what?' I yelped coming to a stop.

'Keep moving there,' bawled Krake. 'Shoulder that pike properly, Dekker. And stop slouching.' Even in my famished condition the bastard had made me carry a pike.

'Don't worry,' said Houndsditch as we marched; 'I told them you died like a hero fighting for – whatever it is we're fighting for.'

I groaned, 'If Elizabeth thinks I'm dead she may go back to my rival.'

'Look on the bright side, Tom. She may cross with the letter at sea.'

'What do you mean?'

'In her letter she said she'd almost raised the money to pay Sarsfield for your release and was hoping to get a passage out here soon.'

That was just like Elizabeth to bring it out herself. That cheered me up until Houndsditch added that a friend had offered to accompany her. Mulcaster, I thought. Who knew what might develop between them on a ship at sea. A gentle swell on a moonlit night. To mutual respect might be added mutual passion. I'm a mercurial character, a pessimist who keeps hoping, but my depression at the brutality I had just witnessed at the edge of the forest was deepened. My belief in and need for Elizabeth gave me an insight into the strength of faith that enabled Catholics and Protestants to die for their faith. Also the hatred that gnawed at the roots of their belief.

Arriving back at the camp, I was greeted by Fat Tim waving his crutch. He was to return to England on the first available ship and his old master had written to say that he would take him back on. He said gleefully, 'No more soldiering for me, I'm going back to old England.'

294

'What's left of you,' muttered Houndsditch, envious at his return to London. He grumbled, 'It should be me 'cos London's wasted on him.'

There was sickness in the camp, dysentery. Sarsfield looked a little sick at my return because he could no longer pocket my pay. But so many others had died that he soon cheered up. This fraud is one of the crying scandals of our day. Haaker, I was pleased to see, had recovered from his wound. We exchanged accounts of our experiences. I told him that the cruelty I had seen, by our side as well as theirs, had made me think England should leave France to settle its differences.

'No, no,' he cried vehemently. 'Do you think that if you go to bed and pull the clothes over your head that this will make you safe, that your enemies will go away? No. If England leaves France, Spain will stay. They will see you as being weak, which will be true. Then when they have settled things in France to their liking they will come over the Channel to you. My country can ill afford soldiers to fight here but the wiser sort know it is most necessary. By fighting in France I am defending the Netherlands.'

Haaker was right, of course. That is until Elizabeth came riding into the camp on a wagon. I ran to greet her and collapsed in the mud. It was dysentery to which sleeping in the open with little food had left me vulnerable; and it was far more serious than the fever I had suffered in the forest. I came close to dying. Elizabeth nursed me through it. They may well call it the bloody flux. While in the grip of the fever I relived all the horrors I had recently witnessed, raving about them like a madman.

When I came to myself, a horrified Elizabeth repeated what I had said and asked if any of it had happened. Not wanting to upset her I said that my raving owed more to the plays I had seen, like Titus Andronicus.

295

'And The Spanish Tragedy,' she said, pulling a face.

'I saw that,' said Houndsditch who had just come into the tent. 'I thought of that part where old Hieronimo bites his tongue out and spits it at the king when Krake cut that Catholic's tongue out.' He chuckled: 'I thought Tom here was going to faint when Krake threw the tongue at him.'

When Elizabeth had got rid of him she said, 'That settles it. I'm getting you away from here before you become as brutalised as him.'

I argued Haaker's case that we needed to be here and that not every soldier was like Houndsditch. Then I asked her what was really on my mind. Where was Mulcaster? To my relief she said she had travelled out with Nicholas Winton on his friend's ship. Nicholas had been unable to come out and see me because the ship had been due to leave on the next tide. It was a trading voyage to Turkey and he had gone to look for herbs for his shop.

My somewhat half-hearted argument for staying faded away when Elizabeth told me she had already paid Sarsfield for my discharge and showed me the paper. The dysentery had left me very weak and I could not be moved for sometime. There was a great deal of sickness in the camp and Elizabeth used the skills learned in handling staff at the Cross Keys to set up a hospital. She organised the heterogeneous group of women who sometimes tended the sick into a much more efficient nursing staff.

Bodin and his wife, who were staying with relatives in Brest while waiting to get a passage to England, came out to see me. Elizabeth told them that the atmosphere of the camp was delaying my recovery. They consulted their relatives then offered us lodgings. It was a house overlooking the harbour and the sea air did me a world of good. It took many more weeks to recover my strength but at last I was able to take ship for England.

As we entered the Thames, Elizabeth admitted she was a little uneasy about my return. Rumours were gathering that Essex might make a bid for power. Anyone who was seen as a threat would be swept aside. She said that during my fever a one-eyed man had tried to enter the tent but hearing me raging against such a man she had kept him out. There was no doubt in my mind that she had saved my life twice over. But now I was re-entering London, a city more dangerous to me than the battlefields of France.

Thirty-Three

Gliding up the Thames on the tide, I sniffed the perfumes of old Mother London; fish markets, tallow chandlers, tanneries. She clasped me in her arms; on one side Southwark with its Rose Playhouse but on the other side the Tower. Ahead was the Bridge. But whatever the dangers, my spirits rose at being back in London. As we disembarked at Billingsgate I even came up with a piece of extempore verse for Elizabeth. I said, 'What Marlowe should have written was:

Come live with me and be my love
And we will all the pleasures prove
That playhouse, bowling alley, inn
Give with the market's raucous din.'

Elizabeth pointed to the Bridge where a line of carts and coaches was streaming southwards out of the city. A passer-by said that the plague (which had been abating in the winter when Elizabeth left London) was reviving. Spring, a time of new life, was bringing death. The playhouses had been closed again and we passed a boarded up house with the red plague cross painted on it.

First we called to see my mother who had helped raise the money for my discharge. She confessed that she had mixed feelings about it since she believed that the powerful Catholic forces must be opposed. I admitted that I had mixed feelings about leaving myself. Even more so when I was now told that there were fresh rumours about another invasion attempt by Spain. There was talk that they would seize the Isle of Man and use it as a base to attack England.

My mother said, 'What I am going to say must not be repeated outside our circle. Many of the Puritan persuasion say that to combat Spain we must purify our church of all Popish idolatry. And that we must have the judicial law of Moses for punishing many sins with death and allow no king or queen to save the sinner. They would execute blasphemers of God's name, soothsayers, heretics, perjurers, breakers of the Sabbath day, neglecters of the sacraments,' getting very red in the face now, mother continued, 'incestuous persons, daughters who commit fornication in their father's houses, adulterers and, and – and some are saying that Protestants need a strong leader like the Earl of Essex.'

This was dangerous talk. But it also showed why Essex might be thinking he had enough support to make a bid to replace Lord Burghley as the Queen's chief minister. While in the army I had heard many soldiers speak of Essex in the same way. He certainly wanted to prosecute the war strongly while it was known that Burghley was looking for a way to make peace.

I called on Henslowe to see if he had any work for me. He was in a very gloomy frame of mind, moaning, 'Why does everyone take a delight in crossing me? Marlowe tells me he is too busy writing a long poem to finish his Faustus play.'

'But the playhouses are closed, Master Henslowe,' I pointed out. He looked at me balefully: 'You'd never make a speculator, Dekker. Trust placed in you as a venturer would be misplaced; money invested in you as a projector would be lost. When everyone is in work I don't sell off my pawnbroker's shop. I wait for better times when they're out of work and need me. The plague will abate, the playhouse will re-open. I want new plays against that.'

'Well I'll be happy to…'

'No, not from you, Dekker. From a popular playmaker like Marlowe. Or Shakespeare, if he were not also writing a long poem. And why doesn't Kyd write another Spanish Tragedy for me instead of translating some French play that no one will pay to see. But it's the Faustus play I want and will have.' His eyes took on an almost dream-like quality as he continued, 'All London is saying that Marlowe has sold his soul to the Devil and has written a play about it. My playhouse will be packed out day after day.'

'If he's not careful his head will decorate London Bridge,' I warned.

Henslowe looked anxious: 'Not before he's finished Faustus, I hope.' He gripped my arm: 'Go to him, Thomas. I've heard he likes you.'

'Oh no,' I said backing away. 'I've got a sweetheart – a female one.'

Opening his purse he carefully counted several coins into my hand saying, 'I'm sure you could do with something to tide you over, Thomas.'

Feigning ignorance as to his motive I said, 'You are a true friend, Master Henslowe.'

'Yes,' he said dryly. 'When I lend a poet money, I'm a friend, when I ask for it, I'm unkind. Persuade Marlowe to finish his play and that money will be a gift from a friend; fail to and it will be a loan from a moneylender charging full interest.'

I put off going to see Marlowe, who was staying with Thomas Walsingham at his house in Surrey. Money in my pocket always induces procrastination in my mind. However, I would have to make the attempt sometime. Henslowe had told me to tell Marlowe there would be extra money for his play. That showed how desperate he was for it. It was easy to understand why. There was a fascination with magic; with necromancy, witchcraft, conjuring up demons to foretell the future. People were worried about what would happen when the Queen died, she having no heir. They wanted reassurance. And there were plenty of soothsayers and astrologers to give it. Fake or genuine, who could say? And even prophecies of doom seemed welcome. Sixteen-hundred was only seven years away and many were saying it would be the doomsday foretold in the Book of Revelations. So a play about all of these by a rumoured blasphemer would draw people like bats to a belfry.

Peter and Rosie had taken care of my few possessions in Coldharbour Tenements, to which I had now returned. They had all the London news and rumours. Peter said, 'If you want a popular subject for one of your ballads then foreigners it is. Rhymes have been posted up all over town against strangers.'

That was a subject I would not write on; unless against the bigots. There was a feverish atmosphere in London. The churches, of course, were still open. But in my opinion they should also leave the theatres open. Plays give people a vent for their feelings. Peter wanted them open again as much as Henslowe. Rosie too, as a source of customers. She was always urging me to write plays about lustful lads and wanton wenches.

With Elizabeth I visited Bodin and his wife in the Huguenot quarter. He had let his hair grow to cover the loss of his ears but there was nothing he could do to conceal his disfigured nose. People did not know whether to look him in the face or not. With a slit nose being a common punishment for criminals in England it made finding employment difficult. Ragueneau had also left a mark on Bodin's mind. He repeated to me Ragueneau's boast about spiriting away the assassin and said that many felt Ragueneau's evil spirit had escaped from the corpse hanging on the tree. It disturbed me and I wished that Nicholas Winton, with his sceptical mind, was back in his

301

apothecary's shop to consult. But then he had been unable to say how the old woman had been murdered while alone in a locked room.

Even the Huguenots were talking about Essex as being the man to help their leader in the war. Many still hoped to return to France. There seemed to be a groundswell in England moving Essex towards power. But Raleigh and Burghley would not go under without a struggle.

The weeks passed and I had still not been to see Marlowe about Faustus. As well as Henslowe's money I had sold some more street ballads and a pamphlet on the plague. And I had begun a play about Mother Wingfield's murder. I hoped to find out how she had died before I reached the end. Meeting Henslowe I assured him that Faustus was proceeding apace. Well it cheered him up. He even began to calculate how big a bribe he would have to pay to get the Rose opened for a few performances. Never mind Faustus, Henslowe would sell his soul for a full house.

It could be put off no longer. I hired a horse in Southwark and rode down to Thomas Walsingham's house. A servant showed me into a room where Marlowe was writing behind a thick cloud of pungent tobacco smoke. As I fanned the fumes away Marlowe had a fit of coughing. Clearing his throat he said, 'I have no doubt that my inside is as black as Henslowe's soul.'

'It's Faustus' soul he's interested in,' I replied.

'Oh, the theatre. I'm engaged on a work that will bring me greater fame than a mere stage-play.'

'He's willing to pay more than the standard rate for it.'

He sighed: 'That is an argument I am seldom in a position to counter.' Pushing the manuscript he was working on over to me he pointed to some lines, then got up and walked to a cupboard. I read:

"Yet as a punishment they added this,
That he and poverty should always kiss.

And to this day is every scholar poor;
Gross gold from them runs headlong to the boor."

Substitute playmaker for scholar and it described me also. Marlowe returned with a thicker manuscript and threw it on the table saying, 'There it is, with comic scenes for Kempe, as requested. Where's the money?'

'You know Henslowe will want to negotiate the amount with you himself.'

'Yes, and the damned rogue will drive as hard a bargain for my poetic soul as Lucifer did for that of Faustus' scholarly one.'

Marlowe is not the type to invite idle questions but I was impelled by the same curiosity as the rest of London and blurted out, 'Some are saying you've sold your soul to the Devil.'

'And some are saying that I and Raleigh deny the existence of the soul.'

I quoted: '*I count religion but a childish toy,*
And hold there is no sin but ignorance.'

Marlowe smiled: 'Yes, I would expand the seven deadly sins to take in ignorance and superstition. To continue with my Machiavel:
Birds of the air will tell of murders past;
I am ashamed to hear such fooleries.'

'I wish some bird had been perched on the window-sill of Mother Wingfield's room and could tell me how she had been murdered.'

He laughed: 'A raven, perhaps, imbued, as Pythagoras would have it, with the soul of an informer.' He chuckled: 'Robert Poley or Ingram Frizer would fit the bill. So you're still obsessed with that, Thomas.'

'I've got another mystery to go with it,' and I told him Bodin's story of the assassin whose disappearance had been engineered by Ragueneau. Marlowe was fascinated and made me repeat every detail of the story, especially the atrocities of Ragueneau and Krake. There is a cruel streak in Marlowe; it gleamed bright in his eyes. What fascinated and disturbed me about both cases was that they defied reason.

I said, 'If they can only be explained by magic, as so many believe, then magic must be a part of the world. Perhaps Blackbeard killed the old woman with black magic.'

'And perhaps Ragueneau raised his assassin from Hell and returned him there. But if they had such powers why didn't they save themselves from the gallows?'

'Satan claiming his own,' I suggested. Marlowe bit his lip and said, 'Blackbeard, as you call him, was allowed to die because he knew too much about powerful men.'

He picked up his poem and said, 'Will I live long enough to finish this?' With a thin smile he added, 'Perhaps I will die before I've drowned Leander in the Hellespont.'

'Henslowe is worried that you'll die before you've damned Faustus in Hell.'

He laughed uproariously: 'Then I'll finish the play first. I must not disappoint my bawdy-house benefactor, my pothouse patron, by palming him off with an unfinished play. There is only the final scene to write.'

He regarded me with what seemed like concern: 'If you do find out more then you'll need to be much more careful. You're still alive because they cannot kill with impunity. Blackbeard's death by legal execution was convenient for them after the trouble caused by the earlier murders. But if they're desperate enough, Thomas, they'll kill and risk any consequences. After all, we are both of us only poverty-stricken playmakers. Essex is out for power and glory. A sea-captain sailing after a rich Spanish galleon would not hesitate to run down a poor little skiff in his way.'

Now whose side was Marlowe on?, I wondered. He was a friend of Raleigh but here he was staying with

Thomas Walsingham who was connected by marriage with Essex. When Thomas' brother, the spymaster Francis, had died, Essex had inherited most of his secret agents. And Thomas Walsingham employed Ingram Frizer. It was like playing chess with pieces that keep changing colour. There were footsteps in the passage then the door opened and in walked Walsingham followed by Frizer.

Thirty-Four

What is the correct behaviour towards a man who has been trying to kill you, on meeting him in polite society? I don't think Castiglione covered it in his book. We all bowed and exchanged remarks about the weather while I wondered if Marlowe had been acting as the setter for the hunters. When a servant brought wine in I was on guard against being manoeuvred into taking a particular glass.

Walsingham's smooth manners suggested that he had read Castiglione's The Courtier; but the craft in his eyes showed that he had been an even keener student of Machiavelli's The Prince. Frizer did not read books. The cruelty and cunning peering at me through his red-rimmed eyes would have been imbibed with his mother's milk. In a class containing Machiavelli and Nero he would have come top. Walsingham discoursed on the modern drama and said he was honoured to have two such distinguished representatives of it in his house. While he speculated on why revenge plays like The Spanish Tragedy and Titus Andronicus were so popular now, Frizer sipped his wine and looked at me as if he wished it were my heart's blood.

I finished my wine and said I must get back to London. Frizer followed me out of the room. At the front door he said, 'I'm sure you know the rhyme going the rounds about treason never prospering. A powerful man is going to become more powerful. Then all who opposed him will become traitors. The most your friends could do for you then, Dekker, would be to bribe the hangman to let you die quickly on the gallows. But I would pay him more to

306

cut you down alive so that you could feel the knife disembowelling you and slicing out your heart. I would take a deep pleasure in watching your still-beating heart jumping in the hangman's hands.'

'Then we'd both be heartless,' I retorted as I walked away without turning round. Having once seen a man hanged, drawn and quartered I did not want Frizer to see how queasy I looked. Having returned the horse to the stable in Southwark, I crossed London Bridge, averting my eyes from the heads above the gate.

When I reported to Henslowe I brought him double cheer. Marlowe was close to finishing Faustus and he had included comic scenes for Kempe. The company, having undertaken another tour to the West Country, were due back in London in a few weeks. Everyone in the profession was hoping that the plague would not be too bad this summer. But it had persisted, though at a lower level, through the winter. So the outlook was not very hopeful.

Walking through Cheapside, the city seemed to me like a man in a fever. Although many of those who could had escaped to the country, many others had chosen to remain. Now they were in the shops and taverns getting rid of their money as if it were red-hot. They surged from the shops in satin and velvet with hoods and hose, feathers and farthingales, ruffs and rings. The crowds convulsed the streets like the limbs of the invalid while their voices, as in his delirium, raved of plagues and papists, of being invaded by Spanish Catholics and flooded with French Calvinists; and always plots; plots against the Queen's life, of Raleigh against Essex, of Essex against Burghley, of parliament against government, of Puritans against the Church. Through this hubbub rang the cry, 'Stop thief! '

Then I saw Peter dodging in and out of the throng. A big, florid-faced man ran past me shouting, 'Cut my purse you bastard, I'll cut your throat.' He was accompanied by several men in the blue coats of servants. I followed.

To make sure he was not stopped by anyone Peter used the old trick of shouting, 'Stop thief,' and pointing ahead. He ran along Paternoster Row and into Paul's Churchyard ducking and weaving among the booksellers. His pursuers stuck to him. Out into Ludgate Street he ran then down Ludgate Hill. Still closely pursued Peter opened the purse and scattered the coins behind him. A few of the crowd stopped to gather them but the owner directed one servant to stay and with the others continued in pursuit. Peter was trying to get to the sanctuary of Whitefriars but at Fleet Ditch his luck ran out. A large wagon completely blocked the bridge. The crowd were on him and the man he had robbed pushed him against the parapet and held a knife to his throat. I caught his arm and shouted, 'If you kill him it will be murder.'

Sullenly he lowered the knife. A man peered into Peter's face and said, 'No need to cut his throat, friend, he'll hang for sure. That's Prigging Peter. Tyburn's been crying out for him for years.'

Peter's hands were bound and he was carried before a magistrate who committed him to Newgate to await trial. In the few words I managed to exchange with him he said, 'They've got me this time for sure, Tom. Tell Rosie...' then he was hustled away. When I got to Coldharbour Tenements and told Rosie, she echoed Peter's words adding, 'His time has come,' then burst into tears. We agreed a time to visit him next day and I asked her if anything could be done to save him. She shook her head: 'You remember I told you he'd used his neck verse. They'll see the brand on his thumb. He don't know any powerful men to get him off. The lord I used to see has left London 'cos of the plague.' She looked at me desperately: 'Do you know any through the theatre, Tom?'

'Not nearly well enough to get this kind of favour from. I was, in a way, employed by Sir Walter Raleigh. But he's out of favour now.'

She caught at my sleeve: 'Try him, Tom.'

I nodded and set off for Durham House, though with little hope. Raleigh was out. I called on the morrow and was told to call in two days. Time was running out for Peter whose trial was almost due. On my third call a servant showed me into an anteroom where I was kept waiting for hours. This is how it is when you are forced to attend on great men. When I was finally taken into Raleigh's study it was to see him enveloped in the usual cloud of tobacco smoke. He said:

'Friends tell me there is a story going round London that the first time one of my servants saw me smoking a pipe he thought I was on fire and threw a bucket of water over me. Have you heard it?'

I said I had. Raleigh went on: 'My friend Spenser says it is an allegory. That if my passion for Bess Throgmorton had been doused like the fire in the pipe, I would not have lost Her Majesty's favour. Sir Robert Cecil would apply the story to my Lord of Essex, saying his ambition needs to be extinguished.' Leaning back in his chair he eyed me closely. I of course was kept standing. Having taken another puff of his pipe he said, 'Have you come to tell me how your play on the murder of Mother Wingfield is progressing? Have you found any links with a certain ambitious gentleman?'

There seemed to be a chink in the armour here that I could work on. I said, 'I've written a good deal of the play. Of course, Sir Walter, you will appreciate that I cannot be too explicit. But if the play is staged the audience will see where the finger of blame is pointing.'

Waving me to a chair with his pipe he asked, 'Do you know how it was done?'

Putting on the conspiratorial air as acted by Ned Alleyn playing Mosby in Arden of Faversham I leaned forward and lied, 'I'm close to it. But my informant is a cutpurse known as Prigging Peter and he is about to stand trial for theft. He knows where to go and who to see for information. So I need to have him out of prison.'

Raleigh nodded. It was easy to guess what he was thinking. If he could supply Lord Burghley and his son Sir Robert Cecil with evidence implicating their rival Essex in treason it would help in his rehabilitation. Time for the clincher. I said, 'This Peter has also picked up hints that Essex was in league with the man who libelled the bishops in the Marprelate pamphlets.'

'The Welshman, Penry,' said Raleigh with satisfaction. 'There's a warrant out for his arrest. I suppose this thief is likely to be found guilty?'

'Caught red-handed, I'm afraid.'

'I'll see if I can get a pardon.' After this uncertain pledge Raleigh dismissed me with a curt nod. He took his loss of power hard.

Next day I accompanied Rosie to Newgate to see Peter. Before going in I warned her not to mention Raleigh. It was all too uncertain to raise any hopes. Peter was in good spirits, helped no doubt by the flagon of beer he had just finished. I asked him if he knew anything more about the Milk Street murder in case I was asked by Raleigh to demonstrate Peter had fresh information. Peter was quick-witted enough to see an opening and soon prised from me what had happened. The cheerful stoicism fuelled by the beer was now replaced by a feverish hope of life. If his pardon was not forthcoming now it would be harder for him to die.

From Newgate I called at the Cross Keys to see Elizabeth. A letter from home saying her mother had been unwell was worrying her. Although the letter said the illness was not serious enough to warrant her returning home, she was still uneasy. Also the present mood of the city was having the same effect on Elizabeth as on me. Things were not helped when Sim Hicks got up from the table he was drinking at and came over to us, his face split by a malicious grin. He said, 'Your family are Dutch, aren't they, Dekker.' He thrust a paper at me and added, 'I copied this down from a notice pinned to the Dutch Church in Broad Street.' It read:

"We'll cut your throats in your temples praying
Not Paris massacre so much blood did spill.
Signed Tamburlaine." And underneath:
"You strangers that inhabit in this land,
Note this same writing, do it understand;
Conceive it well for safeguard of your lives,
Your goods, your children and your dearest wives."

Elizabeth tore it up and threw the pieces in Sim's face saying, 'You and your hateful messages are not welcome here.'

When he had left, trying to carry it off with a swagger, I said, 'We need a break from the city.' I told her about the pardon I was trying to get for Peter and added, 'As soon as it's obtained let's go for that trip on the river that was so rudely interrupted last time by my army service.'

That evening while drinking in the Saracen's Head with Tarlton, Cod and Wheedler I heard the tap, tap, tap of a wooden leg. It was Fat Tim. He joined us and we swapped stories of the campaign like a couple of old soldiers.

When I called at Durham House it was to be told by the porter that Sir Walter was not at home. The look he accompanied his words with implied, especially to you. Now the day of Peter's trial was here. Of course, the guilty verdict was inevitable. And given his reputation, so was the sentence; hanged by the neck until dead. While he was taken down to the condemned hold I hurried off again to Durham House. The same answer. Back to Newgate.

311

Peter and Rosie were holding hands through the bars. They looked at me hopefully. It was hard having to shake my head.

Peter said, 'Not your fault, Tom. You can do nothing against fate.' He beckoned to an old man with a long white beard and introduced him as a necromancer, saying, 'Tell my friend what you told me.'

The old man mumbled, 'A drop as one looks up in hope;

One's saved, one dangles from a rope.'

Peter took a swig of wine and said, 'The drop is me dropping off the cart at Tyburn to dangle from the rope.'

'What about the one who's saved?' I asked. Peter nodded at the old man: 'He says that's him.'

'It could be the other way round,' I objected. Peter took another swig of wine then said, 'I'm being trussed up for theft. I'll be left dangling for half an hour. He's being done for treason because he keeps saying the spirits of the dead have told him the Queen will die in her Grand Climac...'

'Grand Climacteric,' said the old man, nodding solemnly. 'She'll be sixty-three in three years. Seven times nine, which the astrologers say is dangerous.'

Peter went on, 'Well, for treason he wouldn't be left dangling, would he? He'd be cut down for the butcher's knife.'

It sounded a bit strained to me. I said, 'If he's wrong he'll be able to take it up with the dead he says told him.'

The next execution day was in a week's time. When I was again turned away from Durham House I decided to try the Mermaid Tavern. Raleigh sometimes drank there with writers; select ones, that is. He was seated at a table in close conversation with Marlowe. They called me over to join them. Raleigh, who seemed in a cheerful mood, said, 'I haven't got anything for your friend yet but Master Marlowe has got something for Henslowe.'

312

Marlowe threw the manuscript of Doctor Faustus on the table.

'Peter's to be hanged in a week, Sir Walter,' I persisted. He frowned: 'Do you have anything fresh for me? Has he linked the libeller Penry to the gentleman we discussed? Has he found out how the murder was committed?'

'If he were out of prison,' I said desperately, 'he might...'

'Don't try to lead me by the nose, Dekker. I've been in politics too long. Having loyalty for a friend is commendable; having a thief for a friend less so.'

'I owe my life to...'

'If he can serve Her Majesty he will be rewarded with a pardon. If not then he must pay for his crimes.' He tapped the manuscript. 'My friend Kit has written his best play yet. Go and send Henslowe here. At least we can make him happy with the money it's going to make him.'

Once again I was dismissed. With Peter unable to supply Raleigh with any fresh information there was little I could do for the moment. I had promised Elizabeth a trip on the river and I thought it might clear my head, give me some new ideas. Just before we left the Cross Keys a blue-coated young man said in a low voice, 'I'm a servant of Master Seldon. You stayed at his house in Chelsea with the players. He visited the priest in prison and might be able to help you with information.'

I studied him closely. It might be a trap. I asked, 'Do you remember what play we put on?'

'It was about two magicians, Friar Bacon and Friar Bungay.' He left saying it was not wise for him to be seen with me.

'I'll have to look into this,' I said to Elizabeth; 'it may help Peter. But I'm sorry you're losing your trip on the Thames.'

'Don't worry, Thomas,' she replied firmly. 'The quickest way to Chelsea is on the river and I'm coming with you.' I began to protest but she took my arm and down to the Thames we walked.

'Westward ho,' shouted a waterman resting on his oars and in we climbed. When I said Chelsea he grumbled that it was a long pull against the tide. I promised him extra which made Elizabeth look at the sky and roll her eyes. It was good to feel the wind in our faces and to be away from the city streets. But there was the fear that we might be falling into a trap. There was little conversation from the waterman who seemed a melancholy fellow. At the landing stairs at Chelsea we saw another boat tied up. The waterman raised his pipe to us but got no response from our man. Asking him to wait we made our way up to Seldon's house. We rounded a corner and saw Warthog standing outside the house. Looking as startled as me he ran to the door and shouted into the house.

'Back to the boat,' I cried. Elizabeth gathered up her skirt and we ran. Jumping into the boat I gasped, 'Away,' and looking back saw Warthog accompanied by Frizer and Cyclops running towards us. As the waterman pulled off he growled, 'Bloody bailiffs. That one with the wart-encrusted nose has been chasing me. I'll get you clear of the bastards.'

Our pursuers piled into the other boat and gave chase. The doublets of Frizer and Cyclops bulged with what looked, to my military-trained eye, like pistols. We were maintaining our lead but not increasing it. That was going to be a problem when we had to land. One dagger against two pistols was poor odds. The tide was with us now and flowing fast so we were skimming along. Passing Westminster soon we raced past Durham House then Blackfriars.

The waterman shouted, 'Do you want to shoot the Bridge?'

I looked at Elizabeth and we both looked at our pursuers. We had increased our lead a little but they were still too close. But with this fast flowing tide shooting the Bridge would be dangerous. Elizabeth was my chief concern. A woman, with her thick skirt and petticoats, has little chance when cast into the water. Already I could hear the water roaring under the arches. Catching me eyeing the landing stairs the waterman shouted, 'Too late for that now.'

Elizabeth clasped my hand and said to him, 'You can do it?'

'Oh it can be done.'

'After all,' I said, 'you don't want to lose your boat or your life.'

'The bailiffs are going to take my boat,' he said bitterly. 'They've taken my house and my wife has left me. What have I got to live for?'

We were about to shoot London Bridge on a raging tide with a suicidal boatman.

The Bridge is built on great piles or starlings which jut forward like tiny islands with the water foaming around them. We were heading straight for one. Desperately plying his oars the waterman steered us away and towards the archway. But a sudden eddy swept the boat against the opposite pile and we were flung into the water. Pushing Elizabeth up onto the starling I scrambled after her. Still in the water the boatman flung out a hand which I grabbed. Elizabeth caught it too and slowly we began hauling him onto the islet. There was a crack and a bullet sang over our heads to smack into the Bridge. I looked up to see the other boat bearing down on us. Cyclops was lowering a smoking pistol while Frizer was still aiming his at me. It spat flame as the boat bucked. The waterman jerked, groaned, 'Bloody bailiffs,' and slid into the water to be swept through the archway. The other boat followed

315

him with Cyclops glaring at me out of his one eye and Frizer out of his two red ones.

There was shouting from above. We looked up to see people leaning out of the window of a house on the Bridge and lowering a rope. I tied it around Elizabeth's waist and she was hauled to safety. As I looked up at her being pulled through the window a drop of water from her dress fell into my eye. Then I knew how old Mother Wingfield had been murdered.

Thirty-Five

In the house we were loaned dry clothes and given mulled wine by our rescuers. I escorted Elizabeth to the Cross Keys then hurried off to Durham House to see Raleigh. Now I had some information for him. How the murder had been committed. The more I thought about it the more certain I became. The Roman writer I had been trying to think of was Martial. From one of the bookshops on the Bridge I had bought a copy of his epigrams. Searching through it as I walked along the street I found the poem I wanted; Book IV Epigram XVIII.

While passing St Paul's I caught up with Rosie and told her my errand. She said, 'They've brought some executions forward to tomorrow. Peter's among them.' She held up a bottle of wine: 'This will help him through the night but he'll need more for tomorrow. He'll want to make a good end in front of his friends so try and bring something when you come, Tom.'

'I'll bring a bottle, Rosie, for the three of us to celebrate his pardon with. But you'd better not tell him just in case...' I hurried away.

At Durham House the porter refused to admit me. Turning down the relevant page I gave the book to him: 'Ask Sir Walter to read number eighteen.'

He took it reluctantly and entered the house. Returning, he growled that I was to go in. Raleigh was seated behind his desk writing with the book open before him. He was Englishing the epigram. He threw it across to me.

"Winter has formed a sharp dagger of ice
Suspended from an aqueduct. A face
Looks up and Fortune throws the deadly dice
That sends the weapon plunging down to slice
Straight through the throat and melting leave no
trace."

For an extempore translation it was quite good. Raleigh showing that he was also a poet. I said, 'Substitute crossbow bolt for dagger and you have the weapon that killed Mother Wingfield then disappeared.'

'Where did you get this information?'

It was time for a free, a very free, translation of the truth. I replied, 'The cutpurse I told you of. If he were out of prison he could supply you with much more. But he is to be hanged tomorrow.'

'Follow me,' barked Raleigh standing up and striding out. We went down to the river where he kept his own boat and he quickly had us rowed to Whitehall.

Then followed a nightmare of waiting with the time slipping away. Emelia Lanier, nee Bassano, passed by with her husband, a court musician. Lord Hunsdon had quickly married her off when she became pregnant. I had heard she was discontented and she looked it. When she said to Raleigh, 'We are both cast-offs, Sir Walter,' his face looked almost as black as her hair. But she had some reason to be bitter.

Raleigh needed to see Sir Robert Cecil. Perhaps, when the clerk said that Sir Robert was, for the moment, engaged, it was true. Or perhaps Sir Robert was showing Sir Walter that he was no longer the power at court he had been. The clerk was very respectful. Raleigh might regain the Queen's favour at any time. Hours passed. I was painfully aware that Rosie and Peter were in Newgate Prison waiting, hoping that I would bring a reprieve. As Raleigh grew angrier with the frustration of being kept waiting I feared that he might abandon the whole enterprise.

At last the clerk showed us into Sir Robert's office. He came from behind his desk walking awkwardly with his humped back and took Raleigh's arm, all the time apologising for having kept him waiting. Raleigh was escorted to another chair behind the desk while I was left facing them. They questioned me closely then I was told to wait outside. For all of us it was an evening of waiting. Eventually Raleigh came out and said, 'We both think you'd make a good agent, Dekker, because neither of us is sure how much of what you have told us is true. However, Marlowe has told me that he thinks you're basically honest so you can go on digging for us.'

'But the pardon, Sir Walter?'

'Sir Robert Cecil will resolve you on that in the morning.'

'But Peter may be hanged in the morning.'

'Then he'll get his just deserts,' said Raleigh coldly. He added in a friendlier tone, 'Come back to Durham House and I'll tell my steward to find you a bed. Then you can return to Whitehall first thing in the morning.'

A beautiful dark-haired young woman was waiting for Raleigh when we got back to Durham House. Everyone else was forgotten as he took her up the staircase with an arm around her waist. I spent the night on a hard pallet thinking of Rosie and Peter in Newgate.

Early next morning I was at Whitehall asking to see Sir Robert and again being kept waiting. At last a clerk brought the pardon and said, 'Give it to the sheriff in charge of the executions.' I snatched the document and hurried out through Whitehall's maze of corridors. I ran back towards Charing Cross then up through Leicester Fields to Tottenham Court. There I asked a woman if the condemned had passed for Tyburn.

'Yes, dear. If you hurry you might see the last batch being hung.' As I ran along the Oxford Road she called cheerfully, 'There's a quartering today.'

I ran flat out with the thought pounding in my head that if I arrived too late my genuine reprieve would be no better than Frizer's fake one. When I heard the crowd singing "The Lord Is My Shepherd", I knew the end was near. Over the people's heads I could see the condemned standing on the cart with the chaplain talking to them. Forcing my way through the crowd I shouted, 'A reprieve.' A path was made for me and my cry was taken up. When I burst through into the space around the gallows I saw that the first batch were already dangling from one of the crossbeams. I could not make out whether Peter was among them or those on the cart. When Rosie ran from among the crowd and shouted, 'Thank God,' I knew it was all right. I gave the reprieve to the sheriff who examined it carefully then ordered Peter to be released. As he jumped down from the cart the chaplain called, 'Give thanks for the chance God has given you.'

'I'll say a prayer for every purse,' replied Peter to the cheers of his friends; but his bravado was belied by his chalk-white face and unsteady legs. Rosie took one arm and me the other and we helped him away.

'So the old necromancer was wrong,' I said.

'Yes,' agreed Peter. 'I expect he's telling the spirits off now.'

'But was he wrong?' asked Rosie thoughtfully. 'He said that out of him and Peter one would be saved the other left dangling. He's still dangling there. They decided to let him die before cutting him up in consideration of his age.'

I said, 'So he may have just misinterpreted it in regard to who would be saved.' Then I told them how the drop of water falling into my eye had led to Peter being saved. At that he sat on the ground and laughed until the tears rolled down his cheeks. Just as I had worked out a rational explanation for the Milk Street murder, this prophecy seemed to plunge us back into the supernatural. And still outstanding was how that assassin had disappeared in France.

I got on with writing my play and finally finished it. Henslowe would want to call it 'The Murder in Milk Street: Being a True Account of the Strange and Bloody Tragedy' and so on. Well, as long as he paid me.

Henslowe was seated at his usual table in the Mermaid poring over his accounts. His reaction when I presented him with the play was sarcastic: 'Perhaps you haven't noticed, Dekker but the playhouses are closed.'

'But when they re-open you'll want…'

'Besides,' he tapped my manuscript, 'this play might not be allowed a performance. I am not paying you six pound for a banned play. I was bitten by Sir Thomas More. I've got Marlowe's Faustus and I hear Shakespeare has finished his long poem so I may get something from him. But that fool Kyd has gone from translating unprofitable French plays to writing the libels on foreigners being pinned up all over London. Well now he's in prison for his pains.'

'He's been tortured,' said a man at the next table. 'The word is he has accused Marlowe of blasphemy.'

'It's true,' cut in another man. 'Marlowe's got to report daily to the Privy Council. This time he's in real trouble.'

Henslowe groaned: 'If only I could put his Faustus on now I'd make a fortune.'

I made my way to Durham House to show Raleigh my play. When I was shown into his study he was taking a glowing coal from the fire with a tongs to light his pipe. He took his time, getting the pipe going well, before turning to me. I gave him my play. He browsed through it for some time, smiling now and then. Looking up he said, 'You have some talent for playmaking; but your lines lack the passion of a Tamburlaine, they do not burn, as thus,' and he threw my play onto the fire.

When I leapt forward shouting, 'It's my only copy,' he brandished the tongs then used them to cover the manuscript with burning coals.

'Times change,' he said. 'My Lord of Essex is reconciled with Sir Robert Cecil. So now any talk that there was a plot on his Lordship's part is absurd and treasonable. A one-eyed soldier has returned to the army in Brittany and I shall return to my wife in Dorset. You should return to writing comedies, Master Dekker. Marlowe should stick to poetry instead of telling all London that he knows important secrets of powerful men. Powerful men can arrange to have mouths stopped.' He returned to his pipe and I was dismissed.

A few days later I was in the Cross Keys when Nicholas Winton came in, having just returned from his voyage. We discussed the present situation with me telling him that the Essex plot was off. He nodded: 'It agrees with what I've heard since I got back.' He lowered his voice: 'But if I were to prophesy I'd say that one day Essex will try to seize power by force. He is an ambitious and unstable man.'

I told him of the necromancer's prophecy and how I believed Mother Wingfield had been killed. He said, 'Yes, that's how it must have been done. I was sure there was a rational explanation.'

'And the necromancer's prophecy?' I asked. Winton shrugged: 'Coincidence.' So I told him about the disappearance of the French assassin. Winton seemed to feel a belief in the supernatural as a personal affront and never looked happier than when he was demolishing such a belief. As now: 'If you remember, Master Dekker, I told you that I once travelled with a troupe of performers who did tricks that looked like magic.'

'Sometimes people thought it was witchcraft and drove you away.'

'That's right. Disappearing was one of their tricks. Doubtless it varies in detail but I'll tell you their method. The whole troupe would run into the arena dressed in white except for one man who would be in red. A screen would be held between them and the audience for a very short time. When it was removed the man in red had disappeared. How? Simple. His red clothes were made of paper. He could tear them off in seconds and stuff the pieces into the pockets of the white clothes he wore underneath. Then of course he blended in with the rest of us.'

'But,' I objected, 'Bodin insisted that they searched the friars thoroughly.'

'Do you know if there was a fire nearby?'

The darkness of superstition dispelled by the light of reason, I thought. Then Christopher Marlowe came in shouting that he knew atheists in high places and fornicators in the church. Men scattered from him as if he had the plague. With the number of informers swarming about London, no one wanted to be seen in the company of a man voicing such opinions. Still less to hear any names. Winton and myself were sitting in an alcove and I skulked there while Elizabeth went forward and asked Marlowe to leave. Confronted with a man in such a mood, Marlowe's dagger would have been out. But like so many others he was disarmed by Elizabeth's quiet firmness and left, albeit still cursing the great men who had betrayed him. Winton said, 'Those same great men will be his death.'

A few days later when I called at the Mermaid to see if Henslowe had any work for me, I found him in a state of great excitement. Ned Alleyn had sent a message to say that he and the other players would be back in London within a week. And Henslowe had obtained permission for a temporary use of the Rose.

'Less plague victims,' he explained. More bribes, I thought. Marlowe was still being investigated and having to report to the Privy Council. Speculation was rife about whether he would be brought to trial and name names or be disposed of beforehand. Such talk was like the music of the spheres to Henslowe who rubbed his hands saying, 'And I can stage his Faustus.'

I had a long talk with Elizabeth about our future. She wanted me to meet her parents and was still concerned about her mother's health. We agreed that she should arrange time off with the Cross Keys owner while I looked around for a carter who could take us to Cambridgeshire.

Playbills began appearing around London announcing that The Tragical History of Doctor Faustus by Christopher Marlowe was to be played at the Rose on the 31st of May with Edward Alleyn in the title role. The regular bookholder was back so there was no work for me there. I returned to my old trade, street ballads. Peter, who had been given a bad scare, was doing honest but hard work loading ships at Deptford. Rosie sighed and said it would not last. She, as Cleopatra, was now being kept by a rich merchant who enjoyed abasing himself as her Egyptian slave.

The not so merry month of May was going out in a fever of rumours about plague, invasion, refugees, plots and Marlowe's horrid blasphemies. It was a fact that the Puritan John Penry had been tried and sentenced to death. Finally there was a wild rumour that while the actors were rehearsing a scene where Faustus conjures up devils an extra devil had appeared on stage.

On the last day of the month I set out with Elizabeth to see the first performance of Doctor Faustus. The Bridge was clogged with people and carts so we decided to take a

324

boat across. Since many others had the same idea boats were scarce. At last one pulled in and we ran towards it arriving at the same time as another young couple. The waterman settled the argument over who had got there first by ascertaining that we were all bound for the Rose and telling us sharply to get in. The young gallant had more than the one feather in his hat ruffled at the boatman's tone. He tried to assert his superior social rank by looking down his nose at my plain clothes and dropping the names of several noblemen. The trumpeter on top of the Rose blew a loud blast and I got the chance to assert my superior learning when the waterman groaned, 'The Devil Tavern's ale and that damned playhouse trumpet will be the death of me.'

Leaning back I drawled, 'Then you can take Charon's job of ferrying dead souls across the Styx, boatman.'

'Hey, Jack,' he called to a passing boatman. 'I've just had my first Charon joke of the day.'

'I've had three bastards crack it,' growled the other. 'Next one goes into the river.'

Elizabeth was still smiling as we pushed our way into the playhouse. The air was thick with expectation. Rumours buzzed around the packed audience. Marlowe had been imprisoned in Newgate, the Fleet, the Marshalsea, the Clink; he had been seen boarding a ship at Billingsgate, Wapping, Deptford. People found as much drama in the lives of writers and actors as on the stage. But Faustus had been long awaited and now it was about to begin.

The chorus entered to deliver the prologue, ending it by drawing back the curtain at the rear to show Faustus in his study bent over his books. Now Faustus moved to the front of the stage and ran through the subjects he had mastered; going beyond Aristotle in logic, Galen in medicine, Justinian in law. In divinity he recoiled from,

"*Stipentium peccati mons est. The reward of sin is death: that's hard.*"

When he moved onto the metaphysics of magicians and necromantic books he gazed into the distance like a voyager to the New World or like Balboa standing on a peak in Darien staring at the Pacific. So into the dark interior of magic he trekked ignoring his Good Angel, following his Evil Angel:

"Go forward Faustus in that famous art
Wherein all Nature's treasure is contained."

Kempe as the clown gagged and tumbled, his fooling reflecting as in a distorting mirror the heroic foolishness of Faustus. The whole play seemed to hold up a mirror to our modern age with its new ideas and new learning. We have powers of destruction undreamt-of by our forefathers. Cannon, as I have seen, can wreak devastation on a town; gunpowder can blow up a ship with a thousand men in it. Faustus embodies our age; and signing away his soul with his own blood symbolises our commitment to the quest for knowledge, no matter what triumphs or disasters it brings to our future. The play caught the danger but also the excitement of the search:

"Had I as many souls as there be stars
I'd give them all for Mephistopheles."

When Faustus first conjured up Mephistopheles he rose onto the stage in a cloud of sulphurous-smelling smoke emerging from it into a shocked silence broken by a woman's scream. The decay of the grave seemed to drip from the scales covering his body. Faustus threw a hand in front of his eyes and ordered him to return in the shape of a Franciscan friar. When he conjured up devils some of the audience carefully counted them and sniffed the air for brimstone.

And so the tragedy moved inexorably on, brightened towards the end only by the lovely lines on Helen of Troy:

"Was this the face that launched a thousand ships

And burned the topless Towers of Ilium?

Sweet Helen, make me immortal with a kiss."

As Faustus' last hour approached, his Good Angel departed while his Evil Angel gleefully assured him that he would indeed be immortal; in Hell. While he brooded in deep despair I felt a tug at my sleeve. It was Peter. He said:

'Marlowe's dead. Stabbed through the brain with his own knife in a struggle with Ingram Frizer. I saw his body at Mistress Bull's in Deptford.'

Heads turned as the news ran through the audience like a snake through grass. The clock on stage began striking. Eleven. Faustus said:

"Ah Faustus.

Now hast thou but one bare hour to live,

And then thou must be damned perpetually.

Stand still you ever moving spheres of heaven,

That time may cease and midnight never come."

He begged for mercy:

"See, see, where Christ's blood streams in the firmament."

He pleaded for more time; but the half hour struck. Soon it would all be past. He cried for his body to dissolve, to turn to air and again for more time. But for him time had melted away like snow falling on a fire. The clock struck twelve. There was thunder and lightening and two devils entered. "My God, my God, look not so fierce on me," and Faustus was dragged away in a cloud of foul-smelling smoke shrieking for Mephistopheles.

The epilogue

"Cut is the branch that might have grown full straight

And burned is Apollo's laurel bough,"

washed over a stunned audience. Great actor though Alleyn is, there seemed an extra dimension to his playing that day. When he entered to make his bow he looked drained, as though, someone said, he had lost a soul.

327

As we streamed from the playhouse a slack-mouthed man pointed to a raven perched on the roof and giggled, 'Black enough for Faustus.'

'Or Marlowe,' muttered Elizabeth. Then something happened none of us will ever forget. Two ravens appeared flying up the Thames and alighted on either side of the one on the roof. We watched all three rise into the air. As they flapped away the raven in the centre emitted a blood-freezing shriek.

We walked slowly down to the riverside to take a boat. In a narrow street we passed a boarded up house with the red plague cross painted on it and a white face pressed against a window.

I was bundling up my few belongings in Coldharbour Tenements when Rosie and Peter came in to say goodbye. Rosie twirled around the room showing off her new skirt. Peter was looking at it and grinning. Catching my censorious glance Rosie protested, 'I told him not to, Tom.'

'What have you been loading at Deptford, Peter?' I asked.

His grin broadened: 'Skirts and', holding up another piece of clothing, 'bodices. Just the thing for that girl of yours, Tom.'

'No thank you. If Elizabeth found out where it had come from she'd crucify me. You'll be another Faustus, Peter, repenting too late. You took nothing from the play.'

'I took plenty from the play,' he chuckled pouring out three glasses of wine. From its quality I guessed that he had been unloading a cargo from France. We said our goodbyes and I set off for the Cross Keys where I was meeting Elizabeth. When I arrived the carter we were travelling with had just finished tying down the bales on his wagon.

'We must pray he does not cut it so fine on your wedding day,' said Mistress Brayne to Elizabeth. She and her husband had come to see us off. We said our farewells and Elizabeth and I climbed up beside the carter and off we set through the quiet streets of the city on the first leg of our journey to her home in Cambridgeshire. It was just after dawn but the sun was hidden in the mist rolling in from the Thames.

With the plague worsening day by day, my mother had gone into the country to stay with her brother. The inquest on Marlowe had found that Ingram Frizer had acted in self-defence. Marlowe, it was claimed, had snatched Frizer's dagger in a quarrel over who was to pay for the dinner the four men had just eaten. In the struggle, it was said, the dagger had pierced Marlowe's brain. The other two present were Poley the informer and Skeres, a spy and close friend of Frizer. One thing is certain, between them they extinguished one of the poetic lights of the age.

As the wagon climbed Highgate Hill I looked back at London where the mist was thinning. Fires had been lit in many of the streets to try and burn the plague infected air. Red flames licked and curled while the black-plumed ravens croaked and dived in the grey smoke drifting across the stricken city. Out of the mist and smoke rose the solid bulk of St Paul's and beyond it the Tower. As the freshening breeze cleared the air, I made out the Bridge; and the Thames, gleaming in the sun, down which a white-sailed ship was under way. On either side of us the fields were bright with flowers. London would blossom again and I would return with Elizabeth. She, like me, was now a Londoner.

The End

More Titles
From Accent Press Ltd

The Fevered Hive Dennis Lewis   ISBN 095486736X
A cutting edge collection of Cardiff-based, urban writing.

The Last Cut F.M. Kay   ISBN 0954867378
A powerful and provocative collection of erotic poetry

Red Stilettos Ruth Joseph   ISBN 0954489977
An intriguing and provocative collection of short stories by a
Cardiff-based Jewish writer.

Why Do You Overeat? Zoë Harcombe   ISBN 0954489933
The Diet Cookbook   ISBN 0954867394
 Zoë Harcombe/Rachel McGuinness
The result of 20 years researching, why people struggle to lose
weight, these books explain the cause, and provide delicious
recipes to help conquer overeating.

Notso Fatso Walter Whichelow   ISBN 0954489969
A tongue-in-cheek, ruthless and very funny take on the world of
dieting.

How to Draw Cartoons Brian Platt   ISBN 0954709209
Fun, simple and entertaining – this book will help even the
complete novice turn out professional cartoons in minutes.

Triplet Tales Hazel Cushion   ISBN 0954709217
Beautifully written in rhyming couplets with full colour
illustrations, this book is sure to be a children's favourite.

The Shorts Range – collections of short stories each raising £1
per copy sold for the designated charity. For full details log on
to www.sexyshorts.info.

Titles Available By Post

To order titles from Accent Press Ltd by post, simply complete this form and return to the address below, enclosing a cheque or postal order for the full amount plus £1 p&p per book.

	TITLE	AUTHOR	PRICE
☐	Sexy Shorts for Christmas	Various	£6.99
☐	Sexy Shorts for Lovers	Various	£6.99
☐	Sexy Shorts for Summer	Various	£6.99
☐	Scary Shorts for Halloween	Various	£6.99
☐	Why Do You Overeat?	Zoë Harcombe	£9.99
☐	The Diet Cookbook	Zoë Harcombe & Rachel McGuinness	£9.99
☐	How to Draw Cartoons	Brian Platt	£7.99
☐	Notso Fatso	Walter Whichelow	£6.99
☐	Triplet Tales	Hazel Cushion	£5.99
☐	The Last Cut	F.M. Kay	£6.99
☐	The Fevered Hive	Dennis Lewis	£7.99

All prices correct at time of going to press. However the publisher reserves the right to change prices without prior notice.

PO Box 50, Pembroke Dock, Pembrokeshire, UK. SA72 6WY
Email: info@accentpress.co.uk   Tel: + 44 (0)1646 691389

Cheques payable to 'Accent Press Ltd'. Do not send cash. Cards not accepted.

NAME _____

ADDRESS _____

_____ POSTCODE _____